also by
Laura Thalassa

THE BARGAINER SERIES

Rhapsodic

A Strange Hymn

The Emperor of Evening Stars

Dark Harmony

THE FOUR HORSEMEN

Pestilence

War

Famine

Death

LAURA THALASSA

Bloom books

Cover design by Story Wrappers by K.D. Ritchie
Cover images by YAYImages/depositphotos, THPStock/depositphotos

Published by Bloom Books, an imprint of Sourcebooks
P.O. Box 4410, Naperville, Illinois 60567-4410
(630) 961-3900
sourcebooks.com

Cataloging-in-Publication Data is on file with the Library of Congress.

Printed and bound in the United States of America.
LSC 10 9 8 7 6 5 4

For Astrid, who brews potions, dances with skeletons, and howls at the moon. You have magic in your blood, love.

The Law of Three

The magic you cast,
In use be wise and true.
Do good unto others,
For threefold it shall return to you,

If ill will moves your hand,
And woe strikes in your wake,
Threefold it shall return its might.
Threefold the curse will take.

PROLOGUE
Memnon

I am trapped.

I have been for a very, very long time. My body and mind are bound by spells both suffocating and comforting. I cannot escape them, no matter how hard I try.

And how I have tried.

This is not as it should be. I know that. I remember that.

Someone did this to me.

Someone…but who?

The answer evades me.

My thoughts are…fragmented. Broken apart and scattered by the very wards that shroud me.

There was a life before this shadow of an existence. Sometimes I catch glimpses of it. The memory of the sun, the heavy weight of a sword in my hand, the feel of a woman—*my* woman—beneath me.

Even when I cannot recall much of what I look like, I can see the slope of her shoulder and the curve of her smile and the mischief shining in her sharp blue eyes.

Her image…it cuts deeper than a wound.

Need her.

My queen. My wife.

Roxilana.

Need to leave this place. Need to find her.

Unless…

What if…what if she is truly gone?

Lost to me forever?

Terror eclipses my longing and clears some of the haze from my mind. I release what magic I can, funneling it through the few holes I've found in these spells.

Roxilana cannot be dead. So long as I exist, she must too. I have…taken pains to make this so.

I relax.

She will find me.

One day.

One day.

So I call to her, as I always have.

And I wait.

CHAPTER 1
Selene

Today will be the day Henbane Coven accepts me.

I exhale as I stare up at the sprawling Gothic buildings that make up the coven's campus. The property sits on the coastal hills north of San Francisco, bordered on all sides by the Everwoods, a thick coastal forest composed of evergreen trees.

There's no placard that announces I'm now standing on witch-owned land, but this place doesn't really need one. If a person lingers for long enough, they'll see something out of the ordinary—like, for instance, the circle of witches sitting on the lawn ahead of me.

Their hair and clothes float every which way, as though no longer bound by gravity, and plumes of their magic thicken the air around them. The color of their individual magic varies—from bright green, to bubblegum pink, to turquoise, and more—but as I watch, it all blends, creating an odd sort of rainbow in the air around them.

A wave of longing moves through me, and I have to tamp down the panicky, desperate feeling that follows in its wake.

I glance down at the open notebook in my hand.

Tuesday, August 29

10:00 a.m. meeting with Henbane Coven's admissions office in Morgana Hall.

*Leave an extra twenty minutes early. You have a bad habit of arriving late.

I frown at the note, then glance at my phone: *9:57 a.m.*

Well, shit.

I begin walking again, heading toward the weathered stone buildings, even as my eyes flick back to my notebook.

Beneath my scrawled instructions is a drawing of a crest with flowers rising from a cauldron atop two crisscrossing brooms. Next to the drawing, I taped a Polaroid picture of one of the stone structures in front of me, and I've scrawled the words *Morgana Hall* beneath it. At the bottom I've written in red:

Meeting will be held in the Receiving Room—second door on the right.

I head up the stone steps of Morgana Hall, growing breathless with my churning emotions. For the past century and a half, any witch worth her weight in magic has been an active member of an accredited coven.

And today I'm determined to join that list.

It didn't happen last year or when you reapplied at the beginning of this one. Perhaps they simply don't want you.

I take a deep breath and force the insidious thought away. This time is different. I'm on the official wait list, and they arranged for this interview only last week. They must be taking my application seriously, and that's all I need: a foot in the door.

I open one of the massive doors into the building and head inside.

The first thing I see in the main hallway is a grand statue of the triple goddess. Her three forms stand back-to-back—the maiden, flowers woven into her unbound hair; the mother, her hands cradling her pregnant stomach; and the crone, wearing a crown of bones, her hands resting atop her cane.

Along the walls are portraits of past coven members, many of whom have wild hair and wilder eyes. Mounted in between them are wands and brooms and framed excerpts of famous grimoires.

I breathe it all in for a moment. I can feel the gentle hum of magic in the air, and it feels like home.

I *will* get in.

I stride down the hall, my determination renewed. When I get to the second door on the right, I knock, then wait.

A witch with soft features and a kind smile opens the door for me. "Selene Bowers?" she says.

I nod.

"Come on in."

I follow her inside. A massive crescent-moon table takes up most of the space, and on the far side of it, half a dozen witches sit patiently. Across from them is a single seat.

The witch ahead of me gestures to it, and despite all my encouraging thoughts, my heart hammers.

I take the proffered seat, folding my hands in my lap to stop them from trembling while the woman who led me in takes her own seat on the other side of the table.

Directly across from me is a witch with raven-black hair,

thin downturned lips, and shrewd eyes. I think I've spoken to her before, there's something vaguely familiar about her features, but her identity lies just beyond my reach…

She looks up from her notes and squints at me. After a moment, her frown deepens. "You again?"

With that question, I swear the entire mood of the room shifts from inviting to tense.

I swallow delicately. "Yes, me," I say hoarsely before clearing my throat. I'm frightened this interview is now doomed before it's even begun.

The witch who spoke returns her attention to the papers in front of her. She licks her finger and flips through them. "I was under the impression we were interviewing a different applicant," she says.

What am I supposed to say to that? Sorry I'm not someone else?

Short of shape-shifting into another person, I don't think I can appease her.

Another witch, one with a hooked nose and wiry gray hair, says gently, "Selene Bowers, it's lovely to meet you. Why don't you tell us a little bit about yourself and why you'd like to join Henbane Coven?"

This is it. My chance.

I take a deep breath, and I dive in.

For thirty minutes, I answer various questions about my abilities, my background, and my magical interests. Most of the witches nod encouragingly. The only notable exception to this is that hawk-eyed witch who looks at me like I'm a spell gone bad. It's all I can do to answer the questions I get without letting her intimidate me into silence.

"It's been a dream of mine to be a part of Henbane Coven for as long as I can remember."

"How long *can* you remember?" says the witch in front of me.

I squeeze my hands together, a wisp of pale orange magic slipping from between them. I've danced around this topic in my previous responses, not quite sure how to handle it.

"It...depends," I say now. "But my memory in no way affects my determination or my abilities," I say.

"But it would," she counters. "It would affect your ability. Spellcasting costs you your memories, correct?"

There it is, out in the open.

I tighten my jaw. "Yes, but—"

She flips through the papers in front of her before pulling one out and placing it on top of the others. "The medical records you released suggest that, and I quote, 'It is believed that the patient's memory loss is a magic-based disease with no known equivalent and no known cure. It appears to be a progressive disease. Prognosis: terminal.'"

The silence that follows her words is somehow very, very loud. I can hear my own breath leaving my lungs. More magic has slipped out of me, rising from my hands like a wisp of smoke.

"So," she continues, "every bit of power you use chips away at your mind, am I correct?"

After a moment's hesitation, I give her a halting nod.

"And with every use of your magic, your brain deteriorates."

"It doesn't *deteriorate*," I protest, annoyed by that word. I lose memories, not functionality.

Now the witch's expression softens, but it's pity I see on her face. I hate that, more than anything else. I hate it so much, it's hard to breathe.

"At Henbane Coven," she says, "we don't simply embrace

all manner of disabilities—we hold those witches in particularly high regard."

She's not lying. There's a reason some of the most powerful witches have been blind, and the first recorded witch in Europe to fly a broom—Hildegard Von Goethe—did so because she had limited mobility.

"But at Henbane Coven," she continues, "you will be asked to rigorously perform magic. If your magic use is directly related to your memory loss, then being here will undoubtedly speed up your…condition. How can we, in good conscience, ask that of you?"

I swallow. It's a fair question. It makes me feel panicked and desperate, but it's fair all the same.

I glance down at my hands. I've had to think over this very thing so many times. Do I walk away from magic simply because using it will one day kill me?

I look up at the woman across from me. "I've had to live with my memory loss for the past three years," I admit. "Ever since my powers Awoke. And yes, spellcasting eats my memories, and it can make my life very complicated.

"But I cannot live without magic. Surely you understand that," I say, my gaze sweeping over all the witches sitting across from me. "And there's so much more to me and my magic than my memory loss." Like the fact I'm organized as hell. I'm so goddessdamned organized, it would make her head spin. "I would like the chance to show Henbane that side of me. I have a lot to offer."

By the time I'm finished, my magic has swathed me in its soft sunset glow. I'm wearing all my emotions out in the open, and it's making me feel uncomfortable and exposed.

The head witch stares at me for several seconds. Eventually, she taps the table, then stands. "Thank you for your time," she says. Everything about her expression and posture looks solemn and guarded.

Fuck.

Today was supposed to be my day. I spent so many months working toward this. There is no backup plan, except to reapply again in another four months.

I mean to get up, but my ass is rooted to this chair.

"Selene?" the head witch says. "Thank you for your time." Just the way she says it is supposed to be hint enough. She wants me to leave. The next interviewee might already be waiting out in the hall.

Emotion tightens my throat, and my hands are clasped so tightly, it hurts.

"I contest your rejection," I say, staring up at the head witch.

She pauses a moment, then lets out an incredulous laugh. "You're a soothsayer now? You peered into the future and saw your results?"

I didn't need to, though her biting response is confirmation enough.

Before I can let it get to me, I straighten my spine. "I contest it," I repeat.

She shakes her head. "That's not how it works."

Now I do stand, placing my palms on the desk. "I may not have the best memory, but I am persistent, and I can promise you one thing: I *will* keep applying and keep coming back here until you reconsider."

It's my toxic trait not to give up.

"If I may interrupt," says one of the other women. It's the witch with the wiry hair. "You might not remember me, but I am Constance Sternfallow."

She flashes me a tight smile. "I think you are a fantastic candidate," she says, "but your application is flawed in a couple of critical places. You need a better magic quest than the one you've submitted, and you need a familiar. I know it says that's optional, but really, we do require it in most cases."

Constance glances at the other women sitting at the table. One of them gives her a slight nod.

Returning her attention to me, Constance says, "If you can provide those two things—"

"*Constance*," the head witch cautions.

"—then, Selene Bowers," Constance continues, ignoring her, "you will be formally accepted to Henbane Coven."

CHAPTER 2

All magic comes at a cost.

For sorcerers, it's their conscience. For shape-shifters, it's their physical form. For me, it's my memory.

I'm a bit of an oddity among witches. For the vast majority of them, the spell components pay for their magic. And if it doesn't, the rest comes from their ever-replenishing life force. And while my own power follows the same rules, it also takes a few memories while it's at it.

It wasn't always this way for me. I had a normal childhood—well, as normal as one can have when their mother's a witch and their father's a mage—but ever since I hit puberty and my magic Awoke, it's been this way.

I step out of Morgana Hall, staring up at the cloudy sky, excitement and gut-churning anxiety twisting my insides.

I pull out my notebook and flip to the first blank page. As fast as I can, I scribble down the important bits:

August 29

Had the interview. A witch named Constance Sternfallow said you will be accepted if you can meet the following two requirements:

1. Go on a bomb-ass magic quest
2. Get a familiar

I try not to hurl as I stare down at what feel like two insurmountable demands. Magic quests are incredibly subjective; I'll be at the whim of whoever reads my paper on the experience. And finding a familiar, a witch's magical animal counterpart, is much harder than it seems on the surface.

I take a deep breath.

It'll be fine. It's *always* fine. I'm smart, and creative, and crafty as hell. I'll manifest the shit out of this.

Shoving the notebook back into my bag, I glance at another dark Gothic building to my left. This is the coven's residence hall for attending witches, and it's where my best friend currently lives.

I cut across the grass to it.

As I approach, I pass two massive *lamassu*—sphinxlike stone statues with a woman's head and a lion's body—that stand on either side of the porch, the hybrid creatures protecting the threshold of the house.

Ahead of me, the door opens, and a group of witches pours out, chatting among themselves. I rush over before the door can close behind them, and after catching it, I slip in.

Today, the residence hall smells like mint and fresh bread, and I can see wisps of red-orange magic drifting from the spellcasting kitchen to my left, where one of the coven sisters must be baking something literally magical.

All supernaturals have some identifying marker to their

magic—a color, a smell, a texture. It varies depending on the type of being you are. Witches and mages in particular are known for having colored magic—supposedly no two hues are exactly alike. And only witches and mages—and a few other select supernaturals—can see these magical differences.

I nearly go snooping around the house, drawn in by the sight of magic and the cozy feel of the place. It's been a long time since I lived among other witches, and I miss the way their power calls to my own.

Instead of exploring, I cross the foyer to the staircase ahead of me and climb it. Sybil lives in one of the many rooms on the second floor. When I get to it, I call out, "Sybil—it's me!" then promptly enter.

At first, all I see is the greenery. Her room is a mess of plants, shelf after shelf filled to bursting with whatever species she's currently fascinated with. The vined plants snake around the room, twining around framed photos and light fixtures. It's probably some sort of fire hazard, but then, from the faint pale purple shimmer of magic above me, Sybil might've already warded the room against that.

She sits at her desk, her barn owl, Merlin, perched on her shoulder. When she hears me, she swivels around in her chair, causing her familiar to flutter his feathers before resettling.

"Selene!" she says. "Shit, is your interview already over? How did it go?"

I drop my bag and shake my head. "I don't know."

Sybil's face falls a little. "Is that 'I don't know because I don't remember' or 'I don't know because I don't know how to feel about it'?"

"The latter one," I say.

I glance out her window, where I can clearly see part of Morgana Hall.

A coven is a strange thing—it's a bit like a university for witches but also offers affiliated jobs and continuation classes for witches who've graduated. There's also housing for those who prefer to keep their own company, and there's even a graveyard for witches who want to stay with the coven even into death.

The truth of the matter is that joining a place like Henbane means joining a sisterhood, one that supports you and walks alongside you throughout your life. Who wouldn't want that? Friendship, belonging, education, and a life that revolves around magic. I've yearned for it for as long as I can remember.

"You'll get in," Sybil says, drawing my attention back to her.

I give her a sad smile. "They told me my application was missing two requirements: a magic quest—"

Her brows furrow. "But you already had one of those," she objects.

I lift a shoulder. "I don't think they liked my Yosemite camping trip experience."

Sybil makes an annoyed noise. "What more do they want? Mine was one of those group magic quests that the Witches' Club offered back at Peel Academy," she says, reminding me of our high school years at the supernatural boarding school. "That was the saddest excuse of a magical quest."

After a moment, Sybil says, "So they want a different magic quest. Okay, that's easy enough to arrange. What else?"

"They want me to find my familiar."

"What?" Now she's starting to look outraged. "But that's not even a requirement. I know *five* witches personally who don't have familiars. These things take time."

Sybil's own familiar tilts his head at me, like he too doesn't understand.

I press my lips together, not saying what to me seems obvious.

The coven is making me climb these hills because, at the end of it all, they don't trust that I have what it takes.

Sybil grabs my hand and squeezes it. "Fuck them. You've *got* this, Selene, I know you do. You are a witch—you can literally make magic happen. So go home. Have a pity party. And then it's time to plot."

I do go back to my apartment in San Francisco, which is really nothing more than a basement converted into a studio flat, but it's my little slice of heaven.

I close the door, leaning back against it while I debate giving in to that pity party Sybil talked about.

At my back, something crinkles. I turn around to see a sticky note pressed to the door.

> Return Kyla's call and apologize profusely. (She's still mad at you for forgetting her birthday.) Also, buy groceries.

Damn. I pull out my big-ass planner from my satchel, making a few vials of something or other clink at the bottom of the bag.

The planner is engorged with extra sheets of paper, and a flurry of sticky notes stick out from its sides. I flip to a blank page and take the sticky note from my door and place it inside.

I'll deal with you later.

For now, I have admission requirements to complete.

I walk past my bookshelf, which is filled with more of these notebooks and makeshift planners. I go through them like potato chips. These journals of mine *are* my memory, each one meticulously labeled.

There's another mounted shelf across the room packed with homemade, handwritten grimoires, each one organized by subject.

My tables and counters are lined with stacks of blank sticky notes, my wall is covered with a zoomed-out map of the Bay Area, and all my most important places are pinned and labeled on it—my apartment, my work, Henbane Coven, and so on.

I was serious when I said I'd be an asset to Henbane.

Witchcraft is my purpose. I want to study it. I want to excel at it. I want to go out into the world and do big things with it. And I will, with or without the coven's help, I reassure myself. But that doesn't change the fact that I badly want to get in.

I cross to my desk and drop my bag next to it, then head to my kitchen.

I need tea before I settle in to work.

Unfortunately, when I get to my cupboard, a sticky note stuck to it says:

Buy more tea bags—you prefer the fancy herbal kind.

Well, damn.

I open the cupboard anyway, and sure enough, there's no tea. There is, however, a bottle of wine.

There's a sticky note on this too, only this one is not in my handwriting.

The booze-fairy was here!

<3 Sybil

Hells' spells, I love that sneaky friend of mine. I grab the wine, thanking the triple goddess that it's a twist-off cap.

I unscrew it then and there and pad back over to my laptop, drinking straight from the bottle.

Probably not the best habit to drink alone, but whatever, I'll call this my celebratory drink for standing up for myself and getting a foot in the door.

I set the bottle down and pull out my notebook before reading over the two requirements I scribbled down back at Henbane.

It's the second one that's going to give me hives.

Get a familiar.

I drink half the bottle of wine while I ponder how the fuck I'm going to do this. It's not as though I haven't already *tried*. The thing is, a familiar isn't just any animal. It's a particular creature whose spirit resonates with your own and literally binds itself to you. Supposedly, familiars are the ones who find their witches, but that hasn't happened to me yet, and I'm increasingly skeptical that it will happen anytime soon.

Okay, screw number two for now. I take another swig of the bottle, feeling the first stirrings of a buzz. I'll focus on the other requirement, the magic quest.

Every witch has to participate in one of these quests. The idea is you go out into nature, connect with your magic on a deep, spiritual level, and then you write about your experience. In theory, it's supposed to be life changing, but now that it's a requirement for coven membership, it's been cheapened and commodified.

But whatever, the coven wants me to give them an exciting quest?

Fine.

I open an airline site, musing over where exactly I should go. I'm sure the admissions board believes an exciting quest begins with an unusual destination.

Siberia? The Kalahari Desert? The Gobi Desert? I could go to the North Pole, ride a narwhal, and call it a day.

Only, when I scroll through international fares, everything is so *damned* expensive. My god. I'd need to sell a kidney to afford the airfare alone.

Oh, wait. They have deals on flights under this little tab.

I click it.

Oklahoma City—that's…hmmm. Could I make that work?

Nah, probably not.

I filter the results to just international flights and begin looking again.

Reykjavík—don't they have natural hot springs? Sounds nice.

Venice—I don't know. It *seems* magical, but not in any sort of wild, natural way.

London. Paris. Athens.

I rub my head. All these are faraway destinations, but none of them fit the bill.

I take another swig of wine. Perhaps tonight is not the night.

I'll sleep on it and hopefully come up with something tomorrow.

"Great Goddess's left tit."

I stare at the receipt for the nonrefundable plane tickets *and* the nonrefundable cruise I booked to the Galapagos Islands.

I mean, high-five drunk Selene for finding a destination I would legitimately love to visit.

But also, what in the actual fuck, drunk Selene?

A *cruise*? How did we even afford this?

One look at my credit card alerts me that we did *not*, in fact, afford this. Drunk Selene simply decided that future Selene would have to figure it out.

I spend a good ten minutes trying not to hyperventilate.

Maybe I can work overtime until kingdom come so I can pay this off. Or I could try to find more magical odd jobs. Those helped pay the bills this past year when money from my restaurant work didn't quite cover it.

I take in the trip itinerary again.

This is what I get for drunkenly buying myself a magical quest.

It'll be all right—I'll fly to Ecuador, board the boat, enjoy the hell out of the cruise, try desperately to bond with some creature—*any* creature—willing to be my familiar, and then return to the States, where I'll present my magic quest and my newly acquired familiar to the coven. Wham, bam, thank you, ma'am.

I write all this information down in my journal and blow out a breath.

South America, here I come.

CHAPTER 3

I gaze out the airplane's window, taking in the thick mass of clouds stretching off in the distance. Now that I'm actually in the sky and on my way, my excitement is sinking in.

I'm going to *the Galapagos Islands*. Forget travel expenses or magical quests—these largely uninhabited isles have been on my bucket list for a while.

When the view of clouds, and more clouds, and oh, look, *more clouds*, gets boring, I let my mind drift back to when I first became a witch.

Over three years ago, shortly after I began attending Peel Academy, a boarding school for supernaturals, I—and every other new student—went through an induction ceremony: the Awakening. For supernaturals this is an age-old tradition, one that manifests our latent powers.

We're given a draught of bittersweet, and the potion brings to life our paranormal aspects. That's when I first felt my magic stir within me, and it was when I learned of the steep cost it demands.

I return my attention to the book in my lap—*Multifunctional Magic: Ingredients and Rhymes to Apply to Everyday Spellcasting.* Because my mind is not always reliable, I have what I fondly like to call *adaptive magic.* Fancy for *I'm just going to feel things out and wing it.* I don't mean to brag, but it has about a 62 percent success rate.

And honestly, that's better than nothing.

But I'm hoping the more I study and learn, the more I can actually ease off my innate abilities and draw on things like lunar phases, crystals, spell ingredients, and incantations. I have to believe that the more knowledge I commit to my mind, the harder it will be for my power to completely erase it.

Empress…

I pause, a scowl pulling at the edges of my lips.

Did I just hear something?

A whisper of magic brushes against my skin, drawing out goose bumps.

Come…to…me…

I set my pen down.

Okay, what the *fuck* was that?

I glance around to see if anybody noticed. Most of the other passengers are sleeping or watching something on their personal TVs. I do, however, catch sight of a plume of indigo magic snaking down the aisle.

Is someone spellcasting—?

EMPRESS!

The plane lurches, and the deep-blue magic now lunges for me, the cloudy wisps of it twining up my legs and around my waist. I bite back a yelp when I see the dark strands of it moving higher and higher by the second, obscuring the bottom half of my body.

I spare the people around me a quick glance, but though a few passengers are looking around, no one else seems to see the magic causing the disturbance or the fact it's only clinging to me.

I make an absurd attempt to push it away, but the magic is as ephemeral as smoke, and my hands move right through it. The man seated next to me gives me an arch look. Nonmagical humans can't see power the way witches can. I'm sure I look ridiculous swatting at nothing.

Before I can explain myself, the magic holding me in its grip tugs downward, *hard*, and the plane dips again. I swear it feels as though it's trying to rip me right out of the sky.

The aircraft lurches to the right, and my book tumbles off my lap. I can't see where it landed; the blue-hued magic hides it from sight.

Above me, the Fasten Your Seat Belt sign dings on. The overhead intercom crackles to life. "Hello, passengers..." the flight attendant begins.

Come to me!

I grab my head as the booming masculine voice drowns the intercom announcement. I can't tell if it's coming from within me or not, but it seems to be everywhere, and I have the oddest urge to give in to its demands. All the while, that distinct blue-hued magic is making its way up my torso.

The overhead lights flicker, and my stomach drops as the plane loses altitude. A few people cry out.

"This is just turbulence," the flight attendant continues, translating the reassurance into Spanish and Portuguese while the sky outside seems to darken. "Please remain in your seats. Someone will be by shortly to take another beverage order."

I peer out the window again, but I can't see the clouds

anymore. Instead, thick plumes of indigo magic press against the outside of the plane.

Empress, heed my call!

Maybe it's panic, or maybe it's this strange hold the magic has on me, but before I'm even fully aware of what I'm doing, I've unbuckled my seat belt and risen to my feet. Muttering distracted apologies, I angle my way past the surrounding passengers and into the aisle, and the churning smoky power moves with me.

More deep-blue magic is pouring in through air vents and seeping in from the walls themselves, rapidly filling the cabin.

"Hey!" a nearby flight attendants calls, catching sight of me. "Get back in your—"

My queen!

I gasp, putting a hand to my head as the plane jerks downward. I fall against a nearby seat even as I feel more of that magic wrapping its tendrils around me.

I pause, my heart galloping, and I have a moment of absolute clarity.

This is a magical attack.

My eyes sweep over the plane and all its passengers, even as that one flight attendant starts yelling at me to sit back down. I can't tell if the attacker is inside the plane or somewhere on the ground, but I don't think I have time to find the culprit and deal with them.

The aircraft hasn't righted itself; it's still plummeting, and my stomach has a sick, weightless feeling to it.

The offending magic is everywhere, and it's growing stronger by the second. It looks like an indigo cloud, the great plumes of it darkening the cabin. No one else seems to notice this, which means I'm probably one of the only supernaturals on board, and I may be the only one who can do anything to stop it.

Ignoring the flight attendant still calling out to me, I focus on my own power, letting it rise to the surface. It presses against the underside of my skin, and I swallow, my heart pattering away nervously. I love my magic, I relish the freedom and strength it gives me, but there's always a prick of terror, knowing that each time I use it, memories will vanish—and I don't get to choose which ones.

I have no magical ingredients to mitigate the cost of this magic—nothing but the incantation itself. For whatever reason, spells like the neatness of a rhyme.

"I call on my power to fend off this attack," I say, summoning my power. "Force out the enemy and beat their magic back."

I open my eyes as my magic pours out of me. The pale orange hue of it makes it look like clouds at sunset, and as it meets the deep-blue magic, that image only strengthens, the two opposing powers looking like the day giving way to night.

My magic pries the offending one from my torso and slowly but surely pushes it out of the cabin. As I watch, the last strands of it slither out the vents and the seams around the windows.

Once it's all gone, I draw in a shuddering breath, sagging a little when the plane evens out. Around me, other passengers visibly relax. Then I grit my teeth as I feel the slightest tug in my head. It's the only indication that I must've lost a memory.

"...I said, get back in your seat!" The flight attendant's voice is shrill, and she's pointing at me and giving me a look I think is supposed to scare me.

Too late for that. I'm already terrified.

Overhead, the intercom comes on.

"Sorry, folks." The pilot chuckles. "Just some local turbulence. It looks to be—"

My queen…I felt *you…*

My magic lingers the air, shimmering just the slightest. But as I watch, that insidious blue magic seeps back into the cabin.

"*No,*" I whisper.

When it brushes again my own, the contact is gentle.

I swear I hear disembodied laughter.

Yes. My queen, there you are.

Within seconds, it weaves itself through my magic, blending them together until it's the color of a bruise.

How I have searched for you.

The fuck is this voice?

Now heed my call, Empress, and COME TO ME.

The plane bucks, then begins to fall in earnest. This doesn't feel like a little turbulence; this feels like the pilots have lost control of the plane.

People are screaming all over again, and the flight attendant has taken her eyes off me long enough to instruct passengers on proper safety protocol.

While she's distracted, I dash up the aisle, falling against the seats to my sides as the plane bounces and sways. I haven't figured out exactly what I'm doing until I'm storming through the first-class seating area.

Whoever I'm up against, their magic is stronger than my own. I can't hope to stop the attack. The best I can do is mitigate it. If someone is really trying to drag the plane out of the sky, then all I can do is try to help land it.

Give in to this…to us…

The alien magic coils around me, and it feels as though it's trying to slip inside me. Like it wants me to breathe it in so it can get as close as possible. The experience is fucking unnerving, and yet some aspect of this magic beguiles my senses.

More flight attendants shout at me, demanding I turn around and return to my seat. So far, they haven't physically tried to restrain me since their attention is divided between me, the other passengers, and the hazardous walking conditions in the cabin. However, the closer I get to the front of the plane, the more frantic their voices grow. As I near the cockpit, one of them finally moves to cut me off. I think he means to tackle me.

"Stop this man in his tracks." I lift a hand toward the attendant. "Be my arms and push him back."

I flick my magic out at him. The flight attendant stumbles away, falling into the lap of a nearby passenger. I can feel terrified gazes at my back, and I sense a few people rising from their seats, clearly assuming I have bad intentions.

More of my magic lashes out, shoving these misguided heroes back in their chairs.

There are stronger and more terrifying forces at play right now than a young witch.

Come, little witch. We were never meant to part.

The voice is like velvet, coaxing me. It halts the very breath in my lungs.

I force myself onward, toward the locked door of the cockpit.

I reach a hand out and don't even bother with a snappy incantation. "*Open.*" My magic leaps out of me, causing the lock to tumble and the door to swing open.

Come to me, Empress.

I nearly fall into the various switches and buttons on the dashboard as the indigo magic yanks on the airplane again.

One of the two pilots glances over at me. Then she does a double take.

"What in the—?"

The other pilot barks out, "Get back to your seat. *Now.*" Behind me, I can still hear several people shouting at me to get back to my seat.

I push away from the dashboard and lift a hand to the door. *"Close."*

It swings shut, and the lock tumbles into place, sealing us off from the rest of the cabin.

The male pilot glances between me and the door several feet away that seemingly shut itself. His eyes widen with incredulity and perhaps a touch of fear.

"Someone is trying to take us out of the sky," I say, as though that explains my own magic.

To punctuate my words, the plane jerks violently, throwing me forward. I barely manage to catch myself on the pilots' seats, trying to regain my bearings.

"I'm here to help land the plane."

The woman laughs, the sound containing all sorts of skepticism. And honestly, I'd probably laugh too if some little shit who collapsed onto my dashboard claimed she could help.

Come to me…Empress…

The ghostly voice whispers in my ear and against my skin. The hair on my arms stands on end. There's something perversely alluring about that voice.

"Listen, I don't care how experienced you both are—you're working with forces beyond your senses, and you're not going to be able to land this plane without my help."

I'd like to say they were roused by my words, but the truth is, both pilots have returned their attention to flying the plane, and the woman is telling her companion about some course of action that might work.

Right.

I close my eyes and take a steadying breath, focusing inward.

"Use my power. Ignore my pain. With this spell, I'll land the plane." I incant the rhyme over and over as my power flares, then spreads out from me.

When I open my eyes, I see it clear away the deep-blue magic that obscured the view out the front window. Once I can see our surroundings, I try not to scream. There are rolling mountains and a sea of trees beneath us, and they're growing closer by the second.

Oh Goddess, we're going to die.

I take a deep breath and force the insidious thought away.

I just need to help land the plane. It's not impossible. I concentrate on my power again, letting it unspool from within me, and continue to repeat the incantation.

My power rushes out of me and flows to the underside of the plane. I cannot see what it's doing, but I vaguely sense it pressing against the aircraft's smooth metal underbelly. And then I feel it ripple as though it's becoming its own air current. Hell, maybe it is.

It strains, working to shift the angle of the plane.

Not enough! Not enough!

I grit my teeth, my head throbbing from my exertion.

"I call on magic most arcane. Protect these people. Land this plane." My voice grows louder, even as the turbines roar and muffled screams filter in from the cabin.

With each utterance, more magic pours out of me. That opposing magic is still present, but rather than battle for dominance, its magic *melds* with mine.

Once it does so, I feel the nose of the plane inch up, just a little. And then a little more.

The pilots give rapid-fire commands—either to each other or someone on the other end of their headset. Maybe it's all going to be okay, maybe—

"Mayday! Mayday! Mayday! We're going down!"

Fuck.

The trees out the window grow larger and larger.

I keep forcing my magic out, straining to level the aircraft. Now that that other magic is helping, it's working. I'm just not sure it's working fast enough.

I groan, then scream at the exertion.

Empress, I sense you drawing near.

Slowly, slowly, the front of the plane lifts.

"Whoa!" the pilot says, glancing down at the wheel, his hands slipping off it for a moment. Even without him steering, the aircraft continues to pull up. "What the fuck?"

He glances at me, but I'm too busy incanting and directing the power to spare him a look.

"Matt, grab the damn thing and help me land this plane!" the other pilot calls out.

He does reach out for the wheel as the foliage below rises to meet us. I can see leaves on trees and the glisten of rainwater.

It's happening too fast, and I'm not strapped in—I'm not even in a seat. There is nothing to keep me from being thrown across the cockpit and out the window.

In response to the thought, my magic wraps around me, anchoring me to the spot. I'm not sure I even needed to protect myself. This foreign, insidious magic is there a moment later, cocooning me. It too feels oddly protective.

I know we're going to crash. I can see it plainly enough from the view, but I still force out more magic in a last-ditch attempt to save us. My head feels like it's splitting in two from the exertion, and I won't let myself think about the sheer quantity of memories my magic is dissolving.

A cluster of birds rises from the trees below us, scattering as we close in on the misty jungle below.

"Get ready!" the pilot shouts.

The plane hits its first branch. There's a sickening snap, then—

Whack, whack, whack—

Wood splinters and metal shrieks as the plane's underbelly grinds across the treetops. We bounce, and only my magic and this alien power hold my body in place.

The front of the plan dips, then—

BANG!

Despite the magic tethering me in place, I'm still thrown forward onto that damn dashboard, and then everything goes dark.

CHAPTER 4

"...but I thought she forced her way into the cockpit..."

"...I swear to god, she helped me guide the plane..."

"...wasn't wearing a seat belt..."

"She doesn't look hurt..."

I blink my eyes open. Above me, I see the concerned faces of several people, though I recognize none of them. One wears a pilot's uniform. The others seem to be flight attendants.

Pilots? Flight attendants? What's going on?

I frown, my gaze moving from person to person. Beyond them I can hear the soft patter of rain and the murmur of many voices.

I draw in a deep breath, the action causing my head to throb.

I know this pain—and I know the accompanying confusion.

Shit. I must've used my magic—probably a lot of it too, if my headache is anything to go by.

I take a deep breath and go over my list of basics.

I am Selene Bowers.

I am twenty years old.

I grew up in Santa Cruz, California.

My parents are Olivia and Benjamin Bowers.

I am alive. I am okay.

The people clustered around me have been asking me questions. I try to focus on one of them. "What?" I say dazedly.

"Does anything hurt?"

I frown again, then touch my temple. "My head," I say hoarsely. My muscles ache, and my clothing is growing damp from whatever is beneath me, but those are minor inconveniences. Even the headache will disappear eventually.

"What's going on?" I murmur.

"You were in a plane crash," one of the flight attendants says.

"What?" I sit up too fast, and I have to place a hand on my head as a wave of vertigo washes through me.

There was a magical attack—our plane was being pulled out of the sky—I tried to stop it.

I suck in a breath when it all vaguely comes back to me. But the tattered memory feels more like a dream than something I lived through, and when I try to pry details loose, it seems as though they disintegrate.

I blink around at the gathered crowd; then I focus my attention beyond them.

I make a small noise when my eyes land on our massive plane, which rests on a bed of flattened trees. Some of its siding has been ripped free, and the tip of the wing has been torn apart.

"I…survived that?" I say.

"We *all* survived that," the pilot corrects. He's giving me a look, like he has so much more he wants to say. "Every single one of us."

I continue to stare at the mangled plane, struggling to wrap my mind around that.

Our plane crashed. It *literally* crashed. And we all survived.

And I must've helped. My confusion and my pounding headache are evidence enough of it.

Unfortunately, I don't remember much of the experience. Except...except...

Empress...

My breath stills.

I remember that coaxing masculine voice. I—I heard it on the plane. I think, though I can't say what role it played. And trying to piece it together is only making my head pound harder. I press my fingers to my temple, trying to ease the pain.

"There's a doctor making the rounds," the pilot says, drawing my attention back to him. "Can you sit here and hold tight?"

I swallow, then nod.

He pats my leg and stands, moving away to, I don't know, do whatever pilots do when they crash-land. He does throw me one last glance over his shoulder, and there's a question in his eyes. He must've seen something or heard something, something unexplainable, and now he has questions.

I'm grateful I cannot remember whatever it is he's remembering. I have no idea how I would explain my magic.

While I get my bearings, one of the flight attendants fishes out some aspirin and a tiny bottle of water. She too gives me a look as she hands the items over, only hers is less curious and more...*rankled*. I get the distinct impression we had some sort of unpleasant encounter, and it leaves me wondering just what went down in that plane right before we crashed.

Once I've taken the medicine and established that I really am okay, she and the other flight attendants leave my side. I watch them head toward other people who are sitting or lying down. There are dozens—if not hundreds—of people milling about. Some are crying while others are holding one another or staring off into the distance.

I let my own gaze drift over our surroundings. Densely packed trees tower above us, blocking out most of the sunlight. Shrubs have found their homes here on the forest floor, fitting themselves into every available nook and cranny. The ground is wet, the plants are wet, and judging by the steady patter of rain, the air itself is wet.

A strange whooping call echoes in the distance. Beneath that sound, there are birdcalls and fainter noises that must belong to frogs or bugs or whatever else inhabits this place.

So we crashed somewhere in the rainforest, which is somewhat alarming when I realize there must be hundreds of miles of wilderness around us.

How long will it take for anyone to find us?

Around me, the jungle seems to literally darken with my thoughts. I touch my head, wondering if beyond the memory loss, I sustained some trauma to it. It's only when I see a band of deep-blue magic twisting through the trees that I realize I'm not imagining things at all.

The sight of magic out in this jungle should frighten me; it certainly looks ominous as it creeps between the trees. But it stirs something in me, something is right there, at the edge of my mind—

Empress...

My skin pricks. That voice again!

Come to me…

Without thinking, I rise to my feet. I've heard of sirens luring people to their deaths; this must be what it feels like. There's a stirring in my blood at the call of that voice. I don't know what it wants with me or if it means to do these other passengers harm, but I have the pressing need to draw closer to it.

And so I do. Before the doctor or anyone else can come check on me, slip away into the rainforest, letting the trees and the shadows swallow me up.

I don't know how far or how long I walk. I'm in a daze, pulled by the intermittent calls of that voice and the ribbon of dark blue magic that seems to be leading me onward.

Part of me is almost painfully aware that following strange voices and unfamiliar power is a bad idea, and yet there's an entire other part of me held captive by this beckoning magic.

I run my fingers over a waxy leaf and duck under a vined plant dangling from a branch, swatting away an insect that's been buzzing around me. I've been in this jungle for less than a day, and I can already tell that the world's freakiest bugs live here, I'm certain of it. I've seen at least one spider as big as a salad plate, and not five minutes ago, a beetle the span of my palm skittered by.

I wipe the sweat from my forehead.

The trip's gone tits up, but hey, I *am* getting the whole magic quest experience.

I glance over my shoulder, wondering not for the first time how I'll manage to find my way back to the crash site. Undoubtedly, I'll have to use more magic. I assumed

I'd follow the magic for twenty paces or so and find the mysterious being behind it all, but that hasn't happened.

The prolonged walk does give me time to think, namely about the freshly lost memories. There's no way for me to know which ones or how many of them burned away with the spell. That knowledge is haunting—because I could've lost something formative or wonderful or important, and I wouldn't know it. On the other hand, if I don't know what I've lost, it's hard to grieve it.

I feel a tingle of power along my skin, distracting me from my thoughts. At first, I think it's the same magic that has been calling to me, just, well, *louder.*

But it feels different in some intrinsic way. I halt when I see the magic itself. Unlike the indigo power I've been following—which even now lingers above me—this magic glints like iridescent dust motes in the air. As I stare at it, the magic coalesces, thickening around me.

My queen…

The compulsion in those words nearly gets me moving again, but I can't seem to look away from the magic right in front of me. Movement catches my eye, and I lift my gaze just as a massive shadow leaps from the tree directly in front of me, lunging right for my body.

I don't have time to move or scream. It slams into my chest, throwing me to the ground and pinning me beneath its weight.

Can't breathe.

A massive set of black paws rests on my sternum, holding me in place. I let my eyes drift up, taking in the silky dark fur that coats the animal's forelegs and chest. My attention snags on the creature's terrifying serrated teeth for a moment before my eyes rise the rest of the way, and I meet the amber-green gaze of a panther.

CHAPTER 5

Oh, my fucking goddess on high.

This strange magic led me right to a *panther*. I repeat, a *panther*.

I would scream, except my throat isn't working.

I'm going to get eaten and then shit out by this ferocious hellcat, and no one is ever going to know what happened to me.

Pull yourself together, Selene. You have magic at your disposal. No overgrown pussycat is going to end you, no matter how terrifying it is.

The panther opens its jaws slightly—enough for me to get a whiff of big-cat breath, which is as awful as it sounds.

The panther leans forward, bringing its head close to my face. The entire time, it stares at me.

I feel something then, something that gathers in the very center of my body. It takes another second for me to realize it's my magic. There's something in the air—or maybe it's in my bones—that calls to this creature. It has the same ageless feel as my magic does.

And the longer I look, the more I sense some aspect of myself behind those eyes. My fear is gone, replaced by an instinctual familiarity.

My magic hums at the thought, moving out from the center of my body and flowing into my limbs. The urge to touch the great cat, to pet it, is nearly overwhelming.

Tentatively, I lift a hand, feeling my power gather in my palm. My inner skeptic is still positive this is where I die, but my intuition is saying something different, and I trust it above all else.

The magic coiled in my palm builds, driven by some primeval witchy instinct. It makes my flesh tingle and causes my fingers to twitch a little.

The panther closes the last of the distance between us, pressing its face into my outstretched hand, as though desperate for the touch of my magic.

And that's exactly what the creature gets.

Power bursts from my palm at the contact, turning the air around us a glittering pale hue of orange. It slips into the panther just as easily as a breath of air, and I feel it *connect*. Something deep within me snaps into place then, magically linking me to the creature.

I stare up at the big cat as it gazes down at me, its face still pressed against my palm.

After a moment, it moves from my hand, leaning in as though it needs to get a closer look at my eyes. Then, all at once, it gives my cheek a lick that feels like it took off a layer or two of skin.

I reach up and dazedly pet the animal, my hand shaking a little, while inside...inside, I sense our freshly forged bond.

Holy shit, I think I just bagged myself a familiar.

I stare at the big cat for the dozenth time as I brush myself off and get my bearings.

The coven is going to *shit bricks* when they see my familiar.

Shit. Bricks.

I actually smirk a little at the thought. The phrase "be careful what you wish for" came from witches.

The panther—*my* panther—is massive. I'd never truly appreciated that about these great cats until now, when I'm standing next to one.

Of all the animals I could've gotten matched with, I got this one. He—and uh, dude's *definitely* a boy—is much prouder and scarier than the familiar I imagined for myself. To be honest, I was thinking I was more of a chinchilla girl.

Apparently not.

Even now, I can feel the soft hum of my connection to the great cat. It's a strange feeling, being bonded to another essence—and to that of an animal, no less. It's like discovering you have an extra appendage, only this one is sentient.

I close my eyes now and focus on that sentience and the bond that binds us together. The longer I concentrate on our connection, the more I feel a pull to slip down it.

So I do.

One moment I'm sensing the magical bond, and the next, I slide into the panther's mind.

Most of the creature's thoughts are barred from me, but I can feel his mild hunger, and I sense that he's otherwise in good health. His strength simmers just below the surface, and inside his head, I feel stronger, more athletic.

I breathe in, and through his nose, I smell a dozen different scents, each with its own nuanced meaning. Most shocking of all, when I blink and the world comes into focus, I can *see* myself through his eyes.

Freaking trippy as hell.

I swing his head around, taking in our surroundings. His vision is sharper yet less vibrant, and I can see all sorts of things in the shadows of the jungle.

I slip back into my own head, and it's like moving from one room to another—no magic needed, no memories devoured.

I have to place my hand on a nearby tree while I catch my breath.

"You are… This is…" *Unbelievable. Extraordinary.*

And most of all, *unexpected*.

Really, really unexpected.

Despite how desperate I was to find my familiar, I hadn't truly believed it would happen on this trip.

Tentatively, I step forward and stroke my panther's fur, still half expecting him to bite my hand off. But he lets me pet him, even closing his eyes and leaning into my touch.

"What should I name you?" I ask him.

The big cat says nothing, just continues to lean into me.

"Phantom?" I try the name out. I mean, he *is* scary.

No reaction. I think that might be a no.

Goddess above, I'm trying to read the thoughts of a wild cat.

"Onyx?" That one's pretty literal.

No reaction from my familiar.

"Ebenezer?" I throw out.

Now he gives me a look, and it's not a nice one.

"I'm *kidding*," I say. I take in the panther all over again. "Hmmm…you're a serious guy." Serious enough to deserve a powerful name, one of a ruler.

From the foggy wisps of my memory, I drag a name forth. "Nero."

The big cat turns his head and licks my palm with that abrasive tongue of his.

"Do you like that?"

The panther butts his head against my hand, and I think that's a yes.

I pet his fur. "Yeah, I bet you get a thrill being likened to some ruthless Roman emperor."

It's as I'm straightening that movement above me catches my eye. I glance up in time to see that line of indigo magic twisting in the air. It snakes through the trees, toward what looks to be a body of water.

My queen… Find me… Claim me… Save me…

The deep-blue magic reaches for my arm, wrapping itself around my wrist as though it were a hand and tugging me forward.

I stare at it, momentarily confused. I think I assumed finding Nero was the driving force behind the plane crash and this very literal magic quest I'm now on. But, of course, that's not the case. Familiars don't actually put out any magic of their own; they simply amplify and conduct it. The voice and the insistent power pulling me toward the murky water ahead of us are something else entirely.

The magic tugs on my hand again, and I feel compelled once again to find the source of it.

Empress…

"You better not be some swamp monster set on devouring me," I call out, "because now I have a badass familiar who looks like he would happily eat swamp monsters for breakfast."

I glance at Nero, who doesn't look like he's on board with eating swamp monsters at all.

"I'm obviously bluffing," I whisper. "Just go along with it."

Languidly, the big cat stretches, then prowls forward, his tail brushing against my side as he starts after the magic.

I follow him, reveling in the subtle thrum of our connection. Though I cannot see the thin magical cord that connects us, I can still sense my familiar on the other end of it.

This is so wild.

Nero slips between the trees on silent feet, moving like a shadow through the jungle's underbrush.

We haven't gone far when the trees give way to a large, winding river.

Could this be *the* Amazon River? Because that would actually be really fucking awesome. Random, but awesome.

I stand there, hands on my hips, my combat boots splattered with mud and my skin sweaty, and I savor the ridiculous irony of the situation. I'm now getting the wild magic quest I was too broke to afford. I mean, technically I'm also too broke for the quest I purchased, but what are details?

The line of blue magic cuts directly across the river, disappearing into the trees on the other side.

I let out a sigh, then turn to Nero. "You wouldn't happen to know of any nearby bridges, would you?"

CHAPTER 6

It's not a bridge, but Nero does lead me to a boat. Well, a dinghy. One that's rusted over and partially submerged into the muddy riverbank. Inside, it's filled with decaying shrubbery, a murky puddle of water, and what looks to be a thriving, self-contained ecosystem. The floor of it is also partially rusted through. And it's missing its oars.

But you know what? It's *something.*

So I spend a ridiculous amount of time and magic repairing the *Tetanus Express* and prying it out of the riverbank. By the end of it, my head, which had stopped hurting thanks to the aspirin, begins to throb again.

I ignore the pain and my rising anxieties about the amount of power I've used today. I'm on a magic quest; I can be a little indulgent with my spellcasting.

With that thought in mind, I release another burst of my power, one that cleans the interior of the dinghy. All the while, the dark blue magic circles me.

Empress...

I ignore the voice and the restlessness it stirs in me. Instead, I drag the boat into the water, grimacing a little when my boots squish into the riverbed. I nearly whoop with joy when the dinghy stays afloat, rocking gently in the shallows of the river. It's still badly rusted and missing oars, but it floats.

I turn to Nero, who's been watching from the riverbank, and I hesitate. I've spent a lot of time thinking about how to acquire a familiar but not what to do with one once we bonded.

"Do you...want to come with me?" I ask.

Nero stares at me for a moment. Then, in response, he prowls to the lapping edge of the river and leaps into the dinghy. The force of his landing nearly capsizes the boat in the process.

"*Dude,*" I say, grabbing the edge of the vessel and holding it as steady as I can.

If Nero was at all worried about being thrown overboard, he doesn't show it. The panther plops on the floor of the boat and begins cleaning himself.

I glance one last time at what I can see of my magical repairs to the dinghy, then at the far side of the river.

Taking a deep breath, I gather my courage and hoist myself into the boat.

Before I can even attempt a spell to get this thing moving toward the far side of the river, the magic circling me now pushes at my back, propelling us across.

I let out a shaky exhale.

Well, that solves that.

It's only when we've reached the center of the river that I have my misgivings.

What in the goddess's name am I doing? Magic quest

or no, I shouldn't be wandering around in this unfamiliar jungle, letting some mysterious being lure me closer. I don't even have my notebook, so if I forget my memories from earlier today, I'm F-U-C-K-E-D.

I glance overhead at the afternoon sun.

And if I don't get back before sundown…

Doubled fucked.

But my intuition isn't warning me off this trail, and I *did* find my familiar by listening to it earlier. Technically, this *is* what a magic quest is—listening to that untamable inner voice that leads all witches.

Nero lunges toward the river, nearly capsizing the boat. *Again.* I grab the sides of the dinghy for balance while the water near us churns. I hear a crunch, and then the panther is backing up, dragging some writhing thing along with him.

What in the…?

Nero turns toward me, and clamped in his jaws is the biggest motherfucking snake I've ever seen, its head and neck hanging lifelessly, even while the rest of its body still spasms.

Ho-ly shit.

"Good boy," I croak.

He gives me a look like he might eat me next if I treat him like a pet again. He pads back to the middle of the boat and flops down, the huge twitching snake tumbling in along with him.

I grimace.

Clearing my throat, I say, "I feel like we need to go over some boat rules. Rule one—"

Nero sinks his teeth into the creature's belly.

Going to hurl.

"No eating animals on the boat."

Ignoring me, the panther continues to chomp on the dead snake.

What am I supposed to do if my familiar doesn't listen to me? Aren't familiars supposed to give their undivided loyalty to the witch they're bonded with?

I take a few deep breaths and decide this is not the hill I want to die on today.

"Fine, ignore boat rules, just don't get any blood on me—"

I feel something warm and wet hit the back of my hand.

I glare at my familiar—who is *still* absorbed in his meal. "Don't make me turn you into a housecat," I warn him.

He pauses eating to flash me his fangs.

Guess he doesn't like the idea of that all that much. "Then behave."

He stares at me for a moment longer, then goes back to eating his nasty snack.

The blue magic pushes us along, and slowly but surely, we cross the river. Overhead, the rest of the magic hangs above us like a contrail, the line of it disappearing into the trees on the approaching side of the riverbank. I swear it looks denser than it did at the crash site.

I can still feel the power pressing against my back, but it's begun to creep over my shoulders and around my chest, and a strand of it brushes against my jaw, feeling for all the world like the light stroke of knuckles against my skin.

I think it would be better if I found the touch repulsive, but I…don't, and that leaves me confused.

Eventually, we reach the riverbank. I wait until the dinghy has nearly beached itself on the shore before hopping out with Nero and dragging the boat as far ashore as I can.

Dusting my hands off, I turn to the dark jungle beyond.

Come to me…

I pause. That phantom voice is so much stronger now.

The air around me seems to vibrate. I can feel the magic as though it were alive.

Calling to me. Calling…

I pick my way through the vegetation and the looming lush trees, that insistent pull getting stronger. I stop only when I get to a dense, almost-impassable cluster of foliage.

I'm about to move away from it when I sense…more magic. Only this doesn't have the same elements as the blue magic above me.

The spell here—and what I'm sensing is a spell, not unspooled magic—is unlike the one pulling me onward. This power is so subtle that I would have missed it if I weren't looking for magic in the first place.

Now that I *am* looking right at it, I see the shimmery lines that its spellcasting left behind. Sometimes these can take the shape of writing, but other times, like right now, the spells look like nothing more than glittery string woven together.

This spell, however, is not simply a few magical strings; it's a whole tapestry. The spells—*wards* technically—hang in the air like a giant web, one so complex and so intricately wrought that it must've taken weeks if not months to create.

I study the layers and layers of protective spells, in awe that someone created this.

The most prominent of these wards are ones that will a person to leave this place. There are still more that form a magical barrier of sorts, one that would be impenetrable to a nonmagical human. Finally, I sense several overlapping enchantments that obscure whatever's beyond from view. It's all so hopelessly complicated.

Unfortunately for me, the magic I've been following cuts directly across these wards, as though they weren't there.

My queen...

That voice stirs my blood and prods my back, and if I have any hope of finding its source, I'll need to get past these spells.

I give the web of them another once-over. After a moment's hesitation, I reach out with my fingers, unsure how the wards will react. Hexes and curses could be woven into these things, and I really don't want to walk away from here with some curse that rots me from the inside out.

Help me...

I'm emboldened by that plea. There may be someone on the other side of these spells that's in true peril. And while I'm in no position to be some knight in shining armor, I am the only one who's here, so I can at least try to be brave.

I take a steadying breath, then press my hand to the web of spells.

At my touch, the entire cluster of them disintegrates, as though it were no sturdier than an actual web. But even as my hand slips right through, I feel the massive amount of power these spells released, the wave of it slamming into me and causing me to stagger back. The shock wave spreads out into the jungle, dissipating as it goes.

I frown. Spells that strong should've put up *some* sort of fight.

But I only linger on that concern for a moment because now that I've removed this section of wards, I can see the area in front of me for what it really is.

Ruins.

I stare at the toppled columns and the smashed remains of hewn arches, the white marble covered in vines and vegetation. The stone itself appears to be inlaid with golden floral patterns, and the ends of the columns morph into what look to be the boughs of trees.

I'm no expert but...I swear this architecture has the touch of the Otherworld to it, the realm where fairies reside. So what is it doing hidden away in South America?

My heart thumps harder.

Maybe I'm wrong. Maybe it's some sort of failed resort that was left to molder...

That would make some amount of sense, even if it doesn't explain the protective wards.

Tentatively, I step forward and move through the ruins.

Come to me, my queen...

That masculine voice sounds clear and close, and there's something about it that is gut-wrenchingly intimate. It makes my breath come out shaky.

I head toward it, the line of blue magic still guiding my way. It weaves between the structure's fallen features. My gaze snags on a bit of smashed stone and what appears to be part of a marble branch, the end of it morphing into what looks like a real leaf. But that can't be right.

The more details I take in, however, the more certain I am that this isn't some failed resort. Instead, it appears to be an unearthly palace left to rot. Most of it is thickly buried beneath strata of vegetation, but here and there I catch glimpses of what once stood here.

I step up to one of the more intact walls, pushing aside a curtain of plants. Underneath them, I take in the marble, my eyes lingering on the gold inlay of a coiling flowering plant decorating the wall.

This definitely seems made by the fae. Maybe one of them even lived here.

Empress…

I step away from the wall, letting the foliage drop back in place, the haunting voice luring me to it once more.

All around me, I feel more of those wards. They're everywhere, glittering in the air, wrapped around toppled columns, coating the few standing walls. Someone went to pains to cover every square inch of this place in spells. It would take me hours to figure out what each one's purpose is and longer still to remove them all.

Ahead of me, the inky-blue magic slopes downward from the sky, the strip of it eventually sinking into the earth. I follow it all the way to where it meets the ground.

Reaching out, I run a hand through the indigo magic. My fingers tingle pleasantly as they pass through it, but nothing else happens.

I toe the damp earth right where the power meets it. All I see is mud, yet I sense wards deep below—wards and something else, something I am antsy to uncover.

I raise my palm to the mud, and I force my power through it.

"*Unearth your secrets from below,*" I incant. *"Reveal to me what you know."*

My power hits the ground with so much force, it blows thick globs of mud far and wide. Under the direction of the spell, my magic peels away the soil layer by layer. It takes several seconds, but eventually, I uncover a section of marble flooring that looks identical to what I've seen in other parts of these ruins.

Well, identical save for the swath of magic slipping down along its seams.

Save me…

I swallow. The voice is coming from *beneath* the floor in question. I figured as much, but now…now I'm having to make sense of that.

The deep-blue magic gathers around me, coaxing me to uncover whatever lies beneath that slab. I open my mouth, scrambling to fit together another spell, when something else entirely pours from my lips.

"*Buvakata sutavuva izakasava xu ivakamit sanasava,*" I incant, my voice deepening with my power. *Open and reveal that which is hidden.*

The words raise the hairs on my arms, not only because they're foreign and haunting but because they came as naturally to me as English.

Beneath the touch of my power, the stone slab vibrates as it begins to pry itself free. As I watch, tendrils of blue magic slip between my own, and on some level, I feel that contact. A heady shiver courses through me.

With a groan, the marble slab lifts from the ground and slides aside.

I exhale, my nerves on edge.

Now that the floor has been removed, I can make out an opening and steps leading down into it. The dark ribbon of magic descends into the darkness below.

Do I dare go down there?

Come…to…me…beloved…

The voice whispers like a lover, brushing against my ear and raising the hairs at the nape of my neck. The words should be off-putting, but I'm too bewitched by the voice to turn back now.

Even if I were, it wouldn't matter because my familiar slips past me before heading down the steps, like forgotten subterranean chambers are not at all scary or troubling. As he descends, mounted torches flare to life, revealing a long set of stairs and a hallway far below.

"Nero!" I call out. I'm supposed to be the one taking the risks here with the strange voice, not my familiar.

If he hears my voice, he doesn't listen. My familiar disappears, and while I can still hear torches lighting somewhere beyond my line of sight, the sound grows more and more distant, presumably as the panther moves deeper into the chamber.

"Nero!" I call out again.

Nothing.

I slip into his mind just to make sure he's okay. One second, I'm staring down at the dark opening, and in the next, I'm inside, prowling forward, claw tips clicking against the stone flooring. Through Nero's eyes, I see massive walls and flickering shadows, and I can smell…something.

Something *alive.*

In an instant, I'm back in my own head.

I had understood that some being was behind the magic and the voice that called to me. Still, it's obvious this place has been long forgotten, bound in wards that have outlasted the spellcasters themselves.

And yet, despite the forgotten state of this place, something still lingers here alongside these wards, something sentient and magical, and my brand-spanking-new familiar is heading straight for it.

Not good, not good, not good.

Before I can think better of it, I plunge down those stairs after Nero, following the torchlight and the trail of indigo magic.

About halfway down, I notice how dry everything is. Even

the air, which was so humid aboveground, is parched here. On either side of me, torches flicker and hiss, giving off not just the smell of smoke but also frankincense and cinnamon.

I trail my fingers over the walls, where I see the iridescent sheen of spells. The same magic I met earlier is here again, hanging heavy in the air. I don't believe it belongs to that disembodied voice, but that only deepens the mystery. The power fills the space, coating the air and walls like honey, and the blue magic seems to twist and contort—just a little—around it. Odd.

Odder still, I sense it's supposed to keep people away, and yet it seems to welcome me, brushing against my flesh like the softest silk.

Once I get to the bottom, I cast my gaze down the long hallway in front of me. It curves out of sight, that ribbon of magic disappearing with it.

"Nero?" I call.

Nothing.

I look back up the stairs and give the sky one last remorseful look before continuing.

The walls here are carved with images of trees and beasts and warriors on horseback, the firelight and shadows making them dance. Draped over it all are more shimmery webs of spells.

Farther down the hall, the images give way to lines of text. The letters seem to jiggle a little as I look; the words themselves are spells. The writing appears to be...Latin. However, the longer I stare, the more I realize *this is not actually Latin.*

It's the Latin alphabet but not the actual Latin language.

And the only reason I know that is because *I can read this text.*

I say a line out loud. *"...azkagu wek div'nusava. Ipis ip'na-sava udugab..."*

...bind fast within. Keep safe for all eternity...

One of the nearby spells flares to life, stirred by my invocation.

My eyes pass over the rest of the text. Whatever this language is, it's something else, something from far away and long ago that seems to make my blood sing and my heart awaken.

An itchy, restless feeling stirs beneath my skin. It's that same feeling I get when I come across a hole in my memory. I feel turned inside out.

There may be things I can no longer remember, but then there are things I do inexplicably know.

Latin is one of them.

Latin and apparently whatever this language is.

I want to linger here and read this spellwork, just to taste this language on my tongue again. It...evokes some dear but unnamable emotion in me, something I've only felt in dreams.

But the longer I stand still, the more that blue magic coils around me. I can now sense the presence it belongs to beckoning me closer.

I tear my attention away from the wall and move on.

The narrow hall eventually opens into a chamber as large as my apartment, the entire space already lit by torches.

The room is decorated from top to bottom with more writing and images of fantastical beasts. I see griffins and deer with antlers that morph into the branches of nearby trees. I only spare it all a passing glance.

It's what lies at the center of the room that grabs my attention.

Nero lounges on a massive block of white marble, the

stone intricately carved to resemble a massive tree trunk. The fae who surely carved this went to great lengths to capture the texture of the bark and even what appear to be tree rings on the exposed end.

The trail of magic ends there, disappearing into the carved stone through a seam that runs the length of it.

It's not simply a block of stone stylized to look like a massive felled tree.

It's a *sarcophagus*, and this chamber, a *crypt*.

And yet…there's something *alive* in this place. Something that lies in that stone coffin beneath Nero.

Horror rises in me as I muse on that. Whatever's inside that coffin is alive enough to call to me.

How long have they been trapped here?

My queen…

Goose bumps pebble along my skin. The voice is so much louder and more intimate here in this room.

At last, you have come…

It is only now that I realize this voice has not been speaking to me in English. I just understood it as such. In fact, I understood it so well that I hadn't even *thought* to question what language it was. But I think it's the same one written on the walls.

That deep-blue magic pushes at my back, interrupting my thoughts and urging me toward the sarcophagus.

A chill sweeps over me as, reluctantly, I return my gaze to that coffin. As though I can't help myself, I step closer.

Nero stands then and hops off the lid, exposing a smooth rectangular section of marble inscribed with more lines of text, though it's hard to make out what it says from here. Ropes and ropes of spells cover the entire sarcophagus, the torchlight flickering off the phantom sheen of them.

The sheer quantity of spells looks excessive, but then, I don't know what sort of being it contains, only that they were able to lure me here while trapped beneath it all.

I lick my dry lips, more of my misgivings bubbling up. I close the last of the distance to the coffin, peering down at the lid.

I run my fingers over the writing inscribed there, feeling the divots where someone painstakingly carved them into the stone. That simple brush of my hand is enough to release the knot of spells. The threads of them split and unravel, and the released magic blows my hair back as it passes through the chamber, making the flames dance wildly in their sconces for a second before resettling.

My fingers trace the inscribed letters, and I form the words on my lips. *"Zoginutasa vaksasava vexvava ozakosa pesaguva ekawabiw di'nasava."*

For the love of your gods, beware of me.

Beneath that is a name.

NU'SUWNUSAVUVA MEMNON

MEMNON THE CURSED

Conflicting emotions roil within me like sand kicked up in the tide. Fear, anticipation, *desire.*

Empress...

More than anything, I have the overwhelming urge to open the coffin. It goes against good judgment and rational thought, but then, most of today has gone against good judgment and rational thought. Why break from precedent now?

I didn't come all this way to stop at the last moment.

Decision made, I splay my hand against the cool marble surface.

Closing my eyes, I draw in a deep breath and focus on my power.

"Spells unbind. Lid be cast aside. Reveal what lies within."

Magic surges from me, slicing through the last of the spells coating the coffin. The pale orange plumes of it gather around the stone lid. It's eerily silent as my power lifts the carved slab into the air, then slides it aside. Only once it's completely clear of the sarcophagus does it fall.

BOOM!

The lid hits the ground, cracking apart. Clumps of dirt trickle from the ceiling and the earth tremors, just a little. I wave my hand at the cloud of dust it kicks into the air.

Once the dust and the magic settle, I peer into the open sarcophagus, my pulse racing.

Resting within it is a man—a stunning, *flawless* man.

This is no mummy—this isn't even a fresh corpse. His chest isn't rising or falling, but his olive-toned skin has a ruddy, sun-kissed appearance. It's almost as though he were out in the sun hours ago and merely came in here to rest. And yet, if it were that simple, he would have woken up by now.

Even asleep, this stranger is the most mesmerizing person I've ever seen. I stare at his sharp high cheekbones, then his subtly hooked nose. His coarse black hair curls around his ears, and his lips…I can already tell those full, curving lips were made for wetting panties and ruining girls' hearts.

A wicked scar cuts from the corner of his left eye toward his ear before sharply plunging down to the edge of his jaw.

Memnon seems like a badass. A hot, violent badass.

My pounding pulse grows louder and louder as I continue to stare. Something is happening inside me, something that has little to do with this man's dangerous beauty.

Over my heart my magic gathers, the sensation so sharp, so visceral, I have to place a trembling hand over my chest just to tamp it down.

I move my gaze to Memnon's broad chest, which is covered in scale armor. Unlike his physical form, the armor he wears appears brittle and tarnished. His leather trousers and boots look even worse off, the clothing rotted away completely in certain places. The tunic he wears beneath the armor is all but gone. Only the sheathed dagger at his hip looks like it's in decent condition—that and the golden rings he wears.

My love...

My gaze snaps back to Memnon's face, my breath leaving me at the endearment. I'm sure it wasn't meant for me, but I'm moved by it all the same.

As I stare at him, I feel the strangest sort of longing, like my heart is shattering and reforming.

I lift a hand, reaching for him. Whatever force drove me here now desperately wants to touch this man—Memnon the Cursed.

Free him, my mind whispers. *Rouse him from his deathless sleep.*

When my hand is a hair's breadth from Memnon's face, I hesitate, remembering myself for a moment. But then I'm sucked under the spell of this place and the magic surrounding us. Tentatively, I press my fingertip to the edge of that scar near his eye.

I bite back a yelp when the skin *gives* beneath my fingers. It has the icy chill of death clinging to it, but it's—it's *supple* the way living skin is.

Slowly, I trace the scar, following the line of it to his ear, then down, to the edge of his jaw. My hand brushes against his hair, and there is an ache in me so deep. So, so deep.

Free me...little witch...please...

The sound of his voice only sharpens that ache.

How long I have waited…for you…only you…

I place my hand against the man's cheek, ignoring the way that inky-blue magic is filling up this room and that shrewd little voice inside my head is screaming at me to run from this place.

Instead, I draw in a sharp breath, then speak a single command in the same language that surrounds us. "*Obat'iwavak.*"

Wake.

CHAPTER 7

Wind tears through the chamber, nearly extinguishing the torches. A scream rises, and another voice fills the room.

What have you done? it wails.

I pull my hand from the man's cheek, blinking away the strange daze that's shrouded me ever since my plane crashed.

What *am* I doing?

Before I can come up with an answer, the man's eyes snap open.

I stumble back, a hand going to my mouth to muffle my scream.

His irises are a beautiful brown color—dark along the outside edge and light like bourbon on the inside. His pupils dilate as they take me in.

Memnon draws a deep breath, his chest finally rising. As he does so, several scales from his armor slide off his chest, clinking as they fall.

"*Roxilana*," the man breathes, still staring at my face.

My breath catches at his voice. It's no longer echoing

and disembodied, and the rough, human quality makes it all the more intimate.

If longing were a sound, this would be it.

His eyes seem to devour my form. "You found me. Saved me." He's still speaking in the same language written on the walls. I don't know what it is or why I understand it.

Memnon sits up, and dozens more metal scales fall from his chest.

I take a step back, then another.

He places his hands on the lip of the stone coffin and rises.

Oh, Great Goddess, *he's getting out.*

In one fluid movement, he steps out of the sarcophagus. His clothes slide off his body, and his scale armor falls like rain to the ground, tinkling as it goes.

The undead man doesn't seem to notice any of it; his eyes stay fixed on me.

I, however, *do* notice—both because it leaves him naked and because his exposed skin is covered in strange stylized tattoos, the images mirroring that of the artwork around me. Animals and flowers twist up his arms and spill onto his chest and neck. More wrap around his calves and climb his thighs. There are a few others sprinkled onto his lower abs, and there may be more on his back that I can't see. It looks like the ink is slowly closing in on him from his outer extremities to the very center of him.

He strides toward me, staring at me like I'm his oxygen, completely oblivious to the fact he's mostly naked, save for the few remnants of armor and clothing that cling to him like linen wrappings.

"I knew you would come, my queen." The air stirs around him with his magic, it fills the space and brushes against me. "I knew it wasn't true. It couldn't be. A love like ours defies *everything*."

His words evoke images I can't make sense of. I see miles and miles of grass stretching in every direction. I hear the snapping of tents in the wind, the clopping of hooves. There's skin on mine, flickering lamplight, and a voice in my ear. *I am yours forever...*

The images slide away as quickly as they come.

"*Vak zuwi sanburvak*," I say, not needing my magic to respond to him in the same language. It's there, buried in my bones. *You are mistaken*.

"Mistaken?" He laughs, and holy shit, whoever or whatever this man is, he's got a really nice laugh.

He steps up to me and cups my face, and I'm taken aback by how proprietary the touch is. Not to mention the way he's looking at me.

"I'm not...I don't know you." The words don't exactly match up with their English translations. Whatever old language this is, the lexicon doesn't even focus on the same things English does. I feel like a different person when I speak it.

"You don't know me?" His lips twist into a playful smile. "Come now, what sort of game is this, Roxilana?" His eyes twinkle, and he really doesn't give a shit that he's naked right now.

I wrap my hands around his wrists, ready to push him away. But at the contact, he lets out a ragged exhale, closing his eyes briefly.

"Your touch, Roxi. How I have yearned for it. I was caught in a nightmare I couldn't wake from." He opens his eyes, his expression painfully raw. "Long I have languished. Through it all, I held on to the hope that you would come and save me, my queen."

Okay, something is very, very wrong here. I'm not this Roxilana, nor am I a queen or an empress. And I'm definitely not *his*.

I open my mouth to say this very thing when Memnon leans and kisses me.

I suck in a sharp breath.

What in the ever-loving hell?

A naked and newly resurrected man is *kissing* me.

That thought has barely registered when his lips part mine like I'm a lock and he's the key. And then I taste him.

He *should* taste like cobwebs and rotting corpses—but if anything, I swear I taste heavy, decadent wine on his tongue.

My hands move from his wrists to his pecs, my touch knocking away a few more pieces of scale armor. I have every intention of pushing him away, but his tongue strokes mine in the most carnal way, and my fingers decide to dig into his skin instead.

He groans at the pressure, stepping in closer, his naked thigh brushing my clothed one.

And…unwittingly, I kiss him back.

He makes another sexy-as-sin noise and pulls me flush against him, kissing me like he'll die if he stops.

One of his hands has dropped to my waist, and now he's toying with the edge of my shirt, and I know exactly where this will go if don't stop it now.

It takes a whole lot of willpower to break off the kiss, and even then, my feet don't want to move away from him.

Memnon's still cupping my face with one of his hands, his dark eyes searching mine.

"I called to you, Roxi. For so long I called to you, but you never answered. My power grew weak, and then it slumbered, only rousing when…" He blinks, looking down at himself, then at my attire for the first time. "Am I dead?" he asks, his gaze rising to mine once more. "Are you here to lead my soul to the afterlife?"

The afterlife?

"What are you talking about?" I say. I step back, out of his embrace. "My name is *Selene*, not Roxi."

His brows pull together, his mouth twisting into a frown.

This man is obviously confused. He thinks I'm someone else and that we're somewhere else, and I don't know enough about this entire situation to figure out how to handle it well.

His gaze moves to the writing scrawled on the walls. He narrows his eyes as he takes in the inscriptions.

I follow his gaze.

...Memnon the Cursed will sleep the sleep of gods...

...bound to this room...

...powers muted...

...memory cast from the minds of the living...

...forced to sleep...

...never aging, never dying...

I clear my throat. "I...take it you were cursed?"

When Memnon's face returns to me, his expression has changed, hardened, that scar of his looking stark against his skin.

It takes effort not to piss myself at how frightening he appears.

"It was *true*, wasn't it? It was all true. I didn't believe Eislyn, but she was right." He catches me by the chin and tugs me to him. "My queen, *what have you done*?"

"Whoever you are," I say slowly, "you need to let go of me. Now." Only after the words are out do I realize I spoke in English.

"What has addled your tongue?" he demands, tightening

his grip. His scowl deepens. "Or is this some new language you've learned to curse me in?"

All around us, I see his magic thickening the air.

"Whatever it is you have done to me, wife," he says, pulling me in close. "I vow to you that it will not happen again." Despite his nearness, there's no warmth to his touch. Only a punishing sort of possessiveness.

His power closes in on me, and I sense he's readying some awful spell.

Shit, shit, shit.

I push at him, but this time, Memnon doesn't release me.

"Let me the fuck go!" Apparently, I can curse in this language.

Cool beans, I guess.

He laughs low, the sound raising the hairs on my arms. "Let you go? Oh no, no, little witch, you're not going *anywhere*."

The man says something too low for me to hear, but I feel his magic rise.

"Not now that I've caught you. You thought to curse me?" He shakes his head, though I see betrayal blazing in his eyes. *"I will make you pay for what you have done for the rest of our days."*

He steps in close and presses his mouth to mine. I fight against the kiss, but it's not actually a kiss at all.

Memnon's power swarms around us. I feel it slipping down my throat and coiling in my lungs.

"*Sleep*," he murmurs against my lips.

And the world goes dark.

CHAPTER 8

I blink my eyes once, twice, three times.

Above me is the rough surface of an earthen ceiling. I'm lying on my back, and my cheek is wet. I reach a hand to my face just as a big abrasive tongue licks it.

My familiar. Nero.

"Hey," I say softly, sitting up.

I rub my eyes. There's a foggy feeling in my mind, one that often accompanies missing sections of time.

I do, however, remember Nero.

My familiar butts his head against my chin, purring a little as he steps in close.

"I'm okay," I say softly, my voice a little hoarse. "I think."

He pushes himself to his paws, gives me another brief lick on my cheek, then walks away. Pretty sure that was panther for *there, there, now get the fuck up.*

Shakily, I stand, glancing around me. I remember this room, with its strange writing and even stranger carvings. I remember tromping through the rainforest to get here.

My eyes fall on the open sarcophagus, its lid broken on the floor beside it. Nearby I see the shredded remains of the scale-mail armor.

And I remember Memnon, with his bourbon eyes and fantastical tattoos and terrifying scar.

I will make you pay for what you have done.

I have that big bad feeling inside of me. Something isn't right. Something is *deeply* not right.

"Memnon?" It comes out as a whisper. I'm not even sure I want the man's attention. Not after he veered from passionate desire to enraged betrayal.

Save for the soft hiss of the torches, the chamber is quiet. Quiet and gloomy.

I think he's gone.

I look at the walls and the text that runs rampant across them. This was a place filled with spells meant to seal "Memnon the Cursed" in. And it had done a damn good job of it until I came along.

My gaze returns to the broken sarcophagus lid. I can still see the warning scrawled across it.

For the love of your gods, beware of me.

I press my palms into my eyes.

Oh no. Oh, no, no, no.

I released something better left buried. And now I have no idea where he is or why he thinks I'm...*his.*

My queen... A love like ours defies everything... *I am yours forever...*

I rub my temples.

That alone would be problematic, but *no*, he's also convinced I fucked him over.

Ugh.

All at once I have the pressing, claustrophobic need to

flee this place. I stumble across the room, then down the long hallway. The magic that filled this space is mostly gone; I feel the hollow throb of its absence. All that's left are the few tattered remains of spells. They may be enough to ward off people who venture close by, but it's not nearly enough to put Memnon back in that box.

At least he's not here.

Halfway down that curving hallway, I stop. Nero already rests at the foot of the staircase. But the sunlight that should be shining on the steps above him is gone.

Shit, shit, shit.

Is it nighttime already?

I rush over to the stairs, the decorated walls mocking me with one name that stands out over and over.

Memnon.

Memnon.

Memnon.

Goddess, but this guy sucks big time. I trip up the stairs, Nero following me. It's only as I near the top that I notice it's not actually nighttime at all. Or maybe it is—there's no way of knowing for sure because our exit is now covered by a stone slab. In the dim light, I can just make out the spell that covers it, the magical threads a familiar midnight-blue color.

Just by the way the power coats the slab and oozes around its seams, I can tell it's a containment spell.

"Fuck."

I glance back at Nero. "Got any ideas on how to lift this thing?"

He gazes back at me, his tail twitching. I swear the big cat is giving me a look that says, *You're a fucking witch. Spellcraft that shit.* But you know, I probably just reading into my cat's expressions too much.

Regardless, I admit, "I'm afraid that if I use more magic, it'll cost me too many memories."

Nero stares at me for several long seconds, then turns around, descends the stairs, and flops down in the hallway, as though he expects to just…remain locked in here.

"Nice show of faith in me!" I call after him. To myself, I mutter, "You show a cat one ounce of vulnerability, and they assume you're a chickenshit."

Which, full disclosure, I *am*. Still, I don't need judgment like that from my familiar.

I turn back to the stone slab above me. Doing nothing isn't really an option. Nero and I are lucky to have been left here unharmed, but what if the monster comes back?

And shit, what if he *doesn't*?

What if he left us here to die?

Fear closes my throat.

My memory isn't endless, and if I overuse my magic, I don't know what exactly will happen. That's the ominous event horizon.

It won't happen today. I vow that to myself. I *will* get us out of here. Whatever it takes.

I focus once more on the spell. It gives off a glittering sort of light. Unlike the wild plumes of it that I saw earlier, in this form, Memnon's power looks like some indecipherable writing, all of it made by one continuous magical thread. It looks as though it were drawn onto the stone slab above me.

After a moment, I reach out and touch it. It's ever so slightly warm, and I find that, oddly enough, I *like* the feel of it. I stroke the thread, feeling my way around the spell. Definitely a containment ward; I can sense Memnon's intent woven into the magic. *Stay* and *keep* seem to be the overriding words coming off it.

Though it's not the time or place, I can't help but wonder what sort of supernatural he is. There are many who can wield magic, and though there are ways to tell the difference through spells themselves, I don't know them.

My fingers linger on the ward, and as I muse, the intricately wrought thread jiggles and shifts until it eventually moves from its fixed position. The shimmery blue cord coils itself around my middle finger. The spell slithers down my hand, winding around my wrist like a makeshift bracelet.

It's as though the magic likes the feel of my skin every bit as much as I like the feel of it.

I stare at it, half in horror and half in awe.

"This is so weird," I murmur, watching the spell unmake itself as it moves onto my skin.

I should be worried about touching it. It's obvious enough now that this magic belongs to Memnon, the creature I freed from this...prison. Everything about him seems volatile, his magic included. And yet it doesn't eat away at my skin, nor has my touch invoked some secondary spell. It simply peels itself away from the stone and gathers on my hand and wrist until eventually, the entire spell has migrated onto my skin. There it lingers for a few seconds before dissipating.

The magic broke its own spell.

"So, so weird," I murmur again.

Once the magic has completely dissolved, I eye the stone slab once more. I lean my shoulder against it and push, but it doesn't so much as budge.

Below me, Nero yawns, flashing his canines and making a sound that would be cute if it weren't a direct insult to my ability to bust us out of this joint.

I back down two steps and raise my arm, baring my palm to the slab.

"Lift this stone and cast it aside. Let me see what lies outside."

My magic pours from my hand and coats the slab, and then the massive stone lurches upward, then drags itself aside.

I stare at the dying light above me with both relief and a sense of foreboding. Nero and I are free, but now it's nearly night.

Night. Alone in the jungle. Where there is a plethora of predators—and among them, an ancient, *vengeful* supernatural.

I shrink back a little. The deepening shadows beyond the tomb's entrance would be a perfect place for Memnon to lie in wait.

Nero, however, has no such reservations. Now that we're free, the panther slinks past me, picking his way through the ruins.

I hesitate for only a few seconds longer before gathering my courage—and my magic—and stepping out of the crypt.

In the dying light, the ruins look hauntingly beautiful—or maybe beautifully haunted. I can't quite say which it is, only that the sight of them plucks at my heartstrings and makes the back of my neck tingle.

I turn and face the subterranean chamber once more. Raising my hand, I incant, "*Hide what has been found. Place this secret back in the ground.*"

My power sifts out of me and wraps around the stone slab. Even to my own eyes my magic looks weak and sluggish, but it still manages to drag the slab back into place, the stone settling with a *thump*. Nearby muddy earth tumbles and rolls back over the door, then packs itself down. A few seconds later, the ground looks as it did when I found it.

I might've sealed that tomb, but it doesn't matter. The ancient menace it housed is now free.

And I'm at the top of his shit list.

I must not forget about this, I coach myself. *I must not forget.*

As soon as I'm back to civilization, I'll commit an entire sketchbook to this experience, and then I'll make copies of that book and stash them around, so I don't ever forget that *I woke up something I should not have.*

I make my way through the ruins. A few tenacious spells still cling to toppled stones and crumbling walls. The place pricks at my skin. It feels unnatural—too imbued with magic that has grown wild over time.

I rub my arms, eager to leave. And yet, every so often, I pause and glance around, trying to figure out what this structure once was, curious to dig through what little rubble remains just to see what I might find. There's an unnamable feeling running through me, the same sort of feeling certain dreams can give you, the ones you can't seem to shake.

Perhaps it's because this place seems so dreamlike to begin with—enchanted ruins lying in an untamed paradise. And there's a part of me that's sad to walk away from it, even knowing that it was supernatural prison of sorts.

I make my way back over to the riverbank, where Nero is lapping up water. I take in my surroundings in the fading light.

Good news: my boat isn't gone.

Bad news: because the universe hates me, it's in the middle of the fucking river.

I wade in, too annoyed at my situation to even be scared of what may lurk in the water.

"Fuck this trip. Fuck this place. And most of all, fuck that tit-gobbling whore, Memnon."

My entire body throbs from magical overuse, but I still manage to scrape up enough power to blow the boat to shore.

Something brushes against my leg, and I zap it. "Don't mess with me now, fish!" I yell at the water. "Today is *not* the day!"

After an absurd amount of time and effort, the hulking garbage can of a boat reaches me. It's nothing more than a dark smudge on the water, now that sunset has given way to twilight.

At the sight of the vessel, Nero pads over, then hops in before I do. It's only when I hear a wet squish that I remember there's a dead snake carcass on our boat.

Awesome. Really stoked to board this thing.

I have to take a few deep breaths. It could be worse—I could've forgotten there was a dead snake and stepped on it. Or my earlier repairs to the dinghy could've given out and sunk the thing. Or the boat could've drifted away altogether.

So I delicately situate myself on the dinghy and force out more magic to blow the boat across the river.

It's only once we're nearly to the other side that I realize I have no idea where the crashed plane is or how I'm supposed to get back to it from here.

Hells' spells.

I close my eyes and pinch the bridge of my nose.

A minute later it begins to rain.

The universe definitely hates me today.

CHAPTER 9

By the time the search and rescue team finds me the next day, I traveled roughly twenty miles from the crash site, which was in some remote northern region of Peru. It takes another two days to get out of South America and back to the States. The whole thing is a logistical nightmare, and that's not even touching on the personal aspect of it. I still have to talk my parents out of returning to the United States from their prolonged vacation in Europe to help me.

Now I unlock the door to my apartment and flip on the lights. Nero slinks in past my feet, his face tipped up and his nostrils flaring as he takes in the scents of my apartment.

I drop my bags in the entryway, cross the small space, and flop onto my bed.

And then I just lie there, my body unwilling to move.

A moment later the bed dips as Nero hops on next to me. I can't imagine how hard it's been for him. Panthers aren't meant to be taken out of jungles and forced to travel on planes (which is a whole other story, one that involved heavy magic usage) and live in homes. He's been shoved into the world of humans, and I feel rotten for my role in that.

"I'm sorry," I whisper softly, reaching out to pet the top of his snout.

Nero closes his eyes and lets out a contented low sound. It's not a purr—I learned yesterday that panthers can't purr—but it's a happy enough noise.

It doesn't make me feel any better.

I continue absently petting him. "Think I can just lie here forever?" I ask.

He gives me a blank look.

"I want to assume that's a yes, but you seem less the nice-friend type and more the honest-friend type, so I'm going to guess that's a no." I sigh.

Nero responds by stretching on my bed, his body pushing mine to the edge of the mattress.

"Oh, come *on*. You're going to have to share," I say.

He just stares back at me.

I give the beast's body a big push. In response, Nero growls.

"Get *over* it. Until you can pay the rent, I'll be calling the shots. Now *scoot*."

He doesn't.

"Do you want me to turn you into a parakeet?"

Now, *begrudgingly*, my familiar moves over.

I resettle on my bed. "Just so you know, this arrangement isn't going to work when I have boys over."

Nero makes a noise, and I can't be sure, but it sounded like a scoff. Like a fucking *scoff*. As though this random jungle cat—who has probably never been around humans—cannot imagine a situation where a guy would wind up in my bed.

"I *can* get boys," I say. I sound defensive even to my own ears.

A quieter noise comes from my panther. It still sounds disbelieving.

I think my familiar may be an asshole.

"I'm going to ignore your lack of faith in me," I say.

Then I drag myself off the bed. "All right, I can sleep when I'm dead." I pad toward the kitchen. "What we need is some food, some coffee, and some music." I crack my knuckles. "We have a coven to get into."

Armed with a mug of coffee, a snack bag of cookies for me, and some thawed chicken breasts for Nero, I sit in front of my laptop and type out my experience in South America.

I mention my original plans for the magic quest, then how my plane crashed. I describe the disembodied voice that called to me and how, while following it, I discovered my familiar. The paper pours out of me. The only thing I don't mention is the main event: I discovered and freed some ancient supernatural. Not only do I doubt they'd believe me, but then I'd also have to explain why I unleashed a menace and where he is now. And I cannot truthfully answer either of those questions.

I'm just making my final edits to my paper when my phone rings. I glance at the caller ID. *Sybil.*

I bring the phone to my ear. "We're calling each other now?" I answer. "Haven't I told you that my introverted ass only does texts?"

"Ah, my kindhearted best friend," Sybil says. "I knew you missed my voice."

"I always miss you," I tell her honestly.

"Aww, Selene, I love you, babe. I was actually calling to convince you to come to Henbane's harvest party," she says.

Of course, this is why she's calling. It's so much harder to tell her no over the phone than via text.

"That's for coven members only," I say, just in case she forgot.

"You and I both know you'll get in after all you went through," she says.

Wait, Sybil and I already talked?

I spend a frantic moment shuffling through my memories before I vaguely remember the conversation I had with her back at the airport in Quito, back when I was contacting friends and family to let them know I was all right. The plane crash was big news, even internationally.

"So," Sybil says, interrupting my thoughts, "you'll come to the party?"

Of course I want to go to the party. I just...I don't want to feel like an outsider. This is my third attempt at getting into the coven, and considering Henbane's fall semester starts at the end of next week, it's not looking so good for me. I feel like I'm starting to garner people's pity.

I chew on my lower lip, opening the calendar on my laptop. "When is it?"

"This Friday."

That's two days from now; it's doubtful that I'll know if I've gotten in by then.

"I'm tired. I just got back," I say.

"Pleeeeaaase," she begs. "The Marin Pack will be there. So will the mages from Bladderwrack Grove."

Now she's throwing the promise of hot shifters and magical dudes at me.

"I don't know," I say, still wavering.

"Come *on*. We hardly ever get the chance to see each other these days."

Sneaky friend, she knows just how to pile on the friend guilt.

"There'll be witch's brew to drown your regrets in," she continues, "and I heard that Kane Halloway might be there."

I place a hand over my face. "Goddess above, girl, when are you going to let me live that crush down?"

I was in love with the lycanthrope since the moment I laid eyes on him at Peel Academy three years ago. After he graduated, he returned to the Marin Pack, where he'd been born and raised. I don't know whether I have supremely good luck or bad luck that his pack's territory lies right next to Henbane Coven. If I were in the coven, I'd probably see him a lot; the witches tend to freely mix with the werewolves since they're neighbors.

"Live him down? Oh, I'm not going to stop bringing him up until you have your wicked way with him."

"Sybil."

She cackles like the witch she is. "Come on, you know you want to go to the party."

Do I? Because right now, all I want to do for the next month is curl up in my bed with a book and a cup of tea.

I glance at the calendar again.

There will always be time to read.

I sigh. "All right. All right."

My best friend squeals. "Yes! And remember to wear a skanky dress."

"Sybil—"

"And bring a broom, you freak. It's going to be fun!"

CHAPTER 10

The wind moans through the trees, rustling the evergreens that loom all around us. The air has a chill to it, and I can smell woodsmoke somewhere nearby. South America feels like a world away.

I don't have a broom, though my dress is probably short enough to make Sybil proud. I'm one misstep away from everyone getting an eyeful of my coochie.

Nero walks at my side, and I'm so proud to have him there. I feel like he's always belonged next to me, and getting to show off him off in all his hulking, ferocious glory puts my magical insecurities to bed.

People won't pity a witch who's snagged a panther as a familiar. That's the sort of bond that inspires respect—and maybe even a little fear. I wouldn't entirely mind that, if I'm being completely honest.

The two of us cut past the lecture halls and the enormous three-story greenhouse, then head into the Everwoods, the forest surrounding the coven. I follow the distant sound of laughter and music, and for a moment, I pretend I belong here, that I know this campus the way I so desperately want to.

My phone vibrates against my cleavage, which is being used in lieu of a purse.

I pull my phone out, checking the text from Sybil.

Are you here yet? Do you need me to come meet you? We're just past the greenhouse.

I hurriedly respond.

I'm all good. On campus now. I should be there soon.

A gust of wind kicks up, sending a violent shiver through me.

I rub my bare arms and glance over at Nero. "Are you cold, buddy?"

Nero's eyes flick to me just long enough to make me feel like I asked an inane question.

"Fine, fine, forget I asked."

My heels crunch fallen pine needles, and the smell of woodsmoke grows stronger. For a witch, that smell stirs something deep in the bones. This is the magic we're made of—midnight fires and fog-shrouded forests.

The woods open to a clearing filled with dozens and dozens of supernaturals chatting, dancing, drinking, and laughing around bundles of dried cornstalks. Most of the women, I recognize from the coven, but there are some unfamiliar witches, as well as several lycanthropes as well. I take in the mages—the male equivalent of a witch—and the other lycans. Magic shimmers in the air above them, glittering off the light from the bonfire and the enchanted lanterns that float in the sky.

I've missed this.

I've spent the past year maneuvering the regular world filled with nonmagical humans and their nonmagical lives. I forgot how a gathering of supernaturals can make my blood thrum.

I hear a squeal, and then Sybil is running over to me, her drink sloshing in her hand, while her owl, Merlin, lifts off her shoulder where he's been perched.

"There you are!" she calls, her long dark hair swaying behind her. "I was worried you wouldn't show—" Sybil stops short, her eyes landing on Nero. "What in the Tiger King hell is *that* thing?" she says, staring at him. Her own familiar glares at the panther; Merlin looks as put out as an owl can look.

Did I not tell her?

"This is my familiar, Nero." I place a hand on Nero's head, ruffling my panther's fur perhaps a tad more aggressively than I need to.

In response, my familiar growls, probably because he's aware I'm being an ass.

He and I have a love-hate relationship.

"*That* is your familiar?" she says, edging back a little. "I thought you said he was a cat."

Nero gives me a long look, like I've disappointed him. But you know what? He's the one who licks his own butt, so he has no grounds to be judgmental.

"He *is* a cat," I say defensively. "He's just a really, really big one."

"You think?" Sybil says. Her owl flaps his wings in agitation, clearly uncomfortable being this close to a panther.

My friend looks equally uncomfortable, like she's fighting her own instincts to flee from such a large predator. Not that she needs to worry about that. Familiars are fairly safe to be around. As an animal extension of myself, Nero will only attack another human if I command it or if it's in defense of my life. Short of that, he'll act in line with my values, and those don't include maiming best friends.

After a moment, Sybil's expression brightens. "Well, hey, there's no way Henbane Coven can deny you now, not when you have a familiar like *that*."

Among witches, it's commonly thought that the stronger the witch, the bigger and more powerful the familiar. And I am flattered and proud, and I feel redeemed for all the struggles I've faced. But as I glance down at Nero, I bite the corner of my lip. Talking about this has unlocked a whole new worry—that I may have more familiar than I can handle.

Nero certainly seems to think so.

After a moment, Sybil collects herself and links her arm through mine. "Come on. Let's get a drink."

I let her drag me across the clearing, past the sparking bonfire and a fiddler playing some upbeat tune. Next to him is a harpist, though she's currently leaning back on the fallen log she sits on, a drink in her hand, talking to a mage wearing the crest of Bladderwrack Grove, which is the local magical association for mages.

When the fiddler catches sight of Nero, he halts his song, watching my panther with wide eyes. And a nearby group of what must be shifters sniff the air as we pass them. The moment they trace the scent back to Nero, they go preternaturally still, their eyes turning luminous as their wolves peek out.

In fact, little by little, the party goes quiet. I've never had so much attention fixed on me at once. Though, technically, it's not me everyone is looking at. Their eyes are trained on my panther.

Finally, someone shouts, "What in the seven hells is that?" The voice carries across the field.

My stomach roils as though I did something wrong. I don't know why I feel this way. I've wanted people to recognize my worth as a witch for so long; apparently, I have no idea what to do now that they're forced to.

I pause and place my hand on Nero's head as I search the crowd for the voice. "This is my familiar."

Somehow, the silence deepens; the only sounds are the crackling fire and the hiss from another witch's familiar.

Then someone else says, "Man, that's fucking dope as shit."

A nearby witch laughs, and just like that, the tension eases out like air from a balloon.

Sybil grabs my hand once more and continues to pull me along as the rest of the party goes back to chatting.

"So, *have* you heard from the admissions committee yet?" Sybil asks as we make our way to a massive cauldron. Wildflowers grow thickly around its base, and steam drifts up from it.

I shake my head. "No," I say softly, trying not to think about spending another year yearning to be part of the coven.

The two of us reach the cauldron, which is filled with a deep, plum-colored liquid. Herbs and dried flowers float on its surface, and white smoke drifts up from it.

Ah, witch's brew. Exactly what I need to soothe my frayed nerves.

"Another drink already?" a nearby witch says to Sybil, pretending to be shocked. "You *lush*!"

Sybil and the witch cackle together as Sybil helps herself to a drink and grabs me one as well.

The other witch's eyes move to me, and I see recognition spark in them. "Hey," she says, "you're the girl from the plane crash, right?"

I take the cup Sybil hands me. "Um...yeah."

In my mind's eye, I see that indigo magic.

We were never meant to part...

"That's so wild. I heard that the way the plane landed could've only been achieved by magic," she says.

That's news to me.

"Did you help land it?" she asks. The witch has a look in her eye, one that makes me a little nervous. I've hated being overlooked, but between Nero and now this, I'm pretty sure I hate the spotlight even more.

"I can't remember," I say because it's the truth. My memory of the event was wiped.

Still, her words linger with me.

The way the plane landed could've only been achieved by magic.

The witch's gaze moves to Nero, and I can practically see her next question. *Did you find your familiar while you were there?*

Before she can voice it, Sybil grabs me by the wrist and begins dragging me away. "We'll be back for more brew soon!" my friend calls.

I give a helpless wave and follow her. "Are you going to stop manhandling me any time tonight?" I ask.

"Don't pretend like you wanted to stick around to answer Tara's questions," Sybil says.

True.

I bring my drink to my lips rather than answer. This batch of witch's brew is smoky, and it tastes a bit like licorice. It doesn't always taste this way; sometimes it's floral, sometimes it's citrusy, and sometimes it's honeyed. The only consistent part of the alcohol's flavor is the mildly bitter undertone that is *espiritus*, an ingredient that interacts with our magic.

Sybil pulls me in close. "I'm sorry to say that Kane is not here."

I nearly choke on my drink.

"Oh my goddess, Sybil," I say. "Please stop talking about him. I liked him a long time ago."

She scoffs. "If a month ago is a long time."

I narrow my eyes at her, unsure whether she's remembering something I don't or if she's just playing me.

My empress...

The hairs on my arms stand on end.

Holy Mother.

My eyes dart to the trees encircling the clearing, looking for the man behind the voice.

Miss me, little witch?

My breath hitches.

This cannot be real. I left him in South America. He'd been naked and speaking in tongues, confused about where and when he was.

There's no way he managed to make it back here.

"Selene?" Sybil says.

I'm coming for you.

I glance frantically around. Last time I heard his voice, his magic had been everywhere, the dark hue of it filling the crypt. Now, however, the air is saturated with all sorts of magic. If Memnon's is among them all, it's blending in with the others.

And when I find you, beloved, I intend to make you pay.

"Babe, are you okay?" Sybil says, cutting into my thoughts. "You look like you've seen a ghost."

I wet my lips, then focus on her. My whole body is trembling. Nero leans against me, lending his support. I place my hand on his head, slipping my fingers through his fur.

I take a long drink of my brew. Then, lowering my voice, I admit, "When I was in South America, after my plane crashed, I think..." I look around to make sure no one else is listening in. I swallow. "I think I woke something," I whisper.

"What?" Sybil gives me a skeptical look. "What do you mean you *woke* something?"

I remember Memnon's eyes: dark and smoky on the outside, light like honey on the inside. I remember the way those eyes looked at me, as though I were everything Memnon loved and then everything he hated.

"I... After the plane crashed, there was a voice—and magic—that called to me."

"Called to you?" she echoes, her eyebrows rising in disbelief.

I nod. "My memory of it is a little fuzzy. But that magic...it led back to a tomb."

"A *tomb*?" She's looking at me like I've lost it.

"Goddess be damned," I whisper. "I'm not making this up. I found an undisturbed tomb while on my magic quest, and I fucking *disturbed* it." I pause to take a deep breath. "Listen, I know it sounds hard to believe. I'm not Indiana Jones. Still, I followed a trail of magic that led to a crypt, and I entered it."

"*Why would you do that?*" she whispers furiously. Now, finally, she seems to believe me.

"I don't *know*." How can I explain the effect his magic had on me? Even now I remember how it whispered in my ear, and tugged on my skin, and drew me ever closer to the tomb. I...couldn't ignore it. I didn't want to.

"Okay," Sybil says, waving my explanation away. "So you went inside a crypt..." She waits for me to continue.

I take a deep breath. "The place was covered in spells, really arcane ones. I don't know how long they'd been there, but they were still intact."

Sybil nods. "That sometimes happens with old spells," she says. "Age can strengthen well-placed magic." This girl loves magical history.

I continue. "Beyond all the spells, there was a sarcophagus—and I, uh, opened it."

Sybil pinches the bridge of her nose, then takes a large swallow of her drink. She shakes her head. "You're never supposed to open shit like that. Tombs—especially old ones—are full of curses."

About that...

"There was a man inside the sarcophagus, Sybil. He looked just as alive as you or me, except he was sleeping." I lower my voice even further. "Somehow, he was the one who had been calling to me. I don't know how he managed to use his magic when he couldn't wake, but he did. And it looked like he'd been in that coffin for centuries."

Sybil frowns. "Selene, I say this with all the love in my heart, but are you sure you weren't just imagining this? Maybe you got a concussion during the crash..."

I give my friend a look. "My memory may not be perfect, but I *know* what I saw."

If anything, Sybil looks more horrified, not less. "Then what do you think happened to this man?" she asks.

"He was cursed"—*My queen, what have you done?*—"by someone close to him, I think."

"And they buried him alive in that tomb? For centuries?"

It's a terrifying prospect. "I don't know, Sybil. There's

obviously more to the story than that. He seemed…like he might have done something to deserve it."

She stares at me for a long second, her expression strange. "You said earlier that you woke something," she begins slowly. "Please don't tell me that *he* was that thing."

I swallow. "I mean, I couldn't just leave him there."

"*Selene,*" she admonishes, like I forgot a coffee date and not, you know, let loose an evil ancient dude.

I open my mouth to defend myself, but what is there to say? It was a supremely bad idea. One I blithely embraced until Memnon the Cursed decided *I* was the asshole who ruined his life.

I run a thumb over the rim of the cup in my hand and chew my lower lip. "There's one more thing."

Sybil's eyes widen. "How is there *more* to this story?"

I huff out a laugh, even though my stomach is tying itself into knots. "I think Memnon—"

"Memnon? He has a name?"

I nod. I take a deep breath and meet her eyes. "I think he followed me back."

Sybil looks aghast. "Followed you *back*? Why would he do that?"

My empress.

My queen.

I can all but hear his words and see the look in his eyes when he said them.

"Memnon seems to think I was the one who trapped him in the tomb, and now he's after me."

I'm coming for you.

Fuck. I really must not forget this.

CHAPTER 11

The sheet beneath my body is soft, and the room is full of a set of unusual yet oddly comforting smells—cedar and frankincense, smoke and brine.

Soft light flickers from over a dozen terra-cotta lamps set throughout the room, and out the open windows, I hear the calls of summer bugs punctuating the night.

I glance at the bed I'm lying on, the carved wood frame made of Lebanese cedar, though I can't say precisely how I know that. Nor can I say how I know before I touch them that there are two golden fibulas—clasps—that hold my dress together at the shoulders. A couple of deft flicks, and the whole dress could fall away.

Movement on the far side of the room catches my eye.

A man steps into the open doorway, and I start at the sight of his face.

Memnon.

The fear I expect to feel is nowhere in sight. Instead, longing wells in me. I forgot how handsome he is, though, to be fair, *handsome* is too tame a word for his sharp, fearsome beauty. He wears only a pair of loose low-slung trousers, his tattooed upper body on full display.

Those luminous brown eyes are full of desire as he approaches me. He walks right up to the bed and cups my face, even as I wrap my arms around his torso, feeling the hard packed muscles of his back.

"Roxi." He says the name with a deep, guttural roll, the lids of his eyes growing hooded as they take me in.

An instant later, he's kissing me like he's drowning and I'm air. I can't help but kiss him back. I haven't forgotten how well he kissed or how he did it with a possessiveness he shouldn't feel.

I don't mind it either. I know I should. But all I can think about is the fact this man probably fucks like he kisses, and I wouldn't mind finding that out for certain.

I stare up at him, my heart beating fast. I can't seem to breathe, and there's a pain in my chest that I think is happiness, only I've never known happiness to hurt.

He searches my eyes. "My empress. My wife." And then, as though he can't help himself, he leans in and kisses me again, his lips rough and hungry. I'm swept out to sea by the glide of that mouth. I fall into the kiss, enjoying how he tastes like wine.

He drapes his body over mine, pinning me to the bed, and I gasp into his mouth, the action tugging at me.

I break off the kiss, my lips already feeling swollen, and I search Memnon's eyes. "I've…missed you," I breathe.

But no, that's not what I meant to say. Is it?

He smiles, the action showing off one of his sharp canines.

Memnon leans in as though he's about to kiss me again.

Right when his lips are a hair's breadth from mine, he says, "I don't believe you."

He shifts his weight on me, and all sorts of wanton desires well within me. I'm breathless with them, even though there's confusion too.

Something isn't right, but what?

I know I said the wrong thing, and he had the wrong response for it, yet he's still on me, and my hands are still caressing his back, and his hips are lightly moving against mine.

He shifts again so his lips skim across my cheek and brush my ear. "But *I* have missed *you*. I have missed you so fucking much, little witch."

He moves from my ear to press a kiss to my chin. There's a devious gleam in his eyes, and the corner of his mouth curves up in another smile. He somehow makes sinister look sexy.

His hand moves to my waist. "Let me show you just how much," he says, gathering the material of my dress with his fingers.

He pulls my skirt higher and higher, baring my legs. The entire time, he stares at me, his eyes daring me to stop him.

I don't.

I'm too curious and full of yearning.

It's only when my skirt is around my waist and Memnon's hand falls to my inner thigh that I gasp.

"Has our time apart made you shy, my queen?"

His other hand falls against my other inner thigh, and he spreads them, almost obscenely. Only then does he tear his gaze from my face. His eyes seem to feast on my exposed flesh.

Heat floods my cheeks. *"Memnon."*

I'm mortified; I'm turned on. I don't know what to do, but I'm pretty sure I'm too curious for this to stop.

Memnon flashes me another wolfish grin. "Say my name again like that, little witch." His eyes flick back to mine. "I like hearing your voice tremble."

I swallow, and he must notice the action, because his attention dips to my throat.

"*Memnon*," I repeat, and it sounds like a plea. For what, I'm not entirely sure.

He tightens his hands on my thighs. "*Good*, love," he praises me. "Very good."

The man leans toward my body again, as though he means to kiss me. This time, however, his mouth is headed for a very different set of lips.

I only have a moment to be alarmed.

"Memn—" I gasp as his mouth kisses my core, his lips hot against my sensitive flesh.

My hands find his head, my fingers threading through his coarse black hair. I try to push his face away even as I moan.

This should be illegal, it feels so good. I don't understand why exactly this is happening, and I think I should stop it, even though I don't want to stop it.

My head is a mess.

I try to push him away again, and Memnon does stop kissing me—but only so he can laugh lightly against me, his breath hot on my flesh.

"Turning away my kisses, wife?" he says. "How very unlike you."

My chest is rising and falling as I stare down my body at him. "I'm not…" I mean to say, *I'm not your wife*. But my body is aching, and there's still that confusion, like maybe I am? That can't be right though, can it?

So, instead, I say, "Why are you doing this?"

"Because I have missed you, and I want to reacquaint myself. Do you truly want me to stop?"

In the wake of his words, a silence stretches. I gaze at him, the firelight making that scar on his face particularly apparent.

Before I can help myself, I give my head a soft shake.

"Good, Roxi," he praises again.

I tense at the name he uses. It's not mine. Is it?

When I feel the lush press of his lips on my core once more, I stop thinking about other people's names and Memnon's motives and every other thing tugging at my mind. I stop thinking about everything except how goddess-damned good this feels.

Memnon's hands move from my inner thighs, sliding under my legs so he can cradle me by my pelvis.

I thread my fingers into his hair once more, moaning at the sensations he's awakening within me.

Memnon's kisses turn carnal, his mouth moving around my opening. And then he slips his tongue inside me.

I cry out, writing beneath him.

Memnon makes a noise low in his throat as he tightens his hold on me. "You taste so fucking good, little witch. Never want to leave."

"Never, ever have to," I breathe, my words half nonsensical.

He eats me out with unrestrained ferocity, the muscles of his arms bunching and his tattoos rippling as he cups me by the ass. I wantonly grind against his face, and he makes an approving noise, like he really fucking enjoys how dirty I'm being.

My breath comes in shallow pants, and I'm climbing and climbing and—

"Is my queen about to come?" Memnon says against my pussy. "Because"—he sucks on my clit, forcing me to cry out—"if so,"—another suck—"then I'll just have to—" He reaches for something and—

ZZZZZZZ—ZZZZZZZ…

My eyes snap open.

I'm sweating, and my chest is heaving.

Great Goddess, did I just wake up from a wet dream? One starring Memnon the Cursed?

I feel flustered and oddly embarrassed. And hungover. Ugh. I grimace as I taste alcohol and last night's bad decisions on my tongue.

ZZZZZZZ—ZZZZZZZ…

My phone's buzzing rouses me from my thoughts. That must've been what woke me.

I rub my eyes with one hand and use the other to grope around my nightstand—wait, no, *Sybil's* nightstand—for my phone.

Then I pause.

Great Goddess, I had a sex dream in Sybil's room? In her bed? *While she slept next to me?*

Just kill me now and end my humiliation.

ZZZZZZZ—ZZZZZZZ…

My hand brushes my phone, then knocks it to the ground.

"*Fuck,*" I curse under my breath, leaning over my friend's bed. My stomach tumbles with the action, and I force down my nausea as I snatch my phone up.

Behind me, Sybil stretches. "Turn your phone off," she moans.

I grab the phone in question, glaring at it.

I swear if this is spam, I will—

The thought stops dead in its tracks when I read the caller ID: *Henbane Coven.*

I accept the call so fast that I nearly drop it again.

"Hello?" I say breathlessly.

"Selene Bowers?" the woman on the other line says.

I clear my throat. "Yes, that's me," I say, trying not to sound as flustered and hungover as I am. Already, my heart is starting to gallop. Why would anyone from the school be calling me?

Don't get your hopes up. Don't get your hopes up—

"Hi, I'm Magnolia Nisim, from the Admissions Department of Henbane Coven."

Next to me, Sybil sits up, her hair a wild mess around her head.

Who is it? she mouths.

I cover the receiver and mouth back, *Henbane Coven!*

"I and the rest of the admissions committee have read your paper on your magic quest, and…wow." She pauses.

I take shallow breaths to calm my nausea while I wait. *What does that* wow *mean*?

Oh Goddess, what if I screwed my application up again? What will I do now? I don't think I can swing another year scraping by here—

"We are all very, very impressed."

Impressed?

I gasp, and Sybil grabs my forearm, her eyes wide and her face excited.

"We've received word from the Politia," she continues.

"The Politia?" I say, my brows coming together. That was the supernatural police force. What did they have to do with any of this?

"They investigated the crash, and they concluded magic

had to be involved in the plane's landing. You were the only known supernatural on board," she says.

When I don't respond, she goes on. "Do you know how incredible what you did was? You saved hundreds of lives by landing that plane. The media may never hear of it, but you're a hero, Selene."

I lick my dry lips, feeling confused and still nauseous.

A hero?

My mind flashes to the unsealed tomb and the empty sarcophagus.

I...I don't think that's the right word for what I am.

"Selene Bowers," she says, "on behalf of the entire Henbane community, I'd like to formally invite you to join our coven."

Two days later, I stand on the pathway leading up to Henbane's residence hall, Nero at my side.

I'm not entirely positive that this is real, not until I open my notebook and see the printed housing instructions with my name on them taped in my planner. I circled the room number—Room 306—several times.

I head up the pathway toward the front door.

This time, as I approach the *lamassu*, I pause to touch one. I don't know why I love these half woman, half beast statues so much, but I get a thrill when I realize they'll be guarding me every day.

I drop my hand and head the rest of the way up to the front door. The dark water-stained door is fitted with an elaborate bronze knocker held between the pointed teeth of Medusa. Like the *lamassu*, this is another threshold guardian.

As soon as my hand closes over the doorknob, the metal

Medusa moves, the snakes in her hair writhing, and her metal lips part.

"Welcome home, Selene Bowers," she says.

For a moment, I smell rosemary, lavender, and mint, scents associated with protection. Women's voices whisper in my ear, and one of them laughs, the sound morphing into a cackle.

And then, whatever witchy ritual that was, it's done. The phantom smells and sounds vanish, and the Medusa head freezes back into place.

I push the door open and enter the building, Nero following behind me.

Women's voices fill the space. I can't help the smile that spreads across my face.

To my left, there's a living room and a kitchen for spell-work. Beyond them is the house's actual kitchen, where food prep is handled, and across from it is our dining hall.

To the other side of me, there's a library, an atrium, and a hallway I know leads to a study room and the Ritual Room. And straight ahead is the main staircase.

Just like the harvest party, the building slowly goes quiet as the witches catch sight of me and Nero.

Right when the silence is about to feel awkward, Charlotte, a witch I recognize from Peel Academy, leans out of the kitchen and shouts, "Welcome to the family, Bowers!"

Several other women follow suit, calling out their welcomes to me. My shoulders, which had tensed, now relax. Whatever caused that silence, the women here moved past it to make me feel comfortable.

"Thanks," I call out to Charlotte and the others.

I cross the foyer and head up the stairs with my familiar at my side. The wooden stairs creak as we climb them.

I step off on the third floor and head to my right, my eyes scanning the brass room numbers until I get to mine.

Room 306.

The door has been propped open. Inside, there's a single twin bed and a blue velvet chair next to it. Pushed against the adjacent wall is an empty bookshelf. Next to it is a large window that looks out onto a gnarled oak tree.

Across from my bed rests an ancient-looking desk with an equally ancient lamp. Sitting on the center of its surface is a massive iron key.

I walk over and pick up the key.

This is a joke, right? I mean, how am I supposed to put this on my key chain without looking like some old-timey prison warden?

I glance at my door with its ornate bronze doorknob and the large keyhole above it.

All right, so this isn't a joke. The coven just hasn't updated their rooms' locks in a century or so.

Really hoping those *lamassu* do a decent job protecting this place because my lock obviously does shit.

I pocket the key anyway.

"What do you think?" I say, glancing down at Nero.

My panther looks out at the room, then rubs his face against my leg.

My eyes sweep over the place. "I'm glad you approve. I love it too."

CHAPTER 12

"Fuck. Moving." Fuck it so hard.

I collapse onto my bed.

My arms shake from carrying things up three flights of stairs over the course of the day, and my ass and legs are numb from the exertion. And that's not even getting into the fact that many of the notes and labels I put on my stuff have fallen off. And Great Goddess of Earth and Heaven, everything is *not* where it's supposed to be, and my head hurts from it all.

But you know what? It's *done.*

I stare up at my ceiling, hearing the muted laughter of witches in nearby rooms.

A thrill runs down my spine. This is my life now. I attend Henbane Coven. No more waiting and yearning. I get to live here and learn here and lean into all my long-awaited dreams.

I survey my tiny room all over again, and my eyes eventually rest on Nero.

My familiar lounges on a throw blanket I'm pretty sure he dragged off my bed and onto the floor and is chewing on a bone I got him from the butcher's. The bone makes a sickening *crack*; then I hear Nero's rough tongue lapping up Goddess knows what.

"Can you *not* do that on my blanket?" I ask him.

He ignores me.

Defective familiar.

"I should return you," I say to him. "I bet I could buy like fifty cute, fluffy familiars for the price of you."

Now Nero glances up at me, and he licks his lips. Pretty sure that was panther for *sounds tasty*.

I sigh.

After heading over to the window, I shimmy the pane up, letting in a gust of cool air.

Outside, the giant oak tree I saw earlier looms like a dark shadow. One of the tree's thicker branches tees off just beneath my window. The location and sturdiness of it is so convenient that some previous witch must've spelled the branch to be that way, either for herself or her familiar.

I turn to Nero. "I'm going to leave this window open for you so you can come and go as you please."

In response to my words, my familiar rises to all fours. After giving a satisfied stretch, he hops onto the bench seat beneath the window.

"Now, remember, no hunting humans or house pets, okay?" I tell him. "They're not on the menu."

Nero glowers at me.

"Oh, and no eating other witches' familiars," I say. "Oh, and definitely do not attack lycanthropes. It won't end well for you."

Nero gives me a disgruntled look, like I'm the world's cruelest master.

"Just about everything else is free game. I'll leave my

window open so you can get back inside." I chew on my lower lip. "You *can* climb, right?"

He gives me another disgruntled look.

"Geez," I say, holding up my hands. "No offense meant." Well, maybe a *little* offense meant. He is an ass, after all. "I just wanted to make sure."

With that, Nero springs out of my room and onto the oak branch. Without a backward glance, he slinks down the tree before silently dropping to the ground and prowling off into the darkness.

I worry my lower lip as I stare after him. That oaf better not get himself hurt. And he better stay warm.

I sit on the edge of my bed. I'm utterly spent from a day of moving, and I need to take a shower and try to unwind, but my body still buzzes with energy. Now that I have a moment alone, I want to explore. There are new smells, new sounds, and a heady thrum of power in the air itself that I want to acquaint myself with.

Decision made, I push off the bed. I'm nearly to my door when I hear rustling from the oak tree outside. A moment later, Nero quietly hops into our room.

"Back already?" I ask. "I thought you'd be out exploring all evening."

He comes up to me and rubs against my thigh before plopping down on the blanket he stole from me once more.

"I was just about to leave," I say. "Want to explore some more with me?"

In response, Nero yawns in my face.

"Fine. I'll be back in a little bit."

I grab the doorknob and head out of my new room, closing the door behind me. Halfway down the hall, I hear claws scratching against the back of the door.

Fucking cats.

I walk back to my room and open the door. Nero glances up at me, then silently slips out. I look at the inside of door and—

"Holy Mother of Magic Mushrooms, Nero, why do you have to be such a beast?" Several deep claw marks have gouged the base of the door, and wood shavings litter the ground.

Cats, man.

The lights in the hallway flicker. They look like a relic from a century ago, and judging by the magic sputtering off them, I'm guessing they're as old as they appear.

I head down the stairs to the first floor. This level is full of common rooms, most of which I have seen only in passing.

I head toward the house's sprawling library, Nero padding along beside me. When I enter, I don't see anyone inside, all the plush velvet sofas and chairs empty. On the far side of the library, a massive fireplace holds the dying embers of a banked fire.

And then, of course, are the books. Hundreds and hundreds of them nestled neatly into almost every square inch of this place.

I move through the room, stopping to touch this book or that, all while Nero follows beside me. Many of the tomes are moth-eaten, their gilded lettering rubbed half away and their pages yellowed. I bite my lip as I read the spines of books written in Latin and Ancient Greek, the old languages as familiar to me as the face of a dear friend.

Farther in, I see books on Nostradamus's writings and the Dead Sea Scrolls and several other dated texts, some religious, some not, and some occupying that space people like to call *heretical*. It's a space we witches have lived and died in.

There are historical books on witches and witchcraft, as well as books that analyze general spellcraft. It's all very academic, and I relish every bit of it.

When I get to the far end of the library, near the stone fireplace, I hesitate. To my left, an ornately carved door is set deep into the wall. Magic pulses softly from it.

Shimmery wards run along the edges of it, locking the room from supernaturals unaffiliated with Henbane Coven.

I used to be one of them. In fact, the first and only time I tried to open this door was sometime last year when I was visiting Sybil. I can't remember why I came into the library or why I tried to enter the room, but I definitely remember getting shocked. Part of me is certain the same thing will happen now.

Only one way to find out.

I reach for the handle. My hand closes over the metal knob, and I wait for a moment, readying myself for the wards to lash out at me.

Nothing happens.

Below me, Nero nudges my leg, as if to tell me to hurry up. It must be nice for him, not having to worry about getting fried by protective magic.

And I am still worried. I haven't opened the door after all.

I take a deep breath. No time like the present.

I turn the knob and pull. Above me the ward flares brightly for a moment, and yet...no painful spell lashes out at me. Instead, the door creaks as I open it. Beyond the threshold is darkness.

A second later a wave of power crashes into me, and I

stagger back. It isn't a ward striking me or anything of the sort. It's simply *magic.* Lots and lots of cloying, potent magic. I practically choke on it all as I grope around for a light switch.

I don't find one, but in the darkness, I can just make out a lantern set next to the door, a partially melted candle inside. A lantern but no matches.

I sigh.

Going to have to use magic for this.

I pick up the lantern and scowl at the wick. *"Oh, how I hate making up a new spell. Just light this fricking flame from hell."*

Whoosh.

A crimson flame bursts to life inside the lantern, and maybe it's just me, but it looks a little demonic.

Um.

Shit.

Pretty sure I just summoned a bit of hellfire.

I glance at Nero. "You saw *nothing*."

He stares unblinkingly back at me.

I worry my lower lip as I step into the room, lifting the lantern with its red flame. Not even one night in, and I'm already breaking the rules by using dark magic.

I can't focus on those thoughts for too long, however, because the sight around me takes my breath away.

"*Grimoires*," I whisper.

Hundreds of them. They're packed along the shelves, their conflicting magic rolling off them. It's already making my head throb; it's like being sprayed with dozens of clashing perfumes.

There's a long table that runs down the middle of the room, presumably where you can read over the books.

"Can't sleep?"

I yelp, nearly dropping my lantern at the voice behind me.

I swivel around and face another witch, one who probably also lives here.

Her gaze drops to my lantern. "That's some interesting light you've made for yourself."

"Uh…" This is where I get kicked out not a day after I move in.

"It's a head rush, isn't it?" she says, stepping up next to me.

At first, I think she's speaking about dark magic, but then I notice her attention is on the grimoires around us.

"Mm-hmm," I agree, even as the throbbing in my temple increases.

"Many of these were supposedly written by coven members who lived here, though some of them are far older." She gives me a conspiratorial look. "Maybe one day you or I will have a grimoire stored in here."

The thought is so wild, it distracts me from the fact I've been caught almost literally red-handed with dark magic.

"I'm Kasey, by the way," the witch says, holding out her hand.

I take it. "Selene."

"I know. I saw you at the harvest party—you made an entrance with that familiar of yours," she says, her gaze drifting down to Nero.

"Uh, yeah, he's really a sweetheart. Totally misunderstood."

Nero gives me a look like I'm so full of shit, which I obviously am, but Kasey and the rest of the witches living here don't need to know that. I'm sure it's terrifying enough to know you're sharing your house with a panther. Never mind that he has an attitude.

Kasey's gaze moves back to the grimoires around us. She points at one bound in plum-colored cloth. "That one helped me with the potency and longevity of my spells in my wards class—just a heads-up in case you're taking it this semester."

I don't think I am, but—

"Thanks," I say. "I'll be sure to check it out."

Kasey smiles at me. "Well, I'm heading off to bed." Her eyes drop to the crimson flame in my lantern before rising to mine once more. "Oh, and by the way, be careful not to burn anything—magical fires are notorious for not going out, and flames like that"—her eyes flick back to my lantern—"hunger for power."

"Nice meeting you, Selene." Kasey nods and leaves.

"Bye," I call after her.

Once I'm sure Kasey is gone and the house is quiet once more, I speak to the lantern. *"Thank you for the assistance, demon flame. Now go back to hell from whence you came."*

The candle flickers out, leaving behind a vaguely corrosive smell, and some magical black residue smudges the glass panes of the lantern. It's that tar-like substance that gives it its name—dark magic.

It draws from forces of darkness and collects sin and blood as tithe. It's forbidden, evil magic.

And my new acquaintance Kasey saw me using it.

CHAPTER 13

The week following my move-in flies by in a blur. I fully settle into my new room, Nero forms a routine with coming and going from the house to the woods around the coven. My bookshelves are finally all organized with my old notebooks, and my current one is filled with my class schedule and maps. I've picked up my course textbooks and even flipped through a few of them.

I'm ready for my first day of classes tomorrow.

I clomp down the stairs now, Nero prowling next me like a shadow. From the hall to my right, Sybil chats with another witch.

When my friend sees me, she calls out, "Selene! Where are you going?"

I should definitely be doing a better job of getting to know the witches I live with, and now is an opening to do so. I've already chatted with a few of them, and I'm embarrassed to admit that when I've been able to, I've written down their names, their familiar's species, which rooms they live in, and anything else distinct about them, like some sort of obsessed stalker.

I mean, it does work.

"I'm going to take pictures of the different buildings on campus and put together a map."

"Didn't you do that yesterday?" she says.

I hesitate now. Did I?

Sybil uses my hesitation to head over to me. "Babe, you can chill out on the studiousness," she says quietly.

Over Sybil's shoulder, the witch she was talking to now eyes me curiously.

I lower my voice. "You *know* I can't."

I wish it were different. I wish I didn't need to work harder just to be treated normally by my peers. But it is what it is, and Sybil of all people knows this.

She frowns. "It's just, we're finally under the same roof, and yet I haven't even gotten to hang out with you since you moved in."

I swallow, feeling this tension forming between us. I don't want that. I'm adamant about proving my worth here at Henbane, but I also don't want to strain my relationship with my best friend.

"I'm sorry," I say. "I just...don't want to screw this up for myself."

Sybil's expression gentles. "You won't. You're brilliant." She lets out a breath, then nods to the door. "Go ahead then. Map out the coven, and when you get back, let's hang."

I sit on a stone bench at the back of Lunar Observatory, the northernmost building on campus, as the sun dips below the horizon. One of my notebooks lies open on my lap, this one detailing all sorts of information about Henbane Coven, from my class schedule, to notes on where things are, to what times certain buildings are open and closed. There are also notes on the idiosyncrasies that certain buildings have, like the fact the chairs in Cauldron Hall are prone to levitating, thanks to a prank that was never fully reversed.

I smooth my hand over the pictures of Lunar Observatory that I've taped to the page, lingering on the glass dome atop the building that's supposedly spelled to make the heavens appear closer than they are.

There's a thrum building in my veins and tightening my chest. At first, I think it's simply me wishing I had an astrology class this semester—I don't—but...the feeling is persistent. It lingers even after I finish scribbling notes and close my journal. If anything, it seems to grow as I slip my notebook in my bag and glance up at the twilight sky.

I stand just as the lamp in front of me flickers on. I'm slinging my bag over my shoulder when magic brushes against my skin, the touch like a stroke of a hand.

Empress...I have found you.

I suck in a breath, snapping my head up. I glance around, but there's no one in this section of coven property. Yet now that I'm focusing on it, I swear I can *feel* those smoky-ale eyes on me.

There's a pressure forming in my chest, right over my heart. I move my hand to it, trying to massage the tension away.

Right as I do so, that familiar indigo magic billows out from the tree line bordering the buildings, slithering in my direction.

Last time that magic coiled around me, it knocked me out and left me trapped in a tomb.

Can't let it get to me again.

My feet move before I fully form the command in my mind.

Run.

I'm sprinting, my arms pumping and my bag banging against my side as I force my legs faster and faster. Past All Saint's Hall, past Morgana Hall. My thighs burn, and my breath is already ragged. The wind howls in my ear as I push myself harder.

He followed me back.

Goddess above, *he followed me back.*

It was one thing to hear his whispered voice carried on the wind. But to see his magic again and to know he's on the other end of it...

My nausea rises, and I force it down. *Barf later, once you've escaped.*

I feel rather than see a plume of inky-blue magic wrap around my waist like a phantom arm. I cry out, even as more of Memnon's—and it must be Memnon's—power fills the air around me, until it obscures the forest and buildings and the darkening sky.

Come to me, my queen...

I'm breathing harshly as I stop. I feel the tug of his power already, seeping into my skin and slipping into my lungs.

You left me before, but not again...never again...

The compulsion to follow that voice builds within me. I can't tell what sort of spell this is, but it *must* be one.

I follow the line of indigo magic back to the tree line. It continues deep into the Everwoods forest. I take a step toward it, even as my rational mind screams at me that I'm being enchanted.

But my blood is heating, and my skin throbs at every soft brush of Memnon's power.

Don't be a fool, Selene! It's just his magic lulling you into some false sense of safety.

I pinch my eyes shut, keeping my feet rooted in place.

Return to me, Empress. We have been parted for too long…

There's something sensual in those words and that voice, something that reminds me of the Memnon from my dreams. It breaks my resistance altogether.

I take a halting step forward. Then another. It's hard to fight that voice when my deepest, most innate senses are coaxing me toward it.

I think I'm being bespelled. That has to be what this is. I wish I hated it more than I do.

I make it to the tree line, my eagerness mounting. The longer Memnon's magic grips me, the more intoxicating it becomes.

About fifty feet into the woods, the smoky magic dissipates.

I tense, glancing around. My flesh prickles with awareness.

Memnon steps out from the darkness like some nightmarish vision. Only, fuck, this man is real. And he's even more devastatingly beautiful than in my memories.

My gaze moves over his tall frame, and it sweeps over his broad shoulders. I can see the tattoos running down his sculpted arms. Even in a T-shirt and jeans, this man looks all warrior.

My eyes move to his face, and if I weren't still ensnared by his magic, I would've staggered back.

In my dream, Memnon's intense beauty was heightened by desire and flame. Now, however, in the darkness where the shadows are deep and unforgiving, Memnon simply looks brutal—his cheekbones sharp, the curve of his lips cruel, and those luminous eyes wrathful. It's a small mercy that I can't see his scar. I don't think I could take seeing that violence on display right now.

He steps forward, moving with a menacing sort of grace. "Did you really think I was done with you?" he says softly in that old language, his voice rolling and guttural. I understand him with alarming clarity. "That I would leave you in that tomb to rot as you left me?" He shakes his head slowly. "No, no, no."

My pulse quickens. "Why did you follow me here?" I demand in English.

"Speak to me in our tongue, Roxilana!" he snarls.

"I don't know 'our tongue'!" I shout back *in another language.* The words welled from somewhere deep within me just as they did back in Memnon's tomb.

A small sound escapes me, and I clutch my throat.

See, the thing is, that was technically *not* a lie. While I have always been able to understand Latin and Ancient Greek—and even read a bit of Ancient Egyptian—I've never spoken this language. At least, not that I remember.

Memnon stalks forward before grasping my upper arms. "I don't know what game you are playing, but it *will* end."

This close to Memnon's staggering form, I feel particularly small and helpless.

"Let me go," I say in that ancient language. Again, I don't mean to speak it; it just flows from me. I'd marvel at it, but my fear is pushing out every other emotion.

"Not until you tell me what you've done to me," he demands, furious.

I ache as I stare into those eyes. This feels so much like my dream, where confusion overlays reality.

"What are you talking about?" I say, not even flinching this time when the words come out in that other language.

He gives me a bit of a shake. "You dismantled my army. Destroyed our empire, ripped me from our lands, and thrust me into this twisted future where nothing makes *sense*!" He all but roars this last part.

"*Let me go*." My voice rises with my pounding heart, and there's steel in it. My power coils within me, gathering itself. The fear I felt only moments ago is giving way to anger.

Memnon's lips curve into a smile. But his eyes are sharp as swords. "But haven't you missed me, Roxilana?"

"*Who* the fuck is Roxilana?" Again, this strange language.

He gives me an odd look now. "What is this game you're playing?"

"Why would I ever play a game with *you*? I don't even know who you are!"

"You don't know who I am?" His eyebrows lift in disbelief. Then he laughs, the sound chilling. "I have been *inside you* more times than there are stars to count. I am no more a stranger to you than your own skin is."

I have been inside you *more times than there are stars to count.*

I stare at him for a long moment, cold terror washing over me. This creature lured me to his tomb and had me spring him from it. And then he followed me across an entire continent, and now he believes we've been together—like, *together*, together.

I am in deep shit.

"There's been a mistake," I say slowly.

My mind races furiously, trying to recall my memories from South America, several of which have long since washed away. I need to get to the root of this problem.

"*Mistake?*" Memnon growls. His eyes begin to glow like

hot coals, and the air sizzles with power. I jolt, recognizing what supernatural's magic presents like that.

Not a demon. Not a vampire or a fae.

A sorcerer.

They're nearly as bad as demons. A sorcerer's power eats away at their conscience. The stronger one is, the more heartless they'll be.

And Memnon feels staggeringly strong.

Unaware of my thoughts, he continues. "After all you have done to me—after all the *betrayal*—"

"Listen," I say, cutting him off, "whoever you think I am, I'm not her." This Roxilana broad really fucked with the wrong dude. "Please, just let me go."

Memnon's eyes flare a bit brighter. "You *dare* to play ignorant. To call me a liar and what we are a mistake. You, the woman I gave everything to."

"But *I* didn't give you everything," I insist. "You have me confused with someone else."

He ignores my point. "You locked me away, denied me even the basic decency of death. I was never given funerary rites, never allowed to pass from this world to the next. You kept me from the afterlife, where I could ride the skies with my ancestors."

I stare up at the man, who looks like some ancient deity.

"Instead, I lay caged for all this time. But I am caged no longer." The last part comes out grave, ominous. "The world will know my wrath—*you* will know my wrath, my queen.

"I will put you at my mercy," he vows. "And I will destroy your world bit by bit until all you have left is me."

CHAPTER 14

I stifle a yawn as I sit in Spellcasting 101, my first class of the semester. After my encounter with Memnon, I didn't sleep much last night, instead using my time to scribble down what I could remember of the incident. Like the fact that he's a sorcerer and that he happens to want to ruin my life.

I will put you at my mercy. I will destroy your world bit by bit until all you have left is me.

At least he let me go. I hadn't been sure he would after all he had said, but Memnon did release me shortly after his threat, and he retreated into the darkened forest. Somehow, that was even more terrifying than him standing right in front of me. Knowing this vengeful sorcerer was lurking unseen in the Everwoods was partly what kept me up last night.

I rub my eyes, and my tired mind slips. For an instant I am back in my room, sprawled across my bed, my black tail…

Tail?

I snap out of Nero's mind and back into my own, forcing myself to sit up straighter and actually listen to the lecture.

"As you all know, magic is steeped in everything," my instructor says from the podium. Mistress Bellafonte is a middle-aged witch, her coppery locks shot through with white. "Most people barely sense it. Fewer still can access it. Only witches and a few other types of supernaturals can interact with and manipulate it.

"One of the oldest and most basic ways to do so is through invocation. That is, *utterance*," Mistress Bellafonte says, touching her lips. "As we move through this course, we're going to come back to this theme over and over. But for now, let's dig into that."

A thrill shoots down my spine because even though I'm tired and this topic is drier than the Sahara, I'm finally, finally a student at this coven.

"Certain elements of language can add to the potency of an invocation and thus a spell. The most obvious example of this is rhyme. But there are others. An element less commonly known is the use of ancient power words." She gives the room a meaningful look.

"Why is this the case?" she says. "It's the same reason why a witch's power only increases with age—magic is attracted to old things." She pauses again. "You will be more powerful in ten years than you are now. And more powerful ten years after that. Even when your bones are brittle and your muscles are twisted with age, magic will surge within you."

The room has gone quiet.

"The world that values your pretty, youthful face knows *nothing* of your true power. Though in time, *you* will discover it."

Mistress Bellafonte gives us a tight smile. "But I digress."

She paces around the front of the room, her periwinkle magic curling lovingly around her ankles. "In the next several weeks, we shall learn some arcane words and phrases, and we will apply them to spells before we move on to common spell-casting ingredients, the use of writing, and the role grimoires play. We'll discuss what effect seasons and the time of day play into casting, as well as lunar phases and astrological events.

"My hope is that by the end of the semester, you'll have knowledge and some commonsense tools to work with as you come to understand your own power and gifts.

"For now, let's start a basic introduction into the sounds of different dead languages.

"Crack your books open to page twenty-one."

I open my textbook and turn to the requested page. On it is the image of a stone tablet, Egyptian hieroglyphs etched into the stone.

"This is stela found in Karnak. We're not going to translate it all, but I want to recite a portion of it…"

She begins to read it, and no, that's not right. I shake my head absently. She's emphasizing the wrong consonants, and the vowels—

"Excuse me, but do you disagree with something I'm saying?"

I don't realize Mistress Bellafonte is speaking to me until her magic curls under my chin and tilts my head up from my textbook so I can meet her eyes.

My skin heats as the rest of the witches in the room turn in their seats and focus their attention on me.

The silence drags on.

"Well?" the instructor presses.

I swallow, then glance down at the words. I don't know how to voice these murky thoughts of mine, so I simply read what I can of the stela.

"Jenek nedej sew meh a heftejewef. Jenek der beheh meh qa

sa, seger qa herew re temef medew." The words roll off my lips, different from English and different from whatever language I spoke with Memnon. I feel...less certain with Ancient Egyptian, despite correcting the instructor.

I exhale and translate. "I am the one who will save him from his enemies. I am the one who removes arrogance from the haughty, who silences the boisterous so he does not speak."

It's quiet for a long moment.

"You didn't use your magic to read that," she finally says.

I meet her eyes. There's a lot of confusion in them, as well as something else, something that looks like wariness.

She blinks and clears her throat, even as the witches around me continue to stare.

"Exceptional work," she finally says before clearing her throat again. She turns from me then and proceeds to lecture the class about the stela and the power words that could be taken from it.

I frown as I read the rest of the stone tablet. It discusses martial victories against the Nine Bows—the various enemy nations of Egypt. The words on this stela would be better used to invoke dark magic, which is rooted in violence. They shouldn't be in this textbook.

A bloodcurdling scream cuts through my thoughts, the sound coming from somewhere outside the room.

Mistress Bellafonte pauses and gives us all a reassuring smile. "Probably just Mistress Takada looking at all the spells she must grade," she says jokingly before peering down at her notes once more.

But another scream follows it, and this one continues on and on.

"Murder!" someone finally cries. "A witch has been murdered!"

CHAPTER 15

"They say her eyes were gouged out and her heart was ripped from her chest," says Charlotte, the witch sitting across from me. I sit with her, Sybil, and several other witches in our dining room, all of us eating dinner.

I make a face into my food. The details are quickly making me lose my appetite.

"I heard she was naked," adds a witch named Raquel, and she looks as though she wants to hurl.

For the twentieth time today, my heart races. Memnon shows up last night full of ominous threats, and now a witch is dead?

It's just a coincidence, I try to tell myself. *He wants vengeance on* you, *not other witches.*

"Poor Kate," another witch says.

"You knew her?" Charlotte asks, raising her ice-blond brows.

Overhead, the lights in the wrought iron chandeliers flicker, making the gloomy atmosphere all the more intense.

"Mm-hmm. She was a year above me, but she'd taken a leave of absence to work for some company that needed witches. Can't remember the name of it. I didn't know she was coming back to school."

"I think she did move back," Sybil says. "I'm pretty sure I saw her moving into the house—right down the hall from you, Selene," she says, bumping my side.

"She's my neighbor?" I vaguely remember speaking to a few of the girls who lived on my floor, but I don't remember anyone named Kate.

"*Was*," Raquel corrects me.

There are so many wide, spooked eyes around our table. And when I glance at the other tables in the room, the witches present are tense, and their conversations are subdued. I think everyone is considering how the witch found on the coven's property could have been them.

Another witch with wiry hair and a sharp nose sits down, dropping a massive leather journal on the table. "I want to know what her final words were," the witch says.

My gaze moves to her shoulder, where a—*is that a newt?*—sits perched.

"What's that?" Raquel nods at the book.

"It's my own Ledger of Last Words."

"*Olga*," Sybil chastises. "Now is really not the time."

"Actually, now is *exactly* the time." Olga's eyes get a fanatical shine to them. "And I'm in the process of getting approval to pull Kate's final words. It could help catch the killer."

"That's still disturbing as shit," says the witch at the table whose name I still don't know.

Olga lifts a shoulder. "Never said I wasn't disturbed." She laughs, and some of the women at the table laugh with her until it dies away. In its wake is a tense silence, one only punctuated by the scrape of silverware.

Charlotte leans forward in her seat.

"Who do you think did it?" she whispers.

My fears expand in my chest.

It may be my fault. I released an ancient evil, and he may be preying on young witches.

I catch Sybil's eye before I swallow my nerves and shake my head.

"No clue," I say to Charlotte.

No one else at the table has a better answer.

It's only after dinner, when Sybil and I go to her room to work on our first assignments, that I decide to unburden myself.

I try to not let my chin tremble as I sit there on her floor, one of my textbooks open in front of me, while my friend moves about the room, watering dozens of potted plants crammed on shelves or hanging from the ceiling.

Now that a witch is dead—a witch who lived down the hall from me—I can't help the terror seeping into my veins.

"He found me," I say softly, jiggling one of my legs in agitation.

Sybil pauses. "Hmm?" she says, pausing to glance over her shoulder at me.

"Memnon," I say. "He found me."

"Wait." Sybil sets down her watering pail. "*What*?" Her shrill tone has her owl ruffling his feathers before he resettles on his perch.

"Yesterday, when I was getting ready to head back here, he found me. He was lurking in the woods around the coven."

"Are you okay?" she says, alarmed. "Did he hurt you? Threaten you?"

I swallow and shake my head. "I'm fine. No, he didn't hurt me. Yes, he threatened me," I answer.

"He *threatened* you?" Sybil's voice has gone shriller. "Screw the Law of Three and its consequences, I will find a curse so potent, it will shrivel his dick off."

I laugh a little at the thought.

Sybil sits in front of me, pushing my textbook aside. "Tell me everything about what happened."

So I do.

By the end of it, Sybil has paled. "So this guy *actually* thinks you're his wife?"

I nod miserably.

"And he followed you all the way here to Henbane?"

Another nod.

I twist my hands together, chewing on my lower lip. "And now a witch is dead," I say softly.

Realization fills Sybil's eyes. "You think he did it."

I scrub my face. "I don't know. It seems awfully likely though, right? He shows up, and the next day, a witch is dead."

Sybil shakes her head. "That...definitely doesn't look good," she agrees. "But it could still be a coincidence."

I want to believe that. I really do. Otherwise, that witch's death is on my conscience.

Sybil frowns, furrowing her brow. "Just promise me you'll be careful, babe."

I take a deep breath. "I promise."

The coven buzzes with activity as classes come into full swing, and even with the recent murder still fresh, life resettles. Despite all the supernatural aspects of a witch's life, it's the mundane routines that move the days here.

I glance out the window from my wards class. Outside, another class is sitting on the coven's front lawn, growing massive beanstalks in a matter of minutes.

"...the easiest and most durable of wards come in the form of amulets."

I turn my attention back to the front of my class, where Mistress Gestalt, a guest speaker, is giving the lecture. I take in the elderly witch as she leans on the podium. She's what the fairy tales not so lovingly refer to as a *hag*.

Only, the stories didn't get a lot of things right. For instance, hags don't need to have warts and sinister features. This one, in particular, is more of a HAG—a Hot-Ass Grandma.

"Tell me," she says now, "when you think of amulets, what comes to mind?" Her long white hair sways behind her as she walks.

Someone raises their hand, and she points to them. "A stone or pendant you wear around your neck."

She nods. "Anyone else?"

Someone else calls out, "Signet rings."

"Good, good," Mistress Gestalt says. She stops. "What if I told you I was wearing ten different amulets? Do you think you could find them all?"

My eyes sweep over her. She wears a loose royal-blue dress cinched with an embroidered belt, a wrist full of colorful bangles, and leather sandals.

She pulls her hair away from her ear, showing off a copper earring with etched writing. She points to it. "This may be my most obvious example. But I should also tell you that the crowns on three of my teeth are marked with protective wards, and the belt has been embroidered with another spell."

She points to a few of her bangles, a button at the top back of her dress, and a buckle on her sandals.

"Amulets do not need to be obvious or conventional—there are quite a few I've spelled over in the medical field—pacemakers, implants, dentures, and more."

She spends the rest of the two-hour lecture going over the nuances of amulets and all the spells that can be placed on them. I write down notes on everything she says, determined not to miss a single detail.

A bell trills, marking the end of the class.

"Your instructor wants me to remind you all that your amulets will be due at the end of the week," Mistress Gestalt calls out. "I myself will be looking them over. The witch who creates the most exquisite work will be offered a formal apprenticeship at my company, the Witch's Mark."

I gather my things alongside my classmates, my mind turning over the idea of an apprenticeship. Is that what I want? Eventually, I'll have to specialize in some kind of magic. I wonder what a career that specializes in amulets would look like…

"Selene Bowers."

I startle at the sound of Mistress Gestalt calling—and hell, simply *knowing*—my name. Of course, a name is easy enough to procure, if you're a witch.

I glance over at her.

She gives me a soft smile, her light eyes a little vacant. "May I have a word?"

My gaze sweeps over the rest of the witches leaving the room. I don't know what she could possibly want from me, unless it's something I've forgotten.

After a moment, I nod. "Of course." I make my way toward her.

"Good, good." She grabs her notes from the podium and slips them into a bag at her feet.

My heart is picking up speed as I step up to her. I don't even know why I'm nervous. I think it's simply habit that makes me assume I'm being recognized for doing something wrong rather than, I don't know, standing out for my amazing magical talent.

"It's an odd form of witchcraft, yours," Mistress Gestalt says as she zips up her bag.

I raise my eyebrows. She knows my brand of magic? I shouldn't be surprised. Crones are *especially* sharp.

She straightens, and I catch sight of her unusual eyes.

"Incantatrix immemorata." She overenunciates each word. "The unmentioned witch, whose magic devours her memories. Very peculiar. Very rare. I wonder why that is ..."

My brows draw together; I'm taken aback by the fact she knows this about me. "That was just the way I was born."

"Hmm..." Those light eyes scrutinize me, her body trembling a little. Though her magic is strong, her limbs seem light as a bird's. "No, I don't think it is."

My gaze sharpens on hers. Now that I'm looking closely, I realize why her eyes look so unusual. There's no pupil in either of them. *Is she...blind?*

"Who needs sight when the third eye sees all?" she says.

I recoil from her a bit.

Man, elderly witches are spooky. That really is when we come into our highest power.

"Selene, dear girl, you are being circled by vultures. Many eyes are on you. Some of them good, some of them bad, some a bit of both."

"*What?*" I say, alarmed.

"Power is to be celebrated and feared. You have it in spades, but it is locked away. Find the key and *use* it. Don't be a pawn when you're a queen. No one commands a queen."

I blink at her, and my hand twitches from the urge to write this all down before I can forget.

"I don't…understand," I say finally, tightening my hold on my bag.

She laughs, the sound wispy; it makes me think of corn husks for some odd reason.

"There is a lot you cannot remember, but do not fool yourself into thinking you do not understand, Selene Bowers." She gives me a meaningful look with those all-seeing eyes of hers, and for a moment, I think she must know about Memnon.

"Make your amulet," Mistress Gestalt says. "Protect yourself against harm."

Harm?

"And Selene?" she says. "The villains are coming for you. Ready yourself."

CHAPTER 16

Moldy toadstools.

I scrape the charred, flaky goop from the bottom of the cauldron, grimacing as I go.

I've been working on this freaking amulet all evening, and all I have to show for it is this sludge. My hair is singed, I smell like smoke, and the other witches who've entered and exited the spellcasting kitchen have kept their distance.

I was hoping that if I got started on an amulet for myself tonight, I'd manage to both finish my first big class project and wrangle some extra protection against the ominous threat Mistress Gestalt warned me about.

This kitchen has an old cast-iron stove as well as several cauldrons hanging over open flames, one of which is mine. On the opposite side of the room, there are shelves of jars holding all manner of rare ingredients.

I scoop the charred paste from the cauldron and place it into a bowl, ignoring the way Nero's ears go back at the sight of it.

I set the bowl down on the kitchen's butcher-block counter and make a face at my creation. My creation cannot be right. After moving over to my textbook, *A Practitioner's Guide to Apotropaic Magic*, I read through the spell recipe once more.

"Where did I go wrong…?" I ask Nero.

Nero blinks at me, and I swear he's saying, *How am I supposed to know? You're the witch.*

But maybe I'm just anthropomorphizing my panther.

I turn back to my textbook. Could it have been the alyssum? The recipe called for a handful, but that's such a loose measurement. Or maybe I need fresh mugwort and not the dried version.

But then, maybe it's not the mugwort?

I rub my temples.

"You're still here?" Sybil's voice rings out.

I glance up as she enters the kitchen. She came in here with me a couple of hours ago to work on an assignment for a different class, but she long since left to get some reading done.

Apparently, she finished reading.

She crinkles her nose. "What is that ungodly smell?" she says, wandering closer to me.

"That's the smell of protection," I say smoothly.

"Whatever concoction you're brewing, I don't think it's supposed to smell like that." When she gets to my side, Sybil peers into my bowl. "Or look like that."

I gaze down at the lumpy charred paste. According to my textbook, it's supposed to settle into a milky green liquid.

"What are you making anyway?" Sybil asks.

I grimace. "It's supposed to be a protective potion. Once

it's done, I just dip a piece of jewelry into it…and it should come out an amulet."

At that, she laughs. "Dude, that's more likely to attract bad shit than it is to scare it off."

I make a face at her. "It's not done yet."

"Babe, scrap it and call it a night. You can try again tomorrow."

I grab my wooden spoon and stir the grayish sludge. "Does my best friend really have that little faith in my abilities?"

Sybil raises her eyebrows at me. "Uh, when it comes to this particular spell—yeah, I do."

"Pfft." I wave her away. "I'm almost done here."

"All right, Selene, you do you." Sybil pushes away from the counter. "I'm heading off to bed. Want to join me for a run before class?"

I make a face at the thought. "Do I really like running?" I ask her.

For a moment Sybil hesitates, like she doesn't know if I've truly forgotten.

"It's a rhetorical question," I say. "Of course I hate running. But I'm a masochist, so yeah, I'll join you."

She shakes her head. "You have the worst humor, you know that, right?"

I point the wooden spoon I'm holding at her. "I…yeah, I might."

She gives me an amused look. "Night, babe. Don't accidently curse anything with that…potion." With that, she breezes back out of the kitchen.

"Night!" I call out after her.

Once it's quiet, I return my attention to my goop.

Now, where was I?

I glance down the list of steps I've meticulously checked off. All that's left is the final step.

Take the object you wish to coat with your protective mixture and submerge it into the potion.

There's an incantation that goes along with this step, and supposedly, invoking this spell will cause the potion to burn away and leave only the magic-coated amulet behind.

Simple enough.

I add more water to my mixture, whispering the incantation under my breath as I do so. And then I stir and stir until my sludge turns into a lumpy liquid. It looks a little greener as a liquid too, so that's a win.

It'll have to do.

I grab a small clay pendant with swirls stamped onto the front. It was a cheap knickknack I bought at a street fair in Berkeley, but it's unusual and pretty. And if this all goes well, it will be an amulet.

I worry my lower lip as I look at my concoction. After a moment, I drop the pendant into the mixture.

This is going to work, I tell myself.

Taking a deep breath, I hold my hand over the bowl and begin. "*I call on earth and air...*" My power rises, called by my intent and the incantation. "*Wash away weakness*"—the soft orange magic flows down my arm and out from my palm before settling over the liquid—"*from beings wicked and intent unkind...*"

As I watch, my power sinks into the potion, making the liquid luminesce.

I finish the incantation with "*keep me safe; keep me whole.*"

BANG!

The potion explodes like a shot, liquid splattering everywhere.

Shit.

I cough, waving away the odious hazy smoke. Once it clears, I peek inside the cauldron. Then I groan.

Sitting at the bottom is a lump of what looks like fossilized poop.

Do I have to touch it?

After a moment's hesitation, I reach in and scoop the amulet from the cauldron. On a positive note, at least my clumpy concoction is all gone. I mean, the rest of the kitchen is now covered with it, but we're not going to focus on that.

At the sight of the amulet in my hand, Nero curls his lips back.

"Oh, come on, it's not that bad," I say, dropping my smoldering pendant back onto the counter.

But it is. It really is.

I'm at the kitchen's industrial sink, humming while I wash the last of the utensils I used. I try not to notice the heavy disappointment settled in the bottom of my stomach, sitting there like a stone.

This was simply a first try.

I'll get it next time.

"Cleaning cookware, my queen? This is what you gave me up for?"

I scream and spin, throwing the wooden spoon reflexively at the voice.

Memnon leans against the doorway to the kitchen, his frame taking up most of the space. He catches the utensil in his fist, but his eyes remain fixed on me.

How long has he been there?

Now is probably not the time to notice yet again just how smoking hot Memnon is, but *fuck*, the goddess blessed him a little more in that department than she did the rest of us.

Then, at some later date, she must've regretted that blessing and cursed the hell out of his fate to make up for it.

His hair is brushed back from his face, revealing the scar that runs from his eye to ear to jaw. He's frowning, and I'd say he's angry, except there's a touch of confusion in his eyes.

He pushes away from the wall, his bewitching magic unfurling like a flower. "And what in the gods' names is that smell? It's worse than those Roman dishes you made me try—"

"Don't you *dare* come in," I warn him, gripping the counter behind me to hold myself up. My legs want to buckle at the sight of him. This is the man who might've murdered one of my coven sisters.

And he hates me.

Memnon lifts his chin, even as his magic snaps in annoyance. "Or what?" He squares his shoulders, taking a calculated step into the room. "What will my long-lost wife do to me now?"

It's only now that I realize we're, once again, speaking that other language. It stirs strange feelings in me I can't make sense of. The one thing I can identify is my terror rushing through me the longer I stare at this ancient sorcerer.

My heart bangs against the walls of my chest as though it's desperate to get out.

He tilts his head, taking in my expression.

A flash of something enters his eyes, but then it's gone just as quickly.

"Now the fear comes," he says. "Are you realizing, my queen, that you have a reckoning to receive?"

"I swear to the goddess, I will scream so loud, I'll bring this whole damn house down on you."

Memnon pauses, narrowing his eyes. "*That* is your threat, Roxilana? To scream loudly? What game are you playing?" he says.

He keeps asking this same question, and Goddess, but the only thing worse than a vengeful sorcerer is a vengeful, confused one.

"I will tell you what I know," I whisper, "if you stop coming closer."

Memnon must want answers desperately because he does halt in his tracks.

My gaze sweeps over him. He wears a formfitting white shirt, revealing his inked forearms. It's partially tucked into loose black fatigues, which are then tucked into heavy leather combat boots. Gone is the ancient warrior I woke. He looks every inch like some modern special ops soldier.

His power ripples off him like steam from boiling water, and it strikes me all over again that this man is a *sorcerer* of all things; he doesn't seem correctly cast for the role. He's not supposed to have muscles and power. That's, like, cheating.

Shit, maybe that's why he's cursed. Something has to even out the playing field with this man.

Memnon's expression heats at my perusal, but I can still sense his blistering wrath. "I'm waiting."

"Yes, well, give me a moment—you make a girl want to wet herself."

Shit.

Did that just come out of my mouth?

Did that just come out of my mouth?

Memnon's eyebrows rise; then a self-satisfied look spreads across his face.

My cheeks heat. "Because y-you're scary, and I'm t-trying not to pee my pants," I stammer.

Honestly, just bury me now and save me from myself.

He begins to close the distance between us again.

I put a hand out. "Stay back!" I warn him.

Memnon knocks my hand away as though it's nothing more than a nuisance, and he steps into my space.

"*Roxilana*," he growls, gazing down at me. My skin pebbles at the guttural sound of that name on this man's lips. It's not even *my name*, yet it's affecting me. How twisted is that?

"*What game are you playing?*" he demands again, biting out each word.

I lift my jaw obstinately and glare at him. "You need to back up. *Now*." Belatedly, I realize that I once again switched languages. Only, this time, I spoke in Latin.

He smiles at me, and it's so godsdamned wicked. "You think threats will work on me?" he responds *in Latin*. A moment later, his hand comes to my neck, and it grips me softly. "*I* make the threats now, wife," he says, squeezing my throat just a little so his meaning is clear. "Answer my question."

"This isn't some game to me," I say, reverting back to that other, unnamable language, the words rolling off my tongue. "This is my life."

"Your life," he echoes bitterly. "And have you been enjoying our time apart? All twenty centuries of it?" The more he speaks, the more his grip tightens on my throat.

"Have you eaten bad bread?" I say, which is apparently the old-school way of saying, *What are you smoking?* "Listen, my name is Selene, I'm twenty years old, and the first time I ever laid eyes on you was when I opened your tomb. I'm not your wife, and I didn't betray you."

As I speak, Memnon's fury morphs into something colder and more resolute.

He stares at me for several seconds.

"So you're determined to lie to me," he finally says.

I want to scream. Did he hear nothing of what I just said?

He continues. "It's been some time since you were around me, my queen, so perhaps you have forgotten just how I inspired fear into enemies' hearts."

All over again, I remember Kate, the murdered witch. The hand around my throat suddenly feels a whole lot more menacing than I've been treating it.

My eyes dart to my familiar. Nero is curled up on the kitchen rug, his eyes closed.

Why is he sleeping right now?

"Nero," I gasp out, trying to get his attention. His ears flick and his tail twitches, but his eyes remain closed.

"*Nero?*" Memnon repeats. The venom in his voice has my attention snapping back to him. "What does that swine have to do with anything? Did you betray me for him? Even after what he tried to do to you?"

What *the fuck* is he talking about?

"My familiar." I wheeze. "His name…is Nero."

Memnon's frown deepens. "No, it's not."

Wow. The goddess-damned audacity of this man.

"*Nero*," I snap, ready to slip into the panther's mind to wake him.

Before I can, my big cat gets up, stretching his limbs a little, then saunters over.

Fucking *finally*. There's the show of solidarity I've been waiting for—

Nero walks right up to Memnon and rubs his face against the sorcerer's leg.

What the…?

"Really?" I wheeze out. I'm being held by the throat, and Nero thinks he should make friends with Memnon? *Memnon?*

My familiar is defective.

"You expect me to believe any of your lies?" The sorcerer's eyes sweep over the room. "Or this farce of a life you've made for yourself?

"You cannot expect me to believe that you went from ruling the most powerful nation on Api's good earth to *this*." He curls his upper lip as he takes in the kitchen before refocusing his attention on me. "And that mockery of your magic you demonstrated earlier this evening? That was a joke, right?"

The way he says that last part…shit, he must've seen the entire amulet recipe. Not my proudest moment.

"Surely," he continues, "you didn't scheme my demise only to end up as such a pathetic shadow of your former—"

My hand is moving before I've even decided I'm going to hit him. My palm strikes his cheek, making a sharp clapping sound.

Repercussions be damned, that felt *good*.

"I don't know who the hell Roxilana was," I say, switching to Latin again, "but I'll light a candle for her and say a prayer on her behalf that she had to deal with you for any length of time. I bet she laughed gleefully when she buried you in the ground. I know *I* would've."

I went too far.

Memnon's eyes flash, and an ungodly growl rises from his lungs. If he looked murderous before, he looks apoplectic now.

He drags me away from the sink, still clutching me by the throat.

“Forget my former plans,” he says in that other ancient tongue, his voice low and lethal. “I will make you pay *now*.”

He slides his hand from my neck to my wrist, and everywhere his palm rubs against my bare skin tingles in the most unnerving way.

I yank against his hold, but it’s useless. Memnon hauls me out of the kitchen, his magic wrapping around me as I trip after him. Nero trails behind us, prowling along as though none of this is worrisome.

The first floor of the house is quiet, save for the staticky buzz of the flickering lights. Despite the late hour, I cannot be the only person still awake down here. Yet, except for Memnon, it’s been unusually quiet in the house.

I notice why as Memnon leads me into the foyer: the glittering blue residue of wards hanging in the air beneath the two hallways and the house’s library.

Probably made by Memnon earlier, and probably crafted so he could drag me away without anyone noticing.

Is this what happened to Kate?

Intuition is telling me that this man would never dare to harm me, but my intuition has also told me he’s a violent, dangerous man. Then there’s also the fact that he’s grabbed me by the neck, threatened me, and now he’s hauling me to Goddess knows where. Oh, and he’s a sorcerer whose power preys on his conscience.

If I leave out those front doors with him, I may never return.

Thinking fast, I grab a single strand of my hair and pluck it, and then I let the words form.

“With a hair from my head, and the touch of a spurned spouse, I banish you straight from my house.”

My power lashes out, slamming into Memnon and ripping his hand from my wrist as he’s thrown forward.

My magic creates a wind tunnel of sorts, the shimmery orange plumes of it knocking over an unlit candelabra and churning a stack of loose papers into the air. Around us, the house's lights flicker erratically.

Memnon turns to face me, and he smiles now, though it's as sharp as a knife. "*There's* your power, Empress," he says, fighting my magic even as it continues to push him.

Behind him, the house's door opens, like it wants to be rid of Memnon too.

I glare at him, my hair blowing around me. "Get *out*." With my words, another wave of power hits him in the chest, and Memnon staggers back into the doorway.

He grabs the doorframe, holding steady against the barrage of my magic.

"You cannot put off the inevitable," he says. "I *will* be back."

I lift my chin. "Until then, I'll light that candle in your wife's memory."

His eyes burn with his rising magic. Goddess, he is beautiful. Beautiful and angry. Before he can do anything with that power of his, I hear the gravelly growl of the stone *lamassu*, the threshold guardians.

All at once his magic is sucked out of the house, and the front door slams shut.

As soon as he's gone, I sag, leaning heavily against a side table to keep from collapsing.

Fuck.

Nero comes up to me then, rubbing against my leg.

"You're in trouble from now until the end of time," I say, lowering myself to the ground because my legs don't want to hold me up. Nero rubs his face against mine, and I wrap an arm around him. There's a prickly, light-headed feeling in my brain, where my magic is taking its tithe.

I glance up at Memnon's wards, which still shimmer in the air. With a weary flick of my wrist, I send my magic out and tear through them, the action causing me to feel another throb inside my skull. In a matter of seconds, the wards dissolve.

I let out a sigh of relief when I hear the distant voices of coven sisters elsewhere in the house.

I lean my head against Nero's. "Hopefully, that's the last I see of Memnon for a while."

CHAPTER 17

"Tell me you love me."

"I love you," I breathe.

"Tell me I am the only one."

"There has only ever been you," I murmur, my fingers sinking into coarse hair.

Hands slip over the flesh of my torso, and I feel my shirt being tugged up. Warm breath fans against my breasts.

That mouth presses against my nipple, and I gasp, arching into the kiss.

All too soon his mouth leaves, and his kisses trail over my breast and down, down my torso.

"Say you are mine," Memnon demands.

Memnon?

"I am yours," I reply dazedly.

My surroundings and my awareness sharpen. I take in the flickering lamplight, the soft sheets, the naked sorcerer moving down my body, his back tattoos rippling as he goes.

"I lay claim to you before all the gods," he says.

Wait.

What?

"Memn—aaah—" I cry out as his mouth descends to my core, and I arch against him, the sensation of his lips against my flesh nearly too much.

I'm aware of a distant niggle, and I know something isn't quite right. But I cannot place just what that something—

I'm ripped from my thoughts when Memnon tongues my clit, and he moves his fingers to my core, slipping one of them in.

"Goddess!" I'm overwhelmed by sensation. I try to move away, just to get some relief from all those intimate touches.

With his free hand, Memnon holds me fast.

"Memnon—too much," I gasp out.

He laughs against my clit. "And yet you'll endure it all."

I'm forced to feel the persistent stroke of his tongue and the glide of his lips, all while his fingers slip in and out, in and out.

The moment I give in to the sensation is the moment my climax builds. I'm beginning to make helpless, embarrassing noises because, ugh, it feels so damn good. *Too good.*

Memnon moves his mouth away from my clit, but it's almost immediately replaced by the brush of his magic. He uses his power like another set of lips against my clit, continuing where he left off.

While his magic works me, Memnon gazes up the span of my body. When our eyes meet, the world tilts.

"All the lands and all the kingdoms shall be mine once more," Memnon says softly, still moving his fingers in and out of me, "and all shall know my name as they once did. Memnon the Indomitable." His eyes glitter with intensity. "Most of all, you will be mine again."

My orgasm is so close, so, so—

Memnon settles back down between my legs, and he brushes a kiss against my inner thigh. "But first, my queen, you—will—pay."

The alarm on my phone goes off, jolting me awake. I'm awash in sweat, and my core is throbbing with unfulfilled need.

Blowing out a breath, I grab my phone. I'm not entirely sure whether I'm going to take care of my missed orgasm and get up or simply snooze the alarm and go back to sleep. Before I decide, I catch sight of the message on my phone.

Alarm for morning run with Sybil @ 6:30 a.m.

Ugh, that's right.

It's 6:15 a.m. right now, which means I barely have time to change and meet her as it is. So no orgasm and no sleep.

Feeling flustered and grumpy, I grab my clothes and shove myself into them, then tie my hair back and lace up my running shoes.

By the time I knock on Sybil's door, I have two minutes to spare. And I'm still in a foul mood.

When she opens her door, she takes me in. "You look how I feel," she says, slipping out of the room. "Why do we do this to ourselves?"

I rub my eyes and shake my head. "Because we're the queens of bad ideas."

"C'mon then, my fellow queen," she says. "Let's see this bad idea through."

Okay, the run is not half bad.

I mean, it *is* because it's running, and everything jiggles, and I'm somehow sweating in unmentionable places and chilly in others. But the air carries the scent of pine trees and wet soil, and the birds are chirping—and that's to say nothing of the view.

Sybil takes us on a path that winds behind the campus, then continues to the north of it, the dirt path snaking through the coastal hills.

"How much of this does the coven own?" I ask her. It feels like we've been running forever, and we haven't turned back yet.

"Miles and miles—farther up this way are the residences for graduated coven members." Sybil huffs, pointing ahead of us.

I can't see the houses she's talking about, but I know of them. Coven members who prefer living near other witches and away from the hustle and bustle of normal society can choose to live on coven property. The thought of growing old alongside other witches sounds pretty idyllic, but who knows? Perhaps by the time I graduate Henbane, I'll be over it.

The forest around us opens, giving way to a field. Off to my left, I catch a glimpse of the distant coastline and the ocean beyond.

The word *idyllic* was created for days like this.

It's almost enough for me to forget my encounter with Memnon.

He's going to be a problem—a big one too. He's now visited me twice in the past week—to say nothing of my, um, *vivid* dreams. And if Memnon's parting words last night were anything to go by, I'll be seeing him again, and soon.

Only now do I remember one overlooked detail from our encounter.

And have you been enjoying our time apart? he said. *All twenty centuries of it?*

A chill runs down my back as I do the math.

He's two thousand years old?

I cannot wrap my head around that amount of time. And speaking of time, if Memnon knows how many years he slept, then he knows the year it currently is.

What else must he know?

For the first time since he confronted me behind Lunar Observatory, I wonder about his life. How exactly did he get from South America to Northern California? Where did he get his clothes? From whom did he acquire information about the modern world? And where in the goddess's name is he staying?

These questions fill me with a combination of dread and guilt. I don't really want to know the answers to any of them, but I also feel like I released this man, then abandoned him to the world.

Not that I was in any place to help him. Not after how he treated me.

Speaking of how he treated me…

My thoughts turn to my latest dream. I want to wither away at the fact that I've now twice had sex dreams about motherfucking *Memnon.* I mean, he *is* wickedly beautiful, so I guess my eyes have good taste, but come *on,* mind, we do not spread our legs for evil dream men. Even ones who know their way around a pussy.

I draw in a ragged breath.

"Hey, you okay?" Sybil says next to me.

"What? Yeah, I'm good." I rush the words out.

She stares at me for a second. "I'm sorry about the amulet," she finally says.

She thinks my mood is about that mess of an amulet?

If only.

I wave her words away. "It's fine. It really is. I'll just try again."

I can feel Sybil's eyes on me a second longer, but given how uneven the ground is, she eventually has to look away.

We run for a little longer when the dirt path forks, one branch continuing onward and the other curving back the way we came.

"Unless you want to keep going," Sybil says, "we'll want to take this one back to the house." She points to the branch that twists toward home.

"Don't want to keep going," I say. My energy is already starting to flag, and there are still miles between me and my bedroom.

We take the path that curves back the way we came, birdsong and dappled light following us through the Everwoods.

We've got to be less than a mile from campus when up ahead of us, the pathway is roped off by crime scene tape.

Sybil and I slow. There are people in Politia uniforms milling about, their magic filling the air. There's something else lingering in the breeze, something grim and oily and malevolent. Beneath even that, I sense…

Death.

Ruthless, agonizing death. It's just a momentary impression; then it's gone.

"Selene…" Sybil says, a thread of fear in her voice.

Before I can respond, one of the uniformed officers notices us.

"Hey there!" the woman calls.

I think she's going to send us on our way, but instead, she

beckons us closer as she heads toward the crime scene tape. "Can I speak with you two for a moment?" she says.

Sybil and I glance at each other before I call out, "Yes. Of course."

We walk over to the cordoned-off area. Every step closer has my gut churning and my intuition telling me to stay away. Something here isn't right.

"You two locals?" the officer asks, pulling out a notepad and pen.

"We're attending witches at Henbane Coven," I say.

"Do you regularly use this pathway?"

"She doesn't," Sybil says, gesturing to me. "I've been running this trail weekly for the past year."

"Do either of you know of anyone else who regularly comes this way?" the officer asks, looking between us.

My eyes move over the crowd of officers and other uniformed personnel as that sick, uneasy feeling worms its way beneath my skin. The cluster of officers parts, and I catch sight of—of—

My mind can't—*won't*—make sense of what my eyes are seeing. The colors are crimson and pink and beige and black, so much oily black—

The officer steps in front of me, shifting to block my view.

I put a hand to my mouth to fight my rising nausea.

Sybil glances from me to the crime scene to the officer. "What's going on? Has something happened?"

"We're not at liberty to discuss an open investigation," she says smoothly.

But I don't need magic or intuition to know what's going on. I saw it with my own eyes.

Save us, Goddess.

There's been another murder.

CHAPTER 18

The news breaks later that day.

Another killing. Another witch gone too soon.

I try to focus during Intro to Magic, but all I can see is that shape on the ground, the one my mind couldn't make sense of then—the one it *still* can't make sense of. And then there was the oily, terror-steeped magic that clung to the crime scene like awful perfume.

Dark magic. *True* dark magic. The kind people sell their souls for.

It has me shivering even now.

The Politia hasn't released much information about the killing, but it was obvious enough from what I saw that the attack happened sometime between yesterday evening and this morning.

Right after Memnon visited me.

I go cold all over.

Could he, in his anger, have attacked another witch? Could he have murdered her?

I remember the violence of Memnon's power and presence.

Yes, he could have. *Easily*, he could've.

I draw in a shuddering breath, forcing the thoughts away before I spiral. I refocus on Professor Huang at the head of the lecture hall. They have pin-straight black hair that hangs all the way down to their thighs, and when they move, it swings like a curtain.

"As witches, we all draw magic from the world around us," they say, making their way to the side of the stage, where a table rests. On it sit a dozen different items.

"However," they continue, "every single one of you has a unique way of interacting with magic, and as you grow in your abilities, you'll learn how to sculpt your power to fit your use."

They move their hand over the items, touching them one by one. "I've set out several items, each one symbolic of a certain form of magic."

I focus on the items in question. From where I sit, I can make out a potted plant, a loaf of bread, a locket, a dried bundle of herbs, a bowl of water, a crystal, a conch shell, a clay pot, a river rock, a bowl of soil, an unlit candle, a page of writing, and a vial of what looks like gray dust.

"Today, we're going to learn the particular types of magic that call to you," Professor Huang says. "This will give you a good foundational understanding of your own magic, which you can then build on. It's important to know our magical strengths. And later in this course, we will do this again. Only, next time, we will look for the items you want to avoid—those will be your magical aversions.

"But I'm getting ahead of myself." They clap their hands once, their hair swaying with the action. "Now, witches," they say, "I'll have you come down—please form a line in front of the table."

I get up and follow my classmates down to the stage.

"I know what many of you are thinking," Professor Huang says as we all get in line. "Why must you do this again when you have likely done it before?"

We've...done this before?

My mind strains to find a similar memory to this, one that either happened here at Henbane or at Peel Academy. None comes to me.

If the memory once existed, it's become a casualty of my magic.

Our instructor continues. "I recommend repeating this test every few years. As we all know, magic is wily and wild, and it likes to grow and change just as much as we do."

Once we've all lined up, Professor Huang moves to the table and the witch at the front. "Now let's begin."

One by one, my classmates step up to the table and pick out several items that represent their magical preferences. Most end up gravitating to the potted plant—green magic—as well as the loaf of bread and the bundle of herbs, all items that really speak to the life-giving, medicinal nature of witchcraft.

Every so often someone reaches for the locket, or the piece of paper, or the crystal. I watch, fascinated, curious about what I'll end up picking.

When it's my turn, I step up to the table, my magic buzzing beneath my veins. My eyes sweep over the items. I already know what my magic likes best—memories. But the items before me are conduits, allowing magic to be used to its furthest extent.

"Eyes closed, hand out," Professor Huang instructs.

I do as they ask. I can't see the objects clearly with my eyes closed, but I can sense the magic pulsing through each one. I reach out an arm, my palm turned toward the items.

Almost immediately, my hand moves, drifting to the right, then down, until my fingertips touch something wet.

"Water," my instructor murmurs. "Go on."

My arm moves again, now drawn to a different section of the table. When my hand drops into another bowl, I don't even need to hear what my instructor has to say. I can feel the soft soil sifting between my fingers.

I lift my hand out of the dirt. Right next to it is another item tugging at me for attention.

My hand wraps around a smooth stone.

"River rock," Professor Huang says. "Anything else?"

I release the smooth stone. My magic is calling me to two final points on the table. I go with the closest item first, my fingers brushing the rough rim of something and nearly knocking it over. I place my palm more firmly over it.

"The Vinča cup," my instructor murmurs. "Interesting, my dear."

A sharp pull has my arm moving once more. With my eyes still shut, I close my hand around a cool glass vial. This is it, the last item.

"Moon dust," Professor Huang says as my eyes flutter open. Beneath my hand is the vial filled with dark dirt.

"Good job," my instructor says. "What an *unusual* combination."

My disappointment leaves a bitter tang on my tongue.

Water, dirt, a rock, a pot, and...moon dust? *Those* are the things I'm drawn to? Not the herbs? Not the bread? I fucking *adore* bread.

My magic feels cold and lifeless.

"Water may indicate you'll have a knack for potion making," my instructor says. "It's interesting that you picked the river rock but not the crystals and the soil but not the plant. The clay pot is particularly notable as it is nearly five thousand years old, and it contains some of the first forms of writing etched onto it." They point to a small and crudely made spiral. "Finally, the moon dust is an indication that your power may be sensitive to the lunar phases—those can really heighten spells, but you'll need to read up on them."

They pat me on the shoulder.

"Wonderful job," they murmur. "Remember too that there are objects not present that could also tap into your powers—solar magic, astral magic, and numeric magic are just a few. Your homework assignment is to write a paper on your specific magical affinities and how you think they interact with your magic. Due next Friday."

With that, they dismiss me. And now I'm left to wonder what I'm supposed to do with a power that likes dirt and rocks, clay and water, but not plants. Or herbs.

Or bread.

I mean, what sort of twisted magic doesn't like motherfucking *bread*?

It's only as I'm nearly home that I realize there was a very obvious life-giving item not present, one my instructor did not address at all.

Flesh.

Blood and bone can produce life-giving magic just as much as plants and dried herbs can. They also happen to tease that line between light magic and dark.

As I head for the residence hall, I can't help wondering if my power isn't as cold and lifeless as I think it is.

Perhaps it does like life-giving items. Perhaps it hungers for something that comes from the soil and returns to it, something more substantive than plants. Something that grows and dies.

Something that bleeds.

But I'll never find out one way or another. Blood magic is forbidden.

CHAPTER 19

Having a familiar is creating some problems.

Besides the most obvious problem, which is that loose panthers make even witches nervous, there's the fact that feeding a big cat is expensive, especially for a broke girl like me.

I mean, technically, Nero is often out in the surrounding forest hunting wild game—I try not to shudder at the thought—but that comes with its own issues. For instance, he may be doing so on lycanthrope territory, and that could have potentially catastrophic fallout. Not to mention that in the meantime, Nero would be poaching off them.

It's all one massive headache, and it's just easier if I can get him food from the butcher.

So I have to get a job.

I look at the bulletin board hanging in the hallway to the left of my house's main staircase. Pinned to it are several job listings. I stare at them all like they're the Holy Grail.

Before I lived here, I couldn't land a single one of these

jobs. Each one required a coven-affiliated witch, which I wasn't at the time.

Now, however, I can do any of them—assuming they hire me.

I scan the listings. Someone wants a witch to enchant five years off their face. Another one wants a cleaning spell placed on their house. Still another is for some undisclosed need, but it's printed on fancy card stock, which makes me think whoever posted it has money to spend.

Money I could definitely use, especially since I learned earlier today that the amulet I remade for Wards didn't earn me that sought-after apprenticeship.

I jot down the number for each job post. Personally, I'm not sure I could lift five years from a toad, let alone a person, nor do I know a satisfying cleaning spell (my old apartment was proof of that). But I'm willing to learn, so long as it gets me a few extra dollars.

Another witch steps up to the bulletin board, looking at the listings. "There are never enough postings here, in my opinion," she says.

I make a noise of agreement, even though what do I know? I'm new here.

The witch turns to me, and the first thing I notice about her is how white her teeth are. White and straight. Then it's her perfectly arched brows and the way her hair falls in orderly loose waves. Witches are often striking in one way or another. Whether that's a long nose, a short frame, odd eyes, frizzy hair, generous curves, an addled mind, a long face, a prominent birthmark, or—in this witch's case—some pleasing symmetry.

"Are you looking for something in particular?" she asks.

"Not really," I say, turning my attention back to the

bulletin board. Technically, I'm looking for something easy, but I'll settle for what's available.

"So just short on cash?" she says.

I hesitate, then glance back over at the witch next to me.

I mean, yes, my bank account sobs into a bottle of wine most days of the week, but I don't want to come off as desperate.

The witch notices my hesitation. "Sorry, I hope that wasn't rude," she says. "It's just that…" She glances around, then leans in toward me. "There's a spell circle some of us do every new moon that's funded by a few private sponsors. It's a little shady, but it pays well."

That sounds very interesting and 100 percent not up my alley. Listen, I'm all for pushing the rules, but I learned my lesson about not messing with shady shit when I opened a warded tomb and let out an ancient evil who thinks I'm his dead wife and is now stalking me. And maybe killing witches.

A girl can only take so much trouble.

But…I am also desperate—both for quick cash and friendship.

"Thanks for the offer," I say. "I'll think about it."

And then promptly forget. All for the best though.

The witch smiles back at me. "Please do. It's an easy five hundred."

Dollars?

I suck in a breath and nearly choke on my saliva. "I'm sorry, *what*?" Five hundred dollars? That has to be a joke.

Or it's something illegal.

Probably very, very illegal.

The witch flashes me a secretive smile. "Our sponsors pay well."

Seriously. Five hundred dollars is almost enough to make me throw my morals to the wind.

After a moment's hesitation, my coven sister pulls out a notebook, and she scribbles something on it. "I'm Kasey, and this is my number. If you decide to join, you can text me here." She taps the written number, then backs away. "Think about it, and let me know. Next circle is happening on Saturday." She gives me a wave and heads up the stairs, calling out over her shoulder, "I hope you decide to come."

When I walk into my room, the lights are on, music is blaring from my speakers, and there's an overgrown man sitting in my computer chair, his muscled arms and tattoos on display below the sleeves of his fitted T-shirt. In front of him is one of my social media pages. It's open to a photo of me and Sybil wearing onesies and holding red Solo cups. I'm sticking out my tongue and making the peace sign with my fingers, while she's blowing a kiss.

It's…not my best moment. Not that I remember that particular evening.

My gaze slides back from the photo to Memnon. "What the *fuck*?" I say.

I raise my hand, readying my magic, angry rather than scared.

Memnon leans back in my computer chair, snaps his fingers, and poof, everything goes silent.

"Fascinating world you live in," he responds—*in English*. He has a subtle foreign accent, so the words come out guttural and rolling.

His eyes drift over me, taking in the short wrap dress I wore to class. His gaze grows heated.

I angrily toss my bag onto my bed, my pulse rate climbing. "What are you doing in here?" I demand.

Memnon threads his hands behind his head, leaning back in my seat. "I'm seeing where my scheming wife lives," he says, still speaking in English. He glances around him. "Your room is smaller than even our wagon was." His eyes move over the sticky notes that cover the room. "I see you haven't lost your love of writing."

"You can't just…come in here whenever you please," I say, alarmed by the fact he already has.

Not even going to ask about how he knew which room was mine.

Memnon narrows his eyes at me, all while wearing this insufferable little smirk that makes me feel warm in all the wrong places.

Why must I have this reaction to him? He's obviously evil, and the scar and the power he oozes are really driving that home. My body simply isn't catching up to my mind.

"Does that bother you, *est amage*?" *My queen.* Those two words are the only he's uttered so far in his old tongue.

Of course it bothers me. He made himself my enemy.

He also might have murdered two witches.

And once again, I'm trapped in a small room with him.

"Last time I saw you, I banished you," I state.

Memnon drops his hands from behind his head to the chair's armrests. "Yes, well, your magic likes me too much to keep me out for long."

I frown at him, remembering how his spells melted away once my magic touched them. The thought that our powers like each other is perhaps the most unsettling thing I've heard all day.

"You need to leave," I say.

"I'll go when I'm ready."

I want to scream. "I swear to the goddess I will banish you again if you don't leave."

He grins again, and maybe it's the way it tugs at his scar, or maybe it's how it displays his sharp canines, but I shiver at how nefarious that smile is. Nefarious and absurdly sexy.

I get hot and flustered at the sight of it.

Memnon lifts his chin. "Try it, little witch."

I stare at him for a long moment. There's a wild look in his eyes; he's watching me like a snake about to strike.

A banishment spell might be a very, very bad idea.

I'll need to get him out some other way. But first—

My eyes flick to my social media page, where the picture of me and Sybil is still taking up most of the screen.

I cross over to my desk before leaning over Memnon so I can exit out of the page.

Memnon bends forward, skimming his lips against my hair.

I freeze at the contact.

"You came and woke me"—he almost purrs it, his voice is so soft—"and now you continue just existing as though nothing has changed."

I swallow, trying to control the way my body trembles at his nearness. My dreams come back to me then, and I vividly remember how it felt to have him close.

I shut my laptop screen and back away from the desk.

Memnon catches my wrist. "Roxilana, tell me why," he beseeches.

For once, this terrifying supernatural is unguarded, and there's something in his eyes when he looks at me, something beyond heat and anger.

"My name is *Selene*," I remind him.

"You can lie to everyone else, but not to me," he says.

He really thinks this is some elaborate charade this woman, Roxilana, has been keeping up.

No wonder he's confused.

"I'm *not* her," I insist.

He stands slowly from his seat, and I'm reminded all over again of just how large this man is. I have to tilt my head back to look at him. It doesn't help that every inch of him seems to be made of heavy corded muscle.

Memnon reaches out, and I shrink away. He scowls when he sees my reaction, but that doesn't stop him from cupping my cheeks and tilting my head up.

One of his thumbs strokes my cheek. "You have my Roxi's same blue eyes, down to the white line that rings the inside of them." He tilts my face to the side, moving one of his hands to touch something near my ear. "You have the same two freckles she had right here." As Memnon speaks, his eyes soften.

His hand moves to my hair, and it's as though he's forgotten himself and his vendetta for a moment. His touch is almost reverent as he runs his fingers along the strands. I find myself mesmerized by it.

"And this hair," he says, "is the same cinnamon color my Roxi's was." He drops my hair then, his other hand still cupping my face. "You have a birthmark on the back of your left thigh, and your second toes are longer than your big ones. Shall I go on?"

I stare at him like I've seen a ghost. "H-how do you know those things about me?" I say.

His brows come together in confusion. "Why *wouldn't* I know those things? I have spent years mapping you out—*as you have me.*"

What?

Almost instinctively, my gaze moves to that scar of his. Memnon has many distinct features, but that scar is perhaps the most prominent of them.

Seeing where my attention is drawn, he says softly, "You can touch it, *est amage*."

I shouldn't.

It feels at best like a bad idea and at worst, a trap. That doesn't stop me from stepping into Memnon's space and reaching out a tentative hand. The moment my fingers touch the puckered skin of his scar, his eyes close and his nostrils flare.

Memnon stands as still as stone while I draw my fingers along the path of it, moving first to his ear, then down toward his chin.

"This looks like it hurt," I murmur.

He makes a noncommittal sound. Because of course it hurt. It must've been awful.

I get to the end of the scar, and reluctantly, I let my hand drop.

When Memnon opens his eyes again, I don't see any trace of his anger. Instead, there's longing so deep, it makes my stomach flip.

"*Wife*," he breathes, his eyes moving to my lips.

I swallow, my own gaze going to his mouth. I want to kiss him again, just to taste his yearning. I can't remember anyone ever looking at me that way.

But I'm not his wife. Whatever wonderful, tragic love story he had, it wasn't with me.

I place a hand to my temple, trying to clear away my own desire. "How do you know English?" I say distractedly, just to get my mind off kissing him.

"You know my power," he says, almost obstinately, as though he thinks I'm still lying. "You know I can pull what I want from the minds of others, including language."

My eyes widen.

He can do *what* now?

Memnon tilts his head. "Why are you still pretending with me, Empress?" he asks, some of that earlier anger seeping back into his eyes.

"I'm not pretending anything, Memnon."

"Then how do you know Sarmatian, the language of my people? Supposedly, it's been a dead language for many, many centuries."

So that's the language I've been speaking. Sarmatian. "I know several inexplicable—"

"It's not inexplicable," Memnon insists before I can finish. "It's proof of your life with me."

I give him a look. "This may come as a shock, but not everything is about you, Memnon."

His gaze grows intense. "No, nearly everything in my life is about *you*."

He continues to stare at me, and it causes me to squirm.

"I'm *not* your Roxi," I insist, not letting myself dwell on his point about languages. "I can prove it."

I have to at this point, both for his sake *and* for mine. Because that's what memory loss does to you—makes you relentlessly question your reality.

My gaze sweeps over my things, looking for something—*anything*—to convince this man I could not possibly be his traitorous wife. When my eyes land on the spines of my photo albums, I pause.

Of course.

So painfully obvious.

Slipping past Memnon, I move over to my albums and pull out every single one.

Gathering them, I nod to my computer chair.

"Sit," I command.

A split second after I give the order, I'm sure he's not going to listen. But Memnon flashes me an amused look and obediently sits back at my chair, splaying his legs wide.

I drop all the albums on my bed before picking out one that's bound in beige cloth with the word *Memories* written in gold foil across the front.

Memnon watches me with unnerving intensity as I come over to him, album in hand.

A strange tugging sensation rises in my chest as I draw close. I force myself to ignore every last little thing about him because I want to dwell on it all—the burnished bronze of his skin, the twisting form of his tattoos, the rippling bands of his muscles.

I hand the photo album over to him. "Here's your proof."

Memnon scowls at the book in his hands, his narrowed gaze flicking from it to me, as though this is some sort of elaborate hoax.

Reluctantly, he opens it.

He grows almost preternaturally quiet. Drawn in by his reaction—hell, drawn in by *him*—I move to his side, peeking over his shoulder at the images. This album starts on my eighth birthday. There are pictures of me, my friends, the bounce house we rented out in what must be our backyard.

I'm blowing out candles, opening presents, making funny faces with my friends. My hair is wild, my incisors are only partially grown in, and I have a scattering of freckles across my nose that have since disappeared.

I don't remember that day, nor the house. But one of my friends—Em…Emily. Yes, I remember her.

As Memnon flips through the pages, he reaches out one of his hands and absently strokes my arm with his knuckles.

My breath escapes me as I look down at that contact—contact the sorcerer doesn't even seem to notice. I should move my arm. A sane person would.

Instead, I let my would-be husband caress me.

His touch is so soft and so at odds with every violent aspect of him. His hand only moves away to trace the shape of my face in a close-up—this one of me at a family wedding a year or two later. I vaguely remember that event.

One of Memnon's legs jiggles, and the more pages he turns, the more agitatedly his leg moves.

All at once, he tosses the album aside.

"No," he says. "*No*." He stands, running his fingers through his hair. My deviant little eyes notice how his shirt clings to his torso with the action.

"If you are not my Roxi, then *who* are you?" he says, his eyes desolate.

Oh, this one I got. "I am Selene Bowers. My parents are Olivia and Benjamin Bowers. I was born on—"

He's shaking his head, pinching his eyes shut. "No, no, no. I don't believe it. I *won't*."

"The woman who betrayed you is gone. I'm someone else. I was born twenty years ago. What other proof do you need?"

His eyes open, and he looks me over, his attention settling on my upper chest.

"Your skin—I would like to see it, *est amage*."

I frown at him. "I'm not getting naked."

"Not today, no," he agrees.

His answer makes my breath catch, and his words pluck at my magic like a strummed chord.

Memnon rises from my chair before approaching me slowly, like I might take off at any moment. "You have tattoos."

A strange hum starts up between us, a hum that's not really a hum at all. I think it has to do with our magic, but I feel it moving along my arms and spine, and it's making my heart flutter.

"*Roxilana* had tattoos," I correct. I have none. But now my interest is piqued.

Memnon comes up to me and gestures for my arm.

Oh, now he asks for permission before he manhandles me?

I move my arm into his reach. Slowly, as though not to scare me off, Memnon takes my forearm, and with his other hand, he lifts the fluttery sleeve of my dress, revealing my upper arm and shoulder.

I hear his exhale, and my gaze flicks to his face.

He looks…disbelieving.

One of Memnon's fingers comes up, tracing phantom lines on my arm.

"You had a panther tattooed right here," he says, his voice flat, controlled. "And beneath it, a slain deer."

Sounds cute.

Memnon's hand moves from my shoulder and settles on my chest, right over my heart. It's an intimate touch, even though it's only inches away from where it was.

Logic is telling me to knock the sorcerer's hand away. Instinct is telling me to press my hand over his and anchor him to me. So I compromise and do nothing.

"You had my mark right here," he says softly.

For a second, I think Memnon means to move the

neckline of my dress aside. Instead, he reaches for his own shirt before pulling it off in one smooth stroke.

Nobody said you could get undressed in my room.

My protest dies in my throat as soon as my eyes land on his exposed torso. I swallow at the sight of his packed muscles, but it's impossible to notice his muscles without noticing his tattoos as well. Memnon is covered in them—a deer whose horns sprout flowers, a trampled griffin, a snarling panther who seems to be clawing up Memnon's neck. And right over the sorcerer's heart—a winged dragon.

He touches that inked image now. "My family's clan mark," he says, staring at me. His eyes are raw.

Now I do tug aside the neckline of my dress, just to show him my own unmarred expanse of skin. There's no dragon over my heart, just as there were no beasts on my arm.

I hear Memnon's quick inhale, and for an instant, I see something in his expression that I haven't before—despair. It vanishes a moment later.

"You removed them," he accuses, though there's not much force behind it.

I shake my head. "I never had them to begin with."

"You are cunning, Roxi," he says, and I get goose bumps from a nickname that is still not meant for me. "A few conjured photos and some bare skin might convince another man, but I have seen the extent of your mind and your magic. You will have to do better."

"My photos are *not* conjured," I all but growl at him. Those albums are precious to me because they captured much of what my mind has lost—my past.

Judging from the obstinate set of Memnon's jaw, I can tell this isn't even about photos or tattoos or logic. The thought that I am not this Roxilana is unfathomable to him.

But he must be considering it. After all, he hasn't been threatening me, and when I look in his eyes, I see bewilderment instead of malice.

He looks halfway convinced. If I can fully convince him, he may stop accosting me.

A terrible idea pops into my head.

I draw in a deep breath. "Your power allows you to draw information from people's minds?" I ask.

Memnon gives me a long look, like he can't make up his mind whether I'm being deceitful. Finally, he gives a slight nod.

I run a hand through my hair, my heart rate accelerating as I say, "Then I propose a deal: if you can answer a question of mine honestly…then I'll let you use your power on my mind and see for yourself."

I'm actually surprised Memnon hasn't already done something this simple. But when I look at him now, he appears…unsettled by the prospect.

Maybe this man does have some ethics after all.

Or maybe he just really doesn't want to answer my mystery question.

He searches my gaze, looking for who knows what. After a moment, he inclines his head. "Ask your question, little witch."

He's going for it. Great Goddess, he's going for it.

Before I can chicken out, I raise my hand, my power sifting out of my palm. Memnon gazes at the peach-colored magic with something like fondness.

"*Answer the following without deceit,*" I incant. "*Only the truth shall you speak.*"

My power snakes across the space between us, slipping between the seam of his lips and up through his nostrils. He draws in a deep inhale, closing his eyes for a moment.

The corners of his mouth curve up. "Your spell has taken root." He sounds disturbingly pleased by the sensation. His eyes open. "I'm ready."

I can hear my heart thumping as I form the question. I'm so petrified of Memnon's answer that part of me wants to choose another.

But if this man is going to keep showing up, the right answer would really settle part of my nerves.

"Are you murdering the witches found dead on campus?"

Memnon holds my gaze, his face impassive. I see his throat work, as though the answer is trying to wriggle its way free. He holds it back, curving his lips into a defiant smile.

I wait, feeling my spell at work.

Finally, his lips part. "*No.*"

My magic releases him all at once, and I sag with relief.

He's not the killer.

He's not the killer.

I want to sob. I didn't realize what a weight that had been, thinking Memnon had hurt innocent witches.

His gaze flits over me. "I take it you're relieved."

I exhale. *"Very."*

Memnon watches me silently. If he was offended I thought he was the murderer—or disappointed that now I don't—he doesn't say it or show it.

I run my hands through my hair, composing myself once more.

"Come here then, Empress." He gestures me forward. "It's my turn."

I take a hesitant step toward him.

"Closer," he insists.

Oh Goddess, am I really going to let a sorcerer rifle through my head? I didn't think this plan out fully.

I step into his space, trying to banish my nerves. "Is there anything you need?"

Memnon places his hands on either side of my head, and I jolt a little at the touch. "Just you."

That odd humming noise between us grows louder, and my breath comes in shallow pants. It could also be his words. Everything he says sounds like a double entendre.

I don't mean to glance up and meet the sorcerer's stare head-on, but this close to him, with his hands tilting my face up to his, there's nowhere else to look.

His whiskey-brown eyes are tender, affectionate. My heart skips a beat at the sight.

I have been inside you more times than there are stars to count.

Heat rises to my cheeks, and I force away the memory.

Memnon gives me a shadow of a smile. An instant later, however, it's gone. "Close your eyes," he commands.

I stare at him for a moment longer, feeling small and vulnerable with his hands cupping my face, the wall of his body looming over me, and his face so close.

Drawing a fortifying breath, I let my eyelids flutter shut.

Memnon's thumbs stroke my cheeks in silent approval. "Now repeat after me: *Ziwatunutapsa vak mi'tavkasavak ozkos izakgap.*"

I bare my memories for you to see.

The words come easily to me, the sounds of this ancient language both harsh and lilting.

He continues. *"Pes danvup kuppu sutvusa vak danus dukup mi'tupusa. Pes vakvu i'wpatkapsasava kusasuwasa dulipazan detupusa."*

All that I know, I share with you. I willingly give you the truth of my past.

I sense his magic rise, and as soon as I finish speaking, it rushes into me.

Reflexively, I grab Memnon's wrists, ready to jerk his hands away at the first brush of his power in my head, but the sorcerer holds me fast.

Memory after memory flitters by so swiftly, I can hardly make sense of any of them, only that each one is touched by the sharp caress of Memnon's power. On and on it goes, and it could be seconds, or it could be hours. I feel like I'm being turned inside out, like every dirty little truth has been inspected and—

With a curse, Memnon's hands leave me. He stumbles back, breathing heavily, and when he takes me in, his eyes are haunted.

He searches my face, as though it will give him the answers he's looking for. "How…?"

"Do you believe me now?"

He's still searching my face, and while he does so, I allow myself to study his. I'm mesmerized by the black hair that curls at his nape, his pronounced cheekbones, those multifaceted eyes and sensuous lips.

"You're right, *Selene*."

I almost close my eyes when I hear him say my name. This is a small victory, but *I'll take it.* And I can't help but notice how intimate he makes my name sound. As though he knows things about me that no one else does—which, now that he's rifled through my mind, is technically true.

"You remember nothing," he continues. "Your memory itself…" Memnon frowns, a crease forming between his brows.

"My magic feeds off my memories," I explain. "So there are lots of holes in it."

He studies me. "I don't understand our situation," he says slowly. "Not yet at least. But neither, it appears, do you." Memnon grimaces to himself. "So, for now, I'll accept this horrible simulacrum of reality."

Does that mean he really, truly, finally believes me?

The intensity in his gaze has cooled; all that's left is a hollow sort of sadness.

"I had horses, I had warriors and armies, I had palaces and servants and admirers, but most important of all, I had *you*." His voice breaks on that final word, like a wave crashing against the rocks.

"You had *Roxilana*," I remind him softly.

Memnon works his jaw and looks away. "No, in the end, I apparently did not have even her."

His chest rises and falls faster and faster, and I can sense the violent edge of his magic stirring awake.

"You need to leave," I say quietly. Memnon got what he came for. It's not my fault it wasn't what he wanted.

The sorcerer's magic fills the room, and mine mounts to meet his.

Memnon gives me one last baleful look, and then he strides past me and out of my room. The door swings closed behind him, and with that, Memnon the Cursed is finally gone.

CHAPTER 20

I'm on my stomach, my cheek resting against a soft bedsheet. There's someone at my back, peppering kisses up my spine.

"*Est amage*," Memnon breathes against my skin.

I tense at the sound of his voice.

Hadn't he and I parted a few hours ago?

I glance around the room. This one has a low ceiling and close walls made from dark wood. Scattered oil lamps illuminate the intricate red-and-gold design on the blanket beneath me.

My fingers trace the pattern. I…I swear there's something *right there*, on the edge of my mind.

Memnon strokes a hand down my bare spine, and my muscles tighten all over again. I can feel the warm press of his legs against mine, and I can see our magic mingling in the air, the shades going from a rosy orange to coppery pink to dark lavender and a deep sapphire blue.

"Relax, little witch. I only want to make you feel good." A moment later, Memnon gently flips me onto my back.

The sorcerer is naked and on his knees, his cock jutting forward. The lamplight makes his eyes look almost liquid, and I find my breath catching at the sight of him.

He notices me staring, and the two of us hold each other's gazes.

"Tell me what you're thinking," he says softly.

Reveal my thoughts? That sounds terrifying.

But as I continue to gaze into Memnon's eyes, I don't feel terror—not unless you count this strange falling feeling I'm experiencing.

"I want you to kiss me," I confess, dipping my eyes to those lips.

I see them curve into a smile—I even get a peek at those sharp canines of his.

Memnon leans in and presses a kiss between my breasts. "Here?" he whispers against my skin.

A wave of goose bumps moves down my arms.

I shake my head.

Memnon's mouth skims over one of my breasts, stopping to tongue my nipple.

"Here?" he asks.

I gasp, my skin prickling with sensation. "My lips," I breathe.

Memnon smiles against my skin, my nipple still caught between his teeth. That simple devious reaction of his sets my nerves on fire, and I find myself reflexively grinding my pelvis against his.

"Ah, you want a kiss on your lips," Memnon says.

A second later, he's moving. But rather than get closer to my mouth, he pulls away, using one of his knees to spread my legs apart.

Memnon catches my eye and flashes me a grin that promises sin. He bends down, looking like he's about to bow. Instead, he places one of my legs over one of his shoulders, then the other.

His mouth is *inches* from my pussy. Only now do I put together his earlier words.

You want a kiss on your lips.

I feel his exhale against my sensitive folds. Hells' spells…

A shiver works its way through me.

"You are the only goddess I pray to," Memnon murmurs, pressing a kiss to my inner thigh. "You're a fucking *vengeful* one too."

One of his hands strokes the outside of my leg, and he leans in, pressing a carnal kiss to my folds. Another shiver wracks my body.

Memnon must feel it because his hand stops stroking my leg so he can grip me tighter.

A moment later, his tongue slides up my seam. My hips buck at the action, and a breathless cry slips from my mouth.

I'm intoxicated on the sensation he's stirring up within me.

Memnon, voice rough from desire, says, "Let me show you how I pray to you, my wrathful goddess."

With that, he leans forward, and he…*prays*.

I cry out as his mouth moves over my sensitive flesh. His fingers soon find my clit, and he rubs it in circles as his tongue slips between my folds and delves into my core.

I lie there, panting, as Memnon wrecks me touch by touch. One moment I'm desperate to get away from the overstimulation, but then the next, I'm desperate to get closer. It's too much—it's not enough. I need less of his tongue and fingers and more of the rest of him.

I reach for the sorcerer, no longer satisfied with just his hands and mouth working my flesh. I want to feel him *in* me.

At my insistent tug, Memnon stops his ministrations and lets me lead him up my body.

He resettles himself over me, his cock trapped between us.

The sorcerer's eyes glint as he takes me in. "You think I'm going to give you this?" He rocks his hips against mine, and I suck in a sharp breath when his cock slides through my folds.

He laughs, drinking in my expression. "Oh no. You misunderstand, Selene." He kisses my cheek, then presses his lips to my ears. "I will make you ache and ache, *est amage*. You see, I can be wrathful too."

I wake with a gasp. My hand is once again between my legs, and my near orgasm is retreating. My skin is sweaty and heated. I was edged within an inch of my life by a freaking dream. Again.

I blow out a frustrated breath, staring up at my ceiling. Clearly, my subconsciousness thinks I need to get laid. And unfortunately for me, it's set its sights on the worst man for the job.

Even as I think it, a small part of me feels sad that I may not see Memnon again. It's the illogical, masochistic part of me, but it's still there.

But there's also the question of whether Memnon truly *is* gone. I banished him once, and that basically did nothing. I think I'm being optimistic to assume he left for good.

A sound from outside my open window distracts me from my thoughts. The oak tree rustles; then Nero takes shape from the darkness, hopping from the branch to my windowsill, his claws gouging the wood frame.

"Nero." I smile, happy to see my familiar. He was gone for most of the day, and though I know I can always slip into his mind to be close to him and to make sure he's safe, it's not the same as having him right in front of me.

My panther's shadowy form hops down from the windowsill and prowls over to my bed. Without much preamble, he leaps onto my mattress, then immediately begins kneading the blankets.

He's just a cuddly little murder machine.

I reach a hand out and pet his face. Even in the darkness, I can see his eyes closing happily from the scratches.

"You're such a good familiar," I coo, and for once, Nero lets me coddle him.

I run my hand down his neck and flank, pausing when I touch something wet and sticky.

Foreboding washes over me. Pulling my hand away, I rub my fingers together, then bring them to my nose. Almost immediately, I notice the cloying, gamey smell coming from them.

"*Illuminate this room*," I say, drawing hard and fast on my magic. My power lashes out of me, swirling itself into an orb of light.

As soon as my magic brightens the space, I gasp.

My fingers are coated in bright red blood. But it's not just on my fingers; it's all over—

"Nero."

I'm in his head so fast, I get momentarily confused at the sight of my own human face staring back at me.

I can feel wetness against my—I mean *his*—flank and on his legs and paws. But there are no obvious aches or pains.

Not Nero's blood.

I'm back in my own head a moment later. My familiar

sprawls out on his side, and now I can see the blood smears across my checkered comforter.

"What happened?" I ask Nero, even though I know he can't respond. "Is this blood from one of your kills?"

No reaction from him.

"Did you hurt the creature whose blood this is?"

Another nonreaction, except now Nero's tail flicks with irritation.

I'm not asking the right questions.

My mind moves to darker, more terrifying places.

"Was it a human?"

Slowly, Nero's head dips and rises, the action looking unnatural on him. But it was a nod.

"Are they alive?" I ask.

Nothing.

Fuck.

That's a no.

"Can you take me to them?"

Nero gets off the bed and prowls toward the window once more. After grabbing my phone and sweatshirt and shoving my feet into a pair of running shoes, I follow him.

CHAPTER 21

I move like a woman possessed, jogging behind my familiar, my awareness straddled between him and myself.

It only strikes me that this may be a bad idea when we hit the tree line edging the campus.

Oh, we're going in there.

My heart pounds loudly.

You are a powerful witch with a badass familiar. No one is going to fuck with you.

Ahead of me, Nero slows.

Before I see anything at all, I sense the slick, tainted magic that hangs in the air.

Dark magic.

"Illuminet hunc locum." Illuminate this place.

The Latin words flow smoothly out of me, coming from the same shrouded part of me where my stolen memories go. It's a shock to hear them, mostly because lately, it's that other language, the one Memnon speaks, that my mind reaches for. It's like seeing an old friend again, hearing this bit of ancient language fall from my lips.

My magic spins itself into several orbs of amber light, each one levitating into the air above me and Nero. They settle between the bows of trees, glowing softly.

Now that my surroundings are lit, I can see the insidious power ahead of us. It chokes the air and smears the ground. It takes me a moment to realize those smears are *blood*—tainted magical blood.

Next to me, a growl rises from my familiar's throat as he stares straight ahead.

I follow his gaze. No more than twenty feet in front of us lies a body, its limbs twisted, its clothes and skin covered in black-tinged blood. Long hair obscures the individual's face, but it does nothing to hide the open cavity in their chest where their organs should rest.

The meaty smell, the oily magic that glistens and clings to the body—it's overwhelming. I turn and retch.

I figured I would find a body; Nero indicated as much. Yet I find I'm still shocked at the discovery. Shocked and disturbed.

Need to call the Politia. Now.

With a shaky hand, I pull out my phone. It takes me several tries to search for their phone number, my fingers not working as they should.

Finally, I hit the number, and it rings through.

"Politia, Station Fifty-Three—what can I help you with?"

I draw in a lungful of air, but then I taste the dark magic at the back of my throat, and I have to fight another wave of nausea.

All I can manage are a few short words.

"There's—there's been another murder."

I return to the residence hall an hour before daybreak, my body beyond exhausted.

I was questioned for hours, my familiar and I photographed and swabbed for blood and anything else we might've picked up from the crime scene while Politia officers scoured my room for additional evidence. My bedroom is still sealed off, but I'm in no rush to see or deal with the tainted blood all over my things.

I'm going to have to bless the shit out of it once I'm allowed to return.

I spend the first hours of the day crying in one of the shower stalls. Nero is in there with me, rubbing his head reassuringly against my leg. On any other day, I'd find this situation beyond fucking weird—my familiar and I taking a shower together to rinse off the blood and dark magic clinging to us.

Not today, however.

All I can focus on is the memory of that dead individual, their organs ripped out, their very blood infused with dark magic. I didn't see the person's face or the shimmer of their own lingering magic—assuming they had any to being with. Somehow, that lack of distinguishing features makes the whole thing worse. There's no personhood to change my horror into grief or sympathy.

I lean my head against the wall of the shower, letting myself cry until I feel empty.

My hands shake as I grab one of the two towels a Politia officer grabbed for me earlier from my room. I wrap the towel around myself, then use the remaining one to wipe down my familiar.

My bones are weary. I ache in places that can't be healed with ointment and a Band-Aid.

Once Nero and I are dry, we exit the communal

bathroom. If there's one silver lining from this whole shitty experience, it's that I feel a deeper connection to my panther than ever before.

I guess trauma can do that.

Wearing only a towel, I head down to the second floor, where Sybil's room is. Then I pause in front of her door, my hair still dripping. I glance down at Nero. My panther stares up at me. Maybe there's something in my eyes, or maybe he can see my lower lip shaking—something it's been doing on and off for several hours—but Nero rubs his head against my leg, then leans his body heavily against me.

I catch a sob in my throat and force it down at the show of protective affection from my normally distant familiar.

I run my hand down the side of his face and neck. Turning back to the door, I take a deep breath, and then I knock.

From the other side of the door, I hear Sybil groggily shout, "Go away!"

I want to say something snappy back, but it feels like my throat is lodged with cotton, and the words aren't coming.

I wait for my friend to get up and answer the door. When she doesn't, I knock again, this time more insistently.

I hear a groan. "Someone better have died for you to be waking me at this hour." Sybil's words carry through the wall.

I lean my forehead against her door. "They have." My voice comes out softer and hoarser than I imagined. I close my eyes to fight off the images pressing forward in my mind.

There's a long silence, and I almost think Sybil's fallen back asleep when I hear the rustle of blankets.

Seconds after I straighten, the door swings open and a bleary-eyed Sybil is squinting at me.

"Selene," she says, frowning, "what's going on?"

Keep it together. Keep it together.

"It's a long story," I whisper. "Can Nero and I crash in your room for a few hours?"

"You never need to ask," she says, grabbing my wrist and dragging me inside. She holds the door long enough for Nero to slink in behind me.

The window is open, and her familiar's perch is empty. I let out a relieved breath at the sight; I don't want to be dealing with my familiar trying to eat her familiar on top of everything else.

"Need some clothes?" she asks.

"Please," I say as, next to me, Nero noses the plants that seem to explode from every nook and cranny of my friend's room.

Sybil riffles through her dresser before pulling out stretchy pants and a T-shirt.

I remove my towel and hang it up, then tug on the clothes. They're soft and smell like my friend, and once I have them on, I collapse onto her bed.

Sybil comes to the other side of her mattress. "Scooch," she says, nudging me over.

I crawl under the covers of her bed, making myself at home in my friend's room as I have so many other times before. Nero comes to my side before lying down on the floor next to me. Sybil slips under the covers.

After a moment, she runs her fingers through my hair. "Are you okay, babe?" she asks softly.

I shake my head.

"Want to talk about it?"

A ragged breath leaves me.

"No," I admit.

But I end up telling her everything anyway.

The rest of the coven finds out only a few hours later, while Sybil and I watch a baking show on her laptop, the two of us still nestled in her bed.

It's impossible *not* to know about this latest murder, considering the number of forensic specialists I've heard tromping up and down the stairs, undoubtedly heading into and out of my room to collect and catalog evidence.

Eventually, I drag myself out of Sybil's room, taking a pen and a few sheets of lined paper so I can attend classes today and take notes.

I don't know why I bothered to attend today; I sit there and robotically scribble down everything my instructor says. I don't really process any of it, my body tired, my brain fuzzy.

Why did I have to go out into the Everwoods like some sort of junior detective? I shudder when I think about Nero wandering in that forest alongside a murderer, one who practices the dark arts.

Toward the end of class, I get a text from a number I don't recognize.

Forensics is done with your room. You can return.

Relief and trepidation flood my system.

After class ends, I head back to my house, running my hand over one of the stone *lamassu* as I walk up to my front door. Once I enter, my heartbeat quickens.

I don't know why I'm so nervous. It's just my room. I'm ready to be reunited with my things.

I head up the stairs and down the hallway, the rooms in my wing of the house awfully quiet. Usually, there's laughter, or shrieking, or animal vocalizations from my coven sisters' familiars.

When I get to my door, I hesitate, remembering the blood on my sheets.

Drawing in a fortifying breath, I grab my knob and turn. Opening my door, I step inside, and almost immediately, my nose scrunches at the smell of disinfectant and the layers of faded magic still clinging to my room.

The blood has been scrubbed away from the windowsill and floor, and my bed has been stripped completely—someone's even performed a sanitizing spell—but I can still sense the faintest traces of dark magic.

The room feels less inviting than when it was bare of all my things.

I blow out a breath.

There's only one thing to do.

Clean.

It takes several hours to scrub, bless, and ward my room to my satisfaction. Once it's done, I order myself a new comforter and sheet set, wincing inwardly when I realize I charged more on my credit card than I have in my account.

And I still have to buy Nero more food.

I rub my forehead, a throb building behind my temples. The thing about being poor is that you're always one minor problem away from ruin.

The comforter was my minor problem.

I log on to my bank account and count how long I have until I need to pay my bill.

Twelve days.

My stomach twists with unease. Twelve days to figure something out before I officially go into debt.

I scrub my face, feeling lost.

There was something though, wasn't there? Some solution to fix this?

What was it?

I grab my school bag from where it lay and dig through it. When my hand closes over my journal, I pull it out and flip through the last several pages of information.

My eyes flick over assignments, schedules, handwritten directions, and descriptions of locations.

Not that, or that, or that.

Am I misremembering?

On the next page I turn to, a piece of paper flutters out.

I catch it, then flip it over in my hand.

Kasey

Beneath the name is a phone number, and beneath that, in my own handwriting, is an additional message.

Offer to join a spell circle.

$500 gig

Seems shady and is probably a bad idea. Skip unless desperate for cash.

I don't remember writing this note, and I can't quite grasp the memory it came from, but the name Kasey…I think I know which witch that is.

I worry my teeth over my lower lip, my intuition rioting at the thought of participating in anything shady. Entanglements like that have stripped other witches of their coven affiliation.

I glance at my bank account one more time before I decide.

I can look for a job, a student loan, or a grant to cover my needs in the future. But in the meantime…

I enter the number into my phone and send a text.

I want to attend the spell circle.

CHAPTER 22

Witches party. A lot. Normally, I'm all for that.

Tonight I'm not.

"Sybil, you *cannot* be serious," I say when I enter her room in the evening. She's already pulled on a sequined minidress that changes color depending on which direction you smooth out the sequins. It's the kind of outfit that begs for hands to touch it.

"Witches are getting murdered on campus grounds after hours," I say. Already, I heard talk that the coven is thinking of imposing a curfew.

She glances up at me, holding an eyeshadow palette and brush in her hand. Her gaze slides over my lounge pants and loose shirt. "Why aren't you dressed? I texted you about the party hours ago."

"*Because it's not safe*," I say slowly. It's been three nights since I found Andrea, the witch who was murdered in the woods. She'd been unaffiliated with any known coven, simply moving through the area.

Still, her name will be burned into my memory until my magic takes it.

Sybil blows out a breath. "Did you see anyone when you came down to my room?" she asks out of nowhere.

My brows come together. "What does that have to do with anything?"

"Did you?" she presses.

I shake my head.

"Did you hear anyone when you were walking through our house?"

My brows furrow further. "Why does that even matter—?"

"The rest of our housemates are already at the party, which yes, is across the Everwoods on lycanthrope territory, and yes, the world is a dangerous place, but the world has *always* been a dangerous place for witches, Selene."

Other witches were already out in those woods? The thought chills my blood. Why is no one else taking this seriously?

Sybil continues. "The Marin Pack is patrolling the forest, and the coven's head witches have cast protective wards on the area. Whoever is killing witches would be unable to hurt any witch without the entire coven and the shifters knowing.

"Besides," she throws in casually, "they're saying the women weren't killed in the woods, just moved there."

A shiver wracks my body.

As if that's much better.

"And you're going to walk through those woods alone?" I ask.

"Goddess, Selene, I was going to walk over with *you*, but I can find another witch to head over with if you're not coming."

Hell will freeze over before I let my best friend travel across those woods with some random housemate who may not be looking out for her the way I will.

Even if it gets me freaking murdered in the process.

I blow out a breath. "*Fine*," I say, "I'll come along, but only so you don't get yourself killed in your quest to get drunk and laid."

Sybil lets out an excited squeal. "You're not going to regret it."

I highly doubt that.

"Pretty sure the people who invented heels were fans of waterboarding, iron maidens, and the Spanish Inquisition," I mutter as I pull on a thigh-high boot from Sybil's closet. I wear a deep-blue minidress with exaggerated bell sleeves. "And *I'm* the loser who's wearing them," I continue, "all so I can drink cheap booze and make poor decisions."

"My goddess, Selene, stop channeling your inner eighty-two-year-old and cut loose a little."

I make a face as I pull the other boot on. "My inner eighty-two-year-old has figured some things out," I retort.

"Don't you want to see the werewolves' territory?"

Not really.

"Plus, Kane is going to be there—"

I groan. "For the love of our goddess, please stop with Kane," I say.

"Only if you go. If not, I'm going to find him and tell him you're wildly in love with him and want to have his little wolfy babies."

Horrified, I glance at my friend. *"Sybil."*

It might've once been true. Now, when I close my eyes, it's a different face I think about. One that makes my stomach twist with both dread and desire.

Sybil cackles, every inch the villainous witch.

"You wouldn't," I say.

"No, but only because you're going."

Sybil braids a small section of my hair on either side of my temples, then secures them away from my face with clips painted to look like real butterflies. She murmurs a spell under her breath, and the next time I look in the mirror, I see the wings of my clips flutter and resettle, as though they were real.

The two of us touch up each other's makeup, and then we leave the house. Sybil and I cut across campus, past the massive glass conservatory on our right, which is still lit up, despite the late hour. Lampposts around the school bathe the rest of campus in pretty golden light, but the moment we hit the tree line, the shadows swallow us.

"This is a bad idea, Sybil," I say, staring around us at the dark forms of trees. It doesn't help that my familiar is off hunting tonight instead of at my side. There's nothing like having a panther bodyguard to make a girl feel safe.

Sybil bends down and plucks a weed from the ground. Holding it in her palm, she whispers a spell. The plant shrivels and twists before our eyes. In its place grows a ball of pale green light. She blows on it, and it bobs ahead of us, lighting our way. Almost as an afterthought, she drops the dead weed from her hand.

I stare at her for a second longer. "You truly are extraordinary, you know." I'm so proud of her, my friend who will one day change the world.

"Awww," Sybil says, bumping her shoulder against mine. "So are you, Selene."

I draw her words close and let myself believe them. When my memory loss feels overwhelming or when it prevents me from doing the sorts of things other witches take for granted,

I can second-guess my abilities. This is my reminder to tell my insecurities to fuck off.

Sybil winds her arm through mine. "Isn't it wild?" she says. "Just think of all those stories they tell about these woods."

I give her a sharp look. "You mean the ones where witches are being murdered?" I say, my voice rising a little.

"Goddess," Sybil says, exasperated, rolling her eyes at me. "The Everwoods has far more to its history than the recent murders." She glances at me. "Have you heard about the witches claimed during the Sacred Seven?"

According to werewolves, the Sacred Seven are the seven days closest to the full moon, the time when their magic compels them to shift. Normally, packs keep to themselves during those days, usually to stop themselves from accidentally harming nonshifters.

"*No*," I say. "What the hell do you mean there have been witches claimed during the Sacred Seven?"

Sybil lifts a shoulder. "Lycanthropes have been known to lay a claiming bite on witches out late in these woods—if, of course, the witch is unable or unwilling to stop them."

"*What?*" I say, aghast. "That actually happens?" My eyes flick to the sky above us, searching for the moon. But of course it's not there. Even if the trees and the clouds weren't obscuring my view, tomorrow is the new moon, which means there's not much to see in the sky right now.

"That's how lycanthropes claim their mates." Sybil gives me a sly smile. "Ask a shifter tonight how their parents met. Some of them have witch mothers."

Witch mothers who might also shift into *wolves*, if what she's saying is true.

"It's not just lycanthropes either," Sybil continues. "There are stories of fae who've snatched witches from these woods to be their brides."

"Are these stories supposed to make me feel better? Because all I know now is that I should worry about murderers, werewolves, *and* fairies."

"Don't forget your vengeful mummy," she says playfully, a smile spreading on her lips.

My mood darkens at the reminder. But before I can dwell on it too long, the distant thumping of music drifts through the woods.

We continue on a little ways, and then, ahead of us, the forest brightens, and through the trees, I catch sight of supernaturals dancing and mingling in a small clearing next to a cabin.

Sybil and I make it to the revelers, and Sybil's orb floats up and joins dozens of others in the air above us, each emitting light the shade of the caster's magic. It looks ethereal, and the sight of it reminds me of Sybil's earlier words about the fae claiming brides on nights like tonight.

A shiver courses through me.

Next to me, Sybil murmurs, "*Through sweat and salt and musky fear, send the cold away from here.*"

The chill in the air disperses, leaving the night feeling a touch balmy.

"You're welcome," Sybil whispers.

I shake my head and smile. I keep forgetting how much fun it is to openly use magic. I'm still used to living among humans and concealing it.

Sybil and I head inside the cabin, where more shifters and witches are hanging out. I recognize a big group of witches from our house, and I join them while Sybil runs off to grab us drinks.

I listen as my coven sisters chat about how hard premed magic is and nod when appropriate, but I'm distracted by my own unease. This feels like a reenactment of Little Red Riding Hood, only the whole story is flipped on its head, and the wolves aren't going to eat us—whatever is lurking out in these woods will.

In my mind's eye, I see that murdered witch again, with her gaping chest cavity and missing organs—

"I saw Kane."

I nearly jump at the sound of Sybil's voice in my ear.

"Maiden, Mother, and Crone, Sybil," I say, clutching my heart. "You scared me."

"Ease up, Bowers," she says, pressing a red cup into my hand. "I'm not going to bite. Kane, on the other hand..."

"Will you stop?" I whisper frantically.

"Never," she whispers back.

As I speak to Sybil, I catch the eye of one of the witches across the way, her features almost painfully symmetrical.

I'm about 75 percent sure that's Kasey, the shady spell-circle witch. She responded to my earlier text with the time and place of the spell circle.

Now she gives me a little wave, and I wave back at her, my stomach twisting on itself.

Really need to get a respectable job. I don't have the nerves for shady side gigs.

Olga comes over to us, her hair a frizzy tangle of curls and her eyes wild.

"No Book of Last Words?" Sybil says, looking the witch over. "I thought you never parted with it."

"*Ledger*," Olga clarifies. "It's the Ledger of Last words." She holds up her drink. "And I didn't want to spill beer on it. But I've added to it since we last spoke..."

I force myself to tune out the rest of what she has to say. Normally, I'm as curious as the next person about death and last words and all that jazz, but tonight it's not sitting well. Not when I'm already on edge.

So I sip my drink and let my eyes wander over the cabin while my coven sisters chat.

The house is two stories tall, and from where I stand in the living room, I can see the doors that line the second story. Most of them are already closed, and it doesn't take any supernatural sense of mine to know just what is going on behind them.

Without meaning to, my eyes land on a group of lycanthropes across the room, near a roaring fireplace. The magic shimmering off them is translucent and textured, rather than colorful and misty. At the center of them is the one and only Kane Halloway.

My stomach flips at the sight of him chatting with one of his friends, and all those old feelings of excitement and infatuation bubble up. Back at Peel Academy, I *pined* for this guy. And for all that time, he looked right through me.

Kane turns away from one of his friends, and before I can look away, those lupine blue eyes of his catch mine.

Look away, I command myself.

But I can't seem to.

Kane holds my gaze, and the longer I stare, the more I swear I see his wolf peeking out from those irises. Heat rises to my cheeks as the two of us stay locked like that. I don't know much about lycanthropes, but I'm pretty sure staring is a dominance display. And I'm pretty sure challenging a wolf like this is a bad idea.

Across the room, Kane's nostrils flare just the slightest.

Then he smiles.

"Oh my goddess," Sybil says, catching sight of the exchange. "Go over and talk to him like you've wanted to for the past several years," Sybil says.

Finally, reluctantly, I force my gaze away from Kane to give my friend a pointed look.

"He can hear you," I say, my voice low. Even in their human form, lycanthropes have preternatural hearing.

"Then I hope he knows you'd happily fuck him too," Sybil says louder.

Hells' bells.

Out of the corner of my eye, I see Kane grin with the confidence of a man who *definitely* just heard that bit of conversation.

"Why would you do that to me?" I whisper furiously at her.

"Because I love you and you've waited too long for good things to happen to you." Sybil gives me a quick squeeze, then pushes me out of the circle of witches.

I stumble away, flashing her a betrayed look.

"What are you—?" But Sybil has already turned back to Olga, who is only too happy to resume her conversation about last words.

I take a few steps away, chewing on my lower lip, my heart racing. I glance down at my beer. I'm going to need at least three more drinks before my confidence is anywhere near high enough to approach my longtime crush.

"Hey." That deep, masculine voice nearly makes me drop my red cup.

I turn toward the voice, and there's Kane, looking larger and stronger and altogether hotter than my memories of him.

"Hey back," I say. I'm proud the words actually came out because I am drowning in adrenaline. I'm pretty sure the same people responsible for heels and iron maidens and the Spanish Inquisition also invented crushes because there is *nothing* pleasant about this feeling. Which, to be fair, is probably why it's called a *crush* in the first place, because I'm positive Kane is about to pulverize my giddy little heart beneath his boot. I can't imagine this ending any other way.

"Selene, right?" he says, those lupine eyes a little too intense this close. I can practically feel the power radiating off him. Now I do want to bare my neck and look away.

Surprise has me raising my eyebrows instead. "You know my name?"

I can't believe Kane Halloway knows my name.

His own brows furrow. "Of course I remember your name."

I'm screaming inside.

He's so much bigger than I remember—not that my memory is to be trusted. And his voice goes straight through my ears and down to my pussy.

Why are you thinking about your pussy? Pull yourself together, woman!

"I'm glad you came," he says. "I remember you from Peel Academy."

I nearly drop my drink. "You do?"

I feel like the entire history of my infatuation with him shifts on its axis. I always assumed I blended in with the wallpaper.

Kane gives me a strange look, then leans in conspiratorially. "I *did* ask you out on a date," he says. "But you never showed."

"*No*," I say, my voice hushed with horror.

I never showed? Why, universe, why?

"You don't remember?" he says.

I'm still agonizing over the fact I could've been dating this man *since high school.*

"Um, about that..." How to explain my power? "I have this thing, with my magic—"

Before I can finish, some of Kane's friends come up to him, one of them slapping him on the back.

"Kane, man, great party."

One of the other shifters with dark hair lifts his chin at me in greeting. "Hey," he says, flashing a smile.

Hand to the goddess on high, Kane growls. It's so low, I'm not entirely sure I heard correctly, but then Kane's friends back off.

"Easy, boy," the man with dark hair says, even as he backs away. "I meant no harm. Just wanted to tell the witch she has nice eyes." He winks at me, even as Kane growls again.

I guess that's how you fuck with your friend if you're a shifter—you make him seem weirdly possessive of a girl he just started chatting with.

And maybe if I hadn't been pining for Kane for years, I would've let those growls scare me off. But my happy little heart finds the whole thing thrilling, self-respect be damned.

It helps that Kane is grimacing, as though frustrated with his own reaction. He glares after his friends as they walk away.

"I'm sorry," he says, turning to me. "There are things about being a lycan..." His jaw works a little as he tries to find the words.

Kane struggles with people accepting parts of his identity? I didn't expect that.

I wave it off. "Believe me when I tell you, *I understand.*"

CHAPTER 23

The next several hours blur by as I chat and drink with Kane. By the time the two of us move to the dance floor, magic has thickened the air, the various colors of it swirling and blending. I breathe it in, the power calling to my own magic, demanding I let go of my inhibitions.

This is one of the aspects of witchery they don't talk about that often. The wild, nearly frenzied nature of our magic that exposes itself when we gather under a night sky.

I can feel that primordial need for release as I dance with Kane. My clothes feel too heavy and constricting, and I have the urge to strip myself of them. I need…*more.*

Empress…I hear your call…

My blood heats at the sound of Memnon's voice in my head, and my need rises. I don't know when I went from dreading the sorcerer to having this reaction.

I mean to look for Memnon, but my eyes catch on Kane as his nostrils flare, like he scents something. A moment later he cups my cheek on the dance floor, our sweaty bodies sliding against each other.

He stares down at me, and again, I see the lupine glint of his eyes. He leans into my neck, running his lips and nose along the skin there. Whatever he's doing, it feels… animalistic—like perhaps he's smelling me or marking me.

His mouth skims along my jaw before he pulls away. He looks into my eyes for a long second, and then slowly, he leans in once more, his eyes dipping to my lips, giving me plenty of time to back out.

I don't.

His lips brush against mine, and then dancing turns into kissing. I'm unable to stop—my mouth likes the taste of his far too much to stop. Something about it tugs at me, like an itch I can't quite scratch, and that only makes me fall deeper into the kiss, chasing that elusive sensation.

I don't know how long we stand there, making out instead of dancing, before Kane lifts me to carry me off the dance floor and then out of the cabin altogether.

Without really looking, I sense that most of the party has already moved out here. Lycans have paired up with witches and one another; somewhere between alcohol, magic, and instinct, the evening turned carnal.

Kane only puts me down so he can press me against a tree, his hands coming back up to cup my face. I close my eyes as he kisses me roughly, and the dominance, the power, it's stoking a memory…

I open my eyes and frown when Kane's features don't align with what I expected.

A love like ours defies everything… *I am yours forever…*

The phantom words tease out a shiver before I force them away, falling back into the kiss.

Not enough. Not nearly enough.

My hands are moving all over him, and I take a moment to appreciate his muscles through the fabric of his shirt before my fingers dip beneath its hem and run over the rigid planes of his chest.

Kane groans into my mouth, pressing himself deeper into me, and there's no missing the rigid length of his shaft. Now it's his turn to touch, his hands moving up my sides, his thumb skimming my breasts.

I moan. An ache grows between my thighs, one I don't want to resist.

I need…I need…

Little witch, your voice is so pretty when it makes its demands…

I gasp at Memnon's voice in my head, my core clenching for some perverse reason.

Kane grinds against me, and my mind is a mess—is it the shifter or the sorcerer working me to a fever pitch?

I peer over Kane's shoulder, looking for…I'm not sure exactly what. My eyes sweep over our surroundings, and I notice just how many other revelers have paired up with each other. I hear heavy breathing and sounds that would make me blush if I were sober. Even now, I see couples and small groups disappearing into the deep night.

Maybe it's not the men at all—maybe it's simply the intoxicating combo of booze and magic.

Whatever the cause, I'm flush with desire. But our surroundings…

My grip tightens on Kane, and he pauses to see what has me tensing.

"What's wrong?" he says, his voice husky.

I swallow. "Witches have been killed in these woods…" Slipping off into the forest right now is a supremely bad idea.

"None of my pack will let any harm come to your coven sisters."

Unless, of course, a lycanthrope is the one killing them off. The body I saw *was* brutally torn open.

I squeeze my eyes shut against that thought.

"Hey, you okay?" Kane asks, tipping my chin up with his hand.

I nod, maybe a little too fast, before I open my eyes. "Do you want to get out of here?" I ask.

I'm not above shooting my shot with Kane, even when I'm hearing Memnon in my head and panicking about these woods.

Kane's wolf peers out from the back of his eyes. "Yeah, I do."

My heart pounds hard in my chest. Goddess, this is really happening. I'm taking my high school crush home with me.

I take his hand and start leading him away from the party. Then I hesitate. "I came here with a friend, and I was planning on taking her home."

"Then let's grab her," Kane says.

I don't actually know if Sybil wants to go with me at all, but luckily, I spot her across the clearing, making out with a shifter.

"Just a sec," I say to Kane. "I'll be right back."

I head over to Sybil, a little hesitant to interrupt what looks to be a very heavy make-out session.

"Sybil," I whisper.

No reaction.

"*Sybil*," I whisper louder.

Still nothing.

"Sybil!" I finally shout.

My friend pauses, dragging her face away from the

lycan's. "Hey, Selene," she says, trying to pull herself together.

"I was going to take Kane back to the house, but I didn't want to leave you," I say.

"Leave me," she insists, her eyes hazy with booze and desire. "I'll be fine. Sawyer here has promised to walk me home." She smiles and winks at him. Sawyer looks surprised but thrilled at the prospect.

I hesitate. I don't want to be awkward here, but—

"That wasn't the plan."

"Forget the plan."

Still, I'm unsure.

She sighs. "Babe, I say this with all the love in the world, but don't cockblock me. I want this." Her eyes flick over my shoulder, and she smiles broadly. "And I will *definitely* not cockblock you either."

Before I can glance over my shoulder, a warm hand falls to my waist, and I feel Kane's heat at my back. If I were any less intoxicated, I'd be embarrassed that Kane overheard Sybil's words. Instead, I lean into the shifter at my back, my need still building.

"Hey there," Sybil says to him, giving Kane a tiny wave.

"I don't want to leave you," I insist.

"I trust Sawyer with my life," Kane says, jumping into the conversation. "He won't let anything happen to your friend." To Sawyer, Kane adds, "Walk her home at the end of the night." Those words are accompanied by a burst of shifter magic. It brushes my skin and bends the soft light out here before settling on Sawyer's shoulders.

I don't know much about pack hierarchy and dynamics, but I think I just witnessed a bit of the power play involved.

"Kane, man," Sawyer says, "you know you don't have to tell me."

I think I've been given all the reassurances I can. Still, I don't like leaving my friend out here regardless. Sybil must see it on my face because she pulls me in for a tight hug and whispers in my ear, "Babe, go screw the brains out of that man. I'll see you at breakfast tomorrow. *Promise*."

She releases me, then pushes me into Kane, who catches me by the upper arms. To further drive home the fact I've been excused, Sybil drags Sawyer's mouth back down to hers.

All right, message received loud and clear.

I turn from her, and Kane is there, his eyes shining a little too brightly.

"You'd fit right into the pack, you know," he says, as we move toward the outskirts of the clearing.

"What do you mean?" I ask, threading my fingers through his.

"Pack doesn't leave their own behind. You were ready to drag her out of there, and even with all our reassurances, I can still scent your worry."

He can scent *what* now?

Shit, what else has he been smelling over the past few hours?

I redirect my thoughts back on topic.

"Sybil's my best friend," I say as we leave the clearing, the trees looming around us. "She's always been there for me. I'd give my life for that girl."

That wolfish glint is back in Kane's eyes, watching me like he's tracking my every movement. "Like I said, you'd fit right in with the pack."

I'm somehow both flattered and unnerved by the compliment.

Lycanthropes have been known to lay a claiming bite on witches out late in these woods.

"Where did you want to go?" Kane says, interrupting my thoughts.

Right. We hadn't decided on that.

"My place," I say, leading Kane along by his hand.

Three steps later, I nearly twist my ankle when I step on a branch wrong.

Freaking heels.

Kane catches me before I go down and reels me in close. "You okay?"

I swallow and nod at him.

"Good." He smiles and leans in a little closer. "I'm pretty good at giving piggyback rides—if you're interested."

I'm a witch, a symbol of revolutionary feminism. I don't need a man to carry me, or coddle me, or worry over—

"Hell. Yes."

Kane lifts me and swings me onto his back and, ah, provides some relief for the poor, aching balls of my feet.

"Hold on," Kane says, and then he runs.

I yelp, nearly falling off at first. I wrap my arms around Kane's neck and then laugh and laugh.

This is ridiculously fun. Kane is going to get so laid. *So laid.*

"Someone's eager," I whisper into his hair, wrapping one of his sandy curls around my finger.

"Can you blame me?" he says over his shoulder. "I want to get back to kissing those lips."

"It's not fair to be hot *and* have good game," I whisper back into his ear. I follow it with a brush of my lips.

Before he can answer, we pass a naked couple. I yelp when I see a witch who lives down the hall from me getting railed by a lycanthrope.

"Oh my—titties!" I meant to say *goddess*, but I sort of just said what I saw instead.

Beneath me, I hear Kane's booming laugh.

We see another couple and another, each one in various states of ecstasy.

Kane slows briefly partway to campus.

"Why are you slowing?"

Kane points to a nearby standing stone. "These mark the boundary between coven lands and pack lands."

Branching from either side of the stone is a faint luminous line, magically marking the boundary. I try to remember if I noticed them earlier this evening, but if I did, I've since forgotten.

"Why are you showing me this?" Part of me wonders if this is about Nero. Maybe his pack knows my familiar is a panther, and maybe Nero really has been poaching on lycanthrope territory.

Kane is quiet for several seconds, and with each passing moment, I feel more and more like this is about Nero.

But then, he says, "If you ever want to visit me, all you ever have to do is cross the boundary line. My pack mates and I patrol the perimeter here."

That was not at all what I expected.

I peer over his shoulder at him. "Kane, are you…are you saying you want me to visit you even after tonight?"

Only after I say those words do I realize how much *I've* laid out on the line. Because maybe Kane doesn't want to see me after tonight and I got it all wrong. Maybe this is where he really does pulverize my heart.

He hesitates again. "Yeah," he eventually says, "I am."

And then he begins to run once more, and I'm left with my giddy, churning thoughts until we reach my residence hall.

We pass the stone *lamassu*, and Kane sets me down in front of the door, catching me when I stumble a little.

His brows come together, and then he leans in, breathing in my scent. "Are you good?" he asks, pulling away. "If you're not, we don't have to do anything else toni—"

I grab him by the shirt and resume kissing him. He's so noble, and damn it, I like that.

Kane is soooooo getting laid. And then laid again.

"I'm fine," I whisper between one accosting kiss and the next.

That's all the shifter needs to hear. He growls, the sound not wholly human, and presses me back against my front door as his mouth devours mine all over again.

Somewhere in that kiss, I discover Kane doesn't taste like I expect him to, nor does his mouth move like I think it will. Each deviation throws me off.

Clearly, this is me trying to sabotage myself because it can't handle something too good to be true actually, legitimately happening to me.

Right in the middle of the kiss, I start laughing because something too good to be true is happening to me.

"Tell me the joke," Kane says, still peppering my laughing lips with kisses.

I shake my head against him. "I've liked you for so long. I can't believe I get to kiss you now."

In response to that, Kane's mouth returns to mine, and for a brief minute, I'm lost to it. I still have to ignore the nagging thought that something isn't quite right, but I push it away easily enough.

The cold nips at me, reminding me that I'm still outside in the middle of coven property when I definitely want to be doing more of this kissing in my warm room and on my cozy bed.

"Wait, wait, wait," I breathe, placing a hand on Kane's chest and pushing him away. "I need to open the door."

Kane is breathing heavily, his eyes on my lips. His tongue runs along his lower lip, and I bite back a groan at the sight.

I fumble behind me, my hand groping for the door handle. It takes two tries, a small spell, and me nearly falling again before I'm able to get it open.

Kane scoops me up then before leading us both inside. He carries me up the flight of stairs to the third story, all while kissing me. It's only as he heads down the hall toward my room that I break off the kiss.

"How do you know which room is mine?" I say, narrowing my eyes at him.

He laughs at my suspiciousness. "Don't hex me, Selene," he says. "I just followed your scent."

"Oh." *Duh, Selene. Get a freaking grip.*

Kane sets me down in front of my door, and this time I manage not to fumble as I unlock it. I'm about to open it when I feel the brush of magic against the back of my neck and my cheek. It moves over me like a caress, trailing over my mouth. The sensation is so real and so oddly sensual that I have to touch my fingers to my lips, goose bumps breaking out across my flesh.

There's only one person whose power affects me this way.

I am yours forever...

"Selene?"

I blink, remembering myself. I glance up and down the hall, looking for any sign of Memnon. But I don't see him, and the magic I felt a moment ago is gone like it never existed at all.

I shake my head as I open the door. "Sorry," I say, "I lost my thoughts there for a moment."

Kane bends down and brushes his lips against my cheek, and it takes everything in me not to wipe his kiss away.

What is wrong with me?

I hold the door open, stepping away from Kane to put a little distance between us. I draw in a deep breath, trying to sort out my mind.

Kane takes in my place, his nostrils flaring as he breathes in my scent. His eyes touch on the sticky notes that cover my walls and furniture.

My heart races, and I feel vulnerable all over again. People always think they're going to like the weird, quirky girl, but legitimate weirdness isn't always cute and quirky. It's often just…off-putting.

"Nice room," Kane says, and I think he's being sincere. I know I *want* to believe it.

I step inside as well, closing the door behind me.

"Um, there's something you should know about me," I say.

"What?" he says, turning to meet my eyes.

I force the words out. "There's a chance I'll forget tonight."

He raises his eyebrows. "What?" he says again, this time a little more alarmed.

I look him over, unsure just how much he knows about me.

"My magic…it feeds on my memories," I admit. "Every time I use my power, I lose some. I don't get to choose which ones. So…I really might forget tonight."

Kane's brows draw together, and I have no idea what he's thinking.

"I just…wanted to let you know in case that changes things," I add.

Realization sparks in his eyes. "*That's* why you stood me up back at Peel, isn't it?" he says, putting the pieces together. As if the world makes so much more sense now that he knows he was never truly rejected.

Biting the inside of my cheek, I nod.

Kane frowns a little. "Do you *want* me to go?" he asks me softly.

"No—no! I just wanted you to know in case this memory gets taken from me."

Please, magic, don't take my memory of banging my smoking-hot werewolf crush.

Kane's face relaxes, and he steps into my space. "I think I can handle a little amnesia," he says.

Either this dude really wants my pussy, or he's being *exceptionally* understanding. I mean, if a guy told me he'd have sex with me but might not remember it afterward...I just don't know how big I'd be about it.

Kane's hand cups my jaw, and suddenly, his lips are on mine. Just like that, my worry dissipates. I fall into the kiss, sliding my hands to his torso.

Another whisper of magic skims over my skin, feeling like the stroke of a lover. It, more than the kiss, has my core throbbing. I arch into the phantom touch, wanting more.

Kane's fingers move to my hair, and my own grip tightens on him. The more intense the kiss becomes, the more I get a niggling sense that something is...*off.* I just don't know what. It's something sensory—like the feel and smell of him isn't right. I don't know what to make of it, so I ignore it.

I slip my hands under his shirt, and ever-loving Goddess, I can feel each one of his abs.

Shifters.

He lifts me, wrapping my legs around his waist, and the whole thing is hitting *all* my buttons.

Kane moves us over to my bed before laying me out and draping himself over me. He buries his face into my neck, then pauses. There's a rumble low in his throat.

"Why does your bed smell like raw meat?" he asks, running his lips and nose up and down my throat.

"My bed smells like *raw meat*?" My voice has risen with my alarm.

"Mm-hmm," he says as he kisses me.

Freaking Nero.

"Um, my familiar apparently has poor etiquette."

Next time I see that panther, he is going to *hear* about this.

Kane smiles against me, then nips the skin of my neck. I gasp, grinding my pelvis against him.

He releases my flesh—though I swear he's reluctant to do so.

"It's bringing out my predator," he admits.

"Is that bad?" I ask, torn myself. While I find the idea of his animal side hot, his teeth on my neck have forced me to think about claiming bites, which is a hard *no* for me.

Kane shakes his head. "It's fine. I'm in control."

I think Kane finds the whole thing oddly erotic.

He grinds against me, and fuck, I think seeing Kane completely let go would be worth the risk of a claiming bite.

Okay, fine, it *wouldn't*, but I'm all for the wild sex that would go along with it.

I stare up at him. "You're not going to be weird about this the next time we see each other?"

Kane pauses, his breath coming in quick pants. "No. Are you?"

"Without a doubt."

He smiles at that. "It's all right, Selene. I like your brand of weird." He punctuates the statement by nuzzling my face, then rubbing his cheek against mine, an action that seems distinctly wolfish.

"Besides," he adds, "you seem to think things will go back to the way they were before tonight."

I frown, turning to him. "They won't?"

Instead of answering me, Kane bends down to kiss me again. It feels like the sort of kiss that's meant to show rather than tell his intentions. And the slow glide of his lips and the sensual rocking of his hips make me think that maybe I'm supposed to believe he really does want more from me than just one night.

Part of me thrills at the thought, but then another part of me is vehemently against that. I don't know why.

Kane reaches for the shoulder of my dress. He moves the material away and brushes his lips along the exposed skin. My breath hitches.

I need more.

I sit up, forcing Kane back so he's kneeling, my legs still draped around him.

Then I remove my arms, one by one, from the stretchy material of my dress to let it pool at my waist.

Those wolfish eyes look hungry as he takes me in. I feel decidedly self-conscious in my tattered nude bra, but whatever, it's not going to be on for long.

My magic stirs, tugging at my heart and skimming over my skin as I reach for Kane's shirt. I feel my power slip past the shifter, reaching for something across my room and out my window.

My attention is drawn back to Kane when he grabs the hem of his shirt and pulls it off, then tosses it aside.

Shirtless Kane is a sight to behold. He's all taut, packed muscle.

His nostrils flare as I take him in, as though he's breathing in my desire.

Crap, he probably is. Lycanthropes can smell *everything*.

Before I can react, he leans into me, cupping my face as his lips find mine once more.

We fall back onto my bed, wrapped up in each other. I'm running my hands up his sides when I feel what I swear is Memnon's magic back against my skin, stroking, stroking…

I gasp at the feel of it, my body electrified by its touch. It creeps up my arms, drawing out my gooseflesh.

I look for the magic, and this time, I do see the indigo plumes of it moving over my flesh—plumes Kane can't see and probably can't much sense either.

It hits me then—beyond the booze and the haze of desire—that the sorcerer who has been *in my head* this evening, has also been using his magic to draw out my desire.

One of those strands of magic now curls in on itself against my upper arm while Kane kisses my neck. It looks so innocuous, and beneath it, my flesh puckers. As I watch, that magic thickens.

If Memnon's power is here, then…then he must be close by.

Shit.

Shit, shit, shit.

I push against Kane's chest, forcing the shifter to sit up as Memnon's magic grows around us.

"What is it?" Kane says, his gaze hooded with desire.

"You need to go," I say, giving him another push to get him moving.

The shifter stays stubbornly where he is. "Did I do something wrong?"

The indigo magic now floods the room, and my intuition—intuition I steadfastly ignored all evening—is screaming forewarnings at me.

"I have more issues than just my memory," I tell him, scrambling to get up and forcing my arms back into my dress sleeves. The power around me has changed, no longer sensual but agitated, *violent.*

"You need to go," I insist. "*Now.*"

At the direct order, I see Kane's eyes flash, and I feel his own dominance rise at the challenge. "I'm not—"

BOOM!

The entire house rocks, and my window shatters. Something slams into Kane, and a split-second later, his body hits the wall, the plaster buckling under the force.

I hear a wolfish yelp at the impact, and as Kane crumples to the floor, a massive man looms over the shifter. I don't need to see the sleeve of tattoos running down his arm to know who it is.

"Memnon!" I cry, my stomach bottoming out as the sorcerer drags Kane back to his feet. *"Stop!"*

Memnon somehow manages to make Kane look small and boyish as he lifts the lycan by the throat.

To my horror, Kane's eyes have shifted, and his teeth have sharpened.

"*You dare to touch what is mine, wolf?*" Memnon roars, his eyes beginning to glow.

His magic is mounting, and I feel the vicious intent of it as it swirls around us.

"Memnon, stop!" I shout as I swing myself off the bed.

Beneath the sorcerer's hand, a partially shifted Kane

now returns to his human form. Only...he's not the one doing the shifting; Memnon seems to be, his power so dense, I taste it on my tongue. Kane growls and yelps the entire time as though every second of it is agonizing. Once he's fully human, he's drenched in sweat and breathing heavily.

"I will castrate you and feed you your own godsdamned dick for what you have done!" the sorcerer bellows.

There aren't words for the terror coursing through my veins. But beneath it brews my anger.

I lift my hand, my rage channeling down my arm.

"Release him!" The words come out in another language, and with it, my power sweeps over the room, the sherbet-orange hue of my magic overtaking the dark blue plumes of his own.

I feel it the moment my spell catches hold.

Memnon must as well because for the first time since he broke in, he turns to me.

"Release him?" he says. He eyes the lycanthrope. "*Fine.*"

Rather than simply let Kane go, Memnon hurls the shifter out my broken window.

I cry out, horrified as I hear Kane's body snap branches and rustle leaves as it falls.

My power flows out of me then, racing after Kane. There's no spell or any intricate design to go along with it, just intent—*save Kane.*

Unfortunately, my power is too slow.

I rush over to the window in time to hear the dull *thump* of Kane hitting the ground, no magic there to soften the impact.

Fuck, fuck, fuck.

My magic recoils into me an instant later, and I feel that

insidious tug inside my head, the one that indicates I lost another memory from using my power.

It doesn't matter. Not when Kane may be out there dying.

I swing my leg out the gaping hole that was my window, but Memnon scoops me up from behind.

"First you trap me in a tomb and fuck me over for two millennia, and now you dare to break our unbreakable vows and *touch* another?" Memnon growls against my ear. The lilt of the ancient language curls around me like one long, unbroken memory.

Has this man forgotten our entire last conversation?

"I—am not—Roxilana!" I kick at him.

Memnon ignores the strikes and, clutching me close, he steps onto the broken windowsill, then leaps off.

For a moment, I'm weightless. Then we land, and my entire body jolts from the impact, my teeth clicking together.

I catch sight of Kane's slumped form, and I let out a horrified scream.

There's a pool of blood around him, and he's lying there, unmoving.

I struggle in the sorcerer's grip all over again, but Memnon holds me fast. And then, he begins to carry me away, just like those captive fae brides Sybil warned me about.

Oh, hell no.

"Let go of me!" The command comes out in Sarmatian, though I barely notice. I'm spitting mad and consumed with worry for Kane.

Memnon ignores my shrieks and my struggles, continuing to stride onward, into the darkened woods.

In the distance I sense my familiar, but when I slip into his mind, all I see is forest.

Come now! I call to him, though I don't know if Nero heard or felt compelled by the command.

Moving back into my own mind is confusing because the scenery is nearly the same—more darkened trees.

Once I get my bearings, I strike out with my power. The sorcerer laughs. *Laughs.*

The fucking *gall.*

"Don't insult me, Empress. You know you'll have to do much more than that if you wish to harm me."

"You *psycho*! Let me *go*!" I twist in his arms, my magic flaring out of me with my panic and anger. It doesn't so much as loosen his hold.

We've long since lost sight of the coven house when Memnon finally stops, reluctantly setting me down.

I'm breathing hard, my heart pounding a mile a minute when I turn and catch sight of him. The moonlight falls upon his features, turning them sinister. They tug at my mind, and for one brief second, I'm somewhere else—

Memnon grabs the long length of his hair and withdraws a knife.

Before I can react, he brings his blade to his coarse dark locks, and with one brutal stroke, he cuts most of it off.

Then the image is gone. The same man stands before me, but his eyes are harder, the set of his mouth harsher. Despite how angry he looks, every inch of my skin buzzes with this electrifying *awareness.*

Empress...you are mine...

I rub my temple, wanting him out of my head. I also want to scream because I thought we'd dealt with this whole mistaken-identity issue.

"I need to go back to Kane!" I can't help the panic that slides into my voice. If he's still alive, he may not be for long. Not unless I help heal him.

"Get *back* to him?" I see murder in his eyes when he glances past me toward the residence hall. "Sure, I will go back. That way, if that beast isn't already dead, I can make good on my earlier threats to castrate him."

Maiden, Mother, and Crone, the man truly is a psycho.

Panic takes over my thoughts, and now I'm the one gripping Memnon, determined to keep him here and away from Kane, even as my heart pounds wildly because the shifter needs help.

"And now you think to protect *him* from *me*? Your mate?" Memnon's eyes are glowing again. I hadn't realized they stopped until now. That only snags my attention for a second because—

"Mate?" I echo.

Things inside me go very quiet and very still.

"We have spoken our vows before your gods and mine," Memnon continues. "You and I were molded from the same bit of earth. The Fates spun our threads together. And we entered our own covenant. Your mind may be addled—"

Addled?

"—yet there are some truths even it cannot deny."

"I am not that woman!" I shriek at him. "You *know* this—you acknowledged it yourself.

"Now," I continue, jerking against him, "let—me—go!"

"Let you go?" Memnon's eyes burn brighter, his expression hardening as his hair snaps about with his churning power. "Even if I wanted to—even if I didn't have *two thousand years of revenge to exact on you*—your life is bound to mine, *est amage*. Not even death will part us. I will never *let you go*."

Just when I think things can't get any worse, Memnon reels me into him and kisses me.

The moment his lips meet mine, my magic comes alive.

It races along my skin and between my bones. If I didn't know better, I'd say it's consuming me.

Memnon's magic joins in, threading through mine. I feel his power on me and in me, and I throb with the ecstasy of it.

It's not even a choice to kiss him back—he's a wildfire, and I'm getting swept up in it.

I kiss him like I'm starving for contact, like everything that was wrong has now been made right. The taste of him and the thrill of his power moving through me scorch my skin and steal my breath.

This is what I was searching for in the touch and taste of another. This is passion.

Memnon makes a possessive noise, slipping his hands into my hair, his staggering body enveloping me. His lips are bruising against mine; he kisses me with the ferocity of a starving man.

He tilts my jaw up to get a better angle.

It's been too long since you've been in my arms, my queen.

I'm not sure Memnon intended for me to hear this—it sounds like a passing thought more than anything else—but the words whisper through my head all the same, and they break the spell.

What in the goddess's good grace are you doing, Selene?

I move my hands to his lower abs and blast my power out, magically shoving him away.

"I thought we had established that I am not your *anything*." Not his wife, not his queen, not his empress.

An angry smile graces his face. "Yes, you almost convinced me of that, didn't you? But I have since had time to muse on it." His tone changes, turning accusing. "I don't know what witchcraft has destroyed your memory and produced those photos—"

"There was no witchcraft involved!" I say heatedly. We're back to square one. I want to scream.

"—but my magic recognizes yours, and my bond is fucking *singing* through my blood as it hasn't for the past two thousand years."

We're so close that our breath is intermingling.

"It's why you can speak to me in Sarmatian when you're pleased with me, and Latin when you're angry," Memnon continues, making me recall an earlier encounter in the spellcasting kitchen. I'd slipped into Latin with him then. "It's why you can scream and fling your oaths and still kiss me as though we have done it a hundred upon a hundred times before—*because we have.*

"So you are wrong, little witch. You are many things to me. You are my queen, my empress, my wife. You are my Roxilana, the woman who awoke my magic and spoke to my mind before we ever met. You are my nemesis, who cursed me to endless sleep."

Memnon's hand cups my cheek. "And you are my Selene, my eternal soul mate, who woke me from it."

CHAPTER 24

Soul mate.

That terrifying, bewitching word echoes in my head.

I stagger back. "I—I am not your soul mate," I say, even though my voice wavers.

I expect my words to be met with annoyance or frustration. This is, after all, a new version of the same old argument we've had.

Instead, his eyes have softened. "I saw your mind, little witch. I understand how you struggle and that much has slipped past your own awareness."

He closes the space between us and places his palm over my heart.

"What are you doing?" I demand. I should rip his hand away. The ugly truth, however, is that I like his touch, even after all the shit he just pulled.

The gall of my body.

Instead of responding, Memnon stares deeply at me.

Empress...why do you think I'm able to speak to you like this?

I don't breathe, my gaze locked with his.

Your heart knows the answer—as does your magic.

I feel that magic he speaks of rise now, twining with his.

Oh Goddess.

I shake my head.

No, no, no.

Memnon's glittering brown eyes are intent on me, and a slow pleased smile spreads across his lips, like he can hear my own shocked thoughts.

We are soul mates, little witch, and we can speak down our bond...

I squeeze my eyes shut, grimacing because I can *feel* his words in me. They seep into my very blood, like a river reaching the ocean.

It felt like this every time he called to me—even when we were kissing only moments ago. I just assumed it was his brand of magic at work. Now, however...now his explanation makes a sick sort of sense.

Bonds are magical cords that connect two entities—like the one I share with Nero. Soul mates have them as well.

Could it be possible? *Could* Memnon truly be my soul mate, and could he speak to me through a bond we share?

No. I reject that thought before it can take further root.

Memnon's eyes twinkle deviously, and it makes me wonder just how formidable this man truly is. I have seen his magic and his powerful body, and I have heard enough of his past to know he must've been a ruler, one who ruled a vast and expanding empire. Yet, even knowing all of that, I still find Memnon's mind to be largely a mystery. And I think it's that very mind of his that is the most terrible thing of all.

"You can talk to me through our bond too," Memnon says softly, his hand still over my heart.

I pinch my eyes shut. "Stop saying that," I whisper.

Bonds, mates—I don't want to hear any of it.

"What, *bond*? Why would I?" he asks, sounding truly baffled. "It is the basis of everything, *est amage*. Your power, my power. All I know of my magic has come from it. Before I ever met you face-to-face, I heard your voice, right here." Memnon uses his other hand to touch his own heart. "I spent countless nights whispering down it to you, and I spent my days letting it guide me across the world to find you."

My skin tingles with his admission, and when I open my eyes, there's a rawness and an intensity to his words that has me ensnared.

"So, enemies or not, *Selene*, please, ask me a question down our bond—project it to me."

I want to deny him because *I* am in denial, but his plea gets under my skin, and a sick sort of curiosity wins out.

This shouldn't work. It really shouldn't.

I close my eyes once again and focus on that place just beneath Memnon's warm palm; supposedly, it's where soul mates are magically bonded. It's terrifying that I *do* sense something there, now that I concentrate on it.

I've heard bonds described as cords and roads, but this feels more like a river flowing both into and out of me.

How did you get the scar on your face? I push the thought out with my power, forcing it down this magical river I sense.

"At fifteen, a man tried to skin me in battle," Memnon says.

I open my eyes, both stricken and entranced not just by what he said but also by the fact *he heard my voice in his head*.

"You read my mind," I accuse. I don't want to believe the alternative. That we're...bonded, our souls inextricably linked.

"I didn't need to when you spoke so prettily down our bond." Memnon stares at me with some emotion simmering in his eyes.

I hold his gaze for a second, then two, then three. My pulse is jackhammering, and I can hear the roar of blood in my ears. My knees are growing weak.

"I'm not your soul mate," I insist.

Are you sure?

As if to emphasize his point, Memnon's power pours into me from that magical river. For a moment, I close my eyes, and I feel the alluring lick of it right up against my heart. I press my palm to the place in question; it's only once my hand comes to rest on Memnon's that I realize he's still touching me, and I'm starting to get confused about where he ends and I begin.

"No," I whisper, the word coming out as a plea.

"Yes, Empress, you are," he says, his voice gentling. He says it with a surety that sets me on edge.

I've spent far too much time fruitlessly convincing him of my own identity. Perhaps it's time for Memnon to do the convincing.

I lift my chin. "Then tell me about who we were," I dare him.

Memnon reaches out and strokes my cheek with his knuckles, this softness so at odds with the man I have come to know.

"I was a king, and you were my queen," he says, his eyes turning soft.

"You don't look like a king," I challenge him. He's too young, too scarred, too handsome, and too well-built.

He narrows his eyes at me but smiles. "Where I'm from, I do." After a moment, he touches his hair. "Except for this," he concedes. His hand moves to his smooth chin. "And this."

As he speaks, my familiar prowls out from the shadows, silently joining my side when it's far too late for me to need him. I spare the panther an annoyed glance.

"Sarmatian men wear their hair and beards long," Memnon continues. He flashes me a conspiratorial look. "But you preferred me shorn like a sheep, and I admit, I greatly enjoyed the feel of your pussy against my bare face when I ate you—"

I cover his mouth before he can finish.

"Nope, I don't want to hear about that," I say, even as my sex dreams come back to me in all their lurid glory.

Beneath my palm, Memnon grins, and his eyes twinkle with mirth. Gone is the angry monster who stormed my room—

Kane.

Fuck, I need to get back to him.

Even as I think it, I'm not sure how to get out of this situation without drawing Memnon right back to the lycan and further hurting the lycanthrope.

The sorcerer removes my hand from his mouth. "Ask me more, *est amage*. Let me prove our past to you."

At least he now seems to believe that whatever past existed for him, I have no memory of it.

I search his gaze, part of me desperate to check on Kane and part of me eager to hear more about this man.

"What land did you and Roxilana rule?" I finally say, edging backward.

"Sarmatia." That word carries a longing with it. "We were an empire of horse lords and warriors, and we moved along the Pontic steppe, with the migrations of herd animals.

Though I overthrew the king of Bosporus so I could settle you in a palace by the sea. The constant traveling was hard on you."

"I've never heard of any of that," I say. I don't dare mention that my own magic might've expunged the information.

Memnon sighs. "Yes, well, much of the recorded history at the time was written by Romans." He curls his upper lip as he speaks. "To them, we were nameless barbarians. We existed in their nightmares and on the fringes of their world but not in their self-aggrandizing histories. But we *did* exist."

"Uh-huh," I say, edging back some more. "Just like my childhood existed."

Memnon narrows his eyes, no doubt understanding what I'm saying perfectly: *I'll believe your word as soon as you believe mine.*

Before either of us can say more, I hear a broken voice call out, "Selene!"

Kane.

Dear Goddess, he's *alive*. Relief courses through my veins.

I take several steps back, the need to get back to the lycanthrope pressing upon me.

Memnon's expression grows cold, so cold—his eyes most of all.

He nods in the direction of Kane, and I can feel the waves of menace pouring off him. "*Est amage*, it is taking everything in me not to kill that wolf where he lies. You touch that boy, and he dies. *Slowly.* The same threat extends to anyone who thinks to pursue you, little witch. Do you understand?"

I lift my chin, refusing to be cowed by this man. "I'll do as I fucking please. This isn't the Dark Ages, Memnon."

The sorcerer's eyes burn a little as his power resurfaces with his rising agitation.

"No, this isn't," he agrees.

I have to hide my surprise that he understood the reference.

"But I am no modern man," he continues. "I have killed for far less, and I will happily do so again, where you are concerned."

I scowl at him, my magic twisting and snapping out of me with my irritation.

His eyes drop to my mouth, like he's actually considering kissing me.

"I'll be seeing you again soon, Empress," he says, backing away from me. "Until then, sweet dreams."

Memnon turns on his heel and walks away into the dark forest, his magic billowing around him.

CHAPTER 25

The moment he vanishes from view, I sprint back to my house, Nero following at my heels.

I haven't heard Kane's voice since he called out to me that once, and while I feel reassured that he survived the fall, I'm frightened by the silence that's followed.

I get to the edge of the forest, and through the trees, I can see my residence hall. I choke on a cry when my eyes fall on Kane's slumped form lying on the lawn between it and me. He's exactly where Memnon dropped him, and he doesn't look like he's moved.

I race to him and fall to my knees, Nero joining me a moment later.

Kane is slumped on his side, his eyes closed.

"Kane?" I say. "Kane?"

He doesn't respond.

I place my hands on his chest, not bothering to check his pulse or rouse him again. Unless he's beyond saving, what I'm about to do should work.

Closing my eyes, I call on my magic. I've never done this before, but I have enough power and determination to give it a shot.

"Seal punctured flesh, mend broken bones, staunch the unbidden bleeding, and heal the wounds within." I speak the words in Samarian, and though they don't rhyme, the power of them—power steeped in age and obscurity—adds a sharp potency to the spell.

My palms tingle, and then thick, viscous magic seeps from them. It settles over Kane's skin before being absorbed into his body.

I sense it healing him, but I don't see the results right away, not until his crumpled form seems to expand, and it looks unnervingly like a balloon inflating. I can only imagine what sort of internal damage would cause his body to collapse in on itself in the first place.

Kane grunts as one of his legs untwists, and I have to stop myself from wincing on his behalf. I know shifters are used to their bodies rearranging themselves, but this looks violently painful.

A minute goes by, and I'm drawing in ragged breaths, my magic taxing me. I can feel a prickling throb in my head as memories are siphoned away. I won't think about how many memories this has cost me.

Kane moans, then lets out a weak cough. Before he even opens his eyes, he calls out, "Selene!"

I release a shaky breath, my relief almost palpable.

"I'm right here, Kane," I say soothingly, smoothing a hand down the side of his face. "I'm healing you. You were thrown a long way down."

The shifter's brows come together and he forces his eyes open. As soon as he sees me, he reaches for my hand. "You're healing me?" he echoes.

I give his grip a squeeze. "Yeah."

A muffled wet sound comes from his body as my power repairs something. Kane makes a pained low growl.

"I'm sorry," I say softly. "So sorry." Not just for the pain my magic is bringing him—pain he might be able to manage if he could shift and heal himself—but also for the fact I brought this upon him. I've known Memnon is a threat ever since he first confronted me.

A threat I *kissed* only minutes ago.

Ugh, what is wrong with me?

Kane closes his eyes. "I just want to know"—he swallows—"that you're okay."

"I'm fine, Kane. As long as you're okay, I will be too."

His hand squeezes mine.

You touch that boy, and he dies. Slowly.

I draw in a deep breath, trying to calm my nerves because I *have* been touching that boy, and screw that sorcerer because I will *keep* touching him until he's better. I want to rip Memnon apart from shoulder to hip. The fucking *audacity* he has to threaten me.

Kane's eyes flutter. "Who was that who attacked us?" he asks, his voice hoarse. "And how did you get away?"

I glance over at the tree line, my skin still tingling from all the places Memnon touched it.

"It's a long story," I say. "He's"—*I was a king and you were my queen*—"an old enemy."

Briefly his eyes slide to my familiar, who stares back at Kane with a bored expression, as though he'd rather not be here. Which, he probably really would like to return to harassing cute little forest creatures, or whatever it was Nero was doing in the Everwoods.

I face my familiar. "You can go back to the woods, if you'd rather not stick around," I say.

Nero tears his gaze away from the shifter to look at me for several long seconds. I don't know what the look is supposed to mean, but the big cat proceeds to step into my space and rub his body against my own, his tail sliding along my neck as he does so.

Once he's done, Nero prowls away, retreating into the darkness and leaving me and Kane alone.

The shifter returns his attention to me, and I think that maybe he's going to comment on Nero, but instead, he says, "How does someone as nice as you"—the shifter sits up, grimacing a little as he does so—"have enemies?"

I wrap an arm around Kane's back as he sways a little. "You okay?" I ask, ignoring the question.

The lycanthrope grits his teeth. "Good enough—thanks to your magic." He sits up. "You can stop healing me now. I'll do the rest myself."

I do stop, the tendrils of my power snaking back into me. All that's left of my effort is the unnerving throb of it beneath my skull.

"Do you still have your phone on you?" he asks.

I nod.

"Good," he says. He leans forward, getting on his hands and knees, his blond hair hanging a little in front of his face. "Call the Politia and report this."

I don't think Kane used any magic in the order, but I feel a strange compulsion to promptly do as he says.

Maybe that's why I hesitate. Or maybe it's that I don't really believe the Politia is going to stop some ancient sorcerer from doing as he pleases when it comes to me.

Kane's pauses to gaze at me. "Selene, please. Call them.

This man can't think to abduct you from your home whenever he wants."

He has a point—and that's not even touching on the fact this same man threw Kane from a three-story window.

"Okay," I say quietly.

The shifter's back ripples in a way that's not natural, and he groans. "If you're squeamish about nudity," he bites out, "you may want to look away."

I feel a pang of regret that this topic even has to come up. If Memnon hadn't been the world's biggest cockblocker, this man would be several inches deep in me and I would have seen every last bit of him.

I sigh regretfully.

I don't turn away, but I do use the moment to pull out my phone from my boot and call the Politia.

"Hi, this is Selene Bowers. I'd like to report a break-in and an assault at the Henbane Coven residence hall ..."

My words die away as, out of the corner of my eye, I see Kane's form shift. I nearly drop the phone as pelt replaces bare skin, and Kane's face extends, his teeth sharpening, a snout replacing his nose. His hands and feet become paws, and his torso narrows and rounds.

When it's done, all I can see of Kane in this animal are my crush's ice-blue eyes, and even those...those eyes don't look human.

Holy shit, I have to blink several times to make sense of the wolf standing before me. I go still as its gaze locks on mine.

"Hello, miss? Miss? Miss?" the officer on the line says.

"Please come quickly," I breathe, and then I end the call.

I don't move. It's all I can do not to panic as I stare down a larger-than-life gray wolf.

The animal sniffs the air in my direction, and why, oh, why did Kane decide to shift right next to me? And why did I not have the good sense to get the hell away from him before now?

The werewolf approaches me, and he's still scenting the air like I'm his next meal.

"*Don't*," I say, putting power behind my voice. I don't know how much of Kane the man is in control of Kane the animal's mind.

The wolf stops, his ears flicking, and he shakes out his head like he can throw off the magic.

Just as I'm bracing for him to approach me again, shifter magic thickens around the wolf, and then the transformation is happening all over again but in reverse—limbs lengthening and widening, fur retreating—until a very naked Kane is on the ground on all fours, panting from the exertion. I can see his muscles trembling from the effort, and his skin is covered in a sheen of sweat.

"Sorry," he says. His voice is more of a growl than anything else. He clears his throat. "I wasn't thinking. I forgot you weren't"—he glances up at me—"*pack*."

I exhale. I think that was supposed to be a compliment, but considering the fact I nearly shit my pants a few seconds ago, I'm having mixed feelings about the entire thing.

Why does every supernatural have to be so damn scary?

"Lycanthropes don't hunt humans," he adds. "Not, at least, to kill."

When then *would* a wolf shifter hunt a human?

I'm not brave enough to ask.

Instead, I nod. "How are your wounds?"

"Better," Kane says, sounding more like himself. He grabs his clothing and begins to put it on. "I think I'm almost completely healed. One more shift should do the trick, but I'll do that back on pack lands."

I give him a small smile.

I can hear sirens in the distance. Must be the Politia.

Once Kane is dressed—well, mostly dressed, as he's still shirtless—he comes over and sits at my side, wrapping an arm around my shoulders. His embrace is so comforting that I can't help but lean my head against him, Memnon's threat be damned.

"I think we're doomed to just be friends," I say softly, hating the admission but feeling the truth of it.

"What?" Kane looks down at me. "Is this about that asshole?"

I nod against him. There's no point in lying.

He's quiet for a moment.

"And is that what you want?" he says, frowning. "To just be friends?"

I take a deep breath. "I don't know what I want," I say wearily. "I do know that I was ready to have really fun, wild sex with you." I'm not even embarrassed to admit it at this point.

"That's not off the table," Kane cuts in, skimming his lips along my temple.

Those lips feel wrong there. Fuck, *why* do they feel wrong there? I want to carve out my own thoughts because they're all twisted up.

I straighten, pulling away a little from the shifter. "The man who attacked you, he's…been stalking me, and he's made it clear he'll hurt you if we do anything more."

But that isn't the full truth, is it? I kissed the sorcerer, and it felt right in a way nothing else has. And now I'm noticing all the ways other touches don't stack up.

And you are my Selene, my eternal soul mate.

Kane's hold tightens on me. "Fuck him. Some sicko doesn't get to tell you how to live your life."

Yeah, this is true, but the sicko in question apparently overthrew an entire kingdom just to get his girl a summer palace.

That's not the sort of man I want to go toe-to-toe with.

Before I can form a response, two Politia officers, a man and a woman, come around to the back of the house, their flashlights moving over the lawn.

I wave to them, just to get their attention.

The two come over to us.

I pull away from Kane, putting some needed distance between us.

"Are you Selene Bowers?" one of the officers asks.

I nod.

"Would you like to tell us why you called us out here?" the other officer asks, her eyes moving over me and Kane.

For the next thirty minutes, Kane and I recount what happened to the two Politia officers. I covertly glance at their name tags: Officer Howahkan is the man and Officer Mwangi is the woman. They contact Kane's pack to inform them of the incident, and then I take the group of us inside my residence hall.

When we pass the house's library, we catch sight of a witch who sits passed out on one of the wingback chairs, her legs spread and her skirt around her waist. Another woman—a shifter, I think—kneels before her, her head on the witch's thigh. She too appears to be passed out.

Officer Howahkan clears his throat, clearly not cool with what he's seen.

He's obviously not attended too many events with witches. We really do party hard.

I lead the group upstairs, toward my room, skirting around a witch sitting on the landing while singing a bawdy drinking song to her fox familiar, her magenta magic swirling around her.

We head down the third-floor hallway to my room, and once I let the group inside, the officers look over the broken glass, the rumpled sheets, and Kane's discarded shirt. And then Kane and I recount the evening's events all over again, starting with the foiled bang session and ending with Kane shifting. The entire time we recount the events, the coven sister in the room next door has really loud, enthusiastic sex.

Good for her. Should have been me, but good for her.

We all eventually head back downstairs, passing that same witch on the landing, only now she and her familiar have fallen asleep together. The couple in the library is still passed out, and honestly, they'll probably be there until morning.

Officer Mwangi shakes her head at all of it.

I hurriedly escort them out to the front porch before closing the door behind me and giving my sisters their privacy.

"Well, I think that's all we need for now," Officer Howahkan says to me and Kane. "We'll let you know if we apprehend your attacker."

Officer Mwangi scrutinizes me as her partner turns to her, clearly ready to wrap this up.

Her eyes, however, are fixed on me. "Weren't you the same girl who reported the last murder?" she asks.

Um...I have zero recollection of meeting this person.

I swallow delicately. "Um. Yeah."

Kane glances over at me, his brows rising. Officer Howahkan too stares at me with unnerving intensity.

"What a coincidence," Officer Mwangi says, though the way she says it makes it clear she's thinking it's not a coincidence at all. She gives me a once-over, like I've just gotten *way* more suspicious.

I feel my hackles rise.

"Whoa," Kane says, lifting a hand in a placating gesture. "Tonight wasn't Selene's fault. A man broke into her room and attacked us."

Officer Mwangi's attention moves to Kane, and she gives him a look like he's gullible.

I hear an ominous growl low in Kane's chest. I glance at him, remembering how he reacted when I ordered him around earlier this evening. And now he perceived something else as a challenge.

Just where in lycanthrope hierarchy does Kane fall?

Because he's acting like an alpha. A possessive one too.

Officer Mwangi dips her head, and I don't know if she means for it to be a submissive display, but it seems to satisfy Kane's wolf, who quiets at the action.

But placating gestures or not, the damage from the officer's words has already been done. I can sense it in the air like a sick sort of magic itself.

Somehow, between stumbling upon a corpse and getting accosted by an ancient sorcerer, the Politia has determined I'm suspicious enough to take note of.

Goddess, I just hope it doesn't come back to bite me.

When I wake up the next morning, I smile at the sound of birds chirping in the tree outside, and for about two seconds, life is utterly blissful.

Then last night comes rushing in.

I put my hand over my eyes. *Make it all go away.* There are bits of yesterday I can't remember either—getting ready, that's gone. And there are some lost memories from the party last night, but I'm not sure if alcohol or magic is to blame for that.

Still, I remember enough. And in the sobering light of day, one detail in particular catches my attention, one I didn't spend much time musing on last night.

We are soul mates, little witch.

I scramble off the bed, cursing when I step on broken glass from my window.

"Broken glass, stop being a bimbo. Repair yourself and mend this window."

Really need to work on my rhymes…

As the glass levitates off the floor and fits itself back into place, I make a beeline for my bookshelf. My fingers skim over the spines of my journals.

Being a soul mate isn't just some offhand thing. It's an aspect of a supernatural that manifests when their magic Awakens. One that's formally recorded and acknowledged.

So, if I *were* a soul mate, I would have written that down somewhere before my mind stole that information from me. It would have been too important not to.

I pull out the notebooks one by one, and frantically flip through them.

Nothing, nothing, *nothing.*

Of course there's nothing. There wouldn't be because I'm *not* a soul mate. Not to that brutal bastard.

Still, I spend over an hour sitting on the floor of my room, notebooks scattered around me, flipping through page after page of notes I wrote years ago, looking for any clue that I may be a soul mate. It's only as I get to the earliest of my journals that I realize I didn't keep good records until about halfway through my junior year at Peel Academy, *months* after my Awakening.

Regardless, what I do have is thorough enough. And not once do I find any mention of my being a soul mate.

I exhale. I know I *should* feel relieved, but there are those few damnable months that are unrecorded. And then there's the fact I no longer have the memory of my Awakening, when I would've first learned of whether I'm a soul mate.

I rub the skin over my heart, frowning. The more I focus on it, the more I swear there *may* be something there.

It was just the sorcerer's trick, nothing more.

There's one other place I could check that would know for certain.

Peel Academy would have files on hand about my Awakening. They have them for all supernaturals who attend their boarding school. I just need to get a copy of mine.

I open my laptop and head to my email account. Once there, I send out a quick request to Peel Academy's Records Department to forward me my official results.

Goddess, but I hope this settles things once and for all. I'm still holding on to that damnable hope that I'm right.

Otherwise, I'm screwed.

CHAPTER 26

Bzzzzzzz.

The sound of my phone has me rising from my computer chair. I'm not sure where it's coming from, but it's not on my nightstand, where it should be.

Bzzzzzzz.

I follow the sound, pawing through the remains of my outfit from last night.

Bzzzzzzz.

I snatch up one of my boots and flip it over. My phone tumbles out before hitting my floor with a *thunk*.

I have time to see the caller is Sybil, but as soon as I snatch it up, the call ends.

I'm about to call her back—half dreading all I'm going to have to tell her—when I realize there's a nauseating number of texts and missed calls on my phone that I must've slept through.

Oh Goddess, is Sybil all right?

I panic scroll through them.

Did you have a fun night last night?
Was Kane everything you ever dreamed of?
Okay, I'm assuming you're asleep from a night of raging sex, but please text me.
Holy fuck, WHAT HAPPENED?
WHY AREN'T YOU ANSWERING?
IF YOU DON'T TEXT ME BACK NOW I'M COMING TO YOUR ROOM.
Okay, I was totally a stalker and I peeked into your room and you're passed out and snuggling your familiar like he's a body pillow and it's so damn cute.

Beneath the text is a picture my creep of a best friend took of me asleep with Nero.

It *is* kind of a cute picture.

Okay, I'm going to let you sleep, babe. Find me when you wake up.
PS I'm going to let you sleep *a little*. Might start calling you if I get impatient.

Now that I know my friend is okay—despite the fact I freaking left her behind last night to go bang a werewolf (*come on, Selene, do better*)—my whole body relaxes, the tension seeping out of me.

She's good. No murderer is keeping her hostage. She's just worried about me.

As I hold the phone, another text pops up.

PPS I passed on your number to Sawyer who's passing it along to Kane. Whatever happened last night, he's still super into you.

I groan. There's no way in hell Kane is still into me. As for me, setting aside Memnon's threat, in the harsh light of day, after all the booze and bad decisions, I'm not actually sure how into Kane I am.

A worry for another time.

I text Sybil back that I am alive and okay and that I will find her and fill her in about what happened as soon as I can.

After I finish typing out my response, I notice another text from last night, one from another unknown number.

I stare down at the text message on my phone, trying to make sense of what I'm reading.

> Hey, this is Kasey. Can't wait to see you at the circle tomorrow. 10 P.M. Library.

Wait, I agreed to do a spell circle, didn't I?

Shit. Is that tonight?

I grab my notebook and flip to the notes I have written down for this day. Sure enough, I've written *Spell Circle* in red and circled it several times.

I groan.

Goddess, I hope I don't regret agreeing to this.

At 10:00 p.m., after most of my coven sisters have either made their way back to their rooms or headed out to another party this weekend, I sit in the house's library, flipping through a book on Indigenous witchcraft in Peru, jiggling my leg a little.

There are no windows in here, but even without looking, I know the new moon is all but invisible out in the night sky, and I try not to let that spook me too much.

In spellwork, a new moon is good for illusion, hiding the truth, and cloaking enchantments. It also happens to be good for dark magic, when the goddess's third eye has wandered away from the earth.

I hear the soft pad of footfalls, and I set my book down just as Kasey enters the library.

"Hey, good to see you," she says, nodding to me. "Ready to go?"

Nope. Not one bit.

"Yeah," I lie, getting up and crossing over to her. "Where are we going?"

"You'll see," Kasey says cryptically, giving me a wink, as though this is all in good fun and not at all unnerving.

She leads us out of the library and walks down the hall opposite the kitchen. I haven't gone this way much, though on the left is a small attached greenhouse, where even now a witch is watering plants.

We pass it, then continue. I feel the sharp absence of Nero, who is out gallivanting in the woods, too busy being a fluffy forest creature's nightmare to attend some spell circle. That cat, as moody as he is, is my rock. Without him by my side, my nerves are just a pinch more frayed.

At the end of the hall is a door to the Ritual Room. It's where house meetings and official ceremonies are held. We had a brief welcome-back meeting here during my first week and another one about a week ago, so I'm not totally unfamiliar with the space.

Kasey enters the room ahead of me, walking confidently down the makeshift aisle, brushing her hands along the chairbacks nearest her.

I hesitate, looking beyond her at the dark room. The walls and ceiling are painted black, and there are no windows; even the wall sconces and the iron chandelier barely give off light. It's not exactly the room I want to be hanging out in at night.

Not that I'm doing any of this for the fun of it.

Reluctantly, I follow Kasey in, our footsteps echoing around us. Like the rest of the house, various wards and enchantments cloak this space. But in here, with the dark walls that feel like they're closing in on you, the magic feels a bit suffocating.

"Are we meeting other people here?" I ask, eyeing the rows of empty chairs that have been left out after the room's last meeting.

"Not exactly," she says, offering nothing else.

Her cryptic response sets my frazzled nerves further on edge.

Kasey doesn't stop walking until she reaches the back wall of the room.

She pulls out a vial from her pocket and pours a powdered concoction of herbs and who knows what else into the palm of her hand.

She lifts it to her face. "Reveal yourself," she whispers, then blows the powder at the wall.

Where a moment ago there was solid, unbroken wall, now there is a simple black door.

I'm speechless at the hidden door.

Kasey turns to me with a mischievous grin. "Pretty neat, huh? This coven is full of secret stuff." She grabs the doorknob. "Ready to see more?"

I nod, struck by the sight—and the realization that there's *more*.

Kasey opens the door, and on the other side of it is a small white room. The only thing remotely interesting about this room is that it houses what looks like a spiral staircase, one that twists below my line of sight.

Once the breathtaking nature of the illusory magic has worn off, my unease returns. But now it's not just this situation that isn't sitting right; it's the fact there's a hidden door that leads to a hidden staircase that leads to another hidden chamber, and all this is connected to the house I sleep in.

Going to have to ward my room biweekly, just to feel safe.

Kasey steps across the threshold, then turns to face me. Before I cross into the room, I stare carefully at the wall, looking for the spells that hid this room. The magic that covers the walls is complicated and made by many separate hands. It only puts out the faintest shimmer—and I know there must be even more spells that are themselves cloaked from even witchy eyes.

It's honestly beautiful and fascinating, and I wish I had a notebook to jot down all that I see.

Kasey shares none of my wonder. The moment she sees I'm getting distracted, she heads for the staircase.

"C'mon," she says, "they're waiting for us."

Right. The rest of the spell circle.

"How did the rest of them get here?" I ask, entering the room and shutting the door behind me. "Are they also coven sisters?"

"Don't worry about it," she calls over her shoulder. "That's not really what this circle is about."

That didn't give me any sort of reassurance.

I need the money, I tell myself—because it's the reassurance I need to follow through on this.

I head down the staircase after Kasey, the air getting cooler as we go. We descend to a level practically glowing with amber light. When I step off the staircase, my eyes move to the narrow hallway ahead of me, the walls covered in stone masonry, the floor fitted with marble.

It all looks like something made at least a century ago. There's a musty smell in the air that no amount of magic can banish.

My power loves it, even if the rest of me feels trapped down here.

Fitted to the walls are sconces with flickering candlelight, the wax weeping down their sides.

"What is this place?"

"A persecution tunnel," she says. "One of many."

I forgot all about persecution tunnels, but they're a big part of supernatural building plans; they are, in essence, a literal way to escape persecution.

"Henbane is full of these things," Kasey continues. "You know how witches are," she says, lifting a shoulder.

Cautious. Too much of our history has been full of violence against us not to warrant it.

In the distance, I hear low murmuring. As my pulse spikes, so does my curiosity.

The hall curves, then opens into a wide chamber. At its threshold rests another set of stone *lamassu*, keeping guard, and beyond them is a room full of supernaturals.

I lovingly move my hand over the head of one of the *lamassu* as we pass them, and then we enter the massive circular room. Like the hallway before it, the walls are covered in gray stone, and the floors, in polished marble. Several other hallways branch off this one, leading to who knows where.

The space itself is filled with masked and robed supernaturals—all of them witches, I presume, though I can't be positive since no one's magic is giving them away.

One of them wears the mark of the triple goddess on her, the triple moon symbol painted onto her mask's forehead. She must be the priestess, the witch leading the circle.

When she sees Kasey, she picks up what appear to be two folded sets of black robes and pale masks, then approaches us.

"Hey, girlie," she says from behind the mask, and I'm not at all expecting the soft, youthful notes of her voice, nor her familiarity with Kasey, whom she hugs.

The priestess passes over a robe and a mask. "We're just about ready."

Then the priestess nods to me. "Hi there. Glad to have you." She hands me the other robe and mask. "You'll need to put these on—the robe can go over your clothes—then join the circle. We're waiting on the guests of honor, but I think we'll begin before they arrive. They can join us when they get here."

It takes me a moment to realize I'm *not* one of these guests of honor. And then, of course, I feel sheepish because I wasn't expecting to be treated as some special star. I'm just a bit destabilized is all.

The priestess wanders away from us then, leaving me to unfold the robe and pull it on over my T-shirt and jeans.

"Shoes will have to go too," Kasey says, tugging her own robe on. "It helps with grounding and channeling the magic."

"Are you going to tell me now what we're doing?" I say, removing my Chucks and then my socks before setting them aside. I feel slightly better, now that I've met the witch leading the spell circle.

"It's just a spell circle. We'll be holding hands, chanting a little, and joining our power."

Yeah, but for what purpose?

I stare down at the mask, running my thumb over its lower lip; it's obviously meant to give us some anonymity.

Why would that be important? Why would someone pay

for robes and masks and the presence of two dozen witches? If all of us here are getting paid five hundred dollars, then that's roughly ten grand. What sort of magic costs ten grand?

I glance over the other masked members to see if anyone shares my concerns. I can't see any faces, but nobody else *appears* bothered. I try to gain some confidence from that.

Exhaling, I pull on the mask, settling the linen hair covering over my wavy locks, hiding them from view.

Kasey has already moseyed over to the forming circle, though I'm not sure which one of the robed individuals she is.

I join the circle myself, and the girl next to me—not Kasey, judging by her green eyes—nods to me but does nothing else.

Once the circle is fully formed, the priestess moves to the center of it, a chalice gripped in her hands.

"It's time, sisters," she says. "Join me in tonight's spell circle."

My nose wrinkles then as I notice the smell in the room. What I assumed before was simply the smell of a dank subterranean room is…is something else, something vaguely familiar.

Before I can focus any more on it, the priestess lifts her mask just enough to take a drink from the chalice. Once she's done, she lowers her mask again and hands the drink off to a robed witch on the far side of the circle. That witch lifts her mask and takes a small swallow, then passes it to the person next to her. The goblet moves from witch to witch, each one taking a sip before handing it off.

"What's in that?" I ask the green-eyed witch next to me.

She lifts a shoulder as if to shrug it off. "Just a bit of witch's brew—plus a few spices to help heighten our magic."

Spices? Is that what we're calling drugs these days?

Some spell circles use them to enhance the group's collective power and experience, but do I trust the strangers enough in this circle to trip with them?

Hell no.

So when the chalice makes its way to me, I lift my mask and bring the cup to my lips, but fuck this, I am not drinking some random concoction. My life is chaotic enough while sober.

I press the rim of it to my mouth and tip it back just enough for the liquid to brush my lips. After a couple of seconds, I lower the chalice and pass it along. Only once the attention has moved down the line do I discretely reach under my mask and wipe my mouth.

Already, on the far side of the room, I see some witches swaying. Whatever was in that drink, it must be strong to have such an effect.

Once the chalice makes it fully around the circle, the priestess sets it aside.

"Let's join hands."

I clasp the palms of the women on either side of me, and my skin tingles where my power presses against theirs.

The priestess makes a low, guttural noise, then speaks in another tongue, one I understand.

Latin.

"I call on old magic and the darkness from deep beneath our feet. Lend us your power for tonight's spellcasting. From earth to feet, foot to hand, and witch to witch, our circle calls forth your magic."

Power flares across the group, rising from the marble floors and into the soles of our feet. It flows up our legs and torsos before funneling down our arms, moving around and around the group until our powers blend, and it feels as though we are a single unit.

I'm so absorbed in the strange, exhilarating sensation of

being a part of a single larger unit that I don't realize another woman is being led toward the circle, not until the priestess calls out, "Enter our circle and join in the night's festivities. We offer our permission to cross our sacred power line."

Down the circle, two witches awkwardly lift their joined hands, and two more individuals press in between them, crossing into the center of the circle.

I watch the two individuals, my eyes fixed on the larger of them. This person wears a black robe and a mask like the rest of us. It's what lies beneath that mask that catches my eye. The skin of their neck is a smooth pale gray, the sheen of it somehow dull. As they prowl forward, their movements seem jerky and mechanical.

The darkness must be playing with my eyes.

I force myself to look down at that individual's companion. The second newcomer also wears a mask, but that's where the similarities end. Unlike the rest of us, she wears an almost-sheer white shift, one that makes her nipples and pubic hair blatantly visible. I can't see what her expression is beneath her mask, but she leans heavily against the first companion, as though her legs aren't doing so well keeping her upright.

Nothing about it sits right with me.

"What is going on?" I ask the green-eyed witch.

She gives me a look that plainly says to *shut up* but says, "This is just part of the new moon spell circles."

The woman in the shift stumbles a little, and when she rights herself, I notice how small her limbs are.

My heart seizes.

Not a woman but a *girl*. She can't be more than sixteen, which is technically considered the age of adulthood for supernaturals, but come *on*. She looks too young to be out here participating in a spell circle. And definitely not inebriated, which she looks to be.

For a moment, the skin of her forearms shifts, her arm hair elongating. Then it recedes back into her skin as though it were never there to begin with.

I suck in a startled breath.

She's a lycanthrope?

Why is she being led into a witch's spell circle?

Wrong, wrong, wrong.

All of this feels wrong.

The girl's companion moves a hand to the back of her neck and guides her down to her knees.

For a moment I am paralyzed by fear, my horror seizing up my limbs.

What the *fuck* is going on?

My eyes move from witch to witch, but none of them look anxious or agitated.

Why do they not look worried?

"Join hands once more, sisters," the priestess says, stepping into the circle with the two guests of honor.

My heart feels like it's in my throat as I clasp the palms of the women around me, sealing the circle. Magic thickens in the air.

I must be misunderstanding something. Surely I am.

The priestess lifts her arms and speaks once more in Latin. *"I call on the darkness and the old, hungry gods who will bear witness to my deeds."*

She drops her hands and reaches into her robe. From it she pulls a gleaming ceremonial blade.

As the priestess speaks, she lifts a ceremonial blade in one of her joined hands.

Holy fuck, who gave her a knife?

My gaze sweeps over the rest of the circle. Several witches are swaying, and the eyes I can make out in the dim room look a bit glazed, but not one of them appears surprised or uneasy.

Why is no one else freaking out?

Pulling the collar of her robe down, the priestess brings the blade to her sternum. And then she drags it down. I see skin split, hear cloth tear, and when the first drops of it hit the marble floor inside the circle, my magic senses it, rising in my veins like a leviathan, eager to draw on the fluid. And that smell, that earlier smell that's plagued me, I recognize it now—

Dark magic.

It oozes into the air, drifting up like smoke.

The priestess touches her fingers to her wound. Once she's coated them, she approaches the girl, removing the latter's mask.

"*With blood I bind*," the priestess says in English, marking the girl's forehead with her blood. *"With bone I break. Only through death shall I at last forsake."*

At the center of the circle, the girl whimpers, then begins to scream.

No.

I drop my hands from those of my sisters, and the circle's collective magic dissipates away with a *whoosh* as I rush for the girl.

I don't know what I'm doing, only that I should've stopped earlier, when the blade came out, or the dark magic, or hell, even when they mentioned pulling from the darkness of the earth. This situation is all sorts of fucked up, and no amount of money is worth whatever is going on.

I knock the priestess aside before dropping to my knees in front of the girl, distantly aware of the priestess shouting as she loses her balance, her knife clattering out of her hands.

I grab the girl by the hands, terrified for her.

The girl's robed companion turns to me, and from beneath the mask comes a monstrous hiss.

On instinct, my magic lashes out, slamming into the figure and throwing them back.

Empress? Memnon's voice speaks into my head.

Crap. Not him. Not now.

"What the fuck are you doing, Selene!" Kasey yells, coming toward me.

I don't know. I don't know what I'm doing, and this shifter is probably an adult who agreed to this, and maybe I've gotten everything wrong, but her pupils are blown, and she's making wolfish whimpering noises, and I will fucking *fight* anyone who comes between me and her.

"You're okay," I whisper to her, and I wrap an arm under her shoulders and help her rise to her feet.

She sways, placing most of her weight on me. I feel her lean closer and breathe in my scent, reminding me of Kane.

Must be a wolf thing.

Around us, the women are shifting and murmuring, and for the first time this evening, they're starting to look nervous. A few of them have moved over to the priestess, helping her up and trying to staunch the flow of blood from her wound.

"Come on," I whisper softly, urging the girl to move.

If I can get her up the stairs and into my residence hall, I can get her proper help.

"Creature," the priestess calls out, "*avenge me.*"

Across from us, the shifter's original companion now rises from where they fell. Only now, their hood has slipped off, revealing a pale gray face, smooth, lusterless skin, and eyes that are entirely black. Though it resembles a person, it's not human. It doesn't even seem to have a life force at all.

Along its forehead is a single word, one that's been scrawled *into* its skin, written in…in…

Aramaic, my mind whispers to me.

Before I can make out what that word is, the creature rushes us.

All around me, witches gasp.

I throw my magic at the creature, pulling power from the ground just like the priestess instructed. It feels like taking a large breath, then forcing out a powerful exhale. The soft orange plume of my magic leaves me, barreling across the room. It slams into the being, knocking it off its feet and into the stone wall behind it.

Its body makes a dull cracking sound, and the creature collapses in a heap.

Empress, what is going on?

"You fucking fool," the priestess says to me. To the creature, she calls out, "Creature, repair yourself."

The being begins to move, but it's no natural movement. Things are jerking and shifting beneath its robe.

My hold on the girl tightens, and I back us up.

The shifter moans, drawing my attention away from the room for a moment.

"Are you okay?" I whisper to her.

"Don't…feel…so good…" she mumbles, leaning her head against me.

The girl is sweating and trembling and very obviously intoxicated with a drug or a spell or both.

I can barely think over the pounding in my heart. "Can you run?" I whisper. "Or shift?" I'll take an intoxicated wolf over this room of witches *any* day.

"Ungh," she says, her head seeming to roll on her shoulders.

I think that's a no.

I head toward one of the lit passages branching from the room.

"Oh no, you don't," the priestess calls. "Leave if you want, but the wolf is *mine*."

Her magic fills the air, and when I turn to her, her mask is gone. Blood still drips down her chest, and I can still smell the remnants of the dark magic tinging the air. Dark magic I participated in.

"Release the girl," she orders. Beyond her, the creature's body is still shifting and making unsettling scraping noises.

I back up, dragging the poor shifter along with me. Unfortunately, the lit passage is close to the priestess's… whatever that thing is.

The priestess takes a step toward me. "Witch, you have one last warning: release the shifter."

Something is obviously really wrong here. Something more than just shady.

Something evil.

I messed up by being here in the first place, and I messed up again by not stepping in sooner. But over my dead body is this creep of a woman touching the girl.

My expression hardens as I look at her. "*No*."

The priestess draws in a long breath. Then, spreading her hands like she's encompassing the room, she says, "Sisters, Creature, *get me the wolf*."

The entire room of masked figures charges me.

My fear spikes—

Empress, what is going on? I could swear Memnon's voice sounds alarmed, but maybe those are my own emotions talking.

I swing around with the girl and rush us toward the tunnel I was eyeing.

The girl is tripping over her feet, and I'm dragging her more than anything, and if something doesn't change fast, those witches and that...that...monstrosity are going to catch us.

With that panicked thought, I funnel my magic into my hand.

"*Explode*," I whisper, and then I toss the magical grenade behind me.

BOOM!

The girl and I are thrown forward as the earth bucks, and the blast hits our back. Screams sound from behind me, and I grunt as I take on the full weight of the shifter, the two of us slamming into the ground.

Empress, what is happening!

That...didn't go as planned.

I scramble back to my feet, hauling the girl up with me. I knock away my skewed mask, finally able to see my surroundings better. Singed wisps of peach-colored smoke waft through the air.

I glance down at my companion. One look at her dazed expression, and I know she's not going to be able to run. And I don't stand a chance fighting over a dozen people and a monster.

Only one option left.

I close my eyes, calling on my power. *"Magic, magic, make me strong. Help me carry this girl far...and long."*

All right, not my best rhyme, but fuck it, it'll do.

Power rushes down my arms and legs. I feel it winding about my lungs and pumping through my heart.

I sweep the girl off her feet, and cradling her in my arms, I run.

CHAPTER 27

The tunnel we enter is small and dank. The walls here are bare earth, and the marble gives way to flagstone. There are lit candles—probably from when the others passed through, and I just go off the assumption that if I follow the candle-light, it'll lead me out. I have to assume that's what'll happen. If I'm wrong…

Can't think about that.

As I'm running, I second-guess myself again. Maybe I overreacted back there. Maybe I saw a little blood and dark magic and blew everything out of proportion.

But my intuition is telling me I read the situation correctly. That something violent and bad was going on. Something I almost got duped into completing.

That spell the priestess had been uttering, why did it sound so familiar…?

Behind me, I hear the distant footfalls of my pursuers. Crap, they're truly giving chase.

They haven't caught up to me yet, but who knows how

long that will last. I'm carrying another entire human being, and despite the power boost my magic is giving me, I don't think I'll have an edge for long.

Can't think about that either.

In front of me, the tunnel branches off. Following the light, I turn right.

My black robe keeps tangling around my legs, and in my arms, the girl's head lolls.

I hope she's all right.

My eyes fix on the smear of blood on the shifter's forehead, and the priestess's incantation comes back to me.

With blood I bind. With bone I break. Only through death shall I at last forsake.

A chill snakes down my spine.

A binding spell.

That's why the priestess's incantation sounded familiar. She was performing a *binding spell*. The horror of it is only now hitting me.

There are natural bonds, like those of soul mates and familiars. Those require no spells. Their magic is innate; it initiates and executes the binding all on its own.

Other types of bonds require spells, and they can be consensual or—the shifter whimpers in my arms again—not.

"I see her!" a feminine voice shouts from behind me. I hear what sounds like a whole stampede of witches pounding down the hallway after us.

I pour more power into my limbs, aware that I'll probably spend tomorrow sleeping off the magical use and bracing against the killer headache the exertion is going to give me.

Even with the added power, I can hear them closing in on me.

I hear one of them whisper a spell, and instinctively, I

twist away toward the wall to my left. A ball of acid-green magic whizzes by me.

I right myself and continue. As I run, I call on magic from the earth beneath my bare feet. I feel it sift through the stones and touch my skin, and I yank desperately on it, hauling the gathered power up through my body like water from a well. I funnel it down my arm and into my palm.

"Immobilize!" I don't even bother whispering the one-word spell before twisting around and awkwardly tossing it while still balancing the girl in my arms.

Awkward or not, it does its job. I hear a cry as my magic hits someone.

As fast as I can, I face forward and draw more magic into my palm.

Selene, are you okay? I nearly trip at hearing Memnon's voice in my ear. Now he sounds more than just alarmed. *What is going on?*

I can't talk to him and get myself out of this situation, so I ignore his call.

"*Immobilize*," I say again. That's literally the only spell I can think of beyond the screaming in my head.

Again, I turn and awkwardly throw it at my pursuers. The spell smashes into the group. I face forward again, hearing one of them curse behind me, followed by the sound of people falling. I don't allow myself to rejoice before I'm calling on more power.

My muscles are trembling, my lungs are heaving, and I can't think about anything beyond drawing up another spell.

The ones I'm making are crude, and as a result, I'm burning through an alarming amount of magic, but it's the best I got.

I hear the whisper on the wind a second before a spell slams into my shoulder.

I cry out as the magic burns through my clothes and sears my flesh. It's hot as fire, but it feels like acid on my skin, eating away at it.

Another spell is lobbed at me. The violet orb whizzes past my head, and I have a moment's relief as it hits the ground ahead of me, the magic flaring on impact.

I barrel onward, ready to run past it when—

Bam!

The shifter and I slam into a magically erected wall.

I stumble back, then fall on my ass. The shifter girl moans in my arms.

I don't even have time to assess how badly she's hurt; our assailants are closing in on us.

I call forth my next spell.

"Explode." I twist my torso and throw my magic as well as I can at the incoming cluster of supernaturals. It hits the closest pursuer in the shins—

BOOM!

I cover the shifter's face and my own against the fiery heat of the explosion. I can hear the witches' screams as they're thrown back.

Before they can retaliate, I lift my hand, palm facing them. *"I erect a wall from floor to ceiling."* The words come out in Sarmatian. *"Protect me and the shifter from those who would harm us."*

Soft orange magic shimmers in front of me, thinning and stretching until it's formed a transparent wall of sorts. On the other side of it, robed witches are getting up, though they sway and stumble, and I remember all over again that they were given something to drink.

My heart falls when I see there are at least ten of them. So many. And they're all so determined to get this girl and help bind her to that priestess.

The thought sends a fresh bolt of terror through me.

Empress! Memnon's voice is demanding and laced with panic.

I'm busy. I force the message down that river between us.

What is going on? he demands.

Ignoring Memnon, I turn from the rising witches and face the magical wall. It's violet hued and semitransparent.

I kick at it with my heel. It doesn't budge.

I draw on more magic, my limbs shaking from exertion. I try to pull it from the ground and into my flesh so I minimize taxing my own limited well of power.

The magic sifts into the soles of my feet, and when I start to hear witches banging on the barrier I erected, I coax the gathered power up my legs and down my arm.

A small pale orange ball of it bursts to life in my hand.

I throw it at the magical wall in front of me. The wall ripples, the violet sheen of it fading a little, but it holds.

At my back, the other witches are doing the same thing to my wall, pummeling it with spell after spell. So far, it's holding out better than the one in front of me, but there are many of them working on bringing it down.

I spare a glance at the shifter. Before, she'd been dazed but awake. Now she lies limp in my arms. I shake her a little, willing her to wake, but though her chest rises and falls, she remains unconscious.

Not good, not good, not good.

I draw on my magic in a panicked burst and slam it against the wall. The spell shifts, then reforms.

Another pull of magic, another throw.

Another ripple when it hits the wall.

Again and again I do this, ignoring the sounds of the spells hitting the wall at my back.

After one final hit of my power, the violet-hued barrier in front of me shatters. I nearly cry out in relief.

I haul the shifter back up into my arms, wincing at the pain in my shoulder as I stand and bear her weight. My injury has gone from burning to throbbing, and I can tell that once the adrenaline leaves my system, it's going to hurt like a motherfucker.

At my back I hear my own protective wall cracking. That's all the incentive I need to get moving.

I sprint once more down the hall. It curves, the candles burned down almost to their bases.

Okay, but where the hell is the exit?

Ahead of me, the corridor opens to a chamber full of shelves of what appear to be grimoires, judging by the hazy brown mixture of magic thickening the air.

The flagstones give way to more marble, and my feet slap across a solar image as I enter the chamber.

Almost immediately my head begins to pound at the conflicting magic.

I move to the far end of the room, where a set of stone *lamassu* guard a rounded archway. Beyond it looks to be another spiral staircase.

In the distance, I hear the pounding of footfalls.

Fuck.

Frantically, I look at the stone threshold protectors, an idea sparking. I move to the first step of the stairs, then turn back to look down at the statues that are part woman, part lion, part eagle.

"*Lamassu*," I call to them, "*I summon you to protect us. Let no one with wicked intent cross your threshold*."

In an instant, the stone guardians come to life. They rise from their haunches and prowl forward, away from the stairs, their gray tails flicking. It's the oddest sight.

Magic, man. Don't do drugs when you can do this.

I swivel forward and ascend the stairs, gritting my teeth against the strain of lifting the shifter.

I whisper another strengthening spell just as I hear the witches enter the grimoire room beneath me.

Go, go, go, I urge my body. My magic is reaching its limits. My arms and legs are still holding out, but the spell that was supposed to help has barely taken the edge off my strain.

Low, gravelly growls fill the chamber beneath me, the sound raising the hairs on the nape of my neck. I hear one of the *lamassu* snarl and a witch shriek.

An explosive spell shakes the ground, and I nearly lose my balance, wobbling with the shifter in my arms.

I'm more than halfway up the steps when I hear someone near the base of the staircase. I barely have time to process that they've managed to get past the *lamassu* when a spell slams into my back.

I scream, briefly collapsing against the railing as the same flesh-eating curse burns against my skin.

EMPRESS! Memnon roars in my head, and now there is no question about it: he *is* panicking on my behalf.

Keep going. Keep going.

Beneath me, I can hear the witch whispering another spell. I tense, but the hit never comes. Instead, one of the *lamassu* snarls.

A moment later, the witch screams, and I catch sight of her falling, the *lamassu*'s teeth piercing her leg. She and I make eye contact, and hers are full of terror as the beast drags her out of sight.

I take a shuddering breath, ashamed of the relief I feel,

and I force my legs to keep going. As soon as I do so, I have to grit my teeth against the cry that wants to work its way out. I manage to bite it back, but I can't seem to stop the tears from slipping down my cheeks.

Goddess, but the pain. It's all-consuming.

I force myself up each step by sheer will, repeatedly banging the girl's legs into the railing.

"Sorry, sorry, sorry," I gasp, even though I know she can't hear me. She still hasn't woken up.

Beneath me, there are prolonged screams.

I'm nearly to the top of the staircase when another spell ricochets against the wall and crashes into my calf, slicing it open. I scream as my leg gives out.

EMPRESS! Memnon bellows. *HOLD FAST! I AM COMING!*

Just before I hit the ground, I cover the shifter's head, and it's my own skull that cracks against the top stair.

Everything whites out for an instant.

Then I'm blinking the world back into focus, and I hear screams, and the scent of magic is pounding in my head, and above it all, fear that isn't my own floods my system.

TAKE IT.

"Memnon?" I whisper out loud.

I'm still blinking, still trying to make sense of the world even as I'm forcing myself to my feet, dragging the shifter up with me. I can't stop the cry I let out as I force my injured leg to bear our weight.

There are a dozen different spells I could use to alleviate the pain or help the wound mend itself, but between the fear and the pain and my growing exhaustion, I can't seem to think of a single one.

Need to get the shifter to safety.

I stumble up the last of the stairs. My legs shake, my lungs and shoulder and back burn, and I can feel my hot blood running down my leg and warming my skin.

TAKE MY MAGIC. I wince at the sound of Memnon's voice inside me.

Is that what he meant? Take his magic?

NOW, MATE.

Ugh, "mate."

EST AMAGE. *TAKE IT.*

"Stop yelling at me," I moan, staggering away from the stairs and toward a carved wooden door ahead of me. I've only taken two steps when the blood seeping from my calf wound begins to bubble and boil against my skin.

I cry out from the fresh new pain.

Now why would my wound do that...?

The spell must've been a curse. A really shitty one.

I stumble the last few feet to the door and awkwardly grab the knob, nearly dropping the limp girl in my arms. I just manage to twist it open, and then me and the shifter fall through it. I barely have time to twist my body so I'm the one who hits the wet earth and not the girl.

We're outside.

I let out an exhausted huff. That feels like a win all on its own.

I smell the forest around us, and when I look back toward the open doorway, I see the door itself has been carved into the trunk of a tree, though the interior of the tree appears to be far larger than its exterior.

Magic, man...

I still hear the distant sounds of witches fighting and screaming inside, but I doubt the *lamassu* will hold them all off for much longer.

I try to get up, but my entire body is protesting. I whimper at my various wounds. My magic and my adrenaline are wearing away. I don't know how much more I have in me.

By the love of all our gods, little witch, Memnon says, *please—I am* begging *you—take what I am offering!*

What you're offering? I feel it then, through that magical river that seems to flow right to my heart.

Power. Endless power. More than anyone has any business handling.

I don't understand how he's siphoning it to me, and I don't bother to consider the repercussions of using this sorcerer's magic. I reach for it.

I gasp as it pours into me. The pain from my various injuries grows dull, and my fatigue vanishes entirely.

I rise to my feet, picking up the unconscious girl once more.

And then I run.

Need to get to shifter territory. That's all I can think as I sprint.

I sense the boundary line ahead of me, but it feels like it might as well be in a different country.

I stumble over roots, and twigs and rocks cut into the soft pads of my feet. I clench my teeth against the sensation of blood dripping down my calf.

Later. I'll deal with it all later.

I can't hear the witches behind me anymore, and I'm starting to gain confidence when the girl in my arms begins to gag.

I don't want to stop running, not when bloodthirsty witches who practice the dark arts want to enslave this girl's will to another.

But I also don't want her to choke on her own vomit.

I stop and let her down. She's not even conscious. Shit. Shit, shit, shit. I lay her on her side, focusing my attention on her.

Whatever they gave her, I'm afraid she's been given too much.

She gags again, and it's clear that the substance in her system needs to come *out*.

Gently, I press a hand to her stomach. "*Purge*," I command, pressing my borrowed power into her flesh.

The sunrise-orange magic billows out from beneath my palm, then sinks into her skin.

She lunges forward and retches violently. I try not to make a face at what comes up, but I can smell the tainted magic lacing her vomit.

She throws up again. And again.

"I'm so sorry," I say, combing her hair back, wincing as I feel a tug in my injured shoulder.

There must be more poison within her, poison that's entered her bloodstream. It too needs to be removed from her system.

Placing a hand on her chest and another on her back, I grab Memnon's power and coax it down my arms to my palms.

"*Dissolve the poison within*," I command in Sarmatian.

Then I force my power into the girl.

Her back arches, and her eyes snap open. She begins to scream, and I have to grit my teeth and brace myself as magic battles magic within her.

I continue to force as much healing power into her as possible, overwhelming the toxin slipping through her veins. I sway a little, the sustained effort making me feel faint.

A branch cracks somewhere in the distance. Then I hear the crackle of crunching pine needles.

They're still coming.

Beneath my hands, the girl is shaking, but her cries have tapered off to whimpers. She's still not awake, not in any real sense. I swallow as worry engulfs me.

She's defenseless like this.

I lean toward her and whisper an incantation under my breath, one that feels as old as the language I'm speaking in. *"I offer you my protection. My magic will defend you. My blood will spill before yours does. This I vow."*

The oath feels like a memory, like déjà vu.

The footsteps draw near, no doubt because the witches heard the girl's cries.

I can still sense the slick poison slipping through her, but I have to let her go and hope the magic I pressed into her will be enough.

I force myself up on shaky legs, turning to face the approaching witches.

In the darkness I can barely make them out. There aren't as many of them now, maybe five or six. And the monster is still unaccounted for.

I pull magic up from the earth and draw it down from the dark moon, and I siphon still more from that magical river flowing into me. My power gathers and builds, forming just beneath my skin as I face the witches.

They're no longer wearing masks, but unfortunately, the darkness hides their features.

"*Attack*," I whisper, releasing my magic. It snaps out of me like serpents. The mental visual must be doing something because I see my magic pull back, then strike much the same way a snake would. Witches yelp and cry out.

A spell hits me, one that causes my attack to dissolve. Another follows, striking me square in the chest and knocking me back into the earth. This second spell locks up my muscles, and in mere seconds, I'm frozen; I can breathe but not much else. I can't even move my eyes.

A third spell hits my hip as I lie there, this one a dirty crimson color. I know just by the look of it that this one is bad. And then I feel it.

If I could scream, I would.

It's as though I'm being stabbed in twenty different places. Maybe I am. I'm choking on blood, or maybe my lungs are simply seizing up.

SELENE! STAY WITH ME. Memnon forces his magic into me, and I reach for it, letting it slip through me and fight off the curse that's flaying me open.

DO YOU SEE YOUR ENEMIES? MARK THEM, EST AMAGE, *THEY ARE NOW MY OWN.*

"She's hit," one of the witches says.

"Does it look like I care? That fucking cunt nearly ripped off my leg."

"Enough," a third one says.

Memnon's power must be working because the pain from the curse is dying down, and I'm able to move my eyes.

So I can see one of the witches prowling over, her toenails painted a soft pink color. For some reason, that strikes me as ridiculous, given the situation.

She crouches next to me, her straight black hair brushing my cheek. "When the others get to you, you're going to wish you hadn't done shit tonight," she whispers, looking down on me.

She lifts her hand, and I'm not sure if it's to slap me or strike me with another spell, but I want to scream because I can't do anything but lie here, prone.

The witch flashes me a nasty smile. "Payback's a bit—" A black shadow collides with her, and I hear her scream. It cuts out, replaced by the meaty sound of ripping flesh.

There are more screams and more meaty sounds. Now I'm able to tilt my head just a little. A massive shadow is pinning one of the witches, and it jerks its head, tearing out a section of flesh. The creature pauses to glance over at me, its eyes glinting eerily in the darkness.

I *recognize* those eyes.

Nero!

I want to cry because he's here, defending me. He roars, then lunges toward another witch.

I see a flash of cobalt-blue magic whoosh toward him.

In an instant I'm in his mind. *Get down!*

His body lowers, pressing flush against the ground, and the spell whizzes harmlessly past him.

I'm out of his head in an instant, dragging as much of Memnon's magic into me as I can, until it's flushing out the last of the spells that cling to my body.

I thought I was panicked before, but now knowing that my familiar is taking on a group of bloodthirsty witches all on his own—I'm petrified for him.

My fingers and toes twitch, then my hands and wrists, feet and ankles. I want to scream at how painfully slow it's going.

Before I get full motor function back, I sense one of the witches grabbing the shifter girl behind me.

No!

I fling my magic out without a spell, letting the cords of it find the witch. As soon as they do, my power wraps around the witch's ankles and yanks her off her feet.

She grunts as she hits the ground hard. Before she can get up, my familiar is on her—

I cringe at the wet sound of him biting into her. I slip into his mind, coaxing my familiar to let the witch go. Reluctantly, he does so.

From his eyes, I peer around us. The witches all appear to be accounted for. Several of them lie on the ground, moaning. Two more are limping away together. Nero's nostrils flare at the smell of so much blood.

I move back from his mind to my own. I've regained enough control of my body to turn on my side and retch, my body wanting to purge the pain and the spells and all the gruesome sights of the evening.

Nero prowls over to me and nudges me onto my back again. I groan as I flop onto my injured shoulder.

My familiar puts a paw on my chest, and he gives me an intense and—I swear to the goddess—irritated look. Normally, I have to guess at Nero's more complex thoughts, but for some reason, this one is clear: *Call on me for help.*

I swallow and nod. "Thank you," I murmur.

It takes another full minute for the immobilizing spell to completely wear off, even with the help of Memnon's borrowed magic.

Once it does, I hobble over to the shifter girl. She's no longer screaming, which is good, but she's not awake, and she's far too still for my liking. Kneeling at her side, I check her pulse.

It's there—and it sounds strong and steady.

I think she's going to be okay.

"*Give me strength,*" I murmur in Sarmatian, the words forming as I draw on more of Memnon's power.

His magic flares through my body, lending me his might.

I lug the girl into my arms once more, trying not to

think about just how much I'm in Memnon's debt. I've used *a lot* of his power tonight.

Got to get to shifter territory. I can worry about the sorcerer later. The most important thing is making sure this girl is safe.

I've taken maybe five steps when a monstrous roar fills the night air.

Well, fuck. There's the monster. Now he's accounted for.

And I think he's after my ass.

CHAPTER 28

I hate running. Hate it, hate it, hate it.

That's all I can think as I trip over roots and half stumble, half sprint through the Everwoods, my wounds so numerous, they've become one massive ache, one that Memnon's power is no longer able to fully dull.

Oh, and there's a monster somewhere in the forest at my back.

Nero lopes next to me, his eyes glinting in the darkness.

Ahead of me, the barrier comes into view, the magical line shimmering just the slightest. The sight of it gives me a final burst of adrenaline.

From the darkness behind me comes another roar.

I eye the barrier again. I'm going to make it—I am—but even so, there's nothing to stop the monster from following me across.

Have to deal with the creature first.

I fall to my knees and lay the girl down as quickly as I can. After rising to my feet, I back away from her.

"Nero," I say, nodding to my familiar, "guard the girl."

In the forest behind me, twigs are snapping and branches are swaying as the monster barrels toward me.

I barely have time to turn toward it before the creature slams into me.

The two of us go down in a tangle of limbs. I hit the ground hard, the air knocked out of me.

Before I can draw in another breath, two monstrous hands close around my neck.

I gasp, my panic rising.

Can't breathe!

Above me the creature's lips draw back, and it hisses, revealing sharpened teeth.

If I could scream, I would. The thing looks human, but everything from its pallor to the odd smoothness of its features is wrong.

I reach for its hands, desperate to pry them from my neck. I startle at the feel of the creature's skin, which feels like…like…potter's clay.

Don't I have a magical aptitude for clay?

The being's hold tightens, and a gurgled sound comes from my mouth.

Selene, use my power! Memnon bellows inside my head.

Power, right.

I yank on Memnon's magic, and for the hell of it, I try drawing on the creature's own essence. To my shock, I feel its magic migrate from its body to my own. After gathering all the accumulated power, I force it down my arms and out my palms, willing the hands beneath mine to loosen.

For a moment, they do, and I drag in a grateful gulp of air.

But then those hands tighten once more, and the creature stares down at me with those lifeless obsidian eyes, its features slack.

A shadow drops from the treetops above us, landing heavily on my attacker. I hear the dull sound of clay breaking, and I swear to the triple goddess that the monster's back *caved in* under the impact.

Nero snarls above us. I see a flash of his fangs, and I feel a stray claw of his accidentally tear at my flesh as he mauls the creature between us. I grunt at the wave of pain that comes a moment later.

Damn the gods, Empress, USE MY POWER! IT IS YOURS! Memnon roars.

My pain and panic and those compelling words are enough to call forth another wave of power.

I don't mean to let my magic make use of my blood; it's simply that my attention drifts briefly to my newest wound, and the magic follows. Once there, my magic *feasts.*

My power comes alive like never before. I didn't know a could feel like this—like a live wire. It's burgeoning more and more as my blood dissolves.

I gather it in my palms and move my hands to the monster's chest. Its own hold is still fast around my neck, despite Nero's attack.

For an instant, I move into Nero's head.

Move away. Now, I command him.

I shift back into my own head as my panther hops off the creature, then prowls back to the girl.

Black spots obscure my vision, but I wait until my magic has finished devouring my blood. I know that's forbidden magic; I know that tomorrow I'll be sorry I used it.

But tonight, I have no remorse.

I stare into those empty eyes, and I speak a single word. "*Annihilate.*"

My power detonates.

The creature blasts into the air, its body shattering as it's thrown across the forest. My spell continues, the last of it hitting a tree and cracking it apart.

Then the woods fall silent, so painfully silent.

There is my queen. Memnon's words seem to echo in the silence, though I know I'm only hearing them in my head.

I take a deep breath of air, then cough, my throat raw. Nero comes over to me, rubbing his head and then his body against my face.

I force myself to my feet, though my body feels incapable of holding me up. I stumble over to where I saw the creature's remains fall.

When I get to where I think it landed, I whisper "*illuminate*" into my hand.

A weak orb of light bursts forth, the light from it flickering. I blow it off my palm, watching it float over the ground.

I draw in a breath when I see dozens and dozens of clay shards. I lift one of the larger pieces, one that resembles a finger. The inside of it is hollow. There's no muscle, no bone, no blood. The thing that almost killed me literally shattered like a broken pot. Still, several feet away, its head and one of its shoulders lie mostly intact.

As I walk up to it, it hisses, snapping its teeth at me.

Yeah, not today, Frankenstein.

I lift my bare foot, then slam it down on its face, grimacing as the sharp, jagged edges of its head cut into my skin.

What's one more injury at this point?

I draw my foot back and bash it in again. And again.

Somewhere along the way, I begin to scream my rage, and I think I may be crying, and I don't care. I don't care because my body feels like this is the last bit of energy I have.

I pulverize the creature's face until nothing remains.

And then I limp my way back to the girl.

I still don't know her name.

I want to laugh. We both nearly died three times over, yet I don't know her name, and she knows even less about me.

Then I do laugh, and I think I'm still crying.

I'm losing it. I know I am.

I bend to pick her up, and it's not going to happen, my muscles are too tired, my body too spent.

Still, I manage to scrape together enough of Memnon's power to lend me the needed strength.

I haul the girl into my arms and stumble toward the boundary separating witch from lycanthrope territory. With a final lunge, I cross the line.

I fall to my knees on the other side of it, Nero next to me.

My arms loosen, and the girl slides out of them.

And then I pass out.

CHAPTER 29

I am cloaked in darkness, my mind wrapped in it like a blanket. It only pulls back slightly when I hear a low warning growl from Nero, who's curled against my side.

I fight my way back to consciousness, rousing only enough to lift my hand in additional warning to whoever is approaching.

My eyes meet the brown eyes of a wolf. As soon as I see it, I drop my hand.

Not a witch.

In the back of my mind, I note the irony that even bloody and weak, I feel safer right now in the presence of a predator than I do a witch.

"It's okay, Nero," I whisper.

My familiar quiets, though he's tense behind me.

The wolf paces forward, and if it's interested in eating me, I'm F-U-C-K-E-D because I'm not moving. I don't think I could even if I tried.

The wolf takes a few steps forward, then soundlessly shifts. In its place stands a naked older man.

He rushes over the last of the distance before kneeling at our side, uncaring that a panther is mere feet from him. I can't see the man's expression, but he must smell the blood on me. I've lost a lot, I think…

I don't know what we must look like.

The man leans into the girl's neck and breathes in her scent. Whatever he smells causes him to whine. Then he leans over and scents me as well, his nose tickling my skin. Nero growls again but doesn't do anything else. I hear another whine come from the man, this one slightly different.

"Are you okay?" he asks softly.

I don't think so, but I don't bother admitting that.

Instead, I reach out and grope in the darkness for his hand. When I find it, I give it a squeeze.

I swallow, beating back the darkness that keeps clouding my vision.

"They tried…to…bind her," I whisper. I feel a pressing need to get this story out now, in case more people come for me and the girl. "She was…drugged… Did…my best…to…get her…here." I keep having to pause to catch my breath. Everything hurts so damn bad. Even pushing out words. And my vision keeps clouding. I think. It's so dark. I don't know. Confused.

The girl, I remind myself.

"Please…" I say, squeezing the shifter's hand, "get her… to safety…before they…come back."

"Who? Who's coming back?"

I try to speak again, but I'm so tired. So, so tired.

I think I drift a little, but I rouse again when I hear the shifter howl, the sound of it raising my gooseflesh. I crack my eyes open—when did they close?—and see the girl is in his arms.

"Thank you for protecting Cara," he says, and oh, he's talking to me.

I try to sharpen my focus.

"I'm going to send some pack mates over here," he continues. "We'll get you healed and taken care of. Just hold tight." That last part sounds a bit like a plea, and I understand why a second later.

The shifter retreats into the darkness, carrying the girl.

I should feel terrified of being left alone, weak as I am. But Nero is beside me, and I know he's keeping watch. Between that and my relief that the girl is now back with her pack, I let the darkness take me once more.

It seems like only minutes later when my sleep is interrupted again. I hear the heavy crunch of pine needles as someone approaches.

One of the shifters, I remind myself.

The footsteps halt when they get to me.

"Only fools and warriors pass out under an open sky. Reckless woman, you are a bit of both."

I jolt when I hear the voice, forcing my eyes open. In the darkness, I can barely make out Memnon's features, but it's him.

How did you find me? I want to ask him, but I'm so tired, and I know if I try to speak—if I dare move at all—then my various wounds will start waking up with me.

We are soul mates. I can always find you.

He reaches out and brushes the hair from my face. It's… nice. I let my eyes drift closed and enjoy the sensation of his fingers on me. Now that I'm vulnerable, I can admit to myself that Memnon's very presence makes me feel safe.

His hand retreats from my hair, and I hate that his touch is gone. And then I think I'm supposed to hate that I hate that, but fuck, I'm too tired to bother caring at this point.

Hands slide under my body. Even that slight jostling has me moaning as my injuries flare to life.

"It's all right, little witch. You're safe. I've got you."

The moment he lifts me fully into his arms, it feels like I'm being attacked all over again. I cry out as pain lacerates across my body.

Memnon curses under his breath. "*Ease the pain from within*," he utters.

His magic seeps into me from that point over my heart. Almost immediately, the pain dissolves. I want to laugh; it feels so good not to hurt. But I'm so tired. Even more so now that I have a true break from the pain.

Memnon begins to walk, and I lean my head into the crook of his arm, nestling into his chest.

"My flawless queen, my exquisite mate," he murmurs, and for once I really don't take issue with the terms he's calling me. "What heart you have."

I don't think we've traveled very far when Memnon pauses, adjusting his grip so he can use one of his hands to feel where my clothes touch his. I don't really know what he's doing, not until he holds his fingers up, rubs them together, then touches them to his tongue.

"Fuck." He starts moving again, only now he's charging through the woods. "How badly are you injured?"

I don't know. I push the answer through our bond because I'm too tired to speak.

He curses again. "I'm going to get you to your room before I heal you, *est amage*. If we linger out here while I mend your wounds, we will draw too much attention, and

I do not trust my rage right now. I will kill anyone who crosses me—friend or foe."

"You…have…anger problems."

Memnon's hold tightens on me. "You are my weakness, Empress," he confesses, his voice gentling. "You always have been."

As he carries me back through the Everwoods, his lips skim my forehead, and for some inconceivable reason, I lean into the action, nuzzling closer to him.

He makes a satisfied sound, and I swear I sense some emotion coming from Memnon—an ache that is so sharp, it hurts.

"You are safe," he murmurs. "Nothing—*nothing*—will ever get you while you are with me. I swear my life on it, mate."

I feel the truth in those words, though I don't understand why he's being this way when he's been so clear that we are enemies.

It's only quiet for a minute before he speaks again.

"How fierce my mate is," he says. "I saw how you laid waste to your foes."

Bile rises in my throat at the memory of all the sliced-up witches scattered across the forest. How did the night turn into this?

"Fear not, my queen," he continues. "Those who survived your wrath will not live long. I will hunt them down myself and make them pay."

Oh Goddess.

"No," I whisper.

"*Yes*," he says. "The marked themselves the moment they attacked you. No one attacks what's mine and lives."

I don't remember passing out, but I wake to the sound of Memnon's boots striding across the creaking wood floors of my house. I'm still in his arms, still cradled like a baby. And man, after the night I had, I can say with certainty that I *much* prefer being the one carried than doing the carrying. Even thinking about that memory makes my arms throb.

I snuggle deeper into Memnon's chest, and uncaring that he'll likely notice, I breathe in the smell of leather and man. It makes my gut clench in the strangest way.

His arms tighten around me again, and I feel another brush of his lips against my forehead.

The house is dark and quiet as Memnon heads up the stairs and down the hall, the only sound the creaking floorboards. When he gets to my room, he opens the door, flicks on the light, and carries me in, heading over to my bed. Gently, the sorcerer lays me out. Nero follows me onto the mattress before stretching out along my side.

I stare up at Memnon, feeling vulnerable like this. I get a thrill at the position because for all Memnon's ferocity, I do feel safe in his presence.

The thrill lasts for only a moment. Memnon's eyes widen as he gets a good look at me for the first time since he found me. Then his expression darkens...darkens until he looks murderous.

"Who *did* this to you?" His eyes have a feral look to them, and his earlier words really register then—about his rage making him kill indiscriminately. He looks like he wants to end lives.

Reaching down, he rips away the tattered remains of my black robe. I hear his sharp intake of breath at what he sees beneath.

"Selene." There it is again. Panic. It laces Memnon's voice.

Then he's reaching for my shirt, grabbing the hem and—

Riiiip.

I gasp as the material splits down the middle, revealing my stomach and bra.

"What are you doing?" I demand. I shiver as the cool air hits my skin.

"Assessing your injuries," he growls, flicking his gaze to my pants.

He pulls out a wicked-looking blade that was strapped to his side.

At the sight of it, I go still.

His eyes move back to mine, and his expression softens. He takes my hand and clasps it tightly, the hilt of his dagger brushing against my palm.

"Don't be frightened, little witch," he says. "This is so I can remove your pants and assess your injuries. Your clothes are"—he takes a bracing breath—"too blood soaked to pull off without jostling you."

Blood soaked?

I don't believe him, not until I glance down my torso and see the massive red stains myself. I didn't realize my wounds were that bad—the robe obscured them from view.

I drag my attention back to him. A muscle jumps in his cheek, like he's only barely holding in some emotion. His eyes run over my face as though he can't help but take me in.

"Can I continue?" Memnon asks.

Swallowing, I nod.

He gives my hand a squeeze, then lays it down with the sort of care that makes me feel breakable. With his knife, he carefully cuts my jeans away, slicing open one pant leg, then the other.

I'm left in nothing but my bra and underwear, but

Memnon only has eyes for my wounds. His indigo magic thickens and coils around him.

"Your enemies' deaths will be slow," he vows, and there is far too much conviction in his eyes.

I'm too weary to argue with him about this when my limbs are trembling, either from shock or exertion.

Gingerly, he lifts one of my feet, inspecting the pad of it. I already know the flesh down there is torn up. I felt the cuts I collected as I ran barefoot. By that point, I was too determined to care.

"You should've used my magic to heal yourself," he chastises lightly. I notice then what I hadn't before—Memnon's foreign accent is gone, though how it vanished is a mystery.

"I was busy," I rasp.

He inclines his head, like I make a fair point, setting my leg back down so he can shrug off the leather jacket he's wearing. Beneath it, he wears a fitted black T-shirt. Even feeling like roadkill at the moment, I still manage to admire his thickly corded arm muscles and the tattoos that run along them.

Memnon tosses his jacket over the back of my desk chair, and that simple action is natural, as though he's at home in my space, and I don't know why I like it. It should tick me off.

It probably will tomorrow when I don't feel like death warmed over.

The sorcerer kneels next to the bed. Gently, he reaches for the wound along my torso, the one Nero accidentally gave me. His touch is featherlight, but I still hiss out a breath at the contact.

"Relax, my wildcat," he says, giving me an endearing look.

The sight of it throws me completely, and my weary heart picks up speed.

Memnon murmurs something under his breath, and I feel the tingling brush of his power against my side.

I grimace as, under his touch, my flesh repairs itself. It's not painful, but it doesn't feel good either. I try to wiggle away from it, but Memnon's other hand braces my torso, holding me in place with a casual sort of familiarity. That too has my pulse picking up, and my brows come together.

"Good woman," he praises, his eyes on my wound. "You're taking it so well. So well."

He's talking about his healing magic, of course, but that's not what I'm *thinking* about. I'm half dead and tired beyond measure, yet somehow my enemy is making me think about screwing his brains out.

What is wrong with me?

My injury finishes stitching itself back together, saving me from my own thoughts.

Memnon removes his hand, which is still smeared with my blood, and rises to his feet.

Before I can ask him what he's doing, he lifts my legs so he can sit where they rested on my bed. Then he places them both in his lap.

Softly, he strokes my legs. Again he murmurs a healing spell beneath his breath.

His magic sweeps over my legs, burrowing into the open wounds of my feet and my calf. The sensation is warm and itchy and uncomfortable. But Memnon keeps stroking my legs, and his hands feel so good.

"Tonight, I intend to heal you, Empress," he says, his attention fixed to my feet. "But tomorrow, I want answers."

I let out a shaky breath. "Why do you have to make that sound so ominous?" I say as the last of the wounds on my legs and feet seal up.

"Because," Memnon says, lifting my feet so he can stand once more, "I *am* ominous. And I *do* want answers."

Memnon kneels next to me, his face tantalizingly close. "And you *will* give them to me, *est amage*."

This close to him, I can see the thick sweep of his eyelashes and those complex brown eyes that seem to glitter. I can even see that wicked scar that trails along the side of his face. He looks like some lost relic.

I lift my chin obstinately at his words, but instead of replying, I reach out and touch his scar. I don't know what possesses me to do such a thing.

Memnon goes still, letting me explore his face. I trail my finger over the line of the scar, following its brutal path along his face. It's a wicked one.

"How did you get this?" I ask.

His brows come together. "I already told you, Selene."

He has?

"Tell me again," I say, continuing to feel my way along the scar's path.

He frowns but answers, "My people were expanding their territory into Dacian land. Their king didn't take that too kindly. He met us in battle and gave me this to remember him by."

My eyes widen at that. "It looks like he nearly took your face off."

"He tried to," Memnon agrees.

I can feel my own horror at the thought that someone would try to take another *still-living* human's face off.

The sorcerer's eyes twinkle, and his lips curve up playfully. "Just when I assumed you could not get any more innocent, you go and hide yourself in a future that is even more… *civilized* than the Roman one you were raised in."

"What happened to the king who did this to you?"

"I ran him through with my sword. And then I made his skull into a wine chalice."

What?

"You're lying," I say.

"I'm not. It was one of my favorites." He says it so calmly that *fuck*, if that's true…

I shrink away from him.

Memnon frowns at my reaction. "It was the custom of our warriors to do such things. Just as it was custom that every Sarmatian woman ride into battle and kill at least one enemy before she was allowed to marry."

What?

He stares at my shocked expression, something sad entering his eyes. "You had the same reactions the first time you learned these things. It is both a wonder and a heartbreak to see it all over again."

I clear my throat. "I'm still trying to get over the fact you drank wine from the skulls of your enemies." Not sure I'm *ever* going to get over that fact.

Memnon gives me a tight smile; then his eyes drop to my body, his gaze lingering on my ravaged shoulder. "I need to finish healing you, Empress. I'm going to have to roll you onto your stomach."

I start to flip myself over, but then his hands are there, guiding me so I don't jostle my injuries.

Gently, he removes the last of my shredded clothing still clinging to my back. Once the cool air kisses my skin, Memnon inhales sharply, presumably at the sight of my injuries.

"To think you never once believed yourself a true warrior-queen," he mutters under his breath. I'm pretty sure the reference applies to Roxilana, not me. "You carry battle wounds that would make the fiercest of my fighters proud."

"It's that bad?" Memnon's earlier spell is still blocking me from feeling pain.

The sorcerer runs a light hand around the injuries, and I close my eyes at the touch. It still feels unnervingly good.

"*Heal these wounds*," he murmurs in Sarmatian. *"Mend the flesh. Remake it as it was."*

His magic feels like a warm breath against my back. And then that warmth seeps into my skin, turning uncomfortable—almost itchy—and I know even without looking that the flesh is reforming, the wounds healing.

I lie there confused about how the evening went from me attending a spell circle for a little extra cash to being nearly killed by bloodthirsty witches and now being healed by my mortal enemy.

The warm press of magic fades, and Memnon smooths his hand down my back. I exhale at the sensation of his palm against my skin. There's just something about the feel of his hands—hands that have led armies and killed and lifted chalices made from his foes' skulls—that's so damn intoxicating.

Pretty sure enjoying this makes me a rotten human. Oh well, maybe I'll care tomorrow.

Memnon pauses, as though he senses my thoughts.

"*Est amage*," he murmurs, "do you like that? I will keep touching you if you do. All you have to say is the word, and it is yours."

Shit, maybe he does know my thoughts.

I squeeze my eyes shut and breathe through my nose. I sense that everything with this man comes at a price. He's not naming it, but it must be there.

But given all that's happened tonight…screw it.

"I like it," I admit.

His hand doesn't move. *Why* is his hand not moving? I wiggle a little, trying to get it going.

"Let me see your face," he demands.

I turn to look at him. "Why?"

His eyes gaze at me intensely. "Because you are the only thing worth looking at, and my eyes have missed you."

I frown. "I thought you hated me."

He leans forward and runs a knuckle down my spine, and I feel myself arch, stretching like a cat against his touch. "It's a little more complicated than that, Empress."

I understand what he means. I want to hate this man's guts—I know I *should*—but I don't.

"Close your eyes and relax, and I will touch you," he says.

I narrow my gaze. "Why should I trust you?"

He flashes me a sly smile. "You make a good point. There is only one person in the entire world who truly can trust me, and I'm staring at her." His hand smooths over my back again, and I bite back the sound that wants to come out.

Going to make the supremely bad decision to trust this man because why not? I've already made fifty other bad choices; what's one more?

So I close my eyes and let myself relax.

Nero must sense the shift in the room because he hops off the bed then. Several seconds later, I hear the click of his claws against the windowsill, followed by the rustle of the oak tree outside as my familiar flees the current situation. And to think that only a short while ago Nero scoffed at the thought of my bringing boys over. I'd say the joke's on him, except I'm the one who's half dead yet still enjoying the touch of my enemy.

So the joke is most definitely on me.

Memnon's hand continues to move over me, skimming along my back, and it feels so damn good, it should be illegal. Up and down, up and down. The longer it goes, the more restless I get.

Not enough.

"*More*," I plead so softly, I'm not sure he can hear me. The truth is that I'm not at all confident in making demands of him. Not after everything he's already done for me tonight.

His hand stills, and there's a long pause.

"What was that?" he says.

I'm not going to say it again. I'm not—

"*More*," I say again, louder.

After a moment, Memnon's hand moves again. "More what?" he says, and now I swear there's a wicked edge to his words, as though he's toying with me. But I can't be sure.

I shift under his hand, my skin so sensitive. "I—I don't know," I admit, my eyes still closed.

I feel the brush of his lips against my ear. "You should never ask me for things you do not mean, Empress," he says, his voice pitched low. "But I think you *do* know what you want more of. And I think it frightens you."

I swallow, goose bumps breaking out along my flesh.

A second passes. Then two, then three.

"Do you still want more?" Memnon breathes against me.

I don't even bother lying to myself. "Yes."

Memnon doesn't respond, but several seconds later, the bed dips, and I feel his powerful thighs on either side of my own.

His hands return to my back, kneading my muscles. It feels erotic, even though it shouldn't. It's just a back massage.

There is no reason why I should be getting turned on

by this. But moldy fucking toadstools, I am getting turned on. There's an ache between my legs. And it's growing and growing.

"Next time, *est amage*, I will make you tell me what you want—"

A moan slips out of me. I don't mean for it to escape, but there it is.

Behind me, Memnon pauses.

"Then again," he says, "that works too."

Blood rushes to my cheeks, but I refuse to be embarrassed.

I begin to flip over, and Memnon lifts himself a little so I can finish turning onto my back. I stare up at the ancient king.

From this position he looks impossibly big, his shoulders massive, his torso made from muscle and sinew alone. And that wicked face, with his sharp cheekbones and gleaming eyes.

I draw in a shaky breath. "You want to know what I want?"

What's one more bad decision?

I sit up, hook an arm around his neck, and pull Memnon to me, and then I kiss him.

He tastes like sin and nostalgia. I thread my fingers into his hair, pulling him down as I fall back against my bed.

With a groan he sinks onto me, his mouth searing against mine. I've kissed him more than once, and yet this feels like the first true one we've had. His tongue strokes mine, and I remember all over again how much more electric everything is with this sorcerer.

I grind against him, feeling his rigid length trapped between us. He moves against me, and I gasp at the contact, every nerve awakening.

Goddess, how had I not noticed before that this man is

pure, unadulterated sex? The muscles, the tattoos, the sheer coiled ferocity that is so tightly restrained.

This is a man who *fucks*. Hard.

And I am here for it.

Unfortunately, the moment I have the thought, Memnon breaks off the kiss.

His smoky-amber eyes are lust drunk as they stare down at me, and his breathing is ragged. He's looking at my mouth like he's about to devour me whole, and I am 100 percent on board with the prospect.

He blinks a few times, then extricates himself from my body.

I want to weep at the loss of his weight and heat. And his mouth. Especially his mouth. I want to kiss him until the sun rises.

"Sleep, my queen. You used a lot of magic and lost a lot of blood," he says, getting off the bed. "You need sleep, not..." His eyes drop to my mouth. "Not anything else," he finishes adamantly.

Memnon reaches for the blankets beneath me and tugs them out from under my body.

I catch his wrist. "Where are you going?" I hate that I sound desperate. I hate that this man has gone from my stalker to my savior. But the truth is this house doesn't feel safe—not since I realized there's a persecution tunnel that opens directly into this building.

Memnon's expression turns fierce, even while his eyes soften. "Nowhere," he vows. "I will stay here, in this room, watching over you and keeping you safe until you wake."

I don't let go of his wrist. I want him in this bed next to me. I'm positive that's the only way I'm going to sleep at all, despite my exhaustion.

Memnon must see it in my eyes.

"Don't ask me for things you do not mean," he warns me again.

I *do* mean what I'm thinking. That's the real problem. My intuition is telling me that this violent, wicked man is safe, and I'm too tired to disagree.

"Stay with me," I say, tugging him closer.

Memnon takes the hand holding his wrist into his own hands, and he presses a kiss to my knuckles, closing his eyes. He looks like he's fighting himself on something, though I cannot say what.

After a moment, he lays my hand on the bed, then presses his palm to my head.

"*Sleep*," he says.

I feel the gentle brush of Memnon's magic and then nothing else.

CHAPTER 30

I blink my eyes open as late-morning sunlight streams into my room. I hear the distant sound of my coven sisters chatting down the hall and in the communal bathroom as they get ready for class.

I stretch, feeling Nero at my back. That's when the pain awakens.

I groan.

Everything hurts. My arms and back and legs ache from the strain of carrying the shifter girl so far. My muscles are overtaxed, but that is *nothing* compared to the stabbing pain in my head and the nausea rolling through my stomach.

I overused my magic. And then I overused Memnon's magic.

I let out another pained sound. At my back, Nero moves, and the arm that's draped over my waist migrates to my forehead.

Wait. *Arm?*

I'm drawn back against a broad hard chest, and that hand

turns my head so a set of lips can brush a kiss against my temple.

"*Ease the pain. Remove the ache*," Memnon murmurs against my skin.

I suck in a breath at his voice. He stayed with me—I asked him to…

Last night comes back to me, even as my migraine and the rest of my bodily pains disappear.

Goddess, *last night*. Despite the massive amounts of memory I must've burned through, last night comes back to me in full detail—the spell circle, the chase, the witches I fought and the monster I shattered, the brief interaction with a man from the Marin Pack, and then Memnon.

Memnon.

Memnon carrying me. Memnon caring *for* me.

The whole night takes my breath away, but this last part most of all. He's supposed to be my enemy, but nothing about last night fit that narrative. He gave me his magic, then came for me and healed me. And I kissed him. And now he's in my bed.

Just as I think it, his fingers run through my hair. There's something so intimate about the gesture. The fact there's no sexual angle to it confuses me more. I've dabbled in physical intimacy with men, but I'm not used to…this. Intimacy without some sexual motivation.

Maybe that's why I melt under the touch. Apparently, I really like this sort of intimacy. And irony of all ironies, it's waking my body in an entirely different way.

"I've got you, *est amage*," he breathes, still stroking my hair, clearly unaware that my mind is in the gutter.

I flip around, wincing a little as I feel the faintest twinge through my various muscles.

My eyes meet his. His hair is mussed from sleep. It's disarming, and it makes him look a smidge less intimidating.

But just a smidge.

Memnon lost his shirt somewhere between last night and this morning, and this from close, I can say with absolute authority that his body is a masterpiece, coiled muscles stacked on coiled muscles. The tattoos and scars only serve to make it look that much more lethal and appealing.

I force my gaze up to his.

"You stayed," I say.

He runs a hand through his sleep-mussed hair, and the action is so goddess-damned sexy. He is so goddess-damned sexy.

"Of course I stayed," he says, as though there was never another option. My blood heats at the fervency in his voice.

I want to touch him. Everything in me wants to touch and feel and mark and claim this man who looks like my own personal wet dream. Before I can act on any of these fantasies, the arm around my waist drags me forward, and then his mouth is on mine.

Memnon's kisses, I'm coming to discover, are just as intense as every other part of him. His mouth moves over mine almost frantically. He kisses me like he may lose me at any moment.

"Little witch," he says against my lips, "you cannot look at me like that and expect me to keep my mouth to myself." The sentiment is punctuated by another devastating sweep of his mouth.

I eagerly meet each stroke of his lips with my own.

"You taste so fucking good, mate," he says. "And you feel real like nothing else has since I woke." He gathers me closer—

Off to the side of the bed, my phone buzzes, interrupting the moment. I bite back several colorful curses as I pull away.

Reluctantly, Memnon lets me go, but the look in his eyes makes it clear that he's not done with me.

I trip out of bed, belatedly aware that I'm still only in a bra and undies and Memnon is getting an eyeful. I reach for last night's bloody, shredded pants, where the sound of my phone is coming from. It's only as I'm digging the phone out of my jeans that I realize I had it with me the entire time last night. Not that I had a spare moment to place a call between the witches and the clay creature.

"Hello?" I say, bringing the phone to my ear.

"Selene Bowers?" the voice on the other end says.

"Yes, who's this?"

"This is Officer Howahkan. We had a meeting scheduled for a half hour ago, but you never showed."

My stomach drops. "What meeting?" What does the Politia want with me?

There's a pause on the line. "We wanted to follow up and ask you a few more questions regarding the death of Miss Evensen."

I know Charlotte was killed, but—

"I'm sorry, but what does her death have to do with me?"

There's another long stretch of silence, long enough for me to realize that whatever the officer is talking about, I should remember it.

"You discovered her body," he finally says.

"*What?*" I nearly yell into the phone. *I was the one who found Charlotte's body?*

Out of the corner of my eye, I see Memnon watching me like a hawk. I cross my arms over my chest and turn away from him, feeling like between my exposed flesh and this conversation, he's seeing entirely too much of me.

There's more tense silence on the other end of the line.

"I'm so sorry," I apologize, staring down at the scuffed-up floorboards. "I… My magic eats my memories." I draw in a long breath. "Did I really find a body?"

I glance over my shoulder at Memnon, but he wears an unreadable expression.

Another pause from the officer. "Yes."

I almost don't believe him. I know there's been a string of killings recently—I do remember that—I even remember running with Sybil and seeing the crime scene tape for one such killing—but to hear I actually *discovered* one of the bodies? That seems like too big a memory for my magic to expunge.

I head over to my desk, where my planner is laid out. But I don't even know what day to look at.

Why do I not know what day it is?

"What's today's date?" I ask, trying to keep my voice steady.

"It's October fifteenth."

I find today's date, and sure enough, there's a 10:00 a.m. interview with the Politia written into it.

Hells' fucking spells.

"Can I come over now?" I ask.

"That's fine." The officer sounds like he's beyond ready to end this call. "We'll see you soon."

I hang up the phone, still staring at my planner, a scowl on my face.

"Little witch, your memory…"

I glance over at Memnon, who's now sitting up in my bed, looking completely at home and entirely out of place.

His eyes are exceedingly soft as they search mine. "It has left you defenseless."

I fold my arms over my chest. "I am *not* defenseless."

He scowls at me. "I have spent my entire life strategizing. I know a vulnerable position when I see one."

I glare at him. "You don't know anything about my life."

"Not this one, no, but your last one...I have it memorized by heart."

The look he's giving me is too intense.

"I'm not Roxilana." Of course, I remember that random name and not, you know, the dead body I apparently discovered some time ago.

Memnon doesn't say anything to that, and his expression gives nothing away. I can't say what his feelings are on the topic.

But that's an issue for another time.

I turn my attention back to my planner. There are other things written in it, like the Samhain Witches' Ball, which is two weeks from now, that I've literally never heard of. And then there's a paper due on Wednesday on the use of fresh versus dried ingredients in spellwork. Sounds boring as shit, and maybe that's why I have no recollection of the thing.

I flip to the previous week, and I read off everything I scheduled. To my horror, I can only remember a couple of events, like the lycanthrope party I attended with Sybil. But even that memory is mostly gone; only the end of the evening stands out, when Memnon attacked Kane. The dozen or so other events I wrote in might as well be for someone else; I recognize none of them.

I make a small noise. Has the memory loss ever been this bad?

"What's the matter?" Memnon's voice is right behind me. I jolt at the sound of it. I don't know how he managed to sneak up on me.

I turn and get an eyeful of his chest.

"Selene?"

I glance up at him. Gone is the vicious man I've come to know. He looks genuinely concerned.

"My memories over the past week," I say softly. "Most of them are gone."

My hands shake, and my eyes well with tears. Damn it, I'm not going to cry. I saved a girl's life last night. What are a few memories compared to that?

This is why I have my system in place. I'll figure it out.

I let out a pathetic sniffle, one that Memnon had to hear.

"Ugh," I say, swallowing. "I'm sor—"

Memnon gathers me to him, pulling me into a hug. "Don't finish that sentence, little witch. You don't ever need to apologize to me—not for this."

My face is pressed against his massive chest, his body enveloping mine. I don't let myself overthink the moment; instead, I wrap my arms around his torso and hold him close. It feels so good to be held.

"Thank you," I say softly. "For your magic—and bringing me back here."

Only now is it really registering that he stayed at my side the entire night. And hell must've frozen over because all I feel right now is relief that this terrifying human kept me safe.

He squeezes me tighter.

Unlike the past week, the events of last night are still very vivid, and the longer I'm in his arms, the more my mind drifts to them. I have a fuzzy memory of a shifter taking the girl—Cara—from me, but where is she now? Is she okay?

I'm not sure how to even go about finding out.

Then there was that monster. I can't even begin to fathom what it actually was or how it was sentient. Only that the priestess seemed to control it.

I don't even know if I actually destroyed it; the priestess managed to repair it once. Perhaps it could be repaired again.

Then I remember the witches who confronted me in the forest and in that odd grimoire room.

Then the rest of the night's carnage comes back.

Nero tore chunks out of several of them. Those he didn't, the *lamassu* attacked.

I can still see the witches' slumped forms lying in the woods.

"My attackers…" I begin.

One of Memnon's hands moves to my chin, and he tilts my face up to his.

"You don't have to worry about that. They're being dealt with."

I go still. "What do you mean 'they're being dealt with'?" My breath is coming in shallower and shallower pants.

There's a calculating gleam in his eyes. "I told you last night to mark your enemies. The ones you did mark, I found. What I do with them now…you don't need to concern yourself with that."

His words, which I think were supposed to be placating, only serve to spike my anxiety.

"Who *are* you?" My gaze searches his.

He smiles at me again, and there's a vicious edge to it, despite the softness in his eyes. "You already know who I am. You may be the only person who truly knows, *est amage*." *My queen.*

I push away from him then and run my hands through

my hair. "I need to speak with the Politia, and I need a shower and to change—and breakfast would be nice."

Memnon stares down at me, and the affectionate look in his eyes is unsettling. I sense that last night changed things between us for him as well.

"My spell took away your pain, but you need to rest, Selene." Already, he's trying to turn me around and steer me back to my bed. "I will bring you breakfast. The Politia can wait."

Crap. You let an ancient supernatural king stay with you for one night and lend you his power, and suddenly, he gets all bossy and presumptuous.

Going to need to nip this in the bud.

"Um"—I put a hand on Memnon's chest, my insides squealing at his warm skin and hard muscles—"*no*."

That sparkle in Memnon's eyes is still there, but he definitely looks irritated. "What, exactly, are you disagreeing with?"

I huff out a breath. "Listen, I don't know how they did things back when they were busy inventing the wheel, but you don't get to tell me what to do. Also—" I give his chest a gentle shove. He doesn't so much as budge. "Last night and this morning were nice, but now you have to go."

Maybe if I hustle him out fast enough, we won't have to discuss the fact I'm seriously in his debt for all the magic he lent me.

Memnon narrows his eyes at me, though the corner of his mouth curls upward. He parts his lips to speak.

"Uh-uh." I shake my head. "You don't get to say whatever evil little thought gave you that look. Just"—another little push that gets me nowhere—"*scoot*."

Memnon catches my hands, trapping them against his

chest. Very deliberately, he steps into my space, and I am suddenly very aware of his naked torso and my skimpy lingerie.

"I will leave you on one condition, *mate*."

I grind my teeth. I didn't realize getting a sorcerer out of my room required *conditions*.

"You must vow to keep yourself safe."

That's...I guess I can do that. "I swear I'll keep myself safe," I say. Then I force a big fake smile. "Good?"

Memnon's gaze drops to my lips, and those eyes narrow again. But after a moment, he nods at my words. And now he's giving me that affectionate look again. It makes my skin heat and my core clench.

He releases my hands, but just as soon as they've left, his mouth finds mine, kissing me with all the command of the warlord king he claims to be.

I melt against those lips, the taste of him intoxicating. My hands fall to his waist, and I draw my fingers over his tattoos.

This man is one big walking Bad Idea, and I'm learning from last night that I have a weakness for them.

Memnon pulls away. He drags the pad of his thumb over my lower lip. "Keep your vow, little witch," he says.

With one final soft look, the sorcerer leaves me.

CHAPTER 31

"What were you doing out in the Everwoods on the night of October tenth?" Officer Howahkan asks, staring at me across the white table, his long dark hair pulled back in a braid.

The interrogation room is small, plain—it looks like every other bland, ominous interrogation room I've seen on TV. The only difference is that the walls of this one are lined with spells. They shimmer and jiggle a little when I focus on them.

I've only been in the Politia's interrogation room for five minutes, but I already feel the magic on those four walls closing in on me.

"I can't remember," I say.

I reach a hand down and stroke my familiar. Nero bumps my hand, giving me the courage I so desperately need.

I still haven't reported what happened last night, and now I'm not sure whether I should. Except for Kasey, I don't know the names of the witches who attacked me.

Officer Howahkan sighs. "In your earlier testimony, you

said the following: 'He tracked blood into my room. When I realized it wasn't his, I decided to follow the trail back to its source.' Do you deny that now?" The officer glances up from his notes, his eyes piercing.

"No, I'm sure I knew what I was talking about at the time."

The officer gives me a foul look, like I'm giving him an attitude. "Yet you can no longer tell me anything about the incident."

"I can't remember anything about it," I clarify. "I'm not trying to withhold memories from you on purpose."

Officer Howahkan holds my gaze. Despite the enchantments in the room that compel me to speak the truth, I get the distinct impression he doesn't believe me.

His eyes drop to Nero. "That's your familiar?"

Nero stares up at the officer, looking wholly unamused with this situation.

"Yeah, he is," I say.

"He's a panther?"

"Yes..." *Don't know where this is going.*

"I imagine your panther hunts in those woods."

My brows come together. "Are you accusing my familiar of killing Charlotte?" The thought is horrifying.

I put a hand on said panther.

"*No,*" the officer says emphatically. "A human killed the witch, not an animal. But still, I'm curious about the order of events you describe in your original testimony."

"The order of events?" I echo.

"You say you saw blood and followed your familiar back to a body. One could rearrange that timeline to suggest you came from the body to your room, then discovered your familiar dragged evidence back to your doorstep, so you returned and reported the incident to make yourself look innocent."

I can't seem to take a full breath of air, and I feel myself paling.

"Are you suggesting *I* killed this woman?" I whisper, horrified.

I thought this was just some routine questioning.

Officer Howahkan shakes his head. "As a homicide investigator, I have to cast doubt on every single person and look at the evidence from all angles. Unfortunately, your memory loss doesn't help clear you."

"I didn't choose to erase these memories," I say hotly. "I don't get that luxury, something you'd know if you pulled any of my files from Peel Academy or from Henbane Coven.

"You want my alibi?" I fish my planner out of my bag. "Here, you can look at this." I plop the thing on the table.

Officer Howahkan slides it over to his side, and after a moment, he thumbs through it.

He stops on a particular day and studies the notes I have written down.

"There's nothing here that covers the time of the murders," he says.

"I have other planners," I respond. I usually have several going at once. This is just my most functional one. "I don't have them with me, but I could bring them here if you need them."

My nerves fray as it settles in: I'm a suspect in a murder investigation.

The officer slides the planner aside. "Let's move away from Miss Evensen's case for a moment, shall we?"

I exhale, then nod.

"This isn't the first time you've seen one of these murdered witches, is it?" he says.

I tilt my head a little as Officer Howahkan flips through

the papers on his clipboard and taps something he sees. "I don't know what you mean."

He grabs a pen and again taps the sheet of paper he's looking at. "I see here that you were interviewed at the scene of one of the other murders."

My breath catches as I remember there was something with Sybil. I have a murky memory of crime scene tape and the forest around Henbane, but as I reach for more, I…I think I might've seen something, but maybe my mind is just making that up? I can't be certain.

"I'm sorry," I apologize. "I—" The spells on the room won't allow me to say I don't remember because, technically, I do have a little memory. "I think there was something in the woods behind Henbane—I remember the yellow tape—but there's really not anything else."

"So this memory is gone too?" His gaze is steady on me, steady and accusing. "That seems awfully convenient."

"No," I respond, "considering we're talking about clearing my name, I'd say it's rather *inconvenient*."

Officer Howahkan's eyes continue to linger on me for a beat too long before his attention returns to his papers. "It says here that you and a woman named Sybil Andalucia were jogging on a trail that bisected the crime scene. One of my colleagues stopped and questioned you."

I'm at the mercy of those notes; I have no recollection of the incident.

I lift a shoulder. "My friend and I sometimes go for a morning run." When we're feeling particularly empowered—or self-punishing. "But I don't remember that one in particular."

"Hmm," he replies. "Seems as though you were in the wrong place at the wrong time on two different occasions," he says.

A sick feeling churns in my stomach at the underlying insinuation—that maybe this was no coincidence at all.

This is just what investigators do, I try to tell myself. *They press at cracks, knowing only the suspicious break.*

Except memory loss makes me particularly brittle, guilty or not.

For a moment, I peer into the dark spots of my own mind, questioning myself. I cannot know what I have forgotten.

Officer Howahkan must sense the direction of my thoughts because he sets his clipboard aside and leans forward, folding his hands in front of him. "Ms. Bowers, I am going to ask you a hypothetical question. This is not an accusation; I am just curious: Could it be possible you were involved with these deaths and simply don't remember?"

The mere thought makes the room tilt. I feel lightheaded and queasy with unease.

I shake my head, forcing down my rising panic. "That's not who I am," I say hoarsely.

"How do you truly know?"

How do you truly know?

I rub my arms, his words making me feel dirty from the inside out. "My mind and my conscience aren't the same thing. I can forget what I've done without forgetting who I am."

Of course I didn't kill those women.

But you might have killed some last night, my mind whispers. *And Memnon may be finishing the job right at this moment.*

"Am I being accused of murder?" I say softly, my insides all twisted. "Because if I am, I need a lawyer."

Officer Howahkan shakes his head, sitting back in his seat. "No, Ms. Bowers, we were merely entertaining another hypothetical."

"Right," I say warily.

"Well, Ms. Bowers, that's all we need for now. Can we keep this planner of yours?" he asks, tapping his fingers on it.

I open my mouth to agree but then hesitate. "I need that for class." To be honest, I need it for *everything*. I have my life in there, and judging by how many memories I recently lost, I'm going to rely on it more than ever. "I can stay longer if you want to make photocopies of it or take pictures of my entries."

Officer Howahkan nods. "We'll do that. You said there were more of these?" he asks.

I nod.

"Would you be open to letting us see those if the need arises?"

If I become a major suspect, he means.

I chew my lower lip. "That's fine." I mean, sharing my notebooks is no small thing—the thought of officers handling them and reading them and possibly keeping them as evidence has my anxiety spiking, but I also don't want to seem guilty.

Because I'm not. I'd know if I were.

I think.

CHAPTER 32

I'm sitting at my desk, the two paragraphs I've managed to write so far on the magical differences between dried lavender versus fresh all but forgotten as I stare at my bank account.

Overdrawn.

My insides curdle at my bank account details.

Empress…

I sense Memnon a second later. I don't know how, but I feel him moving up the stairs of my house like this place is his own, and I swear the witches in the house go quiet in his wake. Guests aren't supposed to freely come and go in this residence hall—but he's not exactly the sort of guy who gives a fuck about the rules.

Less than a minute later, the door opens and Memnon strides in. I try not to notice how damn enticing he looks in a simple T-shirt and jeans. But on his staggering frame, with all his olive-toned skin and elaborate tattoos peeking out, he makes the simple attire look sexy and edgy.

"Knocking would be nice," I say, gathering my legs up on my chair.

Assuming he knows what a knock is. I bet Memnon predates the invention of manners.

"Perhaps it would be if we didn't already have a bond," he says. "It's better than a knock."

"We're not bonded," I say.

Memnon idly kicks my door closed with one of his boots. "We're in denial again, I see."

"It's only denial if it's true," I say, my gaze flicking over him. "And it's not."

He lifts an eyebrow as he crosses the room.

"You know, stalking is a crime," I say.

"You think that would deter me? I have already hunted you once before," he says, a lock of his dark hair slipping over one eye. He looks to be the very definition of a villain.

I shiver.

"What happened?" I ask. "When you hunted me?"

He looks pleased that I asked.

Memnon steps in close. "I took you as my bride." He brushes my lower lip with his thumb, just like he did when we last parted ways. He's gazing at me like he's remembering what it felt like to hold me.

I mean, Roxilana.

"I made you my queen, gave you riches and an ever-expanding empire."

"Yes, yes, we've been over this many times," I say. "And yet you expect me to believe Roxilana screwed you over."

I mean, if someone volunteered to be my sugar daddy and he was this pretty, I don't think I'd bury him alive.

Then again, Memnon is a douche.

I might bury a douche.

Maybe this Roxilana chick was on to something.

Memnon frowns, his previous good humor long gone. "You promised me answers," he says, folding his arms over his chest. "I want them."

Answers…it takes me a moment to remember I did agree to that and a moment longer to realize Memnon doesn't actually know any of the details surrounding what happened last night. He just saved my ass and then patched me up.

As I gather my thoughts, the sorcerer peers beyond me at the web page open on my computer, catching an eyeful of the sorry state of my bank account.

I reach out and close my laptop.

"Money trouble?" he asks, his face unreadable.

"How do you even know about online banking?" I ask him suspiciously. "And modern currency for that matter?"

My gaze flicks over his shirt and jeans and down to his leather boots. Now I *do* wonder how the sorcerer is getting by.

"Do you really want to have that talk right now, *est amage*? I'm not sure you'd like my answers."

I stare up at him warily. I know he can riffle through a person's mind—I remember him doing it to my own—so I know he has ways of seeing the modern world through others' eyes. I don't know why that would worry me…

Before I can help it, I rub my face. "It's fine. Everything will be fine." It's less an answer and more a pep talk.

Memnon doesn't say anything to that, and somehow, his silence makes my money situation feel all the more hopeless.

"The people last night—they were going to pay me," I say. It's a decent enough place to start. "It was some magical gig I agreed to so I could help pay for Nero's food."

Memnon frowns, his attention moving to my panther,

who is sprawled out on my bed. "It costs a lot to feed him," the sorcerer agrees, approaching the bed to pet the big cat. "I remember."

Nero leans his head into the touch, eating up Memnon's attention.

"It's fine," I repeat, though my voice cracks.

It's not fine, and I'm trying not to think about the very real possibility of being unable to feed Nero.

Memnon glances over at me, and he has a look in his eye like he's scheming.

He moves away from my familiar. "Tell me the rest of what happened last night," he demands. "Leave nothing out."

It doesn't take long to tell Memnon the whole story. He leans against one of my walls, arms folded, as he listens to the entire thing, a menacing look on his face.

"...And that's where you found me," I finish.

It feels good to share this with him. I haven't had a chance to tell Sybil, nor have I dared to write the event down—not when there are incriminating details and the Politia is interested in my notebooks.

A muscle in Memnon's jaw keeps jumping.

"The spell circle," he finally says. "It took place in this house?"

I nod. The mention of it has my pulse speeding. I remember all over again how there's a direct tunnel into our house, one those masked witches can easily use even now.

I'm not going to think about the fact they may even be fellow coven sisters. That thought is downright chilling. As it is, I have to live with the fact Kasey was one of them.

Kasey, whom I haven't heard from since last night.

"Take me to where the spell circle happened," Memnon commands.

I should be bristling at the order. Instead, the sorcerer feels like a rudder keeping me on course.

I leave my room and lead Memnon through the house. Several witches see us pass, and one by one, they fall silent as they take in the man at my back. He's huge and ferociously beautiful, and I'm sure they can sense the danger rolling off him.

I catch sight of their expressions, and while some look a little nervous, they also seem…interested?

Immediately, my hackles rise, and a little bit of my magic sifts out of me, thickening in the air.

Shit, Selene, are you getting jealous over your wicked stalker?

An arm wraps around my chest, and I'm drawn back against Memnon.

A moment later his lips are at my ear. "Possessiveness looks good on you, mate," he says, nipping my ear.

I glare at him over my shoulder before pushing his arm away. "I'm not your mate," I whisper under my breath. "And don't bite my ear."

Memnon's eyes twinkle. "At least you're not in denial about being possessive," he says, those sensual lips curving into a smirk. "We can agree on that."

I'm about to argue with him on that, but then we pass another witch who gives Memnon a moonstruck look, and I turn my glare at her.

I hear soft prideful laughter at my back.

"Shut up."

I may be a little possessive.

CHAPTER 33

When we get to the Ritual Room, I let Memnon in first, holding the door open before following him inside.

His boots echo against the floor as he peers around, taking in the dark walls and the rows of chairs.

I head over to the back of the room, the hairs along my arms rising as the previous night comes back to me.

"We went through this wall," I say, touching the solid surface that glimmers faintly as the spells running along it catch the light. For a moment, I marvel that magic can make doorways appear and disappear at will.

Memnon comes over to me before stopping so close that his shoulder brushes mine.

My breath escapes me in a rush, and I feel a fevered urge to reach for him and taste him all over again. I've only kissed him, but I've dreamed of more. How would the real thing hold up against my imagination?

Memnon glances over at me, arching an eyebrow.

"What?" I say defensively.

Did he hear those thoughts?

He shakes his head and returns his attention to the wall. He runs a hand over it, and I get to appreciate the golden ring he wears and his scarred forearms—

Stop getting distracted by the pretty man, Selene.

Dropping his hand, Memnon turns, looking as though he's going to walk away. All at once he spins back around and slams his fist into the wall.

His indigo magic explodes outward at the impact, and there's a sound like hard candy crushing beneath a boot.

A split second later, I realize that's the sound of the ward shattering. As soon as it's gone, the wall disappears, revealing the opening once more.

I stare, aghast, first at the opening, then at Memnon.

"I've never seen someone use their power like that," I say.

The sorcerer catches me by the chin and flashes me a soft, playful smile. "Yes, you have little witch. Long ago."

Before I can argue with him, Memnon drops his hand from my chin and turns his attention back to the archway.

He clucks his tongue. "Someone's been naughty, hiding a back entrance into your house." Despite the light tone of his words, I see his eyes harden and his features grow sharp.

He crosses the threshold, heading toward the staircase.

I hesitate, fear souring the back of my throat. I don't want to go back there.

It feels as though those witches are still lurking at the bottom of that staircase, waiting for another chance to nab me.

Memnon, on the other hand, looks as though he'd enjoy nothing more than a nice confrontation. He begins to descend, not bothering to coax me along.

Without thinking, I reach for Memnon's magic, just as I did last night, needing the reassurance of his power.

It's there, just as endless as it was last night. I don't know how a single body can house so much magic or how much of his conscience he offered up for it all.

"I can feel myself inside you, soul mate," Memnon calls up the bottom of the stairway, a smile in his voice. "You can draw me into you whenever you like."

My core clenches at the offer, and my face heats. "I'm not your—That's not why—" I draw in a deep breath, frustrated that he has me flustered. "I'm just nervous about coming back to this place."

His footfalls pause.

"Come to me, Selene," he says gently, his words soft and enticing.

Despite how much his orders annoy me, and despite my fear, I move toward those stairs, then down them, not stopping until I get to Memnon, who stands to the side of the staircase.

He places a hand on my cheek. "Do I terrify you, little witch?"

"Yes," I say without hesitation.

"And how fearsome would my equal have to be?" he asks.

I shake my head, not sure how to answer. "They'd have to be very powerful and frightening to be your equal," I finally say.

Memnon strokes my skin with his thumb. "I'm staring at her now."

"I'm not—"

"You *are*," he insists.

I part my mouth to protest further, but he says, "I know you are afraid, but you are underestimating your own strength, *est amage*. I have seen that strength many times, and you saw it yourself last night, when you were one against many. *You* are the frightening thing."

He pulls me in closer. "But you can always draw on my power if it pleases you. As I said, I like being in you."

His words should fluster me, but whatever is going on between the two of us, it leaves no room for embarrassment.

I stare into Memnon's luminous brown eyes. "Why are you being so nice to me?" I whisper.

His eyes are soulful. "If there is one answer that should be obvious to you, it's that one."

I sneak a glance at his wicked mouth. As I stare, it spreads into a smile.

"Does my queen wish to kiss me?"

"Maybe," I say honestly.

Memnon leans in close, that mouth no more than an inch from mine. "Have I told you how much I like the taste of your lips?" he says softly. "Like honeyed wine. It makes me eager to taste other parts of you. I bet they are even sweeter…"

Heat rushes to my cheeks. "God damn it, Memnon, you need to stop—" I haven't even finished the sentence when he grabs me around my waist and lifts me into his arms.

I give a little yelp as he carries me across the room and into the adjoining hallway.

"You're so godsdamned pretty when you're flustered. Does my dirty talk embarrass you?" he asks, staring up at me.

Yes. "You're still a stranger to me," I say, as the candles around us flare to life.

"I'm not," Memnon insists, leading us down the curving hallway. "You know I'm not. I'm your mate, and I've waited a very, very long time to reunite with you."

He lowers me just enough to put my ear close to his mouth.

"I really can't wait to taste you again, Empress," he confesses. "I want to know if even after two thousand years, you make the same sounds when you come against my tongue. Or if you can still ride my cock better than I ride my steed."

Maiden, Mother, and Crone.

"I am *not* talking about this with you." I wiggle, trying to get out of his arms.

With a low, husky laugh, he sets me down. I back away from him, feeling all sorts of hot and bothered. But already, his eyes have moved from me to the rest of the room.

And that's about when I realize we're in *the room where it all happened*. He managed to distract me for the entire walk here, and I have no idea whether he did it deliberately to ease my fear or if he simply wanted to taunt me.

Now, as I watch Memnon, I can see his good mood drain away and the cold, merciless king he once was seep through.

He paces around the room, studying the space.

I glance around myself, my pulse climbing. The first thing I notice is that the shoes I wore are gone. First I feel annoyance—I only had a few pairs to begin with, and I have no money to replace them now—but then dread pools low in my stomach.

Witches can use a person's belongings for all sorts of things—curses and hexes among them.

"What is it?" Memnon says, turning to me. "I can tell you're nervous."

I want to be indignant, but instead, curiosity gets the better of me. "How can you tell that?" I ask.

"Bonds go both ways, *est amage*." Memnon flashes me a challenging look, daring me to defy his words.

I'm tired of arguing this with him, so I simply say, "I left shoes down here. They're gone now. That's why I'm nervous."

He gives me a careful nod, even as tension coils in him. Turning back around, he continues to inspect the room. There's nothing here. The room is bare of every single item the witches down here came with. There are no bloodstains left behind from the priestess, and there's no debris from the magical explosion I set off.

"This place has been scrubbed," Memnon says, echoing my thoughts.

He glances down one of the hallways that branch from the room. I think he's going to do more exploring, and I cannot help the dread I feel at moving through those tunnels all over again.

The sorcerer turns instead and comes back to me.

"I've seen enough," he says quietly. "We can go back up, Empress."

After letting out a relieved breath, I try not to hustle too quickly back to the stairs, even though I'm not fooling either of us.

"Why did you want to come down here?" I ask as I head up the spiral staircase.

"Your enemies are my own," Memnon replies. "Some have been dealt with"—that is a terrifying thing to hear—"and some have not. *Those* are the ones I want to understand."

I take a deep breath. "You keep saying I have enemies, but I've never done anything bad in my life." *Besides waking you up…*

"Tell me, *est amage*, how did you learn of this spell circle?" he asks at my back.

This…this is another frightening detail I haven't spent much time focusing on. "A coven sister let me know about it."

"How did she let you know of it?"

I try to focus on that, and the memory feels as though it's just within grasp, but then—

"I can't remember. All I know is that her name is Kasey, and she lives in my house."

"Kasey." He tests her name on his lips. "She lives in this house?"

I swallow. "Yeah."

There's a long ominous silence following that. I don't really want to know what Memnon's thinking.

"She brought you to the spell circle?" he asks as I step off the stairs.

"Yeah," I say again, heading back over to the Ritual Room. It looks especially dark from this angle.

"Did she bring anyone else along?" Memnon asks at my back.

I turn to him. "No."

"So you were singled out," he says, his expression severe. "Someone wanted you and *specifically* you to be at that circle last night. That means you do have enemies, Selene. You just don't know who they are—yet. But they are clearly aware of you."

Goose bumps burst to life along my skin.

Memnon crosses into the Ritual Room and stops at my side. "You have worried enough on this for now, little witch. Stay guarded, but let me shoulder the burden."

That sounds…really nice.

There's that word again. *Nice.* Memnon is not *nice.* It's not in his nature. Especially not to me, regardless of his pretty words about being mates.

"I will find who thought to hurt you," he continues, "and they will *suffer* for it."

"Please don't hurt anyone," I say.

He flashes me an amused look. "Have the years softened you, my queen?"

"I'm not your queen," I say.

He gives me another look like I'm precious, then turns his attention to the archway. "Someone thought to control who can sneak unnoticed into and out of your home. Why don't we turn their little trick back on them?" Memnon says to me, a calculated gleam in his eye.

He holds out his hand to me, palm up. It's an open invitation to spellcast with this man.

I've used his power and fought it too. I've never deliberately mixed mine with it. I find that more than desiring safety and revenge, I'm eager to feel Memnon's magic meld with mine.

I take his hand, facing the opening once more. Beneath my palm, my magic stirs to life. I'm still recovering from the power drain last night, but at the press of Memnon's hand against mine, it wakes, twining around his fingers and wrist like a lover's caress.

The sorcerer glances at our joined hands, his features pleased. His eyes rise and lock with mine, and for a moment, I'm somewhere else, somewhere where endless blue sky meets endless fields of wheat. Memnon wears that scale armor, his hair blowing in the breeze.

Just as quickly as it appears, the image is gone.

"*Est amage?*" Memnon says. *My queen.*

Yes. His queen.

Wait, *no*.

"Are you ready?" he asks, furrowing his brow.

I swallow, then nod, facing the archway.

I feel Memnon's eyes on me for a moment longer before he too turns his attention to the opening.

A second later, his magic blooms to life, the dark blue plumes of it rolling off his body.

"*From the seed of the air and the womb of the earth, I call forth creation. Fashion a wall to match those that surround it,*" Memnon says, reverting to his mother tongue.

I feel our magic mixing where our hands touch. Memnon pulls on it, drawing my power into him.

I gasp at the sensation. Like he mentioned earlier, I can feel him *in* me, his own essence grasping mine, twisting my magic around his own. It leaves me breathless.

He continues. *"Create an illusion made real to all who look upon it and all who touch it. Only we, your creators, shall hold the power to bring down such an illusion. By our command at the word* reveal, *you shall fall away."*

Our joined magic swirls together, making a deep purple color, one you might see at the end of sunset. It's coalescing in front of us, fitting itself to the archway then smoothing out. The smoky appearance of our power solidifies and the color of it darkens.

"And at our command, conceal, *you shall return to your false form."*

Need to write these words down—hell, I need to write this whole *experience* down—before I forget.

"Mask all traces of this spell so they blend in with those around us."

The words Memnon's using are simple enough, but the amount of power and magical precision it takes to actually execute any of this is astronomical.

As more of my magic seeps out and joins with Memnon's, I stare in awe. Memnon is a master at what he does, as talented as he is thorough and devious.

The shimmering residue left behind in the spell's wake

takes on the same pale sheen that matches the other wards and enchantments placed around the room. If I stared really, really hard, I'd see that the edges of it are laced a dusky deep purple—because not even the best spells can completely override their innate truth.

But this one comes pretty damn close.

With Memnon's final words, the last of our magic leaves us, and the wall solidifies. I step forward and run my hand over it. It feels and looks…exactly as it should. Solid. Mundane. Seamless. It's just one long, uninterrupted surface.

"*Reveal*," I say in Sarmatian.

The wall falls away, and my hand slips forward through empty air. I can see the spiral staircase ahead of us once more.

I step back. *"Conceal."*

All at once, the open doorway becomes a wall again.

A startled little laugh escapes me because I helped *make* this.

I feel Memnon's eyes on my face, and when I glance at him, his own features are full of longing.

"That laugh…" he says reverently. Then his expression grows determined.

I clear my throat, trying to break the strange moment. "What we did probably breaks a law or three," I say. I mean, I don't *know* that, but this feels naughty enough for it to be a crime.

"You have forgotten how power works, little witch. It is one of the few things time hasn't changed." He smirks at me, the dim light in the room exaggerating his scar. "Modern people act like they've evolved into something…palatable. They pretend they don't hunger for blood and destruction, and they almost have themselves fooled." The shadows in the room have exaggerated Memnon's features, turning him sinister.

"But, *est amage*," he continues, "there is only one law humans *ever* follow: might makes right. We were strong enough to take this doorway, so now it is ours."

"That's not how the world works," I argue.

His smoky-brown eyes glint. "Careful now, Selene. You're thinking like an idealist. Bad men use such thoughts for their own gain."

Memnon closes the last of the distance between us. Even the way he moves is confident. And why wouldn't he be confident? He is physically powerful, wickedly intelligent, and has enough magic to wipe out a city. I don't think I've ever met someone who possesses so much strength.

He searches my face again, then peers into my eyes.

"Strange," he murmurs curiously.

"What is strange?" I ask, distracted by how alluring he is. Even now, heat pools in me.

"Your memory and my legacy are both gone," he muses. "Mine has been cast from the record, but it still lingers in my mind, while yours has been cast from your mind but still lingers in the record..."

My brows pinch together as his eyes grow distant.

"*Damnatio memoriae*," he says, reaching out and stroking my cheek with his knuckles. "That's the curse you would've used..."

Curse?

"I've never cursed another person in my entire life," I say, indignant.

"That you can remember," he tacks on, his knuckles still warm against my skin.

I narrow my gaze at him.

"But you *cannot* remember," he says again, his gaze far away.

All at once those eyes sharpen as some realization snaps into place.

His hand drops from my cheek. "The Law of Three," he says, like it's all so obvious. "The Witch's Law."

I know what he's speaking of—every witch does. It's our equivalent of the Golden Rule. The Law of Three is the principle that rules all spellwork. It states that any magic you perform—good or bad—will return to you threefold.

His gaze is heavy on mine. "*Est amage*, you cursed yourself."

CHAPTER 34

As soon as we return to my room, I grab a pen and snatch up my notebook.

There are several things I need to remember. I rush to write them all down, starting with the Sarmatian command words I'll need to invoke to open and close the doorway, then ending with *damnatio memoriae* and the Law of Three.

Ever since Memnon uttered these last two concepts, he's been in a peculiar mood—half-broody, half-contemplative.

The idea that I'm some washed-up ex-lover who went to all this trouble…it's the sort of story you spin to make some ridiculous worldview make sense.

That doesn't mean I shouldn't look into it.

I put my pen down and turn to the man himself. Memnon's taken a seat at the chair by my bedside, and he's studying the dozens of notebooks I've shelved on my bookcase.

I don't know why he hasn't left me yet. I expected him

to. What I wasn't expecting was to enjoy his company. He's weird and edgy and just…a lot all at once, but I don't really want to part ways with him.

His attention moves from the notebooks to the sticky notes that pepper my belongings—they're on the covers of my textbooks, one is on my lampshade, another on my desk, and still another on the back of my door. I know that last one is a reminder to check that I've packed my notebook for the day.

Memnon taps on the chair's armrest and jiggles his leg impatiently.

"Stop it," I say.

Memnon's gaze flicks to me. He doesn't say anything, but there's a question in his eyes.

"You look like you're trying to figure something out." He looks like he's trying to figure *me* out. I rub my arms. "It's making me nervous."

His fingers cease tapping; his leg stops jiggling. Not that it does any good. Memnon caged his restlessness, but I can see it still prowling in his eyes.

I move over to my bed and sit on the mattress, so close to Memnon, my knee brushes his.

"Who are you?" I ask. "Beyond Memnon the Cursed."

At my words, the sorcerer seems to tear himself away from his own thoughts. "I was never Memnon the Cursed. I was Memnon the Indomitable. I presume you gave me the new title when you buried me."

I bite my tongue to keep from arguing with him on that point. "What else?" I say instead.

He tilts his head a little, considering my question. "What do you want to know?" he asks.

"I don't know—anything, *everything*."

He stares at me for a long time, those enigmatic eyes seeming to plumb my depths. He inhales, then begins.

"I was born Uvagukis Memnon, son of Uvagukis Tamara, queen of the Sarmatians, and Ilyapa Khuno, sorcerer king of the Moche."

"They ruled different nations?"

"*Est amage*, they ruled different *landmasses*. My father was from the area you know as Peru. The only reason he met my mother is because he knew how to manipulate ley lines."

Ley lines are magical roads that lie like a net across the world. They're areas where space and time wrinkles. If one knows how to navigate them correctly, they can cross entire oceans in minutes. Hell, they can travel to other *realms* in minutes—the Otherworld and the Underworld share these same ley lines with earth.

I don't know much more than that about them.

"You're telling me that two thousand years ago, your dad left South America to visit a continent across the world?"

Because that would upend the entire history nonmagical humans have established about the moment the East met the West. But then, it would also explain why I discovered Memnon himself, a man who lived in Eurasia, asleep in a crypt somewhere in northern Peru.

"He did more traveling than just that," Memnon says. "But yes."

I'd like to linger on this, but the truth is I'm not particularly interested in Memnon's dad. I'm interested in Memnon himself.

I search his face. "What else?"

The corners of his eyes crinkle, like I'm amusing him—or maybe he's simply pleased to have captured my attention.

"I learned to ride a horse at the same time I learned to

walk, and I killed my first opponent at thirteen," he says. "But perhaps most importantly, my power first awoke when you called to it."

Normally, supernaturals drink a concoction called *bitter-sweet* to Awaken their powers. To hear that this didn't happen to Memnon, that instead, a person—Roxilana, I assume—awoke it…

"How?"

Memnon gives me a heavy look. "Trauma. When you were a child, a Roman legion attacked your village and killed your family. In your fear, you called out to me through our bond."

I'm barely breathing. I don't bother correcting him on the fact this is not me he's speaking of.

"I was confused for many moons about the fearful voice in my head. I didn't know who you were or where you lived—or even that you lived. I thought you were a spirit, one who spoke a language I didn't initially know. And you couldn't hear me, not for a long while.

"But once you did"—Memnon smiles—"things got very fun.

"We spoke to each other all the time—sometimes when we didn't even mean to. I remember being in the middle of battle when I heard you curse at yourself for breaking a bowl."

I stare at Memnon, hanging on every word.

"I started searching for you when I was thirteen, but it was only once I was crowned king that I was able to lead my horde west, into the Roman Empire, and find you."

The sorcerer falls silent.

There's an ache in me, a very real ache, at his story. I don't know why. Maybe because it sounds romantic—kings, and hordes, and a search for a woman he was connected to but could not find.

"What else?" I ask.

Memnon's eyes linger on me. For a moment, they are so incredibly desolate. Then his mouth curves into a sly smile, and that calculating gleam reenters his expression. "Curious, Empress?"

My own eyes fall to his lips. "Why do you call me that? 'Empress'?"

He settles back into his seat, and now his mouth curves into a sinful smirk. "Because the Romans subjugated you, and I quite like paying homage to your power in their language. It gives me a petty little thrill. You liked it even more."

"Roxilana," I whisper. "This all happened to Roxilana."

Memnon's eyes are like embers; I can't look away from him. I sense so many pent-up feelings behind that face.

"Yes," he agrees, "it happened to my Roxilana."

This moment feels as though it's balanced on a tightrope. At any second, one of us could fall.

"What do you want?" I say softly.

"Everything," he says. "My empire, my riches, my palace, my adoring subjects. But most of all—I want you."

I don't know who moves first, him or me, only that we come together, and it feels inescapable. There is my rational, orderly mind, and then there is this. Instinct.

Memnon's mouth finds mine, and he ravages it, kissing me with all the intensity one would expect from a warrior-king. I gasp in a breath when suddenly his tongue is there, sweeping through.

My body awakens at the contact, feverish for more of this, whatever *this* is. I delve my fingers into his hair.

Memnon groans into my mouth, then hoists me into his arms, wrapping my legs around him and cradling my ass.

"My queen, my queen," he murmurs. "I *need* you to remember."

"Shut up about that," I murmur back. Memnon's cute little delusions could ruin a perfectly good make-out session.

If I thought the sorcerer would be offended at my rudeness, I thought wrong. He smiles against my lips, then nips my lower one.

I moan.

"That is no way to talk to your king."

On second thought, I could totally get behind role-playing this. "I'll talk to you the way I want."

At my words, Memnon growls, squeezing my ass, his smile searing against my lips. He maneuvers us onto my bed. My back bounces a little as it hits the mattress.

My fingers run over his scar, and he lets out a jagged exhale.

He pulls away, his breathing heavy. "Time to tell me to leave."

Time to leave? I feel as though we've only gotten started.

"And if I don't?"

"Then I find out just how sweet that pussy of yours really is, and I don't stop until I feel you come on my tongue."

Memnon has teased me plenty about intimacy with him, but he's offering the real thing to me now.

I find that I want it more than I've wanted anything in a long while.

I stare at him for several seconds, and I stroke his cheek again. "*Stay*."

His jaw clenches beneath my touch, and the heat in his eyes grows.

He leans back in and kisses me again, only this one is full of carnal promise. "As you command, *est amage*," he whispers.

Memnon grinds his hips against my pelvis, and I gasp into his mouth, the sound eliciting a grin from him.

His hands move to my body then, stroking up and down my sides. Eventually, they find the hem of my shirt. He fingers it, the action reminding me of when we first laid eyes on each other in his tomb. He played with my clothes then too. Only, we never had a chance to take it any further.

Memnon tugs the shirt up, unpeeling it from my body inch by inch.

"So beautiful," he says as he takes in my exposed flesh, the look in his eyes searing. He saw my skin not even twenty-four hours ago, but concern shadowed his gaze then. Right now, he has no such restraint.

I'm still wearing a bra, and his fingers glide over one of the straps. A lock of dark hair slips over his eye as he studies the undergarment, grazing his thumb over the lace cup. I realize then that the sorcerer may have never *seen* a bra before. I don't know what they wore during Memnon's time, but it probably wasn't this.

I sit up, forcing the sorcerer back to his knees. Then I take his hand. "You undo it from the back." I guide his arm behind me to where my bra hooks together.

Memnon watches my face the entire time, more fascinated with my features than he is with the workings of my lingerie. Still, his hand closes on the clasp.

"This feels like something I would *greatly* enjoy breaking, Selene," he admits.

Despite his words, his other hand comes up, and after a few probing touches, he deftly unhooks the bra. He slides the thing off and casts it aside.

"These breasts…" He bends and takes one into his mouth.

I gasp at the intense and unexpected contact, my fingers delving into his hair. Memnon sucks on my nipple, the sensation going right to my core. I gasp again, my grip on his hair tightening as the rest of me goes boneless.

Memnon cradles my back, holding me in place. "Sweet woman, you feel better than memory serves." His lips move away from my nipple, trailing kisses along my skin until he gets to the other breast, which he then promptly takes into his mouth.

"*Goddess*," I breathe, holding him like I'll fall if I let go.

He rolls my nipple between his teeth before releasing it. "Don't praise your goddess—praise *me*, your king," he says, his breath fanning against my skin.

"You want me to call you *my king*?" I mean, I really *could* get into this role-playing.

"*Yes*," he breathes.

Using the fingers threaded through his hair, I turn his head and lean in to his ear. "Would you like me to say it in English or Sarmatian, *est xsaya*?" *My king.*

A shudder works its way through his body.

He shakes his head and flashes me an intense look. "You don't know what that does to me, hearing you say those words in our language." he murmurs, his gaze fixed on my skin.

And then his mouth is back on my flesh, and he's kissing down, down, down my torso.

I grab the back of his shirt, tugging it up. Memnon, after all, is not the only one who wants a glimpse of bare flesh.

The sorcerer pauses. "Does my queen want me to remove my shirt?" he asks in Sarmatian.

Before I even have a chance to answer, he pulls the garment off, then tosses it aside.

I get a sick little thrill at the thought of his clothes casually littering my room. I find I want them to decorate my space just as much as my Post-it notes do.

The sight of his exposed torso has me drawing in a sharp breath. I already knew his body is a work of art, but seeing it up close is an entire experience.

I reach out and run my hands over his thick coiled muscles. Beneath my touch, Memnon's skin pebbles. I can feel those smoky-brown eyes of his watching me as I explore him.

There are lines of scars all over the place, mapping out the violence this man was once exposed to. My hands stop roving when I get to his tattoos.

"Will you tell me what these mean at some point?" I ask. He's already said a little about them, but I'm curious about the rest.

Memnon cups my face, and the look he's giving me makes me feel beloved. I like it far, far too much for my own good.

"At some point, I won't need to," he says cryptically.

He releases me but only so his hands can move to the seam of my pants. In a couple of deft movements, he undoes the top button and zipper.

"Lie back, little witch," Memnon commands.

My pulse is racing, but there's something about this sorcerer that also makes me feel so very…safe.

Maybe it's simply the fact he actually did save my life.

I lower myself back to the bed just as Memnon's hands hook over the top of my pants and my underwear. He pulls them down, his eyes fixed to my flesh.

The sorcerer tugs them off and then skims his palm up my calf and smooths over my thigh. His gaze scours my body, drinking it in for so long that a little bit of nervous magic sifts from my palms.

Memnon's eyes slowly drift up to mine. "You hold me in your thrall, little witch," he says, his voice husky. "It has been a long time since I've seen you this way."

Role-playing—we're just role-playing.

"Does my king like what he sees?" I ask in Sarmatian. It's supposed to be an easy, playful response. Only after it leaves my lips do I realize I've opened myself up for rejection.

A wry smile graces his mouth at the endearment. "Every inch of you is sheer perfection, my queen. Api fashioned the most flawless woman when he made you."

I swallow, unsure how to respond to *that.* It isn't a rejection, but it feels equally hard to accept, for some reason.

Memnon lowers himself between my thighs. "Now, soul mate, let's see this pretty pussy of yours."

Soul mate?

Oh no, no, no.

I press my fingers to Memnon's lips and shake my head. "You can call me your queen and your empress and your witch, but—not that."

I'm only willing to role-play so far.

Memnon arches a brow. Gently, he pries my hand away from his mouth, pausing to give each fingertip a kiss. It's oddly…affectionate.

"All right…Selene," he agrees.

He returns his attention to my core. The way he's looking at it makes me want to shift. Memnon moves first one of my legs, then the other, over his shoulder.

Then he spreads my outer lips apart and stares at my vagina like he's trying to divine the future from it.

"How I have missed this too."

Memnon leans in and peppers kisses along those outer lips. His mouth is so light and reverent, I jolt a little when his tongue finally strokes up my seam, the touch so much bolder than what came before it.

He groans. "Ah, the taste of you, Empress!" His hold on me tightens. "All the liquor in the world cannot intoxicate me the way you can."

I shift under him, digging my heels into his back as my nerves ratchet up.

His fingers knead a little into my hips. "I can feel how tense you are," he says. "Relax, I'm going to take care of you."

I hadn't realized I tensed up, but I *am* fairly rigid. I force my muscles to loosen.

"That's it," he coaxes. "Beautiful Empress, you have nothing to worry about in my arms. I have longed to have you right here."

He begins kissing my pussy again, scraping his teeth against the soft folds of skin. He takes various sections of flesh into his mouth, laving them with his tongue. My hips move of their own accord, finding a rhythm to Memnon's attentions.

As soon as the sorcerer's lips find my clit, I cry out, "*Est xsaya!*" *My king!*

I...didn't actually mean to say that.

Memnon stills, and it's as though he knows it too.

I feel his grin against my flesh, and his hands tighten where they grip my hips.

I like how your pretty voice makes those words sound. Memnon speaks directly into my mind. Then stroke of his mouth turns fevered, demanding. He sucks on my clit, earning moan after moan from me.

This feels light-years better than anything that's come before Memnon. Like comparing water to wine.

I dig my heels into the sorcerer's back again, and that only seems to spur him on more. Memnon moves lower, toward my core. Once he gets there, he slips his tongue inside me, and I cry out once more, tightening my grip on his hair as I press myself into his face.

"Feels so good, Memnon," I murmur. "So, so good."

Grind against me more, est amage. He's still speaking in my mind. *I want you to coat my face by the time I'm done with you.*

I'm too far gone to be shocked by his words.

One of Memnon's fingers slips inside me, and I gasp a little at the sensation.

"Call me your king again," he says against my flesh, "and I'll add another."

Closing my eyes, I shake my head and smile. *"Est xsaya, uvut vakosgub sanpuvusavak pes I'navkap."*

My king, I may die if you don't.

He laughs lightly against me. "It is *you* who will be the death of me."

Another finger joins the first, spreading me wider.

I make a small breathy sound at the sensation. I can hear the wet noises of those digits as he works me.

Memnon's mouth returns to my clit, and now he does something to it with his tongue, something that makes my hips jerk and a cry rip from my throat.

I release his hair so I can prop myself up and stare at him wide-eyed. "What was *that*?"

The sorcerer pauses to glance up at me.

"Don't look so surprised, *est amage*," he says, his gaze flicking over me. "I have spent years memorizing your body. I know what it likes."

His words prickle my skin. Perhaps for the first time, I feel truly worried by them, because I *did* like that move of his, even though *I* didn't know I would. The truth is, I don't know my body well enough to understand what tricks can bring me to orgasm quickly. But Memnon apparently does, and that's…alarming.

"Now, return your hands to my hair, Empress," he says, "and grind that pussy against me once more. I like feeling what I do to you."

Without waiting for me to comply, he returns to kissing and tonguing me. And I do thread my fingers back into his wavy locks, and I do grind against him. I can't seem to stop myself. Everything he's doing is unraveling me bit by bit.

While his fingers pump into me, the sorcerer does that thing again with his tongue—I think he's circling my clit. And again my hips jerk against him.

I gasp. "*Memnon*."

He repeats it again. And again. And again.

I'm writhing against him as he plays me like an instrument, dragging me closer and closer to that precarious edge.

I can feel you getting close, he whispers in my head, never stopping his ministrations.

I don't bother responding. He's right after all.

Call me your soul mate, he continues, *and I'll let you come.*

I'm sorry, what?

I let out a disbelieving laugh.

I thought we went over this. I thought he agreed to drop the term.

And if I don't? I say silently to him.

Memnon stops kissing me, stops fingering me; he goes utterly still.

"Then I won't give you your release," he says, staring up my body.

I meet his gaze. "You bastard."

His fingers begin moving again.

"Close," he says, "but that's still the wrong word. Try again, *soul mate.*"

I grimace at that word, but then Memnon's mouth is on my pussy, doing that same damn thing with his mouth. He's not even being creative at this point. He knows it's what does it for me. And damn it, it's enough for me to get sucked under all over again.

"Feels so good, Memnon," I admit. I'm panting, moving my hips against him.

Still not the right word, little witch, he chastises.

I moan instead of replying, my body tightening in anticipation of—

The sorcerer backs off my clit, moving to a far-less-stimulating area near my outer lips.

I cry out in frustration.

Say it, he commands.

I don't. But if I thought my resistance would make him stop eating me out altogether, I thought wrong. No, Memnon seems happy enough to continue running his lips and his teeth and his tongue over other sensitive portions of my pussy. He even eventually returns to my clit, working me into a frenzy once more.

But just as I'm again about to tip over the edge, he backs off.

"Memnon." I practically growl his name.

I can do this all day, Empress, he says in my head.

I blow out an agitated breath. I'm being edged by a fucking monster who knows *exactly* what he's doing to my body.

Say it. Now it's him who's pleading with me.

Apparently, promised orgasms make me weak because I silently say to him, *It won't mean anything.*

Perhaps not to you, he responds. But it will mean something to him.

He begins working me again, and I let out another annoyed sound because it feels so terribly, exquisitely good, but I know it's going to stop the moment I get close to climaxing.

I could just say it.

It's only a single word. What's a bit more role-playing? It really won't mean anything.

Decision made, I draw a fortifying breath.

"Make me come…soul mate," I say.

Memnon smiles against me.

And then he does.

He sucks on my clit for mere seconds before the wave of my orgasm crashes through me.

"Memnon!" I cry, digging my heels into him as the pleasure stretches on and on. And still Memnon teases me with his hand and his lips, only letting up once the vestiges of my climax have ebbed away.

I'm left breathless, staring at the ceiling as Memnon's fingers slip out of me. He props himself up on his forearms in front of my pussy, then licks those fingers clean, making a satisfied noise, as though I taste like candy and not, you know, a woman.

"I missed the way you taste," he admits. "I fantasized about it many, many times over the centuries. My mind is a mighty thing, but even it forgot just how sweet your pussy really is."

"Memnon." I press a hand to my temple. "You shouldn't talk like that."

He presses a kiss to one of my inner thighs. "Why not?" he says, moving to give the other thigh equal treatment. "It is the truth, whether you believe it or not."

I decide to let the whole thing go. Memnon gave me the most explosive orgasm, and I want the rest of this day with him to be easy, fun.

I reach for him, and he seems all too eager to pull himself up my body and into my arms. I can feel his cock straining against his pants, but he pays it no mind. Instead, his hands come to cradle my face.

"*Est amage*," he murmurs, stroking my skin with his thumb. *"Est amage, est amage, est amage." My queen, my queen, my queen.* His gaze searches my face, a pleased smile curving the corners of his lips. "You make me excited about the future."

"*Est xsaya*," I say, just to see the way Memnon's eyes spark at the term, "has anyone told you that you are really fucking intense?"

He laughs then, gazing down at me like I'm the most endearing thing he's ever seen. "You have. Many times."

Okay, I walked myself into that one.

I wind a leg around his and move my hands to the top button of his pants. The sorcerer is still wearing clothes, and that's a problem because now I want to be the one tasting him.

At my touch, Memnon tenses.

"Relax," I tease, using his earlier words against him as I undo the button. "I'm going to take care of you."

But the sorcerer's hand lands on mine, stilling my movements. "Not today, little witch," he says.

My brows draw together. "Why not?"

"I'm afraid if I let you wrap that pretty mouth or pussy around my cock, that will be the end of us both."

I give him a perplexed look, because seriously, why does he have to be so intense about this?

But already he's extricating himself from me.

"So godsdamned pretty," he says, almost to himself as he gets off the bed, his eyes lingering on me. "Two thousand years, and I still burn for you."

He looks like he wants to say something else, but he bites it back at the last moment. Instead, Memnon grabs his discarded shirt, and I *don't* like that.

"You're leaving?" I say, sitting up. I don't bother covering myself; he's already seen everything.

Memnon must hear the rejected note of my voice because he says, "I have no intention of *staying* away. But yes, I do have to leave."

I frown, and the action causes him to cross back over to the bed.

He grabs my jaw and presses a kiss to my lips. "I *will* see you again soon, little witch," he promises, releasing my face and heading for the door once more. "Until then—sweet dreams."

"Sweet dreams?"

Hasn't he said that before? Why on earth…?

I suck in a breath. "Are *you* sending me those dreams?"

Immediately, I regret asking the question—if Memnon isn't responsible for them, then I'm going to have to lie through my teeth that I meant something innocent and not, you know, the vivid sexual encounters I've been having with this man in my sleep.

Memnon's mouth curves wickedly. "Have you enjoyed them, *est amage*?"

He *has* been responsible for the dreams!

I'm so shocked that I barely have time for my irritation to rise.

"Stop sending them to me," I demand.

His expression only turns more conniving. "Now that I know they're getting under your skin? *Unlikely*."

And with that parting line, he leaves.

Late that evening, my phone pings. When I grab it, I see a notification from one of my banking apps.

> You received money.

What?

I click on the notification and the app opens.

I put a hand over my mouth when I see my account balance: *$5,000.*

Beneath the transaction is a note.

For Nero and you, soul mate.

-Memnon

I cry then, in earnest, the hot tears dripping down my cheeks and over my hands. I won't go into debt or have to take on any shady gigs to feed Nero this month.

I glance at the amount again, and a choked laugh slips out. The thought that this ancient dude has *any* money at all is absurd—let alone five thousand dollars to throw my way.

But he did throw it my way, all because he caught a glimpse of my bank account and my worry. And I'm not going to question the hows and whys of his financial situation right now.

I wipe away my tears and take a deep breath. Once again, Memnon is being *nice* to me. That's on top of giving me the best orgasm I've had…maybe ever. Great sex aside, I know better than to believe he's being kind for the sake of kindness.

All this will come back to haunt me sooner or later.

But you know what?

Tonight, I don't really give a shit.

Tonight, I'm simply grateful.

CHAPTER 35

I haven't seen Kasey. Not for days.

At first, it's a relief. Not seeing her means not having to deal with the fallout from the spell circle. But the longer I don't see or hear from her, the more nervous I grow.

It's not until I'm sitting out on the back patio on Thursday afternoon, drinking mint mojitos and painting my nails with Sybil that my peace is shattered.

"Evanora hasn't heard from Kasey either," a nearby coven sister says to her friend. "Not since Saturday."

I glance over at the woman who spoke, startled to hear Kasey's name on her lips. She wears her snake familiar draped around her neck like a necklace, while her friend is enchanting a broom to make it hover.

Her friend catches her broom by the handle and whispers an incantation into the wood that makes it lower itself to the ground.

She turns to the other witch. "Do you think…?"

Do you think she was murdered? I'm sure that's what she intended to say.

My heart pounds harder, and I can hear my pulse between my ears.

Was Kasey mortally wounded that night? Or did Memnon go after her? I mentioned to him that I was worried about her.

"I don't know," says the witch with the serpent familiar. "I mean, it seems possible, right?"

Sybil nudges me with her shoulder. "Are you okay, Selene?" she asks, watching my face, then glancing at the witches.

I nod, then shake my head. I don't know what I'm feeling. I still haven't processed any of what happened to me over the weekend, and I haven't dared to tell my friend about it. I've carried it all around like a dirty little secret, and I've shamefully hoped my magic might steal away the memories before I have to deal with them.

Abruptly, I stand, knocking over my glittery purple nail polish. "I just...don't feel so well." Not a lie. "I think...I think I'm going to go lie down a bit."

Before my friend can respond, I'm capping my nail polish and grabbing my mojito and fleeing back inside our house.

Sybil calls after me, but I pretend not to hear it.

I cut through the dining room, then down the hall, then up the stairs. I'm nearly to my room when I feel the muffled buzz of my phone from the pocket of my pants.

I ignore it, knowing it must be Sybil sending me a concerned text. I'll be fine once I have a moment to myself.

I just need a moment.

Nero is waiting for me inside my room, curled up at the foot of my bed like some mutant house cat.

After setting my nail polish and mojito on my desk, I move over to him. I wrap my arms around his neck and bury my face in his soft fur.

Beneath me, my familiar makes a put-out noise.

"I love you, you big grumpy cat. I don't care that you're not touchy-feely. You are the best familiar a witch could ask for."

For a long moment, my familiar doesn't move. When he does, however, it's to bump his head against mine and rub his face against me.

Nero lets me hold him for several minutes longer, until the moment is broken by another buzz from my phone.

I sigh, releasing him.

I pull out my phone and see several notifications. Two are texts from Sybil, asking me what's going on and if I'm really okay. Another text is from my mother, who shared a picture from her and my father's extended tour of Europe. In it, the two of them are drinking beer at Oktoberfest—cute. The last notification is an email from Peel Academy.

They got back to me about my Awakening records.

I open my messages and quickly text Sybil back that I'm fine and everything is okay and nothing at all is wrong (because why would anything be wrong?) and I'm 110 percent groovy like a movie.

I bite back my hysterical laugh.

Then I open my email.

There's a response to my earlier inquiry about my Awakening results, but I don't even bother reading it once I see they included an attachment labeled *Bowers_Selene_results*. I click on the PDF file, and my official Awakening record appears.

I scroll past the information at the top, which lists my

name, date of birth, and date of Awakening. My actual results are near the bottom of the page.

The notes are brief.

Awoken Supernatural Categories:

Witch

Soul Mate

CHAPTER 36

Three years ago, I was given a draught of bittersweet, and my powers Awoke. I only remembered one of them—that I'm a witch.

But apparently, there was a secondary one I forgot.

That I'm a soul mate.

It's right there, typed neatly onto the document bearing Peel Academy's seal.

Soul mate.

I can all but hear Memnon's voice in my ear.

Mate.

Fuck, fuck, fuck.

I press my hand to my forehead and push my hair back.

That swamp monster I revived from undying sleep was right this whole time? Memnon is really, truly my soul mate? And I mean, okay, he's not a swamp monster—he's devilishly handsome, and I think I might have fallen in love with him a little after I invited him into my bed, but he also believes we were lovers two thousand years ago.

And now I have to seriously entertain that idea.

Goddess, why me?

I blow out a breath. *Let's take it one step at a time, Selene.*

I go to my shelf and glance down the line of magic-related books until I get to one on types of supernaturals. I pull it out and plop on my bed next to Nero, flipping to its glossary. Then I run my finger over page after page of definitions until I get to the one I'm looking for.

Soul mate

n.

one of a pair or a group of amorous supernaturals who are bonded through an unbreakable magical connection.

I grimace at the word *amorous*, and then my eyes reread the last bit of the definition.

An unbreakable magical connection.

No. No, no, no.

We're in denial again, I see. Memnon's earlier words float through my head like a taunt.

My panic is interrupted when my phone buzzes…then keeps buzzing.

Worst time ever for my friend to call.

I answer without looking. "Sybil, I promise you, I'm fine."

I'm not fine at all. Not even a little bit.

A gruff voice clears their throat, and shit, this is not Sybil.

"Ms. Bowers?" a masculine voice says, one I vaguely recognize.

"Uh…yeah, sorry, hi there," I say, trying to recover the pieces of my dignity.

"This is Officer Howahkan with the Politia. We spoke at the beginning of the week. Do you have a moment?"

My mind is screaming, *I am a soul mate!*I clear my throat. "Yeah, sure." That sounded normal and not hysterical, right?

"We are trying to solidify your alibi"—*that* pulls me into the moment—"and I wanted to follow up with you on getting your notebooks so we can create a comprehensive timeline for you."

This...sounds a lot like I'm a suspect.

And yet I feel a wave of relief. They want my notebooks. Even though Officer Howahkan couldn't clear me based on what he saw in my planner, that doesn't mean something in one of my other planners won't cover my ass. I have two others I'm also using at the moment, and a few others might have some overlap.

As soon as the Politia gets a good look at all of them, it'll be clear I have an ironclad alibi and a large paper trail. This is my chance to get myself off the suspect list.

"Of course," I say, nibbling on a half-painted nail. "Anything you want to look at, you can see." So long as it gets me cleared, I'm fine with it.

"Great," the officer says. "Will you be home tomorrow afternoon?"

"I have class until two. But after that, I'll be home for the rest of the day."

"All right, then I'll have one of my colleagues swing by sometime between then and five to collect them."

Officer Howahkan and I end the call shortly after that, and I drop my phone and rub the heel of my hands into my eyes.

As much as I want to focus on what it means to be a suspect, my mind keeps going to that email. To the fact I really am a soul mate.

I'm going to have to save a copy of those results and write them down in a billion different places just so I don't forget again. I should do that right now.

Instead, I roll onto my back, my shoulder bumping against Nero's body. I place a hand over my heart and close my eyes.

The truth I've ignored has been right here this whole time. That magical river, the one I drew Memnon's magic from, is still there, patiently waiting for me to notice it. It's time I stopped denying its existence.

The moment I focus on it, really focus on it, I can sense the sorcerer's power on the other end, along with a brief glimpse of his mood, which seems to be calm yet determined.

That little insight causes my breath to catch and warmth to bloom low in my belly. I'm literally connected to another person. I can *feel* him.

And for good or for ill, he may actually be my person.

I take a deep breath, remembering the trick he taught me some time ago.

Memnon? I push the word down that magical river, sending it out like a message in a bottle.

I wait, my eyes still closed.

Did it work? Did I manage to—?

Est amage, you are using our connection…

I can hear Memnon's pleasure in his response. I can even feel warmth in his words. That warmth goes against every other aspect about him, and yet something about it makes me want him in an entirely new way, one that has nothing to do with his sex appeal.

I exhale, trying to calm the turbulent storm of my emotions. I focus on what I want to say to him and push it down our…bond.

I don't understand any of this, but I believe you. I take another deep breath and finish the thought. *You're my soul mate, and I'm yours.*

Memnon's initial response isn't a sentence, it's a feeling: *hope.* There's some other emotions mixed with it—triumph, and maybe a touch of regret? It all flitters by too fast for me to make sense of, especially on top of my own tangle of emotions.

Est amage, I have yearned to hear you say those words. I am coming over...

A wave of panic washes over me.

Wait.

I am still processing the fact I'm actually a soul mate at all. I'm not really ready to face Memnon or deal with the reality of what being his mate actually means. Especially considering that the last time I saw him, he had just gone down on me, and that alone has my nerves and my heart all jumbled.

I want to talk, but my head is a mess, I admit. *Can you come over tomorrow instead?*

I may at least have some things sorted out by then.

From Memnon's side I sense a massive amount of emotion being tamped down.

*Tomorrow then...*he agrees. After a moment, he adds, *Sweet dreams, little witch...*

No more sex dreams! I send back down our bond.

In response, I hear an echo of his laughter, the sound of it opening an ache in me so sharp, it's hard to breathe around.

Memnon's presence recedes from the bond, and though I'm sure I could still pass messages to him, it's a clear signal that he's giving me the space I just requested, space that now feels gapingly lonely.

I rub my forehead.

Memnon and I are really soul mates.

Fuck.

The next morning, right as I'm about to leave my room and head down to breakfast, I step on an envelope someone must've slipped under my door.

I bend and pick it up. It smells like rosemary and lavender, and the loopy scrawl of my name is written in iridescent ink.

Pretty.

I open the envelope and read the brief message inside.

> *You've been summoned to the private chambers of the high priestess of Henbane Coven. Please forgo your scheduled classes and come at once.*

This…can't be good.

In group-led witchcraft, there's often a priestess, a witch who leads the spellcasting. Covens too have a version of this, and the witches who lead these regional groups are known as high priestesses.

I've never met Henbane's high priestess before, but I've caught sight of her house several times since I was accepted into the coven. It sits like a castle in the woods to the north of campus. Climbing roses and wisteria cover the sides of the pale stone walls. Birds and butterflies flitter around it. It's the definition of enchanting, though there's an eeriness to it because it's too enchanting, too lovely. It mesmerizes the eyes while unsettling the heart.

Magic, no matter how benevolently used, has that effect.

I step up to the large wooden door, Nero at my side, and reach for a knocker held between the fanged teeth of some primordial goddess. Before I can touch it, the knocker cackles.

"No need for that, Selene Bowers. We've been waiting for you," the knocker says around the metal in her mouth.

Goose bumps break out across my skin at the small show

of magic. The hinges of the door groan, and then it swings inward of its own accord.

I don't know what I expect when I step inside—to be honest, I don't know why I'm here at all—but I'm surprised to see the bare stone walls and smooth floor, the only decoration another primitive goddess figurine sitting in a nearby alcove, her arms raised above her head. Most witches tend to be maximalists, cluttering their walls and spaces with every conceivable knickknack. The lack of it all is strangely unsettling.

There are arched doorways and a myriad of rooms branching from the entryway, but it's the stairway directly in front of me, the one cut like a slash *into* the floor of the foyer that has my attention.

"Down here," a woman calls from below.

The high priestess.

I can tell it's her without even seeing her face or knowing her name. There's power folded into her words.

I take the stairs down, Nero at my side. Despite my familiar's soothing presence, my nerves are set on edge. Dread has long since soured my stomach. I must be in trouble. Maybe it's the murders. Or perhaps this is about the fight in the Everwoods. Or Nero poaching on lycanthrope territory.

I honestly have a lot to account for.

But I try to push those worrying thoughts away.

I reach the bottom of the stairs and enter a subterranean room whose floors and walls are covered in the same pale stone as the rest of the house.

Directly across from me, on the other side of the room, sits the high priestess. She's a crone, her skin wrinkled and paper-thin. Her dark brown eyes shine like gems, and there is something beautiful and strong about her—perhaps it is her power alone that makes her hard to look away from.

Magic loves old things most of all.

She wears white robes, gold clasps holding the garment together at her shoulders. Her hair lies like unspun yarn over her shoulders and down past her breasts. A white raven sits on her shoulder.

"Sit."

I don't think the high priestess used any compulsion on me, but I swear my ass has crossed the room and lowered itself into the seat across from her before the echo of her voice has quieted.

She folds her hands under her chin, leaving only her index fingers out to tap ponderously against her mouth.

"You don't seem like a murderess," she says thoughtfully, "but then again, the guilty often don't."

What?

"What are you talking about?"

She gives me a knowing look. "You don't think I'm so big a fool that I'm unaware the Politia suspects your involvement in the recent murders."

The silence that follows those words is thick and ugly.

"I didn't kill those women," I say softly.

She leans back in her chair, her eyes moving to Nero, who sits next to me.

"I have long found comfort belowground," she says, switching topics. "My own magic is particularly potent when drawn from deeper earth. Bedrock, in particular, is a very grounding, very powerful substance to draw from. Wouldn't you agree?"

She levels those dark eyes on me, and it's as though she can see me entering the subterranean rooms below the residence hall to join that spell circle. As though she can even see me entering Memnon's forbidden crypt.

I twist my hands together. "I don't think I follow..."

"Don't play coy with me, Selene Bowers. You have lost

your memory, not your wits. The oldest, most eternal parts of the universe call to you. Water, stone—even the moon."

How does she know about my magical aptitudes? Even I can only vaguely remember them.

"Many people consider these cold, lifeless things," the high priestess continues. She leans forward conspiratorially. "They call to me as well."

She resettles in her seat, her white raven turning its head and inspecting me with one of its dark eyes.

"Supernaturals—even other witches—worry about those of us bewitched by such things because…well, we are more prone to dark enchantments and perverse magic."

Ah. So that's what this is about.

"I didn't kill those women," I say again, more forcefully this time. "Please, use a truth spell on me if that's what it takes."

"Your own mind hides itself from you, Selene. Such a spell would not fully prove your innocence. You must know this."

I don't know what this meeting is, but it's clear that perhaps I now have to prove my innocence to two different institutions—the Politia *and* Henbane Coven.

I take a deep breath. "I spent over a year trying to get into this coven. Being here has been my dream since I Awoke as a witch. Even if you cannot trust me when I say I hold life to be sacred, you can at least trust that I would *never* want to jeopardize my spot here."

The high priestess scrutinizes me, seeing entirely too much of me with those enthralling eyes of hers.

"Yes," she agrees, "your Awakening profoundly shaped your life's goals—just as it shapes all of us who come into our truest forms. But," she continues, her tone changing, "you are not *just* a witch."

I go still. So still.

She knows exactly what I've only just learned.

"You are a soul mate." The high priestess tosses it out there as though it's something almost mundane and not the earth-shattering revelation I find it to be.

"I wonder how that might affect your life's goals," she muses, "particularly depending on the soul mate..."

Where is she going with this?

Does she know about Memnon?

She stares at me for a long minute before turning her attention to papers sitting on the desk in front of her.

"The Politia officers aren't the only ones who are interested in you. The lycanthropes have been barraging me with requests to speak with you. They say it's urgent, but they will not tell me what it is."

She gives me a sly look. "They forget that witches see much, and we perceive even more. They do not believe you a murderess. In fact, they seem to hold you in quite high esteem."

For a moment, my unease and self-doubt disappears, and my worries diminish.

The high priestess holds my gaze. "Would you like to speak with the wolves?"

Do I have a choice?

"You always have a choice."

Aw fuck, can this broad read minds?

I try to erase the rude thought, but obviously, it's too late.

The high priestess stares at me, her face expressionless.

"*Yeah.*" The word comes out like a croak, so I clear my throat and try again. "I would like to speak to the wolves."

"Very well. I will let them know, and they will contact you. You are to continue to attend classes as usual. You will be watched. I hope that the next time we meet, circumstances will be different. That is all."

CHAPTER 37

When I enter my room, Memnon is already there, sprawled on my computer chair, wearing a shirt with some name-brand bourbon and too many rings to count, all while flipping through one of my notebooks.

I freeze.

"What are you doing here?" I say a little breathlessly. My stomach does a happy little flip at the sight of him, and I remember all over again just what the two of us did in this room less than a week ago.

The sorcerer glances up from my notebook, and his mouth curves into a sly, knowing smile. "I'm happy to see you too, *est amage*. Or would you prefer I called you *mate*?"

I release a shaky breath. He's clearly already enjoying the hell out of my earlier admission. And I find I want to argue with him, even though I already conceded this point.

Nero pushes past me to rub against the sorcerer's leg.

Memnon reaches down and gives my familiar a pet. "You asked to speak with me today," he reminds me. "So here I am."

Right. *Right.*

I close my door, then turn to face him once more. My heart beats fast as I take him in, from the top of his wavy hair to the bottom of his shit-kicking boots. Every line of him is violent and beautiful and intimidating and overbearing.

I'm bonded to that.

"Little witch," Memnon says softly, and his eyes have gentled. "You don't need to look so frightened."

I exhale. He's right. *This is all going to be fi—*

"I promise I only bite when you ask me to," he adds.

A small semihysterical sound slips from my lips, and I take a step back.

I'm not ready for this conversation. I thought I might be, but I think I need more time.

Memnon puts up a hand. "Wait, Selene, fight me, curse me—well, maybe not that one—just please don't run."

I hesitate, unused to this side of Memnon. He's being raw and vulnerable with me. I drop my book bag then and scrub my face with my hands.

"I don't know how to do this."

"Do what, *Amage*?"

I drop my hands and look at him. "Be a soul mate. Come to terms with the fact you're it for me."

Memnon sets my notebook aside. "You say that like this is a burden." He shakes his head and stands, closing in on me. "This is what men kill and die for. What no amount of wealth can buy. Love. One that could set whole nations on fire." He takes my chin then, giving me a look that's as close to adoration as one can get. "You cannot fathom it, little witch, only because you cannot remember that you once had it. But *I* remember."

This close to me, Memnon is hypnotic, compelling.

"It didn't end well for you though," I say.

"End..." he muses, dragging the word out on his lips. "An era ended. *We* did not."

He's looking at my lips now, and an ache starts up within me, one that only he can soothe.

"You threatened me," I say. "And I know you must still be angry with me."

"Oh, I am," he agrees. "But I grow eager for my vengeance to be sated and for this era to end too. You and I, Empress, we are eternal."

My magic is seeping out from my skin, as is his. The two twist and cur around us, the colors blending until a dusky purple remains.

I want to kiss him again—hell, I *always* want to kiss the man—but this feels too much like throwing myself off a cliff. I don't know where I'm going to land or if I'm going to like it at all.

I pull away from Memnon, forcing my magic back inside me.

Memnon's gaze moves over me, and he looks a little sad, but there's also a lot of understanding in his eyes. "I keep forgetting how skittish you are in the beginning," he murmurs.

My brows draw together.

"When I found you in Rome," he continues, "you were nervous around me too. But that changed, and it will again. Once you remember."

"Remember?" I echo.

"Our past," he says, backing away from me.

You give an ancient sorcerer a single crumb of hope, and he starts asking for the whole damn feast.

"That's not possible," I say.

"It's not possible?" he repeats, lifting his brows. "If it weren't possible, you wouldn't be able to speak Latin or Sarmatian. You wouldn't be able to read Greek or Aramaic or Demotic."

What the hell is Demotic?

Memnon grabs my journal from my desk, and immediately, I tense. My mind and life are laid bare in those pages.

He flips to a particular page and turns the notebook to me. It's full of writing crammed together in various colors, some of the text highlighted, some crossed out.

He points to a doodle I scribbled in the corner. "Do you see this?" he asks me.

What he's referring to looks like nothing more than the crests of a wave, except on top of each crest blooms a three-petaled flower. It's a strange design, clearly something I drew while I was zoning out.

Memnon lifts the sleeve of his shirt and points to one of his tattoos. "Those are the horns of a saiga on my arm."

I take a step forward, momentarily transfixed. My drawing *does* look eerily similar to the artwork on his arm.

"This page is from three months ago," he says. "You drew this before you ever saw me."

My heart seems to stop at that. I can deny Memnon's ravings but not my own records.

Could I really be this other woman?

Roxilana?

"I can show you more examples from your books if you'd like more proof," he adds.

I narrow my gaze at him. "Just how many of my journals *have* you gone through?"

Those are private.

"You're trying to change the subject, *Roxi*," he says,

snapping the notebook shut. "What I am telling you is that your memories have not been destroyed. They still exis;, they're simply locked away. But, if you had the key to that lock, you could retrieve them *all*."

My blood pounds between my ears.

Memnon glances at the journal he holds again. "These notebooks are so meticulous, so thorough. How important they must be," he says, running his thumb over the dark blue cover, where I scribbled in gold Sharpie the dates when I used this journal. This one is from June and July of this year.

The sorcerer's eyes flick to the book bag at my feet, and the air thickens with his magic. The flap of my satchel flicks open, and my latest notebook slides out, lifting into the air.

"What are you doing?" I grab for it, but it slips like butter through my fingers.

Memnon catches my planner in his free hand, and now panic rises in me.

"Seriously, Memnon, I need that back." The Politia's coming later today to look at these very journals.

I don't want anyone pawing at them in the meantime—especially not Memnon.

Ignoring me, he sets my journal from the summer on my desk and opens my latest notebook before flipping through it.

"Oh, there's a Samhain Witch's Ball happening at the end of the week." He reads the reminder like it's a diary entry. "Sounds like *fun*."

I fold my arms and force myself to chill out. "Are you done?" I ask. Whatever rise he wants to get out of me, he won't get it.

"I can give you your memory back," he says, not looking up from my notebook.

My breath catches at his words. It's one thing to tell me that my lost memories exist; it's another to tell me I can retrieve them.

"No one can give me that," I finally say. I don't even let myself ponder what life would be like with them back.

Now Memnon looks up from my journal, his smoky-amber eyes glinting. "My queen, *I can*."

"I don't want your help."

"But don't you? Aren't you tired of not remembering? How much easier would life be if you didn't always forget?"

He's the devil in my ear, offering me the one thing I'm supposed to want. The thing I used to have, before my magic Awoke.

My memory.

I shake my head. "What you're saying is impossible."

"It's actually quite simple. Your power is bound up in a curse—the one you placed on us both when you locked me in that tomb."

I frown at him, not liking where this conversation is going. Nero must not either because he slinks over to the window and leaps out onto the bough of the tree outside, then prowls out of sight.

Memnon continues. "The Romans called it *damnatio memoriae*—to condemn from memory. To cast into oblivion. It was one of the worst fates you could inflict on a person of power."

And this is where Memnon's true purpose is coming into focus.

"If the curse is lifted, it's not just my memory that returns, is it? You'll be remembered too, won't you?"

His eyes are alight with the first true stirrings of his power. "*Yes*," he agrees. "My name and my kingdom will return to the historical record. I want the world to remember me. But"—and now he switches into Sarmatian—"my queen, more than even that, I want *you* to remember me. To remember us and our life. I cannot be the sole bearer of our past. That is..." He shakes his head slowly, his smoky eyes burning. "*Unendurable*."

My heart aches at what he's saying.

Assuming I am, by some strange magic and twist of fate, this Roxilana, then—

"Have you ever considered that I may better off not knowing the past?" I ask. "Perhaps some things are best left buried."

Memnon holds my gaze, his own still glowing with his power. "I told you, Selene. Whatever made you curse me, we can work it out. We *will* work it out."

I shake my head. "You say that like I've agreed to any of this."

"You are under a curse, mate. One made by your own hand. Of course we will remove it—for my sake *and* yours. And then you will get your memories back, and we can resolve whatever came between us."

I feel my ire stir, and for some reason, tears prick at my eyes. Why must everything come back to my memory loss? Why must others think fixing it is what I want most? Or that the loss of my memories is the sum of my identity? Why must they make me feel as though I am not enough as I am? Why can't they see that my ambition, my heart, my fucking optimism—all the best parts of me—have been borne and shaped by my memory loss?

And I know Memnon doesn't exactly hold those views—he's made it clear he's really only interested in the memories from our deep past—but he's still willing to cleave away this part of me.

The truth is that I have never been more powerful than I am now. I am kinder, cleverer, and more authentic *because* of my memory loss. Not despite it.

I stare at Memnon for a long time.

"No," I finally say.

Goddess, but that felt good. Cathartic, even.

He raises an eyebrow, watching me carefully with those simmering eyes of his.

I don't bend.

I am a witch, descended from a line of witches who were persecuted for things others couldn't understand. I am their legacy, and *I will make them proud.*

"*No,*" I say again, louder this time. "I don't want my memories—I don't want any of it."

Memnon narrows his eyes. "You misunderstand, *est amage*. I'm not here to bargain with you. I'm not even here to demand something of you. Not yet."

Memnon sets my notebook atop the other one already on my desk; then he straightens. At his full height, he dwarfs me and the rest of the room.

He steps up to me and takes my chin, tilting it toward him. His eyes have stopped glowing, but they are no less intense when he leans forward and kisses me, the action unspeakably gentle.

When he pulls away, there's something like regret in his eyes. "How intriguing you are like this. There *is* something disarming and downright appealing to this side of you. But you are as much a panther as I am. It is time you remembered."

My own power sparks to life at those last words. "*Memnon,*" I say in warning, "don't make me your enemy in earnest."

"Oh, it is too late for that, little witch. Much too late."

He leans in again and whispers, "I still have not had my vengeance. Not until *now*."

I don't know what he's talking about, not until the two notebooks on my desk lift into the air, his indigo magic twisting around them. Then I start to have an idea.

"I think it is poetically fitting that you be lost in this world," he continues, "just as I have been lost."

"*Memnon*," I caution him.

"Gods, but how I have always enjoyed it when you turn my name into a threat," he says. "But I don't want your anger right now, Empress. I want your panic and your desperation. I want you to come *groveling* back to me. I want you to need me the way I have always needed you." He backs up as he speaks.

"Memnon," I say again, "give me back my notebooks." I feel my own magic stirring to life.

"Maybe if you beg for mercy nicely," he says, "I'll spare you the worst of my wrath."

"You motherfucker."

"That's not begging nicely," he says, grinning, like this is all fun for him. Seven hells, I'm sure it is. Memnon is one part violence and one part vengeance. "Try again."

"Memnon, I swear to the goddess—"

My two notebooks go up in flames. Right in the middle of my sentence, as the sorcerer's eyes brighten with devilish delight, *my notebooks go up in flames*.

I suck in a breath.

My memories.

My magic lashes out of me, winding around the journals, desperate to smother the flames. I yank on my power, trying to bring them to the ground, but they continue to hover in midair, burning.

"*Memnon!*" I practically cry, scrambling onto my desk so

I can try to snatch them out of the air myself. "I depend on those."

"It's a terrible thing to see your entire life's work go up in flames, isn't it?" As he speaks, the rows of notebooks that fill my bookshelf catch fire.

I scream, the sound mingling with his laughter.

Years of work is literally going up in smoke. But it's not just my memories he's burning.

"I need these notebooks for the Politia," I say, trying another angle. "They're my alibi." And thus my ticket off the suspect list they have me on.

"You won't need them once you have your memories back."

Ignoring Memnon, I put a hand to my head as I search my mind for a spell strong enough to put out these flames. Desperation is making it hard to think.

I close my eyes and drop my hand. I don't need a freaking spell. I have all the raw power right at my fingertips.

Memnon wraps his arms around me in some sick simulacrum of a hug, stopping my spell in its tracks. It's not love, or care, or reassurance he has to offer.

His lips brush my ear. "Your efforts are wasted, Empress. You have felt my power. You know you will not be able to put out my fire. Not today."

I open my eyes and turn my head to glare at him, a tear slipping out. "Fix this. *Please.*"

He wanted me to plead with him. I'm giving him exactly what he wants. Right now, I don't care.

Memnon holds my gaze, his smoky amber eyes taking in my reaction. There's a moment there where he looks almost perplexed, as though he's not sure what he's doing. The flames around us dim, and I think he will in fact fix this. But then his features turn resolute once more.

"No."

Memnon releases me, moving his gaze to my bookshelf, where my life is burning away. Many of the memories in those books have already been eaten up by my magic. Those notes and drawings were all I had left of them.

Despite his words, I do try to use my power to put out the flames. Just like he warned, my magic does nothing but momentarily make the flames flicker.

The acrid smell of smoke fills the air, the plumes of it mingling with Memnon's magic. Despite that, the fire doesn't seem to be spreading. My shelved novels and textbooks—and hell, the shelves themselves—sit there intact. Only my precious journals burn.

I stare up at the two notebooks still in midair, watching page after page blacken and char, scorched bits flaking off and fluttering to the floor.

In the distance, I can hear another woman saying, "You smell something?"

Her companion replies, "Probably just Juliette burning another spell."

My cheeks are wet. I didn't even realize I was crying. "Why are you doing this?" I say to Memnon. My life was already a dumpster fire before he entered it. "Not even my queen gets away with ruining my life."

I feel myself shaking, though everything else in me is disturbingly calm.

"I hate you," I whisper.

I really do.

A muscle in his jaw jumps, but his eyes look confident, certain. "Only because you cannot remember that you once loved me," he says.

Does he not see? He is standing in my room, ruining

my life, and breaking my heart, and he thinks some lifetime thousands of years ago matters to me?

"Fuck the past, and *fuck you*." There is so much more bottled up in me, so many emotions I can't put words to.

Memnon must feel them churning inside me through our bond because he says, "Do you think this is the worst I can do, little witch?" His eyes are sharp as knives. "I have watered entire fields with the blood of men I've killed. This is the *least* of my vengeance."

His eyes flick to what's left of my two journals that hover in the air.

"Let's see how well you fare without your precious books. You have until the Samhain Ball."

I have until the Samhain Ball to *what*? Beg some more? Come groveling his way? Whatever he wants, hell will freeze over before he gets it.

"You made a mistake crossing me." The words come from deep within me, my power swirling out of me as I speak.

The look Memnon gives me blazes with satisfaction. "*There's* my queen."

I grimace at him. "I would rather spend a thousand lifetimes forgetting my past than spend *one* remembering yours."

I think I might've imagined it, but I swear I saw him flinch.

"You can rot, Memnon."

He steps up to me, his eyes stormy. A muscle in his cheek clenches and unclenches. "Tough words, witch. Let's see if you can stand by them." He moves to the door, even as my notebooks continue to burn.

"I'll see you at the Samhain Ball, Empress."

And then he's gone.

CHAPTER 38

It takes only a handful of minutes before the crackle of fire quiets.

Smoke drifts from the notebooks that now lie in scorched heaps on my shelves.

My levitating notebooks fall to the ground, disintegrating into ash when they hit the floorboards.

I make a small noise at the sight. I can still feel wetness on my cheeks, but I'm too determined to see what's left of my journals to pay much attention to my emotions.

I move over to my notebooks, reaching for the more intact ones. They're still hot to the touch, but that doesn't stop me from examining them to see what's left.

The photos have melted away, and the paper is too charred to make out the writing and sketches that once covered the pages.

I swallow my rising emotion.

The ones that fared the best seem to be the oldest books, the ones least relevant to my life. The only mercy Memnon gave me was that he didn't touch my photo albums.

So I guess that's a win.

I sit heavily on my bed and put my head in my hands.

The oak tree outside rustles. Then Nero hops back into the room, as though he can sense my sadness.

Actually, now that I understand bonds, he probably can.

Nero comes up to me, rubbing his head against my shoulder.

"Fat lot of good you did there," I say, wiping my eyes.

He rubs the rest of his body against my side, shameless about the fact he was a total *traitor*.

Need to write down what I can remember.

I cross over to my desk before pulling out one of the wooden drawers along its side. In it rests a stack of notebooks.

For all my faults, I *am* organized. And optimistic and kind and clever.

But now I'm also determined.

After grabbing a new notebook, I pull out a pen and begin writing.

First my name, my date of birth, and my parents' names. Important phone numbers, addresses, and so on. Anything and everything I truly could not bear for my mind to lose.

Then I write down a warning.

Do not trust Memnon the Cursed.

You woke him from eternal sleep. He believes you're his dead wife who betrayed him. He wants to make you pay.

He is your soul mate, but he is an ASSHOLE. He burned all your previous notebooks. He will fuck you over again if he gets the chance.

You hate him with every fiber of your being.

A tear hits the page. Then another and another. I can't decide if I'm sad or angry.

Nothing to do about it now but move forward and plot my own revenge.

I write out the days of the week on the next blank page of my notebook, penning in the Samhain Ball under Saturday's date. I circle the event in red and write a note next to it:

MEMNON WANTS YOU TO ATTEND.

I'm still not entirely sure whether I *will* attend or not. I hate the idea of agreeing to his demands, but he also woke in me a thirst for revenge that I had no idea existed until now. But every second I breathe in the smell of smoke, I grow more bloodthirsty and bitter.

He will pay for this.

That promise is the only thing warming my cold, dejected heart.

I'm still writing when there's a knock on the door.

"Yeah?" I call out, cringing when I hear the waver in my voice.

"Selene," a witch says on the other side of the door, "there's an officer at the front door who's asking for you."

I take a deep breath, a queasy wave of dread unsettling my stomach.

Goddess, it's time to face the fallout of what just happened.

I stand inside my room, Nero at my side, while Officer Howahkan and his partner, Officer Mwangi, take in the smoldering remains of my notebooks.

Officer Howahkan is the first to speak. "Are those your…?"

"*Yeah*," I say hoarsely.

It's quiet for several seconds.

He lets out a heavy sigh. "You burned your journals?" He asks it like he's not truly surprised, just disappointed. "You realize how this looks."

Yeah, it looks like I'm fucking guilty.

"*I* didn't burn them," I snap.

The officer's face remains impassive. "Who did?"

"Memnon."

I see a flicker of recognition from Officer Mwangi. "Memnon—is that the same man who broke into this bedroom a few weeks ago?" she asks.

I nod.

"And he was here again?"

Another nod.

"How did he get in?" she asks. Because according to official records, last time this happened, he broke in through a window.

"I don't know—with magic, I suspect. He was in my room when I got here."

"And he's the one who burned your books?" Officer Mwangi asks.

"Yes," I say softly.

"Why would he do that?"

I hug my arms. "To be cruel."

"And why would he want to be cruel?" Officer Mwangi asks. I can't tell if she's concerned or skeptical.

"Memnon is under the delusion that I betrayed him, and he wants revenge."

Officer Howahkan pulls out a notepad and a pen and jots something down.

"Do you have his number? Or his address?" he asks, his dark eyes penetrating. "Some way for us to contact him and follow up on this?"

My throat tightens. "No."

Officer Howahkan presses his lips together. "Do you have a last name at least?"

"No," I say softly.

"Ah."

I'm suddenly tired, so tired. I know how this looks.

I rub my eyes as Nero leans his body against my leg. "Is there any way to fix my notebooks? Some spell that can return them to the way they were?" I ask.

The moment I voice the question, my hope flares to life.

A spell, of course.

Officer Howahkan gives me an inscrutable look. "Maybe," he says, watching me carefully. "Magic is capable of lots of things."

I exhale my relief.

"You can check my phone," I say, eager to give these officers *something*. I grab it and hand it to the officer. "I use it for notes and scheduling all the time." It's just not the main thing I use.

"We *have* checked your phone," Officer Howahkan says.

Oh.

He looks almost sorry as he adds, "If we'd found evidence on it that proved your innocence, we wouldn't be sitting here now, having this conversation."

"Are you planning on arresting me?" I say quietly.

The officer shares a look with his partner. "No," he finally says. "Not today, Selene."

CHAPTER 39

I don't spook easily, but I nearly shit my pants after the officers' visit.

Surely I can be placed somewhere away from the crimes during the time they were committed? I mean, I live in a house with a hundred other women. Someone somewhere should be able to vouch for me.

Officer Mwangi calls in a team to collect what they can of my notebooks' delicate remains, and once they arrive, I leave the room so they can do their thing.

I have to believe they'll be able to reverse the damage Memnon inflicted on them.

I descend the stairs to Sybil's room, Nero following in my wake. I notice a few side-eyed glances from other witches in the halls, and I get the impression word has spread that I am a suspect in the recent string of murders.

The thought of my coven sisters turning on me is terrifying. If any group is good at refusing to persecute others, it's witches. We've been on the receiving end of it too often.

But even we witches have our limits. I wonder how close this coven is to reaching theirs.

There's also the nagging possibility that some of the witches I live alongside could've participated in that spell circle. Another terrifying thought.

When I reach Sybil's door, I can hear her on the other side of it, murmuring.

I knock. When she doesn't answer, I grab the doorknob and push it open.

I mean, technically, it's rude to barge into someone's room, but also technically, Sybil does it to me all the time.

Also, the last time she saw me, I was fleeing her with a mojito in hand, trying to keep all my secrets to myself.

I can't do it anymore.

When I step into her room, I see Sybil sitting inside a chalk circle she's made, the soft lilac plumes of her magic swirling around her as she continues incanting a spell in low tones. Nestled along the edge of the circle are lit candles, their flames flickering in time to the rise and fall of Sybil's voice.

The sight of it reminds me all over again of my burning books and Memnon's glee. I draw in a deep breath, forcing myself to keep it together.

On the opposite side of the room, Sybil's owl, Merlin, sits perched on a bust of the veiled maiden that's nearly been overtaken by the vines growing rampant in her room.

I sit on her bed as Nero sniffs the air in the direction of her familiar.

"Don't even *think* about it," I whisper to him. "I will turn you into a newt if you do more than lick your lips in Merlin's direction."

Nero gives me a grumpy look but settles for flopping on the floor.

Not even that alarming exchange causes my friend to open her eyes. She spellcasts for several more minutes, while Nero and I and my anxiety all hang in her room. I move near her bookshelf, ignoring a Venus flytrap that literally snaps in my direction as I reach for a book.

"Don't be naughty," I say, tapping it on its head.

I grab a book on herbalism and flip through it while I wait, though I'm not really seeing anything when I look at the pages.

You're in deep this time, Selene.

Memnon wanted me desperate, and already I'm feeling the first tendrils of that desperation.

Sybil's magic thickens as she finishes her spell, the plumes of it nearly concealing her. I feel the energy in the room shift, and the candles go out all at once.

I hear her deep exhale as her power clears.

"Fuck, I love magic," she says, opening her eyes.

She rubs out part of the chalk circle and begins to pick up the items she had spread out.

I close the book on herbalism. "What was that spell for?"

"I rolled my ankle this morning walking down the steps of Morgana Hall."

I wince. "Did you have to walk all the way back here on it?"

"Actually, I borrowed a witch's broom and flew back here, and honestly, Selene, we've got to do this together..." She takes me in. "What happened to you?"

"Is it really that obvious?" I say, touching my cheek. But it must be—even I can hear the broken notes of my voice.

"What's wrong?" she says instead, her voice growing alarmed. "I can smell smoke on you."

I reach a hand down for Nero, grounding myself with

his presence. "There's a lot I haven't told you," I admit. I take a deep breath. "What I'm about to tell you is for your ears only."

Sybil frowns. "Okay, now I'm really worried, Selene. What haven't you told me?"

I share it all—everything from the spell circle gone awry to Memnon saving me. I tell her about him helping seal off the tunnel entrance—

"I didn't even know there *were* tunnels," she cuts in.

"I'll show you it sometime," I say softly before continuing.

I tell her about how I found out I was a soul mate. A tear drips down my cheek when I admit exactly who I'm bonded to.

"What!" Merlin flaps his wings at Sybil's outburst, then flashes me an owlish glare, like it's my fault I upset his witch.

I press on, mentioning how Memnon turned on me and burned my books, and I finish with my meeting with the high priestess and being on the Politia's suspect list.

By the time I'm done, my cheeks are wet again.

For a long moment, Sybil is silent. Finally, she whispers, "I am so sorry, Selene."

She pulls me into a hug then, and I lean into her, crying into her shoulder as she rubs my back.

"And to think my day sucked because I have a sprained ankle."

"I'm sure the sprained ankle sucked," I say, sniffling a little.

My friend laughs. "It did hurt like a bitch," she says as she continues rubbing my back. "But then I got to ride a broomstick—I even cackled for the sheer hell of it."

I let out a sad little laugh at that. "I'm pretty sure you *have* to cackle when you're flying on a broomstick," I say, pulling away to wipe at my tears. "It's part of the rules."

Sybil smiles at that, but it quickly disappears. "Honestly, Selene, I don't even know where to start with this one, except that, babe, that was a crap ton of secrets."

I laugh again, even though I know she's saying this just to lighten the moment.

She reaches out and tucks a lock of my hair behind my ear. "I know you're innocent."

I pull away to look miserably at her. "I don't think I can prove it," I admit.

"I'll help you," she says. "I'll ask the other coven sisters if they saw you at the times in question. We'll make a new notebook for you and create a timeline, one that I am sure will clear your name."

"You'd do that?" I'm so used to winging it on my own that I forgot I have people in my life willing to help me.

"You're my best friend, Selene. Of course I will. Now," she says, her tone changing, "forget about the Politia and that case for a minute. I want to chat about *Memnon*." She says his name menacingly.

"Ugh." I place my face in my hands, trying to wish away my life.

What hurts the most is that before he burned my notebooks, I had actually started to fall for him. I caught glimpses of what it would be to care and be cared for by a man like Memnon.

You and I, Empress, we are eternal.

But then he wanted me to hurt like him, to be lost and confused in this modern world just like him. His vengeance eclipsed whatever feelings he has for me.

Sybil rubs my back. "So you're bonded to a fucking loser. If he wants to be enemies, let's make him *pay*."

I lift my head from my hands, my magic rising.

Yes.

"Listen," she says, seeing my interest, "this bastard is your soul mate. He may be the dirtiest rim job out there, but he is fated to you, which means the guy is basically walking around with a hard-on every time he sees you.

"So you and I are going to find some killer dresses, we're going to go to the ball, and you're going to enjoy the fuck out of yourself in front of that bastard. Bonus points for flirting and dancing with every mage who's up for it.

"He'll see what he's missing, and it will be *him* who comes groveling back to *you*."

I stare at her.

And then I smile.

CHAPTER 40

Let's make him pay.

That thought sticks to me like a barb through the weekend and into the following week.

It's there when I forget I have a coffee date with one of the witches in my wards class, and it's there when I miss turning in an assignment for spellcasting. I cling to the promise of vengeance every time I see Politia officers on campus, interviewing witches or examining cordoned-off sections of the woods. I reassure myself of it after each weird look a coven sister casts my way, and I bask in the thought of it when Sybil and I go shopping for dresses in San Francisco.

The problem is, the longer I muse on Sybil's plan, the more I realize…it's not settling my demons.

Not by half.

I think of all the burned books—years of life and work meticulously documented—and how the sorcerer relished destroying them. Then I think of how he attacked Kane in my room and how he's repeatedly threatened me.

Despite Memnon's wicked tongue and the budding thing we had between us, he has made it clear since the beginning that we are enemies. And what have I done to stop him?

Nothing.

And now my revenge is supposed to be wearing a sexy dress and giving other men attention in some bid to make Memnon jealous? It's laughably pathetic, and I'm far too bloodthirsty to settle for that.

I need to make the man *truly* pay. But how?

Wednesday evening, I sit sprawled out in one of the wingback chairs in my house's library, Nero at my feet, as I rub my lower lip and muse over my situation.

Right over my heart, I can sense my devilish bond thrum with life. Unfortunately, I've been noticing this bond more and more since I accepted that I'm Memnon's soul mate. Just giving it this small amount of attention is enough for me to feel the sorcerer on the other side of it.

Whatever he's doing, he's some combination of pleased and impatient.

Smug bastard.

Little witch, are you poking around my mind? Memnon's voice is soft like velvet in my head.

Crap, I forgot that he can sense me too.

I ignore him and the way his words stroke me from the inside out.

I can taste your frustration, he says. *Are you desperate yet?*

Screw you. I shove the words down our bond.

Is that a legitimate offer? Because if it is, I'll have to think about it.

Goddess, but I hate him.

I feel his amusement as his presence retreats from our bond, and I'm alone once more—or as alone as I can be now that I'm connected to another.

That's the heart of the issue—being bonded to him.

Being bonded…

Can…soul mate bonds be broken?

The thought makes my breath catch.

Has anyone ever tried?

Before another thought has fully formed, I'm rising from my chair, then giving my familiar an idle pet as I leave my spot and head for the back of the library.

Nero is up and at my heels as though he weren't busy sleeping a minute ago.

This early in the evening, the library is filled with several witches doing homework or reading various tomes. A few of them glance up at me, including one witch I think is friends with the still-missing Kasey, whose disappearance is now being investigated by the Politia. Kasey's friend grimaces at me, then goes back to reading her book.

One nasty look isn't nearly enough to distract myself from the fierce purpose riding me.

I haven't visited the grimoire room since my first night here, but I'll need them now for what I have in mind.

I pass the ornate stone fireplace and reach the door to the sealed room. When I open it, I wince at the clashing magic that fills the air, and Nero's ears go back.

It's only then that I hesitate.

What am I doing?

This idea that's gripped me, it fills all the dangerous, wrathful spaces in my soul, but is it what I really want? Every source I've read on soul mates speaks of the deliberate nature of them. They're each other's perfect other half.

I don't know what it means that Memnon and I *don't* feel perfect. We feel like two misaligned puzzle pieces being forced together.

I take a deep breath, moving my eyes to the lantern lamp that sits there waiting for me.

Maybe the books got it wrong. Or maybe Memnon and I are perfectly awful on our own and even worse together.

Either way, it seems like a good idea to end this now—if I can.

I pick up the lantern. Waving my hand over it, I murmur, "*With a flicker and a spark, light this candle in the dark.*" A tiny flame flickers to life, and I note with relief that this time, the flame doesn't look demonic.

I step fully inside the room, Nero slipping in after me, and I close the door behind us.

Already, my head is pounding from the conflicting magic in the air.

I set the lantern on the table in the middle of the room, and I close my eyes to better focus my senses.

Now that I'm not looking with my eyes, I swear I feel the prickling awareness of all these spellbooks. Magic is semi-sentient; these grimoires may not have lungs or hearts or brains, but in some innate way, they are alive. And right now, they're observing me.

With my eyes still closed, I place my hands on the wooden table. "I would like to sever a soul mate bond." The words feel forbidden. Taboo. "If any of you contain such a spell, I would ask to see it. Please."

For several long seconds, I hear nothing.

My heart sinks, even as a sliver of relief threads through my system. If it cannot be done, then it absolves me from acting—

I hear the soft scrape of a book sliding out.

I open my eyes in time to see a thin black tome leave one of the shelves high above my head. It flutters down to the table like a falling leaf before landing gently right in front of me.

I barely have time to look at the image stamped on its black cloth cover before it opens itself. The grimoire's pages flick by, like some phantom hand is thumbing through them. Near the back of the book, it finally stops on a page. There's an inked drawing of a heart and a handwritten spell penned in German.

I place my hand over the text, taking a moment to compose an incantation.

"Translate to English this spell for me. Make its meaning clear to see."

The letters jiggle, then morph, and suddenly, I can read it all. *A Spell for Severing Amorous Bonds.*

I swallow. This may be a mistake.

What may be a mistake, Empress…? Memnon's voice echoes in my head.

I scowl at the intimate feel of this man inside me. *Why don't you mind your own fucking business?* I snap back him.

On the other end of our bond, the sorcerer seems quiet, pensive. It's better than the cavalier amusement I felt from him earlier.

There's a flicker of something on his end of our connection, and then he withdraws completely.

I exhale, and my eyes move over the page in front of me. The bloodthirsty, vicious side of me gets a perverse little thrill at the sight of it.

I tap the spell.

I'm going to do it.

The wind howls as I stand in the spellcasting kitchen deep into the night, my cauldron bubbling.

It took me hours to hunt down the ingredients for this

spell, including seawater, roses that bloomed under a full moon, tears from a broken heart (using mine—hope they work), and then some mundane herbs. And to be honest, I didn't find all the ingredients. But I think I can still make it work.

Using a mortar and pestle, I crush the dried rose petals, then throw them in. The next part is going to be tricky—the recipe called for a dead man's dreams, but I couldn't find any of those, so I went to Olga and got the last words of a life cut short.

I bite my lower lip as I stare at the words I copied.

Sounds good. Love you—see you soon.

I try not to shiver at how mundane these last words were. It makes death seem all the more grotesque, to rob someone of their life right in the middle of a perfectly average day.

Instead, I focus on the ingredient itself—should I throw the note into the cauldron or whisper the words over it?

Before I can decide, the front door crashes open, wood splintering as it rips off its hinges. I expect to hear a chorus of screams, but most of, if not all, my sisters have gone to bed, save for a group that left an hour ago for some outdoor spellcasting.

Familiar heavy footfalls stride across the foyer, and my stomach fills with dread.

Memnon fills the doorway, his eyes blazing. They move from my face to the wooden spoon I have in my hand, then the cauldron in front of me.

I move in front of the cauldron, ready to defend my spell. "You do not get to just—"

I yelp as he picks me up and sets me on the island behind me.

He puts a finger up to my face. "*Stay*," he growls, his magic coiling around me.

"Don't talk to me like I'm a dog," I snap back at him.

I try to hop off the counter, but damn it, he spelled my ass—literally. I can't get up.

I watch on helplessly as Memnon stalks toward my cauldron and grabs it with his bare hands.

"Memnon, no—"

Before I can even finish my plea, he overturns the thing, dumping its contents out onto the open fire beneath it, dousing the flame and ruining my concoction.

I make a horrified sound and stare aghast at the ruins of my spell.

Memnon turns back to me, his chest heaving and his palms blistered from where he held the cauldron. "You were trying to break our bond!" he roars.

Upstairs, I hear someone yell, "Shut up!"

"Goddess above, lower your voice," I whisper. "You're going to wake up the whole coven." I'm skating on thin enough ice as it is.

"Even after enduring your betrayal and your desertion, *est amage*, I would never *dare* to break what is ours and ours alone!" His voice rises until he is bellowing the words.

"Maybe if you had spent the past several weeks trying to be my friend instead of making my life miserable, I wouldn't be attempting to break our bond."

His expression flickers, like he may feel regret or shame, but I'm not done.

"I swear to the goddess," I continue, "the moment you leave my sight, I will start the process all over again."

It seems like Memnon grows taller, wider. He steps between my legs, looking menacing, lethal.

"No," he says softly, "you won't." The sorcerer places his hands on either side of my head, his eyes flinty.

I jerk against his touch. "Let me go."

"Your mind isn't the only one that can steal memories," he says, those smoky eyes piercing.

I go still at what he's hinting at. "You wouldn't," I breathe.

He smiles. "Of course I would. I already *have*."

"You've taken my memories?" My voice is unnaturally quiet as I speak. Dark, roiling fury builds beneath my veins.

"Your heart isn't the only thing I own." It's as much a confession as anything else.

I don't think—I launch myself at him. Memnon's magic still holds my legs fast to the table, but I manage to claw at his eyes and tear that self-satisfied smirk from his face.

"Fuck," he curses in Sarmatian, staggering out of my reach. Then he laughs. Laughs!

"Ah, *est amage*, I've missed your fiery side," he says, stepping back into my space and catching one of my wrists.

"I will gut you for taking my memories, you asshole!" I manage to drag my nails down the other side of Memnon's face before he's able to capture my other wrist.

He grins wickedly. "I thought you didn't mind losing them? You fought for your curse so passionately a week ago."

"You had *no* right to take them," I say vehemently.

Memnon ignores my words, his gaze moving to the open grimoire next to me. "Ah, is this the hateful spell?" He moves my wrists into one of his hands so he can place his palm on the book.

Beneath his hand, the page curls and blackens, and a wisp of smoke rises from the book.

I jerk fruitlessly against his grip, my mood darkening with every passing second. This spell was supposed to placate my rage, not enflame it. But it's as though I'm reliving the book burning in my room all over again.

"You think you can break our bond and dispose of me as you did two thousand years ago?"

I sense his own rage rising, and his eyes illuminate with his power. I'm reminded all over again that a sorcerer's magic draws from their conscience; as they grow stronger, their empathy grows weaker. I'm sensing that Memnon lost most of his back in antiquity.

"You will never be free of me, little witch. Never."

I stare at the magic sparking in his eyes. I'm coming to find that there is nothing nearly so dangerous as a wronged sorcerer.

Memnon's hand comes up, wrapping around my throat in the most featherlight grip. But between his spell nailing me to the table, his body pinning me in, and now his hand on my neck, I am completely immobilized.

"But you are right, I have given you more misery than passion. Perhaps it is time I reminded you of what it means to be with me."

My eyebrows shoot up. Wait, *what*?

Before that thought has more than crossed my mind, Memnon kisses me.

CHAPTER 41

Hateful, hateful man. With his wicked lips and wicked thoughts and wicked intentions.

He's got some fucking *gall* to dare kiss me after he's upended my world.

So I bite his lip. *Hard*.

Memnon groans as the metallic tang of blood hits our tongues. The monster smiles against my mouth and deepens the kiss, as though the small violence is a turn-on for him. Despite my raging fury—and, oh, how it rages—I kiss him back, hungry for more of him. My fingers slide into his hair and pull it taut enough to hurt.

I hate that I do still want him when all I really want is to hate him.

Memnon's fingers flex just the slightest bit against my throat, reminding me that he has me pinned and vulnerable, though it doesn't make me *feel* vulnerable. I feel as though I'm going to combust. Already, I know that if I open my eyes, I will see plumes of my magic seeping out of me.

"My empress is finally showing her true colors," Memnon murmurs against my lips.

There's nothing true about this at all—this is my worst side. But if my mate wants to cut himself on the sharpest parts of my personality, *so be it.*

When his tongue delves back into my mouth, I bite it. Memnon hisses, but if anything, he kisses me with more fervor. Fervor I return.

I can't explain it. There *is* no explaining it. I hate his guts. I'd love nothing more than to kick him in the balls. But I'm also enjoying hate kissing the shit out of his lips. I'm pretty sure I'd be fine taking this hate all the way to the end of desire.

I think I've just unlocked a new kink.

Memnon pulls away. "You will know me in all ways," he vows.

His thoughts must be in the same vein as mine—that, or he heard me through our bond.

While it's fine for me to fantasize about using Memnon to fulfill my own desires, like hell am I going to let him do the same thing.

I push the sorcerer away, his hand slipping effortlessly away from my neck.

Hate-fucking fantasies be damned—

"If I can't break the bond, I'll simply cast a spell to shrivel up your dick," I threaten him.

Memnon smiles, a bead of blood gathering at the corner of his lip. "It's cute that you think you haven't already tried."

That has my eyes widening.

He wipes the bead of blood away, flicking his eyes over me.

"*Release*," he says in Sarmatian.

Immediately, his magic lifts itself from my body, no longer anchoring me to the table.

His eyes settle on me. "I love you, little witch," he says, his expression a touch sad. "More than all the world. That is my deepest truth, and it's one I should have told you again and again as I once did.

"And I'm sorry you have to bear the weight of that love." His features shift a little, growing determined. "But you *will* bear it."

With that, he heads for the doorway.

"Three days," he calls over his shoulder. "That's all you have left, Empress."

And then he's gone.

Those three days pass in the blink of an eye.

Three days to try to sort out my own tangled emotions. Three days to fixate on my revenge. Three days to wonder what Memnon means to do on the night of the ball.

I now stare at the gown spread out on my bed, my mood grim.

I don't want to face Memnon again.

Maybe that's cowardly. It's still the truth.

He is my worst nightmare, but I'm also coming to find he's a huge weakness of mine because he saved me and he cared for me and a part of me—a twisted, wayward part of me—*likes* him. Fuck, I more than like him. I'm beyond attracted to the man, and I crave the sound of his commanding voice and the feel of those arms around me. All he has to do is kiss me or whisper a few pretty words in my ear, and I'll reconsider every hateful thought I've had of him.

I'm terrified that will happen again tonight when I'm seeking out my revenge.

In the distance, I hear someone tromping up the stairs, followed by the creaking of floorboards as they head down my hall.

Seconds later, Sybil opens the door. "Hey, babe!" she hollers as she bustles in, carrying her dress and shoes as well as a massive tote bag full of what looks to be makeup and maybe hair supplies.

She drops it all on the bed. "Fuck, I'm excited for tonight, aren't…?" Her voice trails off as soon as she sees my face. "No, no, no, Selene," she says.

I touch my cheek. "What?"

"I'm not going to let you panic about tonight. This is your night for revenge. I want to see wicked grins and evil looks only."

I put my face in my hands and groan. "I'm nervous," I admit.

Sybil comes over to me and places her hands on my shoulders. "Your soul mate thinks you're conniving and cruel. The Politia thinks you could be a killer. You're obviously neither of those things, but fuck it." She gives my shoulders a shake. "We're going to embrace it for one night."

She releases me and turns to the items on the bed. From her bag she pulls out a bottle of vodka and two cans of sparkling juice. "We're going to drink, we're going to do each other's makeup and hair and have fucking *fun* dressing up like villainesses for a night. What do you say?"

I take a deep breath. "Pour me a shot."

By the time I reach for my dress, I'm giggling.

I may have had a touch too much alcohol.

Our hair and makeup—done. All that's left is pulling on our dresses. I walk over to mine while Sybil grabs hers, my legs a little shaky.

The black dress is floor-length with a small train and a slit all the way up to nearly the top of my thigh. The back is even sexier, held together by only two crisscrossing straps, leaving the rest of my skin down to the small of my back exposed.

There's a sheen to the material that makes it look a touch iridescent, and it slides around me like a serpent. Now that I have it on, I do feel more than a little wicked.

"I know you have a love affair with high-tops and combat boots." Sybil turns to me in her ruby-red dress, the gemstones on it glittering as they catch the light. "But for tonight, let's do something a bit fancier," she says, moving over to my closet.

"I don't have anything fancier," I say. "Besides, how am I going to crush my enemies beneath my boots if I'm not wearing boots?"

"You're not going to crush them beneath your boots," Sybil says with an exaggerated eye roll. "You're obviously going to impale them with your stiletto heel. Just give me a sec—"

She dashes out of the room, her own nude heels already on. Distantly, I hear something thumping down the stairs, followed by curses.

Uh-oh. This is why stilettos are a bad idea—especially when alcohol is involved.

I rush out of my room, passing other witches in various states of dress. Lying on the landing, her dress basically around her waist, is Sybil.

Another witch is already there, ready to help her, but she waves the girl away. "I'm good, I'm good."

Despite her words, I head down to the landing and help pick my friend up as she smooths her hands over her dress.

"The shoes aren't worth it," I whisper.

"I didn't just eat shit for nothing, Selene," she says. With that, she pulls her hand away and staggers down the rest of the stairs, heading to her room.

I take the moment to visit my own room and grab my phone, which I tuck it into my dress. Nero has been lounging next to my bed this entire time, but now, as though sensing I'm leaving the room for good, he follows me out.

We get to Sybil's room just as she's closing the door behind her, her owl familiar perched on her shoulder and a pair of open-toed stilettos in her hand.

"Here," she says when she sees me, thrusting the heels at me.

I slip the shoes on, and then we make our way downstairs with our familiars before heading out of the house alongside another group of witches—two of whom are wearing Chucks.

Meanwhile, I'm strapped into a pair of stilts.

Wait, this thought feels familiar. Did I have an entire exchange just like this one with Sybil on another night...?

I bet I did.

I exhale. I better be putting off killer-queen vibes, or I'm going to mutiny.

The group of us cuts across campus, following the stream of witches heading toward the conservatory. Nero prowls at my side, acting as my date.

Overhead, the full moon shines down, illuminating the darkness and limning our surroundings in a pale blue light. I draw in a breath at the sight of it, my magic tingling as it too feels the touch of that light. Full moons are for revelation and truth that not even the darkness can hide. And this one, the hunter's moon, is particularly poignant.

It's a good night for revenge and for forcing Memnon to face *my* true feelings of him.

Witches on broomsticks cut through the air, laughing with abandon, their skirts and hair waving in the wind behind them.

An old sense of longing comes over me, and I have to remind myself I'm in the coven and I'll learn how to fly on brooms eventually. That's one more thing I'll get to accomplish during my time here. I just haven't yet.

The conservatory glows in the distance, the all-glass structure lit from within and without by hundreds of levitating lanterns, the flickering candlelight creating a beautiful, almost-Gothic effect.

I've never actually been inside the coven's massive greenhouse. Not until tonight. It's clear as I get closer that I've been missing out. I can see all sorts of wild greenery growing inside, and in honor of Samhain, someone's grown pumpkins the size of chairs outside the building. Many are still attached to their vines, and the plants themselves curl around the massive fruit.

I make my way up the marble steps leading to the door, Nero at my side. I glance at Sybil's shoulder, noticing that Merlin has already flown off into the night. I pause, glancing around as the rest of the witches continue into the building. No one else's familiar seems to be with them.

I chew on the corner of my lip as I take in Nero. "I don't think you're allowed inside as you are," I say.

My panther looks at me for a long time with his

golden-green eyes, as though he's trying to silently communicate something. I slip down our bond and into his head for a moment, and I feel an emotion from him I'm not expecting—affection.

Slipping back into my own body, I kneel so I can place my forehead against my familiar's.

"I love you too," I whisper to him. I pull away and pet his face. "Stay safe in those woods tonight." There are bound to be a lot of drunk, lusty witches making bad decisions out there.

Nero gives me another long look, as if to say, *You stay safe too.*

Or maybe that's just me anthropomorphizing my familiar. I nod anyway.

With one final look, Nero turns from me and lopes toward the tree line. I stand, watching him go.

Empress...

My flesh puckers at Memnon's call. I turn to face the conservatory once more, and I startle when I catch sight of him through the double doors.

He stands with his hands in the pockets of his tux, looking so much larger than the people moving around him.

I suck in my breath at how good he looks, his wildness caged in by the cut of his suit jacket and pants. Well, *mostly* caged in—he's done away with a bow tie, his dress shirt is partially unbuttoned, and I can see that panther tattoo of his peeking out above the collar of his shirt. His hair looks like he's run his fingers through it several times.

If I thought a tuxedo would make Memnon look any less dangerous, I was wildly wrong.

My heart trips on itself at the sight of him, and a light, fluttery feeling fills my stomach.

Revenge, I remind myself. Tonight is for revenge.

His smoky eyes glitter as he takes me in, from the tips of my toes, up along the slit of my dress to my bust, and then, finally, to my face. He looks like someone hit him upside the head.

I see him swallow, his eyes still fixed on me, and holy shit, is Memnon actually…thrown by this outfit?

Guess the revenge dress worked.

I take a deep breath and square my shoulders. All right, I can do this. Already, the fluttery feeling in my stomach is settling.

I head the rest of the way up the stairs and enter the conservatory, hearing some haunting melody fill the air. All around me, witches and mages stand around in formal wear, chatting and laughing and drinking witch's brew from delicate coupe glasses like we're high-society folk and not wild, enchanted things.

I turn to where Memnon stood a moment ago, but he's gone. Unfortunately, somewhere in all the crowd, I've lost sight of Memnon. I glance around.

"Selene!"

I turn toward the voice, only to see Sybil slipping through the crowd toward me. Farther behind her, I catch sight of the group we came here with.

"I grabbed us a table!" my friend says, stepping in front of me. "Want to go sit down, or—?"

"I saw him," I say to her.

"What? Where?" She glances around.

"I don't know, I lost sight of him." As I speak, I realize my hands are shaking. But it's not from nerves; it's from my coiling magic.

I'm ready to face the man.

Sybil's face grows excited. "You know what this means?" she says. "It's revenge time."

Instead of returning to the table Sybil nabbed us, she leads me in the opposite direction, down one of the conservatory's wings.

For a moment, as I take in our surroundings, I forget about Memnon and the vendettas between us.

I cannot believe I haven't visited this place before.

Plants fill every level of the conservatory, growing from massive terra-cotta pots and patches of ground where the floor has been cut away. The only place not completely covered in growing foliage is the dance floor and its surrounding tables, though even that area is dotted with plants. And all of it is illuminated by the levitating lanterns above us.

At the end of the wing, beyond clusters of chatting supernaturals, a massive cauldron smokes. Next to it rests a pyramid of coupe glasses, all filled with the wafting brew.

Right, more booze to loosen my inhibitions and allow me to have a good time tonight. Maybe it'll even make me forget that *having a good time* does nothing to quench my thirst for payback.

Sybil and I haven't made it to the cauldron when I feel the brush of familiar magic on my bare back.

Empress…we have unfinished business…

I stop walking, and Sybil glances back at me.

"What is it?" she asks.

"Memnon."

"Do you see him?" she asks. "Where is he?" She peers around me as though she might spot him.

I have the oddest urge to laugh at her. "Do you even know what he looks like?" I ask.

"No, but all assholes have a look to them. I'm sure I could pick him out of this crowd."

Now I do laugh. "I can hear him," I admit. I touch my temple. "In here."

My friend's brows rise. "Oh—*oh*. Right. You have freaky soul mate powers."

I glance surreptitiously around us, but I don't see Memnon. He's clearly toying with me.

Worse, it's working.

Fun is the absolute last thing on my mind right now. Instead, all my anger and resentment and shame and worry—all those ugly emotions rise in me, along with a few others, like excitement, hope, and a breathless, flighty feeling I won't put a name to.

We reach the pyramid of booze, and the two of us grab glasses. But as I stare at the brew I hold, I scowl.

"I can't do it," I admit.

"Can't do what?" Sybil asks as she takes a sip of her drink.

I can't continue to drink and laugh and *pretend*. Goddess, I don't want to pretend anymore.

"I need to find Memnon and deal with him." As I speak the words, I feel the absolute truth of them. I hand my friend my drink. "Can you take this back to our table and save it for me?"

"But, Selene—"

"Please, Sybil." I give her a beseeching look. "I'll only be gone a moment." I force out a smile. "Then we can have fun together. In earnest."

She exhales but then nods. "Okay, yeah, fine. You deal with the loser and then find me." My friend gives me a playful look. "But don't take too long, or else I'll drink your brew for you."

This time, I give her a real smile. "Deal."

Once Sybil leaves my sight, I prowl the aisles of plants, making my way around whispering couples. I pass them, threading through the conservatory until I reach a lonely corner of it that is clear of all guests.

The notes of some tragic song drifting in the air and the distant murmuring of voices are the only clues that a party is in full swing at the moment.

Where are you? I call to Memnon down our bond.

My hands fist a little, and already, my thirst for revenge is mounting. I'm vividly imagining getting a good swing at the sorcerer or maybe kneeing him in the balls. Magic is leaking from my hands at the prospect.

Around me, the air stirs; then a broad chest brushes against my back.

"Right here, little witch," he breathes against my ear.

My pulse spikes at his voice and his nearness, and I spin to face him.

Now is my opening. If ever I wanted to get a move in while he's unsuspecting, now would be it.

Instead, I hesitate, my vengeance taking a back seat to this breathless excitement I feel at the sight of him. A sobering thought comes to me then: no matter how much I rage against Memnon, he will always be the man my eyes search for in a room, and his features are the ones I'll crave. The crush I had on Kane is nothing—absolutely nothing—compared to this.

Memnon's own eyes drink me in. "You have never needed magic, *est amage*," he murmurs, his roughened voice drawing out goose bumps on my arms. "You are entirely bewitching even without it."

I lift my chin a little. "Were you hoping I'd be a mess tonight now that you burned my notebooks? That I'd be *begging* you to return my memories back to me?"

"Mmm..." The noise he makes sounds more like a growl than anything else. "I *do* like the idea of you begging, *est amage*. You always made such...*convincing* arguments."

I don't know if it's a memory or my imagination, but for a split second, I have an image of myself on my knees before him, his cock in my mouth—

It disappears as quickly as it came, but it leaves me breathless and flushed.

Memnon's eyes drop to one of my reddened cheeks, and he strokes the skin there. "Beautiful, intoxicating witch," he breathes.

He leans in, almost as though he can't help it, those tempting lips skimming my skin, daring me to push him away.

I don't know what spell he's using, but right in this moment, our insurmountable issues seem to dissolve into nothing. When Memnon is this close to me, it all becomes very simple.

He's mine.

His lips skim down my jaw. "Something I discovered after I first met you is that if I kiss you right here—" He brushes his lips against the side of my neck, right under my pulse point, and a shiver wracks my body. He smiles against my throat. "You do just that."

I tilt my head back even as I lean into the kiss, one of my hands moving to his hair. I thread my fingers through his dark locks, wanting to keep him against me. I crave more than his mouth on my throat and our bodies pressed together like this.

I want to push him down and yank open his starched white shirt. I want to hear buttons popping. I want his skin against mine.

I want him to flash me that pirate smile of his while

I have my way with him and put an end to this fire he's lit in me.

He burned your notebooks—your memories. Do not climb the man like a tree. Make him pay.

I nearly gasp at the sobering thought. My fingers loosen from his hair, and I stiffen in his arms—when did his arms snake their way around me?

Fuck, this is exactly what I wasn't supposed to do tonight.

It takes a ridiculous amount of self-possession, but I manage to bring my palms up to his chest, admiring for a moment that his pecs feel so good. Isn't that silly, that pecs can feel—?

Fuck, concentrate, *Selene.*

Roughly, I push Memnon away, adding a little magic into the action to move his massive body.

The sorcerer staggers back, his expression lust drunk as his eyes move to my lips.

"You destroyed my journals and the *years* of memories in them," I remind us both.

Some of the haze fades from Memnon's face.

"Is this your attempt at making me feel regret?" he says, wiping his lip with his thumb. "Guilt? Shame?" His hand drops, and his features grow serious. "Because, my queen, this is absolutely what victory feels like."

"Victory Over what? Our highly dysfunctional relationship?"

Memnon smiles down at me. "I have anticipated this evening for a long, long time."

My brows draw together, even as unease coils in my belly. "What are you talking about?"

"What do you think I've done with all the time we've been apart?" he asks, tilting his head.

I never knew.

He shakes his head slowly. "There is so much you don't know about who I am." Memnon steps in close. "Like you, *est amage*, it is not in my nature to grovel. I am in the business of *power*." He puts a finger beneath my chin and tilts my head up. "And you, *my love*, are wholly unready for it."

I search his eyes. This is where I need to pull away. Or attack. But he has me bewitched, both by his look and his touch.

"Even as a king, I would ride into battle with my horde." His voice grows soft, intimate, and he's switched to speaking Sarmatian. "But sometimes, when I faced a particularly obstinate foe, or one I wanted to make an example of, I would leave my warriors a ways away from the battlefield, and I would ride in alone." As he speaks, the lanterns above us dim, as though shrinking from whatever ominous story Memnon is set on telling me.

"Do you know why I would face my worst opponents alone?"

"I'm sure you're going to tell me," I say softly.

He flashes me a whisper of a smile, though it holds no actual humor.

"Sorcerers have vast amounts of power, but when used in such large quantities, our magic can grow a bit…*feral*."

I think he's about to tell me the story of how he lost his conscience to his power.

Instead, he says, "The stronger the magic we cast, the less we can control who that magic touches. Friends—and family—are always in danger when we let it loose." He pauses to let that sink in. "So I would face my enemies alone, and the fearsome, obstinate rulers I faced would see firsthand the sort of destruction I could wreak."

I feel myself growing cold, terrified by what he's insinuating.

"Fields would be strewn with entire armies, and I would sit there on my steed, untouched."

In my mind's eye, I can see fields of corpses and blood-spattered wheat and Memnon in his scale armor sitting astride his horse. I can practically taste his ominous, overpowering magic thickening in the air.

"And sometimes," he continues, "if I had particularly good control of my power that day, I would save the ruler's death for last. I'd let him survey the ruins of his army. I'd let it sink in that he should've surrendered to me when he first had the chance."

It's obviously a warning, one that leaves me shaking. Distantly, I can hear the music playing and people laughing, and my phone vibrating between my cleavage as someone tries to call me, but it feels a world away.

Through my fear, however, my anger rises, along with my magic. This is my moment—my opening for true revenge.

My power gathers in my palms.

Memnon glances down at my hands. "Are you going to strike me, little witch?" He sounds amused. "I *like* the thought of that. It may even tickle."

My magic burgeons in response to the insult, building and building. I can feel the chaotic movements of it within me.

He nods to my chest. "Your phone's been ringing. I imagine it's urgent," he says, backing away. "Why don't you answer it?"

I glance down at my chest for just a moment, but when I look back up, Memnon's gone.

Damn it.

I stride after him, my power already receding into me now that I've lost sight of the sorcerer. My heels click as I wind through the aisles, searching for Memnon. But he's vanished entirely.

I stop, peering around at one empty row of trees and shrubs and another where a couple is making out against the trunk of a palm tree.

Bzzzz…bzzzz…

I glance down at my cleavage again. Memnon's right, my phone *has* been ringing.

I blow out a breath, then fish the phone out.

I give the caller ID a passing glance, assuming it's Sybil.

It's not.

Kane Halloway, my phone reads instead.

Why is Kane of all people calling me? I haven't heard from him since our disastrous evening together. To be honest, I hadn't even realized I had his number.

I answer the call anyway, putting the phone to my ear as I walk down a row of plants.

"Hey, Kane," I say, bringing the phone to my ear. My eyes snag on a door to a back courtyard. "Now's not—"

"Listen, Selene, I have a lot to say, and I don't have much time to say it." The man who speaks doesn't sound like lycanthrope I remember. His voice is far too low and gravelly. He hardly sounds human at all.

I pause. "Kane, is that you?" I ask softly.

"Full moon. I'm fighting a shift."

My mouth forms an O. To be honest, I didn't know it was possible for lycans to hold off a shift during the full moon for *any* amount of time.

I head for that door outside, wanting some fresh air and a little privacy to handle wherever this call is going.

"My pack knows it was you who saved Cara," he rushes to say. "I confirmed your scent myself."

The shifter girl I saved—that's what he's talking about.

"Okay..." I'm not sure where he's going with this.

I slip out the door to a massive courtyard enclosed on three sides by the glass walls of the conservatory. There's a stone patio, but it gives way to a garden full of overgrown plants. The foliage has mostly overtaken the marble statues and fountains scattered throughout the space, and it's all but engulfed the few lampposts out here.

"I don't know how much about pack dynamics you know, but after what you did, you're now considered a friend of the pack."

The silence that follows that admission is heavy, like what he's saying is a big deal.

"Being a friend of the pack means we extend our protection to you for as long as you hold the title," he adds.

Protection. He's offering me *protection.* Not just any protection either, but the protection of an entire pack. My breath leaves me all at once. That is a damn big deal—and a formidable offer.

I glance at the few other revelers out here, who are sipping drinks or slipping into the shadows of the night while his words sink in.

"We meant to arrange a formal meeting and to tell you all this in person, but I'm afraid there's no longer time for that," Kane says, his voice still inhumanly low.

I frown as I watch a few witches flying on broomsticks now land and make their way toward the back doors of the conservatory.

"What do you mean there's no longer time for that?" I say, not following.

Kane seems to pick his words carefully. "One of my pack mates works with the Politia."

As soon as I hear *that*, my stomach twists on itself.

Kane pauses too, as though he doesn't want to say his next words.

He finally sighs, the sound coming out garbled, as though his throat can't fully make the noise. "The Politia is going to arrest you."

CHAPTER 42

"What?" I nearly drop the phone.

Across the courtyard, a few guests glance over at me as they head inside, clearly startled by my outburst.

I must've heard Kane incorrectly. There's no way—

"Tonight," the shifter adds. "They have a warrant out for your arrest. Apparently, they found a shoe of yours with blood from that witch who recently went missing."

"Kasey," I whisper.

As for my shoes, I *am* missing the pair I left behind the night of the spell circle. Did the Politia find one of them? If so, why would it be in the woods, and how in the hell did it get Kasey's blood on it? I was barefoot by the time the fighting out there occurred.

There must be some mistake.

I'm about to say so when Kane continues. "The Politia thinks you committed the murders."

I can't seem to draw in enough air. It's one thing to be a suspect in a murder case, but they're planning on *arresting* me? *Tonight?*

"Goddess..." I whisper, feeling the world tilt as more guests head back inside the conservatory. "I'm innocent, Kane." I need to say it, even though I can't remember everything.

"If any of us shifters thought you committed these killings," Kane says, "then friend or not, we would turn you in."

I exhale a shaky breath. Packs are notoriously loyal but even more notoriously protective of the innocent—particularly their own.

"We believe someone's framing you."

It feels as though someone kicked me in the stomach.

Framed. I'm being...framed.

I've been so caught up in proving my innocence that I didn't stop to wonder why my name kept popping up in the first place. I just assumed it was some combo of being in the wrong place at the wrong time and being unable to prove my alibi.

I hadn't considered the possibility that someone was deliberately leveraging my memory loss against me.

I should've though.

I press a hand to my brow. "Shit."

Shit, shit, *shit*.

Kane's tone sharpens. "My alpha wanted me to pass along this message: Cooperate with the authorities. We'll send in one of our lawyers to help sort this out once the Sacred Seven are over." Once the lycanthropes can fully control their shifts again.

I put a hand to my head. My mind is screaming, and I can't seem to draw in enough air.

"Kane," I say softly, "I...*thank you*." What he's saying may not prevent me from getting arrested, but knowing I have an entire pack's backing makes the whole ordeal seem a lot less hopeless.

The lycanthrope's voice grows deeper. "Cara told us what happened as well as she could remember. It's not much, but it's still enough for us to know how much you risked, saving her. From what it sounds like, they were going to force Cara into—" His next words get mangled. Kane stops, clears his throat, and continues. "A bond against her will." Another several seconds of silence pass, and I can only imagine he's fighting his need to shift. "We would like to hear the story of that night in your own words, once we sort out the situation with the Politia."

"I can do that," I say quietly.

Hearing Kane speak like this—like the leader he must be getting groomed to be—is throwing me. I had a crush on him for years, but I never *knew* him. And now I'm discovering that maybe he isn't just some gorgeous shifter; even as young as he is, he may be a commanding member.

He hesitates, then adds, "Also, Selene, this is unofficial, but *I'd* like to see you again." His voice roughens once more, nearly to the point of indecipherability. "I've wanted to since I said goodbye to you that night."

He and I left things off in a strange place—somewhere between a fling, a crush, and a near-death experience. At least, I think that's where we left off.

"I—"

Little witch, are you ready to play…?

I press a hand to my heart at the sound of Memnon's voice inside me. I can barely focus on my earlier need for revenge in light of what I've now learned.

"I just wanted you to know where I stand on that," Kane says before I can give him a proper response. He clears his throat. "Anyway, try not to answer any questions until one of our lawyers can speak with you."

"Okay," I say, my voice a little lost.

I'm now vividly picturing Politia officers swarming the conservatory and cuffing me in front of all my coven sisters.

I need to leave and get back to my room. If I'm to be charged and arrested tonight, I don't want an audience. Especially not one that consists of my friends and peers. This will be a bad enough experience to live through as it is.

"When are they going to get here?" My voice wobbles.

"I don't know," Kane admits remorsefully. In the background, I hear a wolf howl, then several more. "In an hour? Maybe later, maybe sooner—I didn't get the specifics."

I rub my eyes, and I can't decide if I want to laugh or cry. This whole situation is nuts.

"I am so sorry, Selene," he adds softly. "I—"

Screams echo from inside the conservatory, and I nearly drop my phone.

I curse under my breath.

Memnon—I know this is his doing.

"Kane, I have to go."

Before he can respond, I end the call, cutting across the eerily silent courtyard, the train of my dress whispering behind me.

I head for the double doors that lead into the main section of the conservatory. Even from here I can see the guests inside, but I don't hear the music playing anymore, and now that my eyes sweep over the supernaturals closest to the windows, they seem unusually tense.

"Selene!" Memnon bellows from somewhere in there.

The hairs on the nape of my neck stand up.

I reenter the enormous greenhouse, brushing past guest after guest. Their eyes are wide, and lots of nervous magic wafts off mages and witches and floats high in the air.

"Selene!" he calls again.

There's such a thick crowd of supernaturals that I don't see him. Not until I slip past the guests ringing the dance floor.

Standing in the center of the dance is Memnon. He's not alone.

In his clutches is a blond witch, her entire body trembling. He holds that fancy dagger with the golden hilt almost casually to her throat. I know in my bones it's an honest threat. He'd slit that woman's throat in an instant if it suited him. He may still do worse.

"Selene!" This time, it isn't Memnon calling to me.

I turn toward Sybil's voice, searching for my friend in the crowd. I catch sight of her red dress, then her panicked eyes. *"Run—"*

"*There* she is," Memnon says, his wicked eyes glittering when they catch sight of me.

Everyone around us stands watching in frozen horror.

For a moment, I'm just as frozen as they are. I was expecting something awful from the sorcerer, but not *this*.

Finally, I find my voice. *"Let her go."* The command comes out stronger and calmer than I thought it would.

Memnon's attention drops to the witch, and he considers my words. Beneath his blade is a thin line of blood.

"No," he eventually says, "I don't think I will."

My pulse thunders in my ears. Around me, the guests are still rooted in place. It's only now that I notice Memnon's magic weaving between them, and I sense it's what's keeping them from intervening or fleeing.

My attention returns to the sorcerer. "Whatever you're thinking of doing, Memnon, you won't get away with it," I say. "This isn't the ancient world, and you aren't a king anymore. You have hundreds of witnesses here. The Politia will get you."

He laughs, the action causing his dagger to shift and the witch in his arms to cry out. Another line of blood forms beneath the edge of his blade.

"The Politia?" Memnon says. "I find it *highly* amusing that you would trust them, considering your own situation."

He tilts his head. "Have you already forgotten our conversation on power? Those who hold it make the rules. And those who don't must follow them—including the Politia."

Around me, I hear people murmuring and the quiet sobs of one or two of them, but in some fundamental way, the room has gone lethally quiet.

"Strange how the murders always seemed to involve you," he says. "How many times have you wondered if you were guilty of them? The Politia sure seems to think it was you. I wonder who could have possibly directed their eyes to such an innocent, law-abiding witch?"

We believe someone's framing you.

I stare at him in growing horror.

"*You*," I breathe. "It was you who framed me."

My stomach roils, and for a moment, I think I'm going to be sick.

"But..." My brows draw together. I asked him point-blank if he'd murdered those witches while he was under a truth spell.

"I didn't kill those witches," he concedes. "That was another. But I *did* move their bodies before they could be destroyed. I found that I could expose the deeds of those who were guilty while implicating you for their crimes."

There it is, his confession, said before a room of hundreds

of my peers. It terrifies me that he's unfazed by that—especially because I'm sensing that his indifference doesn't come from ignorance of our modern ways. I think it may truly come from having enough power to make problems *go away*.

I can't seem to catch my breath. "What have you done?" I whisper.

"So many things I couldn't possibly recount them all to you here." He scrutinizes his dagger. "A warlord is more than just a sword arm, *est amage*. There is so much strategy involved."

My magic rises, pressing against my skin.

"We can't come back from this, you know." Even as I say it, I ache. Ache for something that might've been deep and real but now I'll never get.

What monster does something like this to the one they love?

But the answer has always sat there, right in front of me.

Memnon's wife, Roxilana, went to incredible lengths to hide Memnon from the world. Perhaps she saw this side of him before I ever did.

"We can't come back from this?" His eyes spark with his power, and his grip on the woman in his arms tightens. "*Est amage*, I did not endure in that cold, bleak sarcophagus for two millennia to lose you all over again."

The witch in his arms whimpers. There's a growing number of tear tracks down her cheeks, ruining makeup she probably put on with excitement. Tonight was supposed to be fun, not some sort of nightmare.

"Let the woman go, Memnon," I say again. My magic continues to gather, mounting beneath my skin and sliding through my veins. "This is between the two of us."

Memnon's gaze drops to the witch. More blood drips

down her neck. She shifts, and I see her magic thickening beneath her palms, the emerald wisps of it dissolving inches from her. I don't know what enchantment he's placed on her, but it's neutralizing her powers.

"How badly do you want her freedom?" he says. "What would you be willing to do for it?"

I'm caught off guard by the question. I feel all the eyes in the room on me. This bargain isn't just for the witch in Memnon's arms. It's for Sybil and all the others here who are trapped under the sorcerer's magic.

"What do you want?" I say, my power churning inside me.

"You know what I want."

I suddenly remember his words from a week ago.

You are under a curse, mate. One made by your own hand. Of course we will remove it.

He wants me to remember our past. What would this revenge even be for if I couldn't recall the crime that earned it?

My magic spikes in alarm, a little slipping out through my palms.

I look from him to the witch and back. I know this is where I'm supposed to capitulate, but I *can't.* Not on this point, and not to this fucker.

So I choose violence instead.

"*Explode,*" I whisper.

My magic blasts out of me, and as it leaves, I get a dizzy head rush, my power eating through who knows how many memories. Only at the last minute do I think to hone it like a blade.

It slams into Memnon's shins, knocking him backward. The witch in his arms screams as his dagger drags across her skin, slicing into her shoulder. But the cut is shallow and imprecise.

The moment the witch is free of Memnon, she scrambles away. The woman only makes it a few yards, however, before she gets tangled in the same spell that's locked the limbs of the rest of the room.

I hear her frustrated cry, and the guests near her reach for the woman, murmuring to her in terror-laced whispers.

Memnon regains his footing, then gives a sinister low chuckle, "Naughty wi—"

"Explode." I launch another spell at him.

This one hits him square in the chest, blowing him off his feet.

More magic gathers in my hand. *"Explode."* I fire off. *"Explode. Explode."* I'm forming and throwing the spells as quickly as I can. They hit him in quick succession, detonating against his body and knocking him back. One of them misses, shattering the window behind him.

I stalk forward, a vicious hunger rising in me. For revenge, for blood.

"Slice." The spell slashes through his fancy suit and his skin, making it bloom red.

Thick indigo plumes of Memnon's own magic pour out of him before pooling around his sprawled body and creeping across the floor.

Even with my strikes and the spells he's already placed on the room, his own power seems to be growing.

I step up to him, each hit of mine only making me angrier and more resolved. Hurting him doesn't feel good. I want it to—fuck, how I want it to—but it doesn't, and that only seems to fuel my rage.

I scowl down at him.

The mighty sorcerer touches his chest, where his blood is spilling. He looks at the red liquid on his fingertips, then at me, his eyes glittering. "Have I told you, mate, that battles have always been my favorite sort of foreplay?"

His magic descends on me at once, throwing me back. I hit the ground hard, and the air leaves my lungs as my body slides across the dance floor.

Around us, the other guests are panicking, their shouts and cries filling the air, along with their magic. Memnon's power wraps around the entire building, barricading everyone inside.

I haven't even stopped sliding when my own magic strikes out at him again, the wordless spell lashing against him like a whip.

Memnon grunts at the impact, but then I see him pull himself to his feet.

More magic pours down my arms. *"Explode."* I sling the spell from where I lie.

This time, a tendril of Memnon's power swats it away, and it explodes against a cluster of trees and shrubs, blowing them apart and causing the nearby guests to scream.

I force myself to my feet as Memnon's own shoes click against the ground. He runs his hands through his hair, looking bloody and violent in the most primal of ways.

I try to draw on Memnon's own power through our bond—

"Ah, ah, little witch. That's a cute idea, but I'm afraid I won't be sharing my power for this."

I reach for my own magic before flinging it at the sorcerer with abandon. His power rises to meet mine, the dark blue clouds of it crashing against my lighter orange ones, holding it at bay.

"Exquisite mate," he says, his eyes beginning to glow. "I would fight you all evening just to watch your ferocity," he says. "I hope you know it fills me with pride to see you unleash yourself.

"Unfortunately," he continues, "I still need your help to lift our curse."

I wipe the corner of my lips, where a little blood has slipped out from a cut in my mouth. "I'll never agree to that."

"But you will," he insists. "See, I know your heart, Selene, better than anyone, so I know that while *you* may be willing to take me on alone, you'd never put others at risk."

The first icy tendrils of true fear skate down my back.

"I will harm every single person in this room until you agree to lift the curse," he vows.

My magic leaks out with my panic. *"Memnon."*

"I do so love it when you say my name like that," he says. "Agree to help me lift the curse, mate. Like you said yourself, no one else has to get hurt. This is between you and me."

I glare at him as he uses my own words against me.

"Or we can do this the hard way."

The words are barely out of his mouth when I hear a sharp inhalation.

To the right of me, a witch with dark curly hair clutches her throat. There's seemingly nothing wrong with her, and yet she sways, reaching out and gripping a stranger's shoulder as she tries and fails to draw breath.

On the opposite side of the dance floor, a mage grabs his neck, making pained choking noises as his canary-yellow magic moves restlessly around him.

Guest after guest clutches their throat, their breath seizing in their lungs until the entire conservatory is suffocating on nothing more than Memnon's magic.

The room fills with panicked magic that's tangling together and making the air hazy. All of it, however, is soon overwhelmed by the deep blue hue of Memnon's power.

This time, my magic unleashes before I even consciously choose to fight back. It fills the room, the pale peach hue mixing with Memnon's magic. I feel it pulling at the ends of my mate's power, trying to draw the lethal magic away from the throats of all these supernaturals.

I grit my teeth as I meet resistance.

"Agree to lift the curse, mate."

"*No.*" A wave of power explodes out of me, knocking Memnon's away for a moment. I hear dozens of ragged gasps as, for a moment, people drag in a desperate breath of air.

My head throbs, and the edges of my vision turn hazy as memory after memory burns away. I don't know which ones, but there's a hollow ache in my chest at the loss.

Then the sorcerer's power is back, clogging people's windpipes and tightening like a noose around their necks.

I let out a frustrated cry and redouble my efforts.

I pull from the earth beneath me and the moonlight above me, drawing as much magic into myself as I can.

I form it crudely inside me, then funnel it down my arms and into my hands.

"*Remove Memnon's magic from their necks,*" I incant, only belatedly realizing I've spoken in Sarmatian.

My magic races out of me, once again prying at Memnon's.

Not enough. It's not enough.

I force out more, more, more. My mind feels on fire, my magic straining like an overworked muscle.

"Impressive, my queen," Memnon says across from me. His eyes glow like embers, and his hair ripples with his power. "Truly. I didn't expect to have to give in to my truest nature for this fight."

His magic strengthens against mine, and all the ground I thought I was gaining is undone at once.

I scream from exertion, nearly falling to my knees. Using this much magic all at once is becoming painful. I feel as though I'm ripping my own muscles away from their bones, the magic unmaking my body bit by bit.

Worse, despite my efforts, people are still suffocating; I can see their eyes bulging out and their faces changing colors as they're deprived of oxygen.

I draw on yet more magic. The throbbing beneath my skull has increased, and the haze at the corners of my eyes has spread, obscuring my vision.

The first witch falls, her body hitting the floor with a dull *thud*.

"Stop," I plead.

"Agree, and I will."

Another body falls. Then several.

Now I do drop to my knees, my muscles weak and shaking. I can hardly see him through my blurred vision. "Please, Memnon, end this."

"I will, once you agree to my terms," Memnon says.

Burning away, everything is burning away...my high school memories, then my childhood ones. I'm sure of it.

"Speaking of terms," he continues, his hair billowing in some invisible wind, "there is one more demand I forgot to mention earlier." He strides toward me, magic billowing out of him with every step he takes. "I'll need you to agree to it too."

I stare up at him as he comes up to me, his ominous form looming.

"Marry me."

CHAPTER 43

"What?"

I want to laugh. I want to scream. Around us, bodies are still hitting the ground, and I'm the one on my knees, and this can't *possibly* be an actual proposal.

Memnon's hand slips beneath my chin. "Marry me."

I can't see him well through the strain shrouding my eyes, but my ears heard him correctly.

"Agree to lift the curse and be my wife in earnest, and I will release these people."

"You're sick," I whisper.

His grip tightens on my chin.

"You're running out of time, little witch. Better decide fast."

"No," I say breathlessly. "Choose different terms."

He lets out a laugh, as though there's anything amusing about this moment.

"Why *would* I?" he says. "I have you *right where I want you.*" His expression grows serious, and his gaze burns. "I am still *awfully* bitter about being locked away for fucking millennia."

I glare at him as he kneels before me, putting us at roughly eye level.

"But I love you," he continues, his entire demeanor gentling. "I have *always* loved you. The night I found you half dead in that forest made me face a truth I tried to bury. I cannot live without you." Iron enters his voice. "I *won't*."

My body trembles, and the throbbing in my head only increases. He's given me an impossible ultimatum, one I must agree to if I want these people around me to survive tonight.

"If you do this," I say softly, "I *vow* to make every day of your life a living hell."

A slow, wolfish smile spreads across his face. "I look forward to it, *est amage*."

More magic is pouring out of me, though it's sluggish now, and it's battering uselessly against the sorcerer's. My mind is starting to feel hollowed out. I've overdrawn my power, and still more supernaturals are falling to the ground.

There's no escaping Memnon's demands. Not in any real sense. My hate and anger nearly swallow me whole, but the sorcerer is right. I don't want anyone else to die on my behalf.

Around me, the room has gone quiet, except for a few panicked gurgles and those unsettling thumps.

My shoulders heave with every ragged breath I take. I've done everything I can. It just isn't enough.

"Fine."

With that, I collapse forward, falling into his waiting arms, my breathing heavy, my magic spent.

CHAPTER 44

I lie in the arms of my enemy.

My soul mate.

My future husband.

I stare up at him tiredly as my vision clears.

Memnon brushes my hair back from my face, a soft look on his own. I guess victory has gentled him.

Around us, guests gasp for air.

I whisper, "Is everyone—?"

"Alive?" Memnon finishes for me.

I nod.

"Yes. They are all alive and well."

I relax a little. He made good on his end of the deal—he released these supernaturals from certain death.

Which means I'll have to uphold my end. I grimace at the thought.

The sorcerer's hands slip under my body, and he rises from the floor, lifting me with him.

"My fierce queen," he murmurs, clutching me close. I

don't have it in me to fight this embrace. My body is shaking; my mind is frayed. "You are a warrior at heart. I couldn't be prouder. I may have defeated you tonight, but you have honored yourself and honored me by battling so valiantly."

I'm going to marry this man. That thought echoes on repeat. He nearly killed a room full of people, and somehow that earned him everything he most desperately wanted.

"Selene!" Sybil's panicked voice carries through the crowd.

"*Sybil,*" I call back, my voice wispy and feeble. My friend sounds shaken but okay.

Memnon glances up, his expression turning cold once more as he takes in Sybil and the rest of the guests. Their eyes are frightened, their bodies huddled in on themselves.

The sorcerer's magic sweeps out of him and over the room. Before I can ask what spell he just cast, I see shattered glass lift from the ground and reform in their original panes. Trees and shrubs that were knocked askew now straighten and re-root, and their scattered soil returns to the gardening beds. Shattered coupe glasses repair themselves, their spilled contents returning to the delicate cups before the cups themselves float back into various guests' hands.

Most astounding of all are the guests themselves. They blink and look around, their former fear transformed into confusion.

The sight of Memnon using all that magic after I spent nearly every drop of mine makes my nausea rise. I was never going to win this battle.

"Selene!" Sybil calls out again. This time, however, her voice is gentle and worried.

I catch sight of my friend, her long hair cascading over her dress as she hurries over, eyeing Memnon with suspicion but not fear.

What did he do to her mind and everyone else's here? No one is screaming at him, and though we're drawing a few curious looks, it seems to be because Memnon and I are disheveled, and he's holding me like I'm his war prize.

Which, unfortunately, I kind of am.

"Are you okay?" Sybil asks, her eyes landing on various parts of me where there must be some scrape or smudge.

No. I want to weep. *I'm not okay at all.*

"I'm…fine." I force the words out. "I just…twisted my ankle." I give a weak laugh, one that sends a bolt of pain shooting beneath my skull. "This is why I don't wear heels."

Sybil frowns, searching my face. When her gaze moves to Memnon, it snags on the bloody bit of shirt peeking out above my body. Her expression hardens with loathing.

"You're Memnon, aren't you?" she says. "I knew I'd be able to pick you out of the crowd."

She said something earlier about this, hadn't she? Something that made me laugh, but I can't quite grasp it now…

"*Go back to the dance.*" Memnon gives the words a magical push, and Sybil backs up.

"If you're sure you're okay," she says, her brows drawing together. She's fighting Memnon's magic, her eyes lingering on me.

"I am," I rasp out, the lie tasting bitter as it leaves my lips.

She hesitates a few more seconds before finally turning around and rejoining a larger group of witches, as though nothing were amiss.

Almost everyone else is regaining their bearings.

"What the hell was in that witch's brew?"

"What just happened?"

"Did I miss something?"

"Was that supposed to be part of the evening?"

There's a smattering of laughter, and though I notice a few supernaturals look suspicious—I mean, we *are* witches, so we know a thing or two about magical interference. But overall, people are eager to get back to enjoying themselves.

"What did you do to them?" I ask, staring at the crowd.

"I wiped their memories of the past ten minutes."

He fought me, restrained and suffocated a room full of supernaturals, then partially removed their memories, and he *still* looks primed for battle.

The sheer quantity of power at this man's disposal is terrifying.

"You can't keep compelling people to do what you want," I say, my voice weak with my fatigue.

"You keep forgetting, *est amage*. I hold the power, which means I get to do what I want," Memnon says back, his eyes drinking me in.

My stomach dips at the look he gives me, and if I had more energy, I would snarl and rage that my own reaction to him hasn't been blunted by his recent actions.

"Where are we going?" I ask as the sorcerer carries me out the main doors and into the night.

"Back to your room, where you and I will lift the curse. We *do* also have a wedding to plan."

Oh, how I loathe this fucker.

I narrow my eyes. "Gloating isn't a good look on you."

"That's not what you said two thousand years ago—but then, you wouldn't remember that, would you?"

I loathe him, loathe him, loathe him.

That doesn't stop me from leaning my heavy head against his chest, my body spent.

The sorcerer pulls me in closer, and I can't decide if the

action rankles me—he's the reason behind my exhaustion after all—or if it softens my angry heart.

My gaze moves to the tree line, and I sense Nero lingering in the shadows there.

"She's all right, Nero," Memnon calls. "No need to slice me to ribbons. I'm not interested in hurting her."

"At the moment," I add.

He glances down at me. "*Anymore*," he corrects. His eyes are steady. "No more vengeance, *est amage*. I set my trap and sprung it. Once you uphold your end of the agreement, I will bury the past and look to the future. I have a bride to charm after all." At this last part, his expression shifts, turning almost mirthful.

If I had more energy, I'd lunge at him and scratch the look off his smug-ass face. Bury the past. If he had any interest in that, he wouldn't be trying to resurrect long-lost memories.

My familiar slinks from the tree line, so stealthy and quiet that even under the light of a full moon, he's hard to notice. When he gets to us, his ears are back and a low growl rumbles in his chest. He hisses at Memnon, flashing his fangs.

What a good kitty. I take back every rude thought I've ever directed Nero's way.

"I'm not putting her down, Nero, not even for—"

Nero lunges, slashing at Memnon with his claws.

My body dips a little as the sorcerer reacts, hissing at the pain.

"*Fuck*, Nero. I know you love her. I do too—she's safe with me."

My familiar is still growling in warning, plainly pissed off. Just hearing the menace pouring off Nero, I'm sure my panther will attack Memnon again—he's just waiting for the right moment to do so.

"It's all right, Nero," I say softly, reaching my hand down.

The big cat's growls die away, and a moment later, I feel his head brush against my palm.

I pet him gently. "You are the *best* familiar I could ask for," I coo, even though I'm sure Nero hates that voice. "And I am all right, I promise. Let's plan a better time to attack Memnon, deal?" I feel the sorcerer give me a look, though I don't bother to glance at him and see what the expression is. "For now, we can leave the bastard alone." Enough harm has already been done this evening.

"How merciful of you, Empress," Memnon says, and I can hear the amusement in his voice.

At the sound of the sorcerer's voice, Nero growls once more, but it eventually peters out, and when Memnon begins moving again, Nero falls into step next to him.

"Just be happy I didn't ask him to castrate you—I think he was ready to."

"Selene, you and I both know you are far too curious about my cock to let that ever happen."

I glare at him. "I'm sure, like the rest of you, it'll be a disappointment."

If I expected Memnon to be offended by that, I thought wrong. The sorcerer lets out a surprised laugh.

"I don't see how that's funny."

"Come now, Empress, you're amusing, even when your humor is at my expense. Also, I appreciate the confirmation that you will be seeing my cock at some point in time."

"I did *not* confirm…"

Crap, I did though, didn't I? I made it sound like I would be seeing him naked in the future.

Memnon wears that same smug expression.

"Castration is still not off the table," I insist.

"Neither is fucking, apparently," he responds, his eyes glinting playfully.

I narrow my eyes at him.

"Though we can do it *on* the table as well," he adds. "Really, anywhere that pleases you, *est amage*. I live to serve only you."

My cheeks heat at his words. It doesn't help that Memnon is holding me so close, I can feel the beat of his heart against my cheek.

I exhale, the fight still gone from me. My inside of my skull throbs from all the spent magic and the memories tithed. I lean more deeply into Memnon's chest, uncaring that he's taking every one of these actions as another victory. He may as well enjoy it because tonight I really did lose.

And I'm only just starting to process that.

Memnon leads us around to the front of my house, climbing up the path to the front door. We pass the stone *lamassu*, and though they're threshold guardians, they don't try to defend me against Memnon.

Except for Nero, I'm well and truly on my own.

Memnon steps up to the front door, and my heart nearly skips a beat when the Medusa door knocker moves, the snakes in her hair writhing.

"We don't allow wicked men with dubious—"

Memnon's blue magic slips out from him and blows into the metal Medusa's face.

The knocker coughs as its eyes flutter shut, and the door swings open.

"That was just rude."

Memnon's mouth curves slightly. "I care for manners about as much as I do the law."

He crosses the foyer and heads straight for the stairs,

Nero at his feet. The place is as quiet as it ever gets. If there's anyone still in the house, they're sequestered away.

The floorboards creak as Memnon makes his way up the stairs and down the hall, and it may be my imagination, but I swear I can almost taste the sorcerer's excitement.

The thought makes my pulse spike. I've been trying very hard not to think about what's going to happen once we get to my room, but now that said room is in sight, I can't fully suppress my rising nerves.

Memnon stops at my door, and using his magic, he again swings the door open before carrying me inside. After Nero slinks through, the sorcerer kicks the door shut.

He sets me down on the edge of my bed with surprising gentleness, then grabs the chair next to my bed before dragging it over to me.

I narrow my eyes at him as he sits in the chair, resting his forearms on his thighs, one of which is bloody from where Nero sliced him open.

The familiar in question comes to my side, my big cat leaning his body against my leg. I reach down to pet him, and though I'm weak from exertion and I'm sitting on my twin bed and not a throne, here in my revenge dress, with my panther at my side, I feel like a wicked queen. I hold that image close to me because there's strength in it, strength I badly need.

"Are you ready to begin?" Memnon says. His face is placid, but his eyes have a feverish glint to them. I can see desire and excitement simmering beneath the surface.

I assume he means to lift the curse. Which, fuck no, I'm not. But then my thoughts turn to the other stipulation he had.

Marry me.

I envision this man's skin pressed against mine, his body bearing down…

My heart thunders at the visual, and my mouth goes dry.

It's all too vivid.

The longer I dwell on it, the more my blood heats.

I wet my lips. "When would you want to get married?"

Cannot believe I'm even asking this.

Memnon leans forward and takes my hand, clasping it between his. He is perversely beautiful, and I hate that I notice it, even now.

"Immediately," he says.

My breath leaves me all at once. "*No*."

"*Yes*," he insists. "We are already bonded—your magic claimed mine the moment it manifested in you, soul mate. And though you cannot remember it, we have been married for a long, long time."

I release a shuddering breath. "Then why bother marrying me again?" I say, throwing in one last-ditch effort to steer him away from this terrifying idea of legally binding ourselves together.

Memnon lifts a hand and strokes my cheek, the action disarmingly sweet. "Our magic has always been committed to us, but I want your deliberate commitment as well, Selene. I want to hold your hands under this sky before our old gods and your new ones, and I want us to pledge our vows.

"And even if you don't believe in me, I want you to believe in the sanctity of our union." He scrutinizes me with those luminous eyes of his. "And I think you will."

I don't know how much he knows about me—my memories in general are a bit muddled after our earlier battle—but yes, I believe in the sacredness of marriage.

Which is why I have stayed far, far away from it.

I hear the faint sound of sirens in the distance. At first, I think nothing of the sound. But then, through the bruised, aching recesses of my mind, I remember fragments of a call I had this evening. I strain to remember—

The Politia is going to arrest you.

I suck in a breath as the memory returns.

They're going to arrest me. Tonight—right now.

Fuck.

Memnon must hear the sirens too, because he raises his eyebrows, knowledge alight in his eyes. "Oh no." There is zero sympathy in his voice.

And why would there be? He orchestrated this entire fucking situation.

"We better lift this curse before they arrive," he continues. "Time, after all, is almost up."

I'm seething, but there's one inconsistency my mind snags on. "Why marry me if I'll just be rotting away in jail?" Because it looks like that's where I'm headed.

Memnon's still holding my hand, and now he gives it a squeeze. "Don't worry about reasons, *est amage*. All you need to do is uphold your end of the bargain."

I grimace at him.

There's more he's planned. There must be. Otherwise, the situation doesn't make sense.

"Are you ready, *est amage*?"

Goddess save me, we're going to do this. I think I may hurl.

I force myself to nod. "Let's get this over with."

CHAPTER 45

Outside, Politia sirens draw closer.

"First," Memnon says, "we must make an unbreakable oath."

I draw my brows together as he reaches into the inner pocket of his tuxedo. "An unbreakable oath? About *what*?"

He gives me a look. "About what you promised me this evening. As much as I care for you, *est amage*, I don't trust your word."

From his breast pocket, Memnon pulls out a dagger with an ornamental hilt. I tense at the sight of it.

Before I can further react, Memnon draws the dagger down his hand, not flinching even a little as he cuts himself open. It takes me an extra moment to remember that binding spells require blood.

And that's what we're doing right now. Making the agreement binding.

He wipes the blade on his pants, then hands the knife hilt first to me.

After a brief hesitation, I take it, staring down at the dagger. It's clear the sorcerer is determined to swaddle me in promises until I'm buried so deep, there will be no possibility of escaping him.

We'll see about that.

That's *my* promise.

I drag the blade down my palm, biting my lip at the flare of pain. A line of blood springs up, and for a moment, all I can do is stare at it.

Memnon takes the knife from me while I'm distracted, then wipes it clean again before tucking it away. With his bloody hand, he reaches for my own, threading his larger, darker fingers through mine. The wound on his palm presses flush against my own, our blood mingling.

What little magic I have left rouses at the contact, tendrils of it seeping through my blood and into Memnon's. His own magic reaches for mine, twisting around and around it.

Outside, I hear cars come to a stop, their sirens cutting off. I have minutes—if that—before they close in on me.

Memnon gives my hand a squeeze, silently urging me to speak.

I part my lips and seal my fate. *"I vow before my gods and yours, that tonight I shall lift our curse, and as soon as circumstances allow, I shall marry you. I bind my life to these vows."*

My magic flares as I finish the oath, and I gasp as it melds with Memnon's.

I glance up at the sorcerer.

He's already looking at me, his gaze both soft...and eager.

My heart gallops, and I'm breathless, which I wish were due to my own horror and not this strange curiosity that begs me to stroke his face and give in fully to this oath I made.

"Now for your memories," Memnon says, his voice roughened with emotion.

Outside, I can hear car doors opening and closing.

Memnon releases my hands before cupping my face. "*Est amage*, I know this feels like the end, but I swear to you, this is the beginning. Whatever is between us, we will lift this curse and discover it together. And we *will* fix it. I am still yours—forever."

I work my jaw. There *is* nothing left to fix. This will be a marriage and a bond in name only.

Memnon must see or feel my intentions because his expression grows somber.

He takes my hands in his, our bloody hands pressing together once more.

"Repeat after me." He switches languages then, his voice becoming more rolling and guttural. *"The curse I placed, I now shall lift. I withdraw my will. I end my spell. I bring into balance that which I set askew."*

I echo his words, my head pounding harder and harder with each sentence.

"Reveal the memories that this curse sought to hide. For now and forever."

I take a fortifying breath, then repeat this too. My magic churns restlessly beneath my skin, the growing pressure of it making me fidget.

Memnon and I repeat the lines once more, this time together.

"For now and forever."

My magic explodes behind my eyes, and then—

It begins.

CHAPTER 46

It starts with the most recent memories, this evening and then the rest of the day filling out in such detail, I nearly gasp.

It's…it's actually working.

There was a part of me that didn't think it would.

The previous week comes back in all its fullness, then the week before that—and the one before that. Faster and faster, the memories return, though there's no time to examine each one.

I see the span of my time here at Henbane Coven, and then I see my time before that.

I see myself opening Memnon's tomb—then awakening my trapped mate. And before that, finding Nero and the harrowing plane crash I survived.

My lips have parted, and though I know Memnon is staring intently at me in the present, I'm locked in my past, my unearthed memories demanding nearly all my attention.

The past year comes back to me, and my breath comes out in shaky gasps. There was so much yearning and frustration and self-doubt as I worked to get into Henbane Coven. But there was so much self-discovery over that time too—I was able to live alone and function well in San Francisco. I had my own job and paid my own rent.

Little bits of knowledge come back to me, things I was never sure of before—like the fact I enjoy working out, despite all the bitching and moaning I do about it. And I'm a truly awful cook—my mind has unearthed so many disastrous attempts. I have been intimate with four men—Memnon included—and I've been on far more dates than I imagined. I've reread my favorite books half a dozen times each, and I really did get to relive the joy of them over and over.

My years at Peel Academy, the supernatural boarding school I attended, come back, then the memories I had of life before my power Awoke. Not even these memories were safe from the ravages of my magic.

As a child and a young teenager, I was happy, chaotic, wild. I played outside most of the day, alongside my powerful parents, who—with the help of a little magic—grew our backyard into a wild wonderland. When I wasn't digging my hands and toes into the earth, I was painting or drawing. More shocking still, I was messy, *disorganized*. My room was absolute chaos, and my mom would have me recite a cleaning spell alongside her.

I remember my great-aunt Giselle, who smelled like baby powder and way too much perfume and had an opinion about literally everything, and how she passed away from cancer. My father cried for weeks after, and I thought maybe he'd never smile again, until he finally did.

Further and further back, my mind goes.

My dad taught me how to ride a bike, his meadow-green magic billowing around the wheels when I started to lose my balance. I baked and ate ginger cookies with my mom, the two of us making faces at the sharp sugary flavor.

Young, I was so young. Mom read me fairy tales, and they made me upset. *Princesses* don't *wear dresses—they wear trousers and shoot arrows from the backs of horses. I would know this because I'm a queen. But where's my king? He should be here. He's* always *here. Something's wrong.*

My memories grow indistinct and distorted.

I can see a tire swing. Bushes with strawberries on them, but someone said not to eat them. They looked really good, and I wanted to.

I got old words and new words confused. It was hard. My parents didn't understand. I didn't really either.

Long hallways. An old heavy book that seemed to make the air glitter around it. A checkered blanket, a fuzzy kitty.

I was rocked. Held. Warm arms…

The memories close, and Memnon comes into focus. His hands are no longer holding mine; instead they cup my face. *When did that happen?* I feel the press of his magic and mine.

The throbbing in my head has worsened.

"I remember," I whisper.

He gives his head a shake. "No, you don't," he whispers. "Not everything. Not yet."

His bloody hand presses against my cheek. And somewhere down below, the Politia hammers on the front door.

"Ready yourself, *est amage*—it's coming."

"What is—?" I choke on the last of my words.

My back arches, and my mouth parts as I stare up at the ceiling. I wrap my hands around Memnon's wrists as my mind seems to crack, and a spell held for two thousand years dissolves.

In its wake, there is a single instant of peace. Then memories from another time, another place spill in.

It starts with fire, and blood, and screaming. These memories may be older, but they are far more terrifying than anything I have experienced.

I'm squeezing Memnon's wrists, and I feel tears tracking down my cheeks.

He was right the whole time. I am Roxilana. She is me.

And it's very clear that in my mind, the only true hero in this first life, the only person who loved me and fought for me, defended me and adored me, was Memnon.

Fearsome, powerful Memnon who really did kill entire armies. He loved me more than life itself, and I loved him just as fiercely.

Here in the present, his thumbs stroke my cheeks, and he murmurs reassurances. "It is all right, my love. It is all right. You are here, with me."

But, somewhere along the way, things changed.

My life twisted and twisted, and the walls closed in on me much just as the walls have closed in on me now.

And I did the unthinkable.

I betrayed my soul mate.

I shudder at the truth of it. The memories abruptly end. I gasp as the magic cuts off.

I'm vaguely aware of the Politia officers storming the stairs, their heavy footsteps thundering as they close in on my room, but I hardly care.

I can still feel the wetness of my tears and Memnon's blood on my cheeks.

Memnon's eyes are gentle and unguarded as he peers at me.

"*Roxi?*" he says softly.

The name causes a sob to slip from me. I am both old and new all at once. I have been *reborn.*

"You should've never given me those memories back," I say, my voice barely more than a whisper. "I was better off… and so were you."

The door bursts open, and Politia officers storm the room.

Neither Memnon nor I pay them much mind.

"*Est amage,*" he says, his expression growing fevered, "we will figure it out. *Together.* I vow to fix all my wrongs. Whatever you want, you shall have. I am yours forever."

He tries to pull me to him then, but I'm ripped from his hold.

An officer spins me around and cuffs my wrists, even as Nero growls at the intruders.

"Selene Bowers, you are under arrest…" They keep talking, and Nero keeps growling, but I am no longer aware of anything but Memnon.

I search his eyes. "What have I done?" I whisper.

I never should've woken Memnon from his sleep.

I have set a monster upon the world.

Author's Note

The Sarmatians were a real group of pastoral nomads that lived on the Pontic Steppe roughly 2000 years ago. I first became enamored with these nomads fifteen years ago when, back in college, I studied the grave sites of dozens of girls and young women who were buried with warrior's accoutrements and whose remains showed signs of violence. It's believed that these women were the real life inspiration for tales of the mythical Amazons, as Scythian and Sarmatian women would ride into battle.

Since first learning about these cultures' existence, I've tried to research as much as I can about who they were and what their lives were like. Unfortunately, the Sarmatians have left behind no written record of their own lives, so the language Memnon and Selene spoke in *Bewitched* is made up—though I did try to incorporate the common linguistic sounds that I saw in the words that did survive.

While couldn't find the original Sarmatian word for "queen" I instead used "Amage", which was the name of an actual Sarmatian queen. Likewise, the name "Roxilana" is based on the Sarmatian word "Roxolani" which roughly means "blessed people."

It should also be noted that I drew from other pastoral nomadic tribes—most notably the Scythians—to fill in gaps in the archaeological record, as the Sarmatians shared a great many cultural practices and ideologies with tribes that lived adjacent to them in time and space. An example of this is the word "xsaya," which appears to be the Scythian word for "king" according to one Luwian inscription.

Some additional notable details I wanted to mention: Sarmatian men tattooed themselves, and Memnon's tattoos in particular are heavily inspired by the tattoos found on the remains of a Pazyryk chieftain. Similarly, Memnon's scar is a duplicate of a scar found on the body of a Scythian warrior. The skull chalice was based on true—if macabre—practices as well.

Though this book is a work of fiction, it's been fun to bring to life bits of this culture that has held me in its grip for so long.

Read on for a look at the first book in the Bargainer series,

Rhapsodic

Present

A file folder drops to the desk in front of me. "You've got mail, Callie."

I lower my mug of steaming coffee from my mouth, my eyes flicking up from my laptop.

Temperance "Temper" Darling—swear to God, that's her name—my business partner and best friend, stands on the other side of my desk, a coy smile on her face. She drops into the seat across from me.

I kick my ankles off my desk, reaching across it to drag the file closer to me.

She nods to the folder. "This one's easy money."

They're all easy money, and she knows that.

Her eyes drift around my cupboard-sized office, the twin of hers.

"How much is the client offering?" I ask, propping my feet up once more on the edge of my desk.

"Twenty grand for a single meeting with the target, and she already knows when and where you're to intercept him."

I whistle. Easy money indeed.

"Rendezvous time with the target?" I ask.

"Eight p.m. tonight at Flamencos. FYI, it's a fancy restaurant, so—" Her gaze drops to my scuffed-up boots. "You can't wear *that*."

I roll my eyes.

"Oh, and he'll be there with friends."

And here I was looking forward to getting home relatively early.

"Do you know what the client wants?" I ask.

"The client believes her uncle, our target, is abusing his guardianship of his mother, her grandmother. The two are going to court over the issue. She wants to save some legal bills and get a confession straight from the horse's mouth."

Already, a familiar exhilaration has my skin beginning to glow. This is the chance to potentially help an old lady out and punish the worst kind of criminal—one who preys on his own family.

Temper notices my glowing skin, her gaze transfixed. She reaches out before she remembers herself. Not even she is immune to my glamour.

She shakes her head. "You are one twisted chick."

That is God's honest truth.

"Takes one to know one."

She snorts. "You can call me the Wicked Witch of the West."

But Temper's not a witch. She's something far more powerful.

She checks her phone. "Crap," she says. "I'd love to stay and chat, but my perp's going to be at Luca's Deli in less than an hour, and with LA lunch hour traffic, I really don't want to be forced to part the 405 like the Red Sea. That sort of thing looks suspicious." She stands, shoving her phone to her pocket. "When's Eli getting back?"

Eli, the bounty hunter who sometimes works for us and sometimes works for the Politia, the supernatural police force. Eli, who's also my boyfriend.

"Sorry, Temper, but he'll be gone for another week." I relax a little as I say the words.

That's wrong, right? To enjoy the fact that your boyfriend's gone and you get time alone?

It's probably also wrong to find his affection stifling. I'm afraid of what it means, especially because we shouldn't be dating in the first place.

First rule in the book is not to get involved with colleagues. One evening of after-work drinks six months ago, and I broke that rule like it'd never been there in the first place. And I broke it again and again and again until I found myself in a relationship I wasn't sure I even wanted.

"Ugh," Temper says, her hair bouncing a little as she leans her head back, her eyes moving heavenward. "The bad guys always love to stir things up when Eli's gone." She heads for my door, and with a parting look, she leaves my office.

I stare at the file a moment, then I pick it up.

The case isn't anything special. There isn't anything particularly cruel or difficult about it. Nothing to make me reach for the Johnnie Walker I keep in one of my desk drawers. I find I want to anyway, that my hand itches to pull the bottle out.

Too many bad people in this world.

My eyes flick to the onyx beads that coil around my left arm as I drum my fingers against the table. The beads seem to swallow the light rather than refract it.

Too many bad people, and too many memories worth forgetting.

The swanky restaurant I walk into at eight p.m. sharp is low lit, candles flickering dimly from each two-seater table. Flamencos is clearly a place rich people come to romance each other.

I follow the waiter, my heels clicking softly against the hardwood floor as he leads me to a private room.

Twenty grand. It's a crap ton of money. But I'm not doing this for the payout. The truth is that I'm a connoisseur of addictions, and this is one of my favorites.

The waiter opens the door to the private room, and I enter.

Inside, a group of people chat amicably around a large table. Their voices quiet a little as soon as the door clicks shut behind me. I make no move toward the table.

My eyes land on Micky Fugue, a balding man in his late forties. My target.

My skin begins to glow as I let the siren in me surface. "Everybody out." My voice is melodious, unearthly. Compelling.

Almost as one, the guests stand, their eyes glazed.

This is my beautiful, dreadful power. A siren's power. To compel the willing—and unwilling—to do and believe whatever it is I wish.

Glamour. It's illegal. Not that I really give a damn.

"The evening went great," I tell them as they pass. "You'd all love to do this sometime in the future. Oh, and I was never here."

When Micky walks by me, I grab his upper arm. "Not you."

He stops, caught in the web of my voice, while the rest of the guests file out. His glazed eyes flicker for one moment, and in that instant, I see his confusion as his awareness fights my strange magic. Then it's gone.

"Let's sit down." I direct him back to his seat, then slide into the one next to him. "You can leave once we're finished."

I'm still glowing, my power mounting with every passing second. My hands tremble just the slightest as I fight my other urges—sex and violence. Consider me a modern-day Jekyll and Hyde. Most of the time, I'm simply Callie the PI. But when I need to use my power, another side of me surfaces. The siren is the monster inside me; she wants to take and take and take. To wreak havoc and feast on her victims' fear and lust.

I'd be hard-pressed to admit it out loud, but controlling her is hard.

I grab a piece of bread from one of the baskets at the center of the table, and I slide over a small plate one of the guests hasn't touched. After I pour olive oil, then balsamic vinegar onto the plate, I dip the bread into it and take a bite.

I eye the man next to me. That tailored suit he wears hides the paunch of his belly. On his wrist, he wears a Rolex. The file said he was an accountant. I know they make decent money, especially here in LA, but they don't make money this good.

"Why don't we get right to the point?" I say. As I talk, I set up the video on my phone so the camera can capture our conversation. "I'm going to record this exchange. Please say yes out loud and give your consent to this interview."

Micky's brows stitch together as he fights the glamour in my voice. It's no use. "Yes," he finally says between clenched teeth. This guy is no fool; he might not understand what's happening to him, but he knows he's about to get played. He knows he's *already* getting played.

As soon as he agrees, I begin.

"Have you been embezzling money from your mother?" His senile, terminally ill mother. I really shouldn't have read the file. I'm not supposed to get emotionally involved in cases, and yet when it comes to children and the elderly, I always seem to find myself getting angry.

Tonight's no exception.

I take a bite of the bread, watching him.

He opens his mouth—

"From this moment until the end of our interview, you will tell the *truth*," I command, the words lilting off my tongue.

He stops, and whatever he was about to say dies on his lips. I wait for him to continue, but he doesn't. Now that he can't lie, it's only a matter of time before he's forced to admit the truth.

Micky fights my glamour, though it's useless. He's starting to sweat, despite his placid features.

I continue eating as though nothing is amiss.

Color stains his cheeks. Finally, he chokes out, "Yes. How the fuck did you—"

"Silence."

Immediately, he stops speaking.

This sicko. Stealing money from his dying mother. A sweet old lady whose biggest failure was birthing this loser.

"How long have you been doing this?"

His eyes flicker with anger. "Two years," he grits out against his will. He glares at me.

I take my time eating the last of the bread.

"Why did you do it?" I finally ask.

"She wasn't using it and I needed it. I'm going to give it back," he says.

"Oh, are you?" I raise my eyebrows. "And how much have you...*borrowed*?" I ask.

Several silent seconds tick by. Micky's ruddy cheeks are turning a deeper and deeper shade of pink. Finally, he says, "I don't know."

I lean in close. "Give me your best guess."

"Maybe two hundred and twenty thousand."

Just hearing that number sends a slice of anger through me. "And when were you going to pay your mother back?" I ask.

"N-now," he stammers.

And I'm the queen of Sheba.

"How much money do you have available in your accounts at the moment?" I ask.

He reaches for his glass of water and takes a deep swallow before answering. "I–I like to invest."

"How much money?"

"A little over twelve thousand."

Twelve thousand dollars. He's emptied his mother's coffers, and here he is living like a king. But behind this façade, the man only has twelve thousand dollars at hand. And I bet that money will get liquidated soon as well. These types of men have butterfingers; money slips right through them.

I give him a disappointed look. "That's not the right answer. Now," I say, the siren urging me to be cruel, "where is the money?"

His sweaty upper lip twitches before he answers. "Gone."

I reach over and turn off the camera and the recorder. My client got the confession she wanted. Too bad for Micky, I'm not done with him.

"No," I say, "it's not." Those few people who know me well enough would recognize my tone's changed.

Again his brows draw together as his confusion peeks through.

I touch his lapel. "This suit is nice—really nice. And your watch—Rolexes aren't cheap, are they?"

The glamour makes him shake his head.

"No," I agree. "See, for men like you, money doesn't just vanish. It goes toward…what did you call it?" I look around for the word before snapping my fingers. "*Investments.* It moves around a bit, but that's all." I lean in close. "We're going to move it around a little more."

His eyes widen. Now I see Micky—not the puppet controlled by my magic but the Micky he was before I walked into this room. Someone shrewd, someone weak. He's fully aware of what's happening.

"Wh-who are you?"

Oh, the fear in his eyes. The siren can't resist that. I reach over and pet his cheek.

"I–I'm going to—"

"You're going to sit back and listen, Micky," I say, "and that's all you're going to do, because right now, you—are—*powerless.*"

Acknowledgments

Bewitched is the first time in four years that I've been able to share a new fictional world with you all, and I can't tell you how exciting it is to get to introduce you to this one! Though, to be fair, *Bewitched* takes place in the same universe as my *Bargainer* and *Unearthly* series, so it's more like returning to an old and beloved place, and discovering something new about it. I've been steadily working away on this series for years, and the magic of this world and Selene's unfailing optimism and humor have been such a joy to write.

That being said, it took so much to get this idea out of my head and into your hands. A huge, huge shout out goes to two ladies in particular who really helped make that happen. My agent, Kimberly Brower, and my editor, Christa Désir, were the first two people to read my manuscript, and their support and guidance has made this such an incredible experience for me. I've been a lone wolf in publishing for so long, and both of these ladies have really shown me what it means to not go it all alone. Thank you both from the bottom of my heart for all you've done.

I want to also thank Manu, who has helped me clean up and polish *Bewitched*. Your feedback helped so much and I lived for the little asides you sprinkled throughout the manuscript.

To Pam, Katie, Madison, and the rest of the Bloom team, thank you all so much for all the love and enthusiasm you've put into this book. I'm honestly blown away that I get to work with all you amazing people.

K.D. Ritchie, thank you for the beautiful cover and all the associated art and graphics you've made for this book! I still remember seeing this cover, which had originally been made for one of the series' novellas, and being adamant that this had to go on the cover of *Bewitched*. I'm still mesmerized by it.

Dan, thank you for being my real life love story and being proof that soulmates really do exist. Without, you know, all of the angst and conflict of the fictional ones I write. Astrid and Jude, thank you for the love and cuddles and reminding me every day to notice the magic that exists around us. I hope you never lose your wondrous perspective of the world.

To my readers, thank you for taking a chance on *Bewitched*. I'm always so humbled by the outpouring of love and excitement you all give my books, and this one is no different. Thank you for letting me share my words and worlds with you.

About the Author

Found in the forest when she was young, Laura Thalassa was raised by fairies, kidnapped by werewolves, and given over to vampires as repayment for a hundred-year debt. She's been brought back to life twice, and with a single kiss, she woke her true love from eternal sleep. She now lives happily ever after with her undead prince in a castle in the woods.

...or something like that anyway.

When not writing, Laura can be found scarfing down guacamole, hoarding chocolate for the apocalypse, or curled up on the couch with a good book.